# Amy-Alex Campbell

# The Darkest REALM

I0593201

AAC Publishing Australia

Maps by Amy-Alex Campbell
Cover and title page by Warren Design
Artwork by reendhanasukma

Printed in Australia
First Printing Feb 3, 2022

ISBN 978-0-6486992-5-5

AAC Publishing Australia
Sydney, Australia

Amy-Alex.Campbell@outlook.com
www.amyalexcampbell.com

A copy of this title is available in the National Archives of Australia
Written on Dharug land

*For Marie Willa,*
*Transgender woman extraordinaire.*

*You are such an inspiration and a strong voice for*
*the transgender community. I am so proud of you.*
*Thank you for being you.*

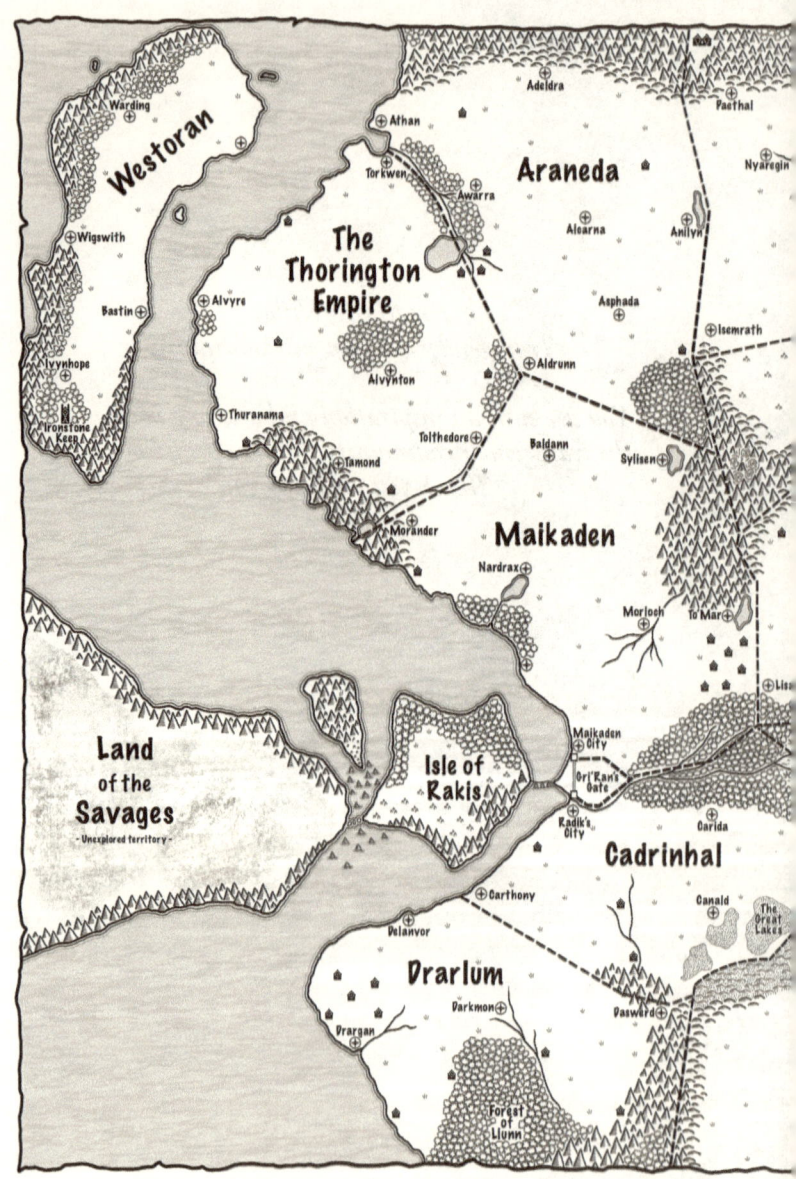

The Explored

Warding

Westoran

Wigswith

Bastin

Ivynhope

Ironstone Keep

Athan

Torkwen

Awarra

The Thorington Empire

Alvyre

Alvynton

Thuranama

Tamond

Morander

Adeldra

Paethal

Araneda

Nyaregin

Alcarna

Anilyn

Asphada

Isemrath

Aldrunn

Tolthedore

Baldann

Sylisen

Maikaden

Nardrax

Morloch

To Mar

Lisa

Land of the Savages

- Unexplored territory -

Isle of Rakis

Maikaden City

Ori'Ran's Gate

Kadik's City

Carida

Cadrinhal

Carthony

Canald

The Great Lakes

Delanvor

Drarlum

Darkmon

Dasverd

Drargan

Forest of Llunn

# Lands of Ayrillis

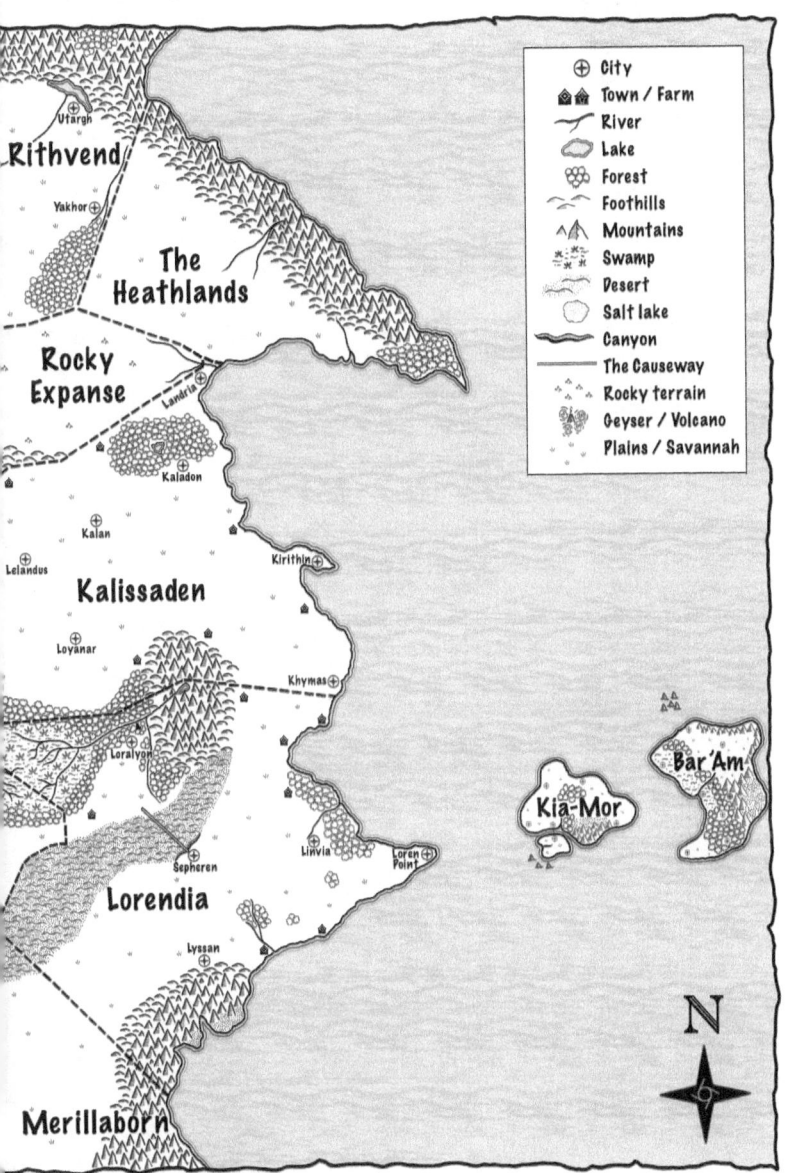

Utargh

Rithvend

Yakhor

The
Heathlands

Rocky
Expanse

Landria

Kaladon

Kalan

Lelandus

Kalissaden

Loyanar

Kirithin

Khymas

Loralyon

Sepheren

Linvia

Loren
Point

Lorendia

Lyssan

Merillaborn

Kia-Mor

Bar'Am

| | |
|---|---|
| ⊕ | City |
| 🏠🏠 | Town / Farm |
| ∿ | River |
| ⌓ | Lake |
| ❁ | Forest |
| ⌒ | Foothills |
| ∧∧ | Mountains |
| ※※ | Swamp |
| ⋯ | Desert |
| ◯ | Salt lake |
| ‿ | Canyon |
| — | The Causeway |
| ⬩⬩⬩ | Rocky terrain |
| ❀ | Geyser / Volcano |
| ⋅⋅ | Plains / Savannah |

N

# Part One

# Lorendia

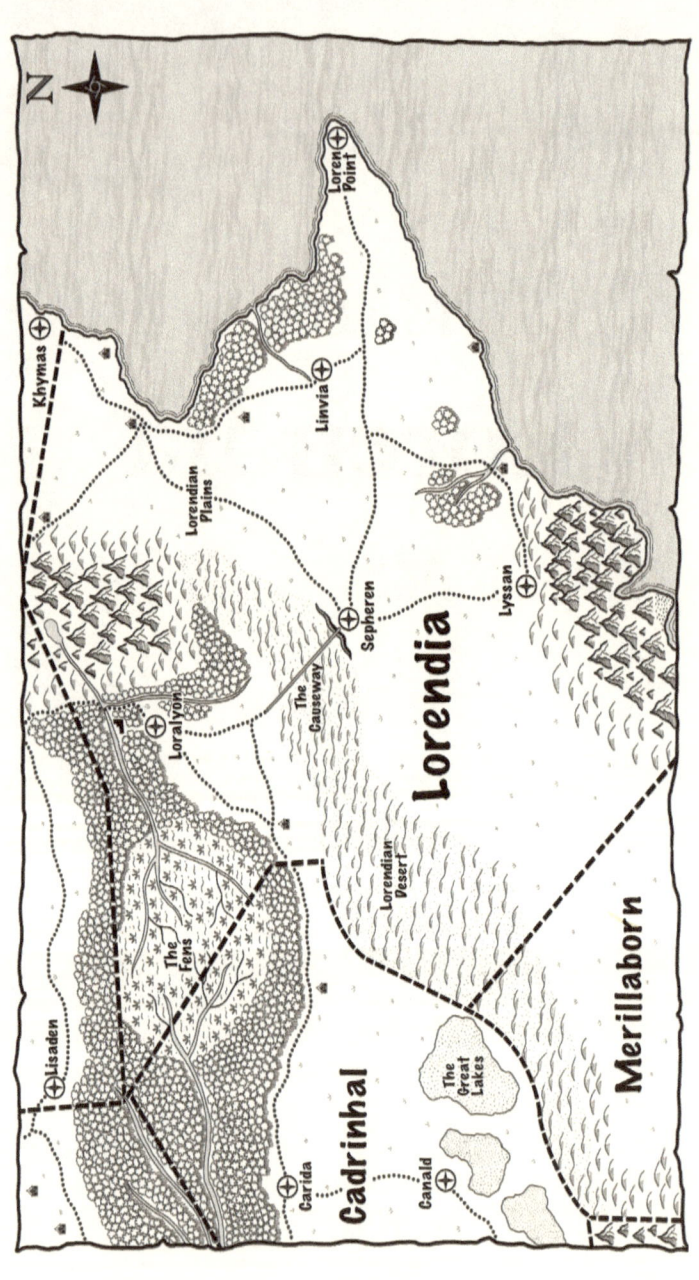

L ord Du'Rakis stood on top of a small rise, glaring across the battle that raged before him. The earth was blanketed in red from both the blood and uniforms of his army. Soldiers were falling to the ground, cut down like wheat before a scythe. The sound of a horn echoed across the battlefield, and the mounted King's Army surged across the bridge of Rarn. The remaining red militia retreated and ran for their miserable lives.

A muffled grunt from behind him hardly earned his attention. He ignored it and continued to watch as the rest of his army regrouped with the bulk of his reserves. The pitiful militia were almost no more; the reserves, on the other hand, were his most loyal followers of the Brotherhood of the Black Ibis. They would succeed or die trying. There would be no excuse for failure.

"My Lord. I bring you grave news."

He turned to face his general, who was breathing heavily from exertion.

"What is it, Ashavan?" he demanded.

The general bowed respectfully, then turned and indicated a dishevelled man being held by two of the Brotherhood.

"One of our spies just made it back through the lines. The cretins you seek are no longer at Rarn, My Lord."

"WHAT?!"

"They left almost thirty-six hours ago with a detachment of King's Army soldiers. They're on their way to Riz'Hra even as we speak." Ashavan's expression changed to anger. "The news that the cretins are being kept in the city's keep was a lie. Nothing but a diversion, My Lord."

Lord Du'Rakis turned and swept his eyes back across the battlefield, his hands shaking as the anger rose within him. His plans ruined yet again by unreliable human filth.

"Those who brought us this news. Were they from trusted sources, or useless plebs?" he asked through clenched teeth.

"They were from the Brotherhood, My Lord. Senior ranks, too. We sent them into the city to gain intelligence as you ordered, and instead they brought us false, unverified lies."

His entire body shook with rage. The fury coursing through his veins started pulsating and he could feel himself subconsciously drawing power from the realm. His mission had failed; his own people had betrayed him. The sky darkened and filled with thunderous clouds as his wrath took over his very being.

He stepped from his body and hurtled himself to the middle of the battlefield. As he made his projection solid, he raised his arms above his head dramatically and called forth a single bolt of lightning to strike the ground at his feet. Thunder roared above the battleground. The armies stopped fighting and gasped, then shrank back from their enraged leader. The silence was deafening, as every eye fell on him.

"Fools! You have failed me!" he roared towards the Brotherhood. "The laziness of some of you have led to all of the deaths here today, including your own. You and your families will all suffer an eternity for your betrayal!"

"My Lord Am–" a shaking lieutenant stepped forward hesitantly.

"SILENCE!" he screamed.

He called forth another bolt of lightning and struck the pitiful man before he could form his next words. In a flash, the man's body spasmed and fell to the ground in a smouldering heap. The Brotherhood gulped and took another step back.

"No one may speak that name. EVER!"

In a swift and deliberate motion, he raised his arms and directed the entirety of the energy he'd harnessed from the realm towards the Brotherhood. Lightning crackled from the skies as he struck each and all of his remaining followers.

Some tried to run.

Others tried to beg for their pitiful lives.

The rest accepted their fate, and as wave after wave of lightning struck them down, the battlefield echoed with the screams of almost a thousand people. Soon, Lord Du'Rakis was the only one still standing with breath in his lungs. The air reeked of sulphur and death. He turned to survey the army behind him, but the superior forces had already retreated back across the bridge. Satisfied, he softened his projection and returned to his physical form.

"From this day forward, we fight this battle alone," he said grimly to Ashavan. "By allowing the cretins to escape, the prophecy will be fulfilled and there is nothing I can do from here. The powers of Am and Gri'Ran together are too much for me to fight. To follow the cretins now would be folly, and my ruse will be discovered."

"What of the advance party you sent?"

"If they're not already dead, they will be when the cretins get there. But for now, it is time to execute stage two of my plan. Gather Enbarak, Belarüs, Rissa, and Ornas, and meet me in the Keep. We will cleanse our chapters of this filth, and I will have my revenge."

General Ashavan crept through the darkened city streets, being careful to remain unseen. He was a large, hulking man, able to whittle bodies into latticework with a single stroke of his sword. To risk being caught roaming the streets after curfew by the city guards would cost him precious time, time he could not afford. He knew that should he slip up in the slightest way, Lord Du'Rakis would show him no mercy. Just as he showed none to the almost thousand-strong army of the Brotherhood. The thought of the smoking bodies littering the battlefield and the stench of the burning flesh made him shudder.

The patter of the heavy rain hitting the weathered bluestone street muffled his footsteps as he hurried down a dark alleyway. Rounding a corner, a lone mutt started barking from the shadows.

"Halt! Who's prowling around out there?" a voice shouted.

Ashavan snatched a key from his pocket and jiggled it in a lock as the sound of running feet grew louder. He slipped inside and pressed his ear to the door.

"It's just a mongrel dog," a gruff voice said. "Let's git outta this rain."

Ashavan breathed a sigh of relief as the guards moved away.

"Who's there?" a voice called behind him.

"It's me," Ashavan said quickly.

A beam of light pierced the darkness as Tysion unshuttered his lantern and placed it on a table. The small room had hardly changed since Ashavan was there last; a cot against the back wall, a wardrobe, a small table with two chairs, and a bench to prepare meals. The air was cold and frigid; the tiny room had no fireplace.

"What are you doing here?" Tysion demanded.

Ashavan eyed him in the dim light; his body looked strong and healthy as always. His brown wavy hair matched the soft curls on his chest, which disappeared into a trail leading below his under garments. Tysion's green eyes twinkled in the light of the lantern, betraying his confusion.

"I had to see you," Ashavan blurted out. "You are no longer safe here. The Brotherhood of the Black Ibis is being expunged by our Lord. He's coming to destroy what's left. You need to get out tonight."

"Our Lord? He's yours, not mine. I left that ridiculous cult years ago." Tysion snapped.

"I came here to warn you, not to argue. If I get caught, I'm a dead man. You and I both know that." Ashavan pleaded. His stomach twisted and turned unpleasantly. "Please. Just pack your things and hurry. We don't have much time."

"And where will I go?" Tysion countered. "You know this place and my workshop is all I have left. You come barging in here and try to uproot my life as though I can just go and start over like nothing ever happened –"

"If you don't leave tonight, you will die!" Ashavan yelled, his frustration getting the better of him. "He is on a rampage, and this whole city is at risk. I may have made some poor choices in my life, but I swore when I did to always protect you no matter what. Now please, start packing. You can hate me while you get ready."

Tysion glared at him for a moment, then huffed and pulled on his tunic and hose.

"Where will I go?" he repeated as he threw some clothes into a pack.

"Head east, as far as you can. Avoid the cities. Hide by day and travel by night." A wave of sadness washed over him as Tysion turned and stuffed a few tools of his craft into another pack.

"I never meant to get in this deep," Ashavan said softly. "We were led to believe that we were doing the right thing. That we were helping to make the world a better place by stamping out corruption and evil. I never thought it could go this far, and that we were the ones doing wrong."

"You need to get out now," Tysion said, his tone changing. He paused and looked Ashavan in the eyes. "Only now are you waking up to the level of brainwashing that goes on in that place. Any cult that defies the gods is going to have evil intent. If only you'd woken up when I did."

"I can't leave, and you know that," Ashavan groaned. "Unless he is killed, I am bound to him until the very end. I'm so sorry. I never wanted this to happen."

"Sorry isn't going to change anything." Tysion pulled on his heavy cloak and boots, then stood and buckled his sword to his waist. "Let's go."

The rain was still bucketing down outside, making it hard to see in the shadows. Ashavan was grateful they at least had some cover to help keep them hidden from the patrols. After a few close calls, almost being discovered by the guards, they made it safely to the entrance of the sewers.

"Down there is the only safe way out," Ashavan whispered.

Tysion nodded and scurried down the ladder. Ashavan followed, pausing only to pull the heavy cover back over the entrance. The smell of human waste greeted his nose, almost choking him. He heard a splash below followed by gagging.

"Disgusting," Tysion retched.

"It's better than being killed," Ashavan said grimly. "Pass me the lantern. We should be safe here."

Tysion unshuttered the lantern and handed it over. Ashavan flinched from the bright light after being in the darkness for so long. He held it up so they could see and sheathed his sword.

"This way. Be careful, it's slippery."

The sewers were ancient and robustly built from large

blocks of basalt stone. The walls and ledges were covered in green moss and grime, and as they carefully picked their way through the gloom, rats fled in every direction. The sound of rushing water was almost deafening; the level in the channel had risen considerably since Ashavan passed through earlier.

Finally, a stairway materialised from the darkness. Ashavan led Tysion up the slippery stairs, then paused once more to shutter the lantern. He handed it back to Tysion, then cautiously opened the door and stepped into a small cave.

"Who's there? Show yourself!" someone yelled. "Hey!"

Ashavan cursed and drew his sword in time to parry a blow from a polearm, throwing his attacker off-guard. Ashavan swung his blade with ease and buried it into the man's abdomen, just below his breastplate. A look of disbelief crossed the man's face; with a gurgle, he fell to his knees and slumped to the ground.

Without a word, Ashavan wiped the blood from his blade, and dragged the dead guard into the sewers. He listened to the thumps of the body as it rolled and slipped down the stairs for a moment, then closed the door and turned to Tysion.

"Are you ok?" he asked.

"I'm standing next to someone who kills without conscience. I'm not even sure how to answer that," Tysion sighed.

"It was us or him," Ashavan said firmly. "He swung at me first. Come on, I have a horse waiting for you."

They walked in silence until they reached the edge of a large forest. Ashavan didn't stop; he led the way deeper into the brush to two horses. Wordlessly, he took Tysion's packs and buckled them to the saddle.

"Take this horse and get as far away from here as you can. There's food and coin in one of the packs. Remember what I said; hide by day, ride by night." Ashavan looked at

Tysion for a moment, then lowered his eyes to his feet. "If things had been different…if I left when you did, do you think we'd still be together?"

"You mean if you had've listened to me when I warned you the Brotherhood was bad news? Or left when your lord tried to kill me? Your heart is ensnared by that cult. Until you can break away from it, your heart will never be your own." Tysion stepped forward and planted a soft yet firm kiss on Ashavan's lips. "If that day ever arrives, come and find me."

Before Ashavan could say anything else, Tysion leapt into the saddle and sped off into the night.

2

His eminence, Worshipful Master Christophe Saul Du Freyne of the Great Monastery of Am, first and only disciple, stood at the bow of the Scruffy Mongrel, watching the dark cliffs as they sailed slowly past. He could make out the haze of the University and Al'Obrel in the distance, and his stomach turned uneasily.

In the almost seven months since he'd awoken from his god-induced reverie, Freyne avoided his past as a man of faith, and the idea of having to face it again in the next day or so terrified him. The thought of running back to his life of solitude in the forest was preferable over having to step foot back in the monastery.

Freyne closed his eyes and drew a deep breath, inhaling the familiar scents around him. He could smell spring in the air, soon to be summer; the soft earthy tones from the morning dew were strong and fresh. He could feel the whispers of nature surrounding him, calling to him.

He slipped his mind into the highest realm, and at once his vision came to life with a burst of nature. Bright sprites of life were everywhere, dancing before his eyes. For the first time since leaving his forest, he felt at peace again. He was home.

*"Welcome back, old friend. We have been waiting for you to return,"* the trees whispered. *"Evil walks among us*

*and draws breath as we speak. It is time for you to awaken fully and protect the true balance of nature."*

*"Danger! Beware the path you walk, death is lurking at every corner,"* the rocks breathed. *"We can feel it stirring on our back."*

*"Troubled seas! We can feel the ash of distant volcanoes disrupting our tides and poisoning our waters. There are unnatural forces tearing holes in our very fabric. Help us!"* the oceans cried.

*"Something has gone wrong. The prophecy of your land has not restored the balance as it should. Balance must be restored, or our world will be destroyed. Not even the heavens can save us from what will be,"* the skies added. *"It is time to find your people and bring them home."*

*"I know, my friends,"* Freyne replied. *"We will do all that is in our power to help restore the balance of nature and destroy the evil."*

*"We will walk with you and Nickolai on your journey. Be well, friend."*

The whispers subsided, leaving him to ponder the words of warning. He knew darkness was coming; Nika would not be alive had things gone the way they were supposed to. Deep down, he was glad that Nika agreed to come back from death to help fight Ami'Khel, and that he didn't have to suffer the rest of his days alone. But he felt bad for Nika, too. He was being forced to fight a battle that wasn't his, in a world that he was a stranger to. Nika already paid the ultimate sacrifice, and still the world wanted more from him.

Nika had changed, there was no question about it. His focus on his training was impeccable, and his aptitude sometimes scared Freyne. He could sense Nika's growing control over the forces of the realms, though Nika still seemed hesitant to embrace them, as though he were holding back, and Freyne knew not why.

He sighed. The pressure of what they had to do weighed

heavily upon him. Where he once had a prophecy to guide him, he was now on his own, the future unwritten, and that filled him with fear and self-doubt. Nika was right; it was the calm before the storm, and when the storm came, by the gods they'd better be ready for it.

The waterfront was the usual hive of activity as the Scruffy Mongrel thudded gently against the dock. The day was already warm, with only a soft spring breeze to keep them cool. Nika had exchanged his usual heavy cloak and travelling clothes for a neat grey shirt over his black trousers. He was freshly shaven and had trimmed his hair and goatee in preparation for their visit with King To'Rel.

A platoon of twenty or so mounted soldiers emerged from the University gates and halted on the dock, forcing sailors and workers to scurry out of the way. One of the soldiers held the king's purple crest high with pride.

"My father is so predictable," Iryna grumbled, joining Nika and their friends on deck.

"How did he know that we're here?" Gaitan asked.

"King To'Rel has listening posts all along these cliffs," Chardi explained. "He's been watching us for days."

"That's creepy." Gaitan frowned.

"Not really. A good king knows what's going on in his lands." Chardi replied.

Nika looked around at his friends, feeling a little sad that their journey together was almost at an end. His eyes landed on the princess, and his heart swelled with pride. Iryna was no longer the brat she was when their journey began; she'd finally seen the real world and matured considerably.

"I'm going to miss you guys," he said sincerely.

"Oh, we'll be around," Ur'Shad shrugged, though Nika could sense a hint of sadness from the big man.

Iryna turned, and to Nika's surprise, drew him into a tight hug and kissed him lightly on the cheek.

"I'll miss you all too," she said. "I wish I could come with you."

She went around the group, saying goodbye one by one. As she finished hugging Gaitan and Priye, Maple appeared on deck and strode towards them.

"We're ready to offload," she said, all signs of her loud and boisterous self gone.

Iryna fell into Maple's arms, and Maple patted her softly on the back.

"It'll be okay, sweetie," she said gently. "Take care of my brother and keep him out of trouble."

"I will, I promise," Iryna sniffed.

Nika bent down and picked up Arnie-Kyn, and followed his friends through the ship to the hold. He could feel the cat purring in his arms, happy to finally reach solid land. As they stepped off the gangway onto the dock, the captain dismounted and bowed deeply to Iryna, before saluting smartly to Chardi.

"Welcome home, Your Highness," he said politely, removing his helm. "I've been asked to deliver you to your father."

"Thank you, Hisley. I see you've been promoted while we were away."

"Why yes, Your Highness. I'm a captain now."

Nika looked closely at the captain and recognised him as the guard who escorted him and Freyne to King To'Rel on their first visit to Al'Obrel. Hisley appeared to sway in Nika's vision; he shook his head to try and clear his head. Instead he felt dizzy, off-balance after being on water for so many weeks.

"We have your private carriage ready, Your Highness," Captain Hisley was saying. "We also brought horses for your party."

"Thank you, but I will ride on a horse with my

friends," Iryna replied. "You may put our belongings in the carriage. Nika and Freyne, you two take Streek."

"Oh, as you wish, Your Highness." Hisley bowed again and motioned to some of his men.

The soldiers took their packs, and another handed them each the reigns of a horse.

"Streek?" Nika asked, confused.

"It means lightning in native Thorington tongue," she replied with a smirk. "I think she has earned her name after that night in Barthra."

A sailor handed Nika Streek's reins. As he mounted, he noticed Freyne's face turn a deep shade of crimson; Freyne quickly hurled himself into the saddle behind Nika.

"The king bids you join him at the monastery, Your Highness."

"Very well, Captain."

Nika felt Freyne stiffen behind him.

*"Are you ok?"* he asked silently.

*"No, not really,"* Freyne replied. *"I wasn't planning on going there so soon. Or at all. I'm not ready for this."*

*"It'll be alright. I won't leave your side, I promise."*

*"Thanks, boo."*

The soldiers formed a protective ring around the group, and together they made their way through the University's gates and into the city. As they passed slowly through the slums, the dishevelled residents gave the royal soldiers a wide birth. Nika rubbed his head subconsciously as he recalled the last time he'd attempted to pass through the slums. He shifted slightly in the saddle so that their bodies touched without drawing attention from the soldiers. Freyne rubbed Nika's hip discreetly; Nika knew he was thinking the same.

His thoughts turned to the upcoming meeting with the king. To'Rel was a fair man, who had vested great interest in the outcome of the prophecy. How he would take the bad news, though, Nika could only guess. His main concern, which kept him awake most nights, was where to go next. He had no idea where to search for Khel or the rifts, or what to even look for. How was he, a mere man, supposed to defeat a mancer who was so powerful he could deceive the gods?

Nika hardly paid any attention to his surroundings as they rode through the city. He did notice a small stone inn as they bypassed the noisy market, and the idea of a hot bath and a decent bed was certainly appealing. The thought of relaxing while Khel was on the loose, though, filled him with pangs of guilt. He didn't come back from the dead to relax; he had a job to do.

Every so often, a soft whispering on the edge of his hearing made him start; each time he looked around to see where it was coming from, but no one spoke. Even Gaitan was quiet for once. With a sigh, he turned back to his silent brooding.

His thoughts turned back to the long voyage back to Al'Obrel. Each day, he and Freyne immersed themselves in Nika's training within the darkest realm. It was exhausting work. Day after day Freyne pushed him to his limits, which slowly helped to increase his tolerance to realm exposure. While he was pleased with how much he'd learnt, deep down he was scared.

Nika knew that he was toying with great powers, and at times he felt like an imposter who shouldn't be messing with such powerful forces. Knowing that he could kill at will while hardly lifting a finger was almost terrifying; what if it became as easy for him as it did to Khel? What if some day he came to enjoy it? Was having access to such power really necessary just to kill one person?

Nika glanced at the busy market, eyeing the merchants and scholars as they went about their business. Each person was a life that represented their own story; they had their own fears, goals, and dreams. To take an innocent life was to snuff out so much more, and Nika didn't want to be responsible for that.

It wasn't until they passed through a set of enormous fancy iron gates set in a high stone wall that he noticed the Great Monastery of Am. Nika sucked in a deep breath, captivated by the beautiful architecture. The monastery was massive; he guessed at least four or five times larger than the temple at Karatha. Large ornate spires cast long shadows across the city, reminding the residents and visitors of Am's importance.

The façade was constructed from blocks of dark basalt stone, broken up by stained-glass windows which twinkled from the flickering lights within. Extending from the main temple were thick walls accented by battlements.

"*It's beautiful, isn't it?*" Freyne asked.

Nika nodded, unable to avert his eyes. He could feel Am's presence emanating from the very walls, calling to him. The soft whispering seemed to come from deep within the bowels of the monastery itself.

"*Those doors lead to the Sanctuary, which is open to the public for worship and contemplation. It's similar to the temple at Ner'Am, only much larger and more beautiful. The rest of the monastery is tucked behind those walls, off limits except to monks and special guests.*"

"*Is the king here to pray?*" Nika asked.

"*I doubt it,*" Freyne replied. "*He'll be expecting a full debriefing on the outcome of our journey.*"

"*Why here, then? Why not back at the castle?*"

"*There are spies everywhere in the castle and any public place. The monastery is perhaps the most secure place in the world. Am's presence is strong here, and no one would dare to go against their word.*" Freyne took a deep breath. "*It also means that the high priests will be there. They're not going to be happy when they see me. Am, give me strength.*"

Captain Hisley called to halt at a smaller inconspicuous entrance further along the wall. Two monks dressed in dark grey robes stood guard either side of the door, their faces hidden beneath their hoods. As the party dismounted, the doors opened, and another monk wearing deep burgundy robes stepped forward and bowed deeply. Without a word, he beckoned for them to follow. Nika bent down and sat Arnie-Kyn on the ground.

*"Why are his robes a different colour?"* Nika asked.

*"The colour signifies their rank,"* Freyne explained. *"That man is the abbot. He's in charge of the monastery and the monks."*

*"I thought the high priests were in charge?"*

*"No. The high priests are beyond the daily grind of monkhood. They are amongst the highest ranks attainable and answer only to Am. I know I still refer to them as monks, but that's just out of habit."*

They walked along a dim narrow passage in silence, with nothing but the gentle breeze whistling past. The sounds of their footsteps were muffled as they kept up with the abbot. At the end of the passage, he opened a creaking door and stood aside to let everyone through.

Nika's eyes swept his surroundings. They were in a hallway lined with doors on their right. To the left, a series of ornate stone pillars formed evenly spaced archways which opened into a large neatly groomed garden. The garden was square, bordered by three other hallways, and in the centre was a marble statue of Am.

*"This is the Eastern Cloister,"* Freyne said, as though reading Nika's mind. *"The rooms along this passage are used for training and instruction. The other three passages that border the garden are the neophyte's living quarters, or cells."*

*"Did you ever live in this part?"*

*"In the early days, yes. My cell was over there."* Freyne pointed across the garden.

A lone bird fluttered onto Am's shoulder and sang its

happy tune, the only noise to shatter the serene silence. Nika felt a sense of peace and calm wash over him. Without thinking, he reached out and took Freyne's hand.

The abbot led them through a small corridor and into a wider passage, lined with evenly spaced alcoves on each side. Each alcove had a marble statue of Am holding a flickering oil lantern. On the left, the wall was broken up by a large heavy door, flanked by more monks. One of them made a hand gesture towards the abbot, and opened the door.

Nika was unprepared for what lay beyond that door.

The Inner Sanctum was a round chamber, the floor mosaiced in geometric perfection; tiger eye, lapis lazuli, and polished quartz made a shimmering swirling pattern. In the centre was a marble altar, similar to the one Nika woke up on all those months ago. A golden bowl of water sat on top, flanked by two candles in gold holders.

The roof was domed, inlaid with polished metals that reflected the candlelight. Directly above the altar, a round stained-glass window cast rainbowed light into the chamber, casting a kaleidoscope of colours around the room. A ring of marble pillars cast shadows behind them, giving the chamber the appearance that it was floating in time and space.

Most overpowering of all was Am's presence. Nika sucked in a deep breath as it washed over him; to speak or make any kind of noise would be to shatter the perfection of that holiest place. Nika and Freyne stood aside and let their friends pass; the effect of the Sanctum did not appear to hold as much pull over the others as it did for them. Freyne looked almost as though he were glowing.

Freyne drew Nika towards the altar, and made that same gesture with his hands. He dipped his finger in the water and dabbed it to his forehead, then turned to Nika and dabbed his also. Nika was bursting with questions, but knew that it was not the time nor place. Freyne paused, and stared at his hands, confused. He *was* glowing.

The abbot paused towards the rear of the chamber and pointed to the shadows behind a pillar. Nika spotted an ornate iron staircase that spiralled into the depths below. One by one they followed the abbot down the stairs. Freyne paused and pulled the hatch closed behind them.

The lower chamber sported more of the pillars that the designer of the monastery seemed to love, and was lit up by oil lamps. The whispering that Nika had been hearing was much louder, and seemed to be coming from a door at the furthest end of the chamber.

*"Where is that whispering coming from?"* Nika asked, unable to contain himself any longer.

*"What whispering?"* Freyne looked puzzled. *"I don't hear anything."*

*"I -"* A knock behind him made Nika jump; the sound echoed throughout the chamber and rung in his ears. He turned to see the abbot standing by another door, this one flanked by two marble statues of Am. The doorknob turned, and the heavy polished door swung open.

A brown hooded monk and the abbot made the same hand gesture that Nika observed upstairs, and without a word, the abbot turned and made his way back up the staircase. The brown monk beckoned the group inside.

Nika could sense Freyne's nervousness grow as they stepped into yet another chamber, only this one was furnished and welcoming. The lush deep red carpets were soft underfoot, and numerous bookcases along the walls held books and artefacts. Three doors on each side of the room broke up the bookcases evenly. With a gentle thud, the doors closed behind them.

"Welcome, friends. Please come and be seated. His Majesty is already here."

At the far end of the chamber, Nika spied a number of red couches spaced out around a cosy fireplace. King To'Rel and Queen Nahal stood up, and Iryna rushed forward into her mother's arms.

"Welcome home, all of you," To'Rel said, moving to shake Ur'Shad and Chardi's hands in turn. When his eyes met Nika's, the colour drained from his face. "I wasn't expecting to see you here, lad. Nonetheless, welcome."

Iryna broke free from the queen's arms and fixed To'Rel with a frown.

"You sly dog, Father. Don't think we didn't know that you lied to us."

"You know as well as I do that you wouldn't have gone along willingly," he said firmly. "Even the prophecy said I'd have to lie in order to get you there. It's sad when even the seers foresaw your lousy behaviour. I hope you learned something while you were away."

"Where's Lana?" Queen Nahal asked before Iryna could bite back.

Chardi's face grew saddened, but he didn't answer.

"Lana didn't make it," Iryna said sadly. "I'll tell you about it later."

"Beloved Lana. My heart breaks for her." A look of sadness came over To'Rel's face. "Who are your new friends?"

"This is Priye, a nurse and midwife. And this is Gaitan, a soldier and artisan who defected from the militia of the Independent District. Both have been most helpful on our journey," Chardi said.

Priye curtseyed formally and Gaitan bowed awkwardly.

"It's a pleasure to meet you both. Moving on, please allow me to introduce their eminences, high priests Darius, Jormond, Maldon, and Braverek. And this here is Brother Orison from Ner'Am."

The monks all drew back their hoods. Nika's heart swelled when he saw Orison's kindly face smiling at him. He recognised another of the monks from when he first stepped into the library.

"So that's where our cat got to," Jormond sneered, pointing first at Nika, then sweeping his finger to Freyne. "Who's your other guest?"

Freyne sighed and stepped out from behind Ur'Shad's larger frame.

"You know who I am, Jormond."

Jormond looked infuriated.

"How dare you address me like –" he broke off suddenly and his jaw dropped.

"Christophe!?" Darius gasped.

"It's Freyne, Darius."

"Where have you been for the last seven hundred years?" Jormond demanded. "How dare you just up and leave us like that! And to come back now after the prophecy has been fulfilled!"

"What happened and where I have been is between Am and I. If you want to know, ask them," Freyne growled. "Do you want to hear the outcome, or do you want to stand here and question Am's authority?"

A frosty silence fell across the room as Freyne stared down the angry looks of the monks. Nika fidgeted awkwardly, but as he promised, he didn't leave Freyne's side. Finally, Jormond cleared his throat.

"This isn't over," he said. "We will commune with Am later and decide your punishment."

"Go ahead." Freyne shrugged. "Now, if you don't mind, His Majesty would like to hear our report."

The monks murmured amongst themselves, and To'Rel motioned to everyone to sit. Nika sat next to Freyne and lifted Arnie onto his lap. He could feel the tension sizzling in the air as Iryna started recounting their journey.

"Punishment?" Nika asked, an uneasy feeling in his belly.

"They like to think that they have the powers to banish me to exile," Freyne replied. "Little do they know of Am's plans for us."

"Why were you glowing back there?" Nika asked, unable to contain his questions any longer.

"I have no idea," Freyne admitted. "That's something that has never happened before."

"Oh. Well, what's that hand thing everyone keeps doing?"

"It's an affirmation to Am. A sign of absolute respect." Freyne shifted slightly on the couch so their bodies touched. "Everything anyone does here is usually some symbol or ritual that means something. You may have noticed how the hallways, and even the cloisters, are all symmetrical. The mosaic in the Inner Sanctum is perfect. Even this room, if you look closely, is symmetrical."

"I see. That chamber out there wasn't, though."

"That is the one place in this entire monastery that isn't," Freyne explained. "In this section, the inhabitants live longer than normal lives, bordering immortality. In that other section, behind that simple door, are the catacombs. Kings, queens, high priests, anyone who was ever somebody important lie through that door."

Nika pondered Freyne's words for a moment.

"It's not symmetrical, but you have life and death, so I guess that still balances things out," he mused.

Freyne turned and looked at him with a slight grin on his face.

"What?" Nika asked.

"You haven't even started any of the most basic of religious training, and you already know and understand more than most brothers do."

"I guess I could say I've had a good teacher," Nika smirked. "Who else here is the lover of a disciple of Am?"

"There is hope for the whelp yet," Arnie-Kyn added wryly.

Nika ignored the cat's dig and turned his attention back to Iryna for a moment; she was describing their visit with King Kaiton. All eyes were on the princess, engrossed in her story. Nika had to admit that she was good at captivating an audience.

"That room over To'Rel's left shoulder is the archives," Freyne said, drawing Nika's attention back. "The room next to it is where I lived for all those years. It's a bit more comfortable than the neophyte's cell. And if you remember that room you stayed in when you came here the first time, the secret entrance is behind that fireplace."

"Wow," Nika replied. "I'm pretty sure I'm not supposed to know that."

"Too bad."

Iryna's tale swung around to Lana's burial and Freyne's prayer. Once again, all eyes turned to Freyne.

"I had no idea that you're a man of faith, let alone a high priest," To'Rel mused, stroking his short brown beard. "Why didn't you say so when we last met?"

"I was somewhat indisposed at the time, Your Majesty," Freyne replied. "A lot has happened between now and then."

"I understand. Please continue, daughter."

Iryna continued her story, earning a frown from the king.

"Once we were inside, the statue of Gri'Ran came to life and spoke. Am and another god appeared, and Nika did what he had to do. He went through with his sacrifice as was required of him."

"So why is he here with us now?" Braverek demanded. "You're supposed to be dead."

"What happened, lad?" To'Rel asked.

Nika gritted his teeth. He sat Arnie on the couch and stood up.

"There was a problem," he started, trying to remember the speech that he'd rehearsed over and over for that very moment.

"Well obviously there was a problem if you're here

with us right now," Jormond snapped. "We were very clear in our letter about what you had to do. How could you possibly stuff it up?"

Nika ignored him and turned his attention to King To'Rel and looked him in the eyes.

"Back when Freyne and I were in your office, you told us the story of Ami'Khel. You told us that he was murdered, and the result was a broken pact with the gods which caused a rift to open."

"That's right. Go on, lad." To'Rel nodded.

"After my death, Am and Gri'Ran summoned the other gods and they held council. Something was wrong. I could sense it even as I slipped into death's cold embrace. The story we knew was a lie, Your Majesty. Khel formed the rift himself using forbidden mancery and used it to escape to my world. Ami'Khel lives."

"PREPOSTEROUS!" Jormond bellowed. "How dare you bring such lies here!"

"They're not lies!" Iryna glowered at him. "I saw it with my own two eyes. To call them lies is an attack on my integrity."

"Your Highness-" Maldon said softly, speaking for the first time.

"Silence, all of you!" To'Rel said firmly. "Nika, please continue."

"Thank you. The rifts that Khel made are still open and are becoming unstable. If they are not closed soon, they will collapse and tear apart the very fabric of our universe. No one can undo a mancer's work, except for that mancer or someone from their bloodline. The gods knew that Khel would never willingly close the rifts, so Am came to me in my death. They offered me a choice." Nika paused for a moment and swept the faces of his friends. They all stared at him in awe; it was the first time he'd spoken of his death since it happened. "I could stay dead and be delivered into the afterlife for the rest of eternity.

Or, I could return to life on the condition that I close the rifts and hunt down Khel and destroy him."

The monks started whispering amongst themselves animatedly. Nika sat back down, and looked at his friends.

"What do you mean you're from a different world?" Gaitan asked incredulously.

"What can I say?" Nika shrugged. "Something happened to me in my world and I woke up here."

"No wonder you're so odd." Priye smirked.

"Gee, thanks," Nika grumbled.

"I'm sorry for my deception," King To'Rel said to Nika. "The letter you brought me said I had to ensure you get to Gri'Ran's Rest and go through with the ritual no matter what. I think by now you will understand the importance of this."

"Of course, Your Majesty." Nika said.

"We need to pray," Braverek said abruptly. "Only Am can guide us from here."

To'Rel sighed and his face creased into a frown.

"I am not leaving this monastery until I have a clear vision of what is to come and what we must do," he said firmly. "If you pray, we all pray. Nothing is to be gained from withholding information right now, especially if Khel really is still alive."

"With all due respect, Your Majesty, we don't have time to sit around in prayer all day," Freyne objected.

"Oh, I suppose you think you can just break protocol now and summon Am at will?" Jormond hissed.

The monks started bickering amongst themselves again. Nika could see that the king and queen were becoming exasperated.

"Fine! I'll do it myself," Freyne said angrily. "These fools have no idea the forces they are messing with. Give me your hand."

Nika reached out and took Freyne's hand obediently. Prayer was one of the many things Freyne had taught him during the long voyage home. He felt Freyne's mind join with his, though instead of slipping into the realm, he looked deep within himself to the tiny spot where he knew Am's presence lived within him. He allowed Am's energy to roam free within his body for a moment, filling him with a warm tingling sensation, before channelling it to join with Freyne. Between them, Am's power was strong.

"My sons. Why do you call me?" Am whispered.

"My God. We seek your guidance in the next step of our journey," Freyne replied. "The high priests are being stubborn as always and refuse to help without lengthy prayer and contemplation first."

"Those fools." Am sighed. "Very well."

The presence drained from Nika's body, and when he opened his eyes, he could see a swirling ball of energy growing and forming in front of the fire. A collective gasp escaped from the monks' lips. All but Orison fell to their knees and prostrated themselves before Am. Orison knelt and smiled fondly at his god.

Freyne gently squeezed Nika's hand and winked; once again, Freyne was glowing, though Nika wasn't sure that he knew. The swirling ball formed into the glowing shape of a spectral being. Nika dropped to his knees as Freyne had taught him, and was surprised to see even the king kneeling before the god.

"My children," Am said softly, gazing around the room. "What is the problem here?"

The monks quivered, terrified. Slowly, Maldon sat up on his knees and looked into where Am's eyes would be.

"I-Is it true, My God? Is Ami'Khel still alive?"

"Of course it's true," Am replied. "You all should know that I would never send you lies. The Miscreant lives, and even now is wreaking havoc amongst the cities on the mainland."

"One of my spies told me they saw an entire army destroyed by a single being at Rarn," To'Rel said slowly.

"Would this have anything to do with Khel?"

"That very being was Khel, my son. His entire army slain out of anger for his failure. He tried to prevent the fulfilment of the prophecy, but luckily I was able to intervene in time. The consequences of my intervention, however, may be catastrophic. Only time will tell."

"What of the Brotherhood of the Black Ibis, My God?" Freyne asked.

"The Miscreant is purging his entire following except for his most trusted generals, and is sweeping the cities to destroy any survivors even as we speak. I fear what his next move will be."

"Is there any hope for the survivors?" To'Rel asked. "I mean, would it be possible for my allies to protect them?"

Am floated across the floor to where To'Rel knelt and touched him gently on his forehead.

"You are a good leader, my son. Your heart is in the right place. Unfortunately, to open your arms to any former cultists would put your entire kingdom at risk, and we can't afford that. As callous as it sounds, we must sit back and let this play out as we await his next move."

"I understand." To'Rel nodded.

"Keep your family safe no matter what. My protection holds for my places of worship, but it is not as strong as it once was. Hold me in your heart, always." Am gently touched Nahal in the same way, then began to make their way around the room one by one, repeating their gentle blessing.

"What about Christophe, My God?" Jormond spluttered as Am reached towards Nika. "He turned his back on us and abandoned his post. He must be punished!"

Am spun around and fixed their gaze on the four monks. Nika could sense a hint of anger radiating from the god.

"You have no idea what my son has sacrificed and given up for me, the prophecy, and indeed this very world.

More than any of you, that's for certain," they said firmly. "Do not think you are above my word just because you sit within the highest ranks of my house. It is not up to you to decide who is punished, especially in my name. Understood?"

"Y-Yes, My God," Jormond stuttered.

"Since the four of you seem to like punishment, you are all to re-read the entirety of my laws, all seventy-two tomes, in each of the four languages, word for word. And until you are done, you are to commune only in the Sanctuary. Understood?"

"Yes, My God." Jormond, Maldon, Braverek and Darius replied together.

"Maybe then you will recall my words that you have so clearly forgotten." Am swept their gaze around the chamber. "You all should know that I have appointed Freyne as my one and only disciple, so you will treat him with as much dignity and respect as he deserves."

Jormond's jaw dropped and his face looked like he was about to faint.

Am turned and touched Nika's forehead, sending a warm tingling sensation through him.

"Nickolai, my son. I have not been successful in my attempts to locate the rifts. I cannot sense them from within the Crystal Heavens. You and Freyne have all the powers you need to find them yourselves." Am turned finally to Freyne. "Take ship across the sea to Loren Point, and begin your search from there. I am sensing something strange towards the west, so that is the direction you should go."

"How will we know if we're going the right way?" Nika asked.

"You will know. I am with you always. But now, I must go. I love you all, my children. Hold me forever in your hearts."

# 3

The sun was sinking towards the horizon by the time the ship was ready to sail again. After a simple lunch with the sullen monks and royal family at the monastery, the king and his soldiers insisted on escorting them back to the ship.

Freyne stood with Nika, Gaitan, and Priye on the dock, waiting to be called aboard. Arnie-Kyn had already disappeared into the hold, irritated that they were once again to travel by sea. Finally, Maple strode down the gangway towards them.

"We're all good to set sail," she grinned. "Oh, hello King!"

"Mar'hea! I almost didn't recognise you." To'Rel opened his arms, and the two embraced fondly.

"That's understandable. I was blessed with the good looks, unlike Ur'Shad," she laughed.

"You old cow," Ur'Shad snorted.

"When your mission is complete, I would like to invite you all back here," To'Rel said warmly. "I have chosen a husband for Iryna. Hopefully you'll all make it back in time for the wedding."

Ur'Shad's face dropped.

"Who?" Iryna demanded.

"We'll discuss it back at the castle. In the meantime, have a safe journey my friends." To'Rel reached out and shook their hands one by one. "I don't think you need me to tell you that the fate of our world hangs on the outcome of your quest. Here is a signed declaration that you are my royal envoys just in case. I have allies in Drarlum and Rithvend, so it might prove useful. I also have some coin to help you on your way, should you require armour or weapons or anything."

Freyne accepted a folded sealed letter and a heavy purse of jingling coins.

"Thank you, Your Majesty."

"Good luck my friends. May the gods bless you on your journey."

Freyne nodded and made his way along the gangway, then hurried up to the deck with the others behind him. As he leant against the rail, the sailors untied the final rope, and the ship started drifting on the current. The king, Ur'Shad, Chardi and Iryna all waved, then turned to head back to Al'Obrel.

"I wonder who To'Rel chose for Iryna's husband," Gaitan pondered.

"It wasn't you, so don't get your hopes up," Priye smirked. "I'm guessing Kaiton's son."

"I wouldn't want to marry a princess anyway," Gaitan said defensively. "Come to think of it, I don't think I want to get married at all."

"It's overrated, trust me," Priye nodded.

"How long will it take us to reach the mainland?" Nika asked.

"Usually around six weeks," Freyne replied.

"Six weeks?" Nika groaned with frustration. "I'm starting to see why Khel uses rifts to get around."

Freyne slipped his arm around Nika's waist and pulled him into a tight hug. The few hours they were on shore, unable to publicly show their affection, was too long. At least they could be themselves in front of their friends with zero repercussions.

*"Patience, boo. We'll get there soon enough,"* Freyne said gently. *"We can use the time to revisit and refine some of your training."*

*"It's so frustrating,"* Nika grumbled. *"I just want to get this over and done with."*

*"I know."*

---

It was dark and humid as the Scruffy Mongrel crept into Loren Inlet, the inland shipping district of Loren Point. The occasional flash of lightning lit up the sky, followed by an ominous rumble in the distance. Dogs barked nervously in the streets of the city, unsettled by the approaching storm.

What should have been a six-week voyage only took them four weeks. Blessed by strong relentless winds blowing directly into the sails, the ship moved along at a steady pace. Nika grew suspicious when he noticed the swells pushing them forward, even when the sea was mostly calm around them. Freyne confirmed those suspicions with a visit to the highest realm. The winds and seas were only too happy to help them on their journey.

The inlet channel was lined by a bluestone wall, topped with a well-lit boardwalk, which ran for miles in each direction. Bordering the boardwalk was a row of tightly packed double-storey houses overlooking the waterfront. Each house was a different shade of yellow, orange, or red, which made Nika think of piles of leaves in autumn. As they slowly drifted towards their bay on the dock, he spotted other ships bobbing roughly in the swells. He heard steps behind him, and turned to see Gaitan and Priye making their way across the deck.

"I didn't think we'd ever see land again," Gaitan said, glancing eagerly towards the city.

"I was starting to feel that way too," Nika agreed.

"Be thankful that Am sped up our trip," Freyne added.

The ship finally came to a stop with a light thud; the sailors rushed to tie off just as the rain started to fall.

"Strange weather for this time of year," Maple noted, joining them at the rail. "It's going to be a rough night on board. There's an inn that overlooks the town square that's not too far from here. Go and rest up there for the night, tell them Maple sent you."

"Are you staying here?" Nika asked.

"Yes. No shore time until the ship is unloaded and cleaned. Once the jobs are done, then we can go have some fun."

"We'll just take our packs for the night then. We can come back in the morning for the horses," Freyne said.

"Good idea. From memory there is a market near the square, you'll be able to restock your supplies there." Maple kissed Nika and Freyne on the cheek, and smiled. "Get going. I'll see you in the morning."

---

The rain was bucketing down as the sodden group made their way to the inn. The strong winds of the storm howled around the buildings; the humidity was rapidly cooling since they docked, and the air was growing colder by the minute. The street was empty as they hurried along the slippery bluestone road. Nika held Arnie under his cloak, and could feel his tail flickering irritably.

Nika breathed a sigh of relief when the inn finally came into view. He followed Freyne inside to the warm reception area, and pulled back his hood.

"Good evening, friends," a stocky innkeeper with short ginger hair and rosy cheeks greeted them.

"Good evening, my lady," Freyne echoed formally. "We're good friends with Maple. She recommended that we spend the night here. Do you have three rooms available?"

"Maple! Is she here in port?" The woman's eyes lit up.

"Yes. She sailed us here from Al'Obrel," Freyne replied.

"I have plenty of rooms available, it's been a quiet week." She smiled. "I'll give you the suites that have their own baths. Friends of Maple are friends of mine."

"Thank you, my lady." Freyne replied.

"That cow had better come and visit me," she grinned. "I'll send someone up right away to fill your baths. I'd imagine you wish to bathe before dinner. I'm Maretta by the way."

"I'd rather eat-" Gaitan started.

Priye grasped his ear and twisted it.

"Ow!" He gasped.

"Like I told you on the ship, you stink. You will be bathing before dinner, even if I have to scrub you myself," she said firmly.

"Alright, alright. Sheesh." Gaitan rubbed his ear.

Maretta laughed and led them through a low-ceilinged dining room and up a flight of stairs.

"You'll find soap and towels are already in there," she said, pointing to their rooms.

Gaitan huffed and disappeared inside, slamming the door behind him.

"You should be gentle with him," Nika said to Priye.

"He's no delicate flower," Priye smirked. "A lesson in hygiene never hurt anyone."

"Except for his ear," Freyne pointed out.

Priye laughed and slipped into her room. Nika opened the door to the third and stood aside to let Freyne past.

"I'll send up your dinner in around an hour." Maretta winked and disappeared back downstairs.

The room was neat and modest, much like every other room Nika had stayed in. It had the usual couch, fireplace and small table and chairs, and a separate bathroom with both a bath and latrine. He carefully extracted Arnie-Kyn from under his cloak and sat him on the bed, then turned and faced Freyne. He felt himself swaying as though he was still at sea, and stumbled as he attempted to balance himself.

"Are you ok, boo?" Freyne asked, peeling off his cloak.

"I'm fine," Nika replied. He removed his cloak and handed it to Freyne to hang beside the door. "I'd forgotten how it feels to be on solid land. It still feels like we're at sea."

"It'll pass soon enough." Freyne helped himself to Nika's shirt.

"So what's the plan now that we're here?" Nika asked.

"We bathe, eat and sleep," Freyne replied, tugging at Nika's belt. "We'll worry about the rest tomorrow."

---

Nika woke to the sound of heavy rain lashing against the windowpanes. A chill hung in the air, and the wind whistled eerily around the eaves. Arnie-Kyn was curled up in a ball between his neck and shoulder, sleeping soundly. Nika reached out and patted the bed beside him; it was cold and empty. For a split second, a feeling of dread pooled in the pit of his stomach.

"Morning, boo."

He opened his eyes to see Freyne seated on the couch by the empty fireplace with his journal and pencil in hand.

"Oh. There you are." Nika breathed a sigh of relief. He shifted slightly to avoid disturbing Arnie, and sat up and stretched. "How long have you been awake?"

"Not long. We both overslept by around an hour. Breakfast won't be far away."

Freyne stood up and opened the heavy drapes, letting in the dull light of the day.

"What a miserable morning," Nika grumbled. "Will the market still be open on a day like this?"

"The markets are open every day regardless of the weather," Freyne replied. "Come on, let's get you up and dressed. We have lots to do today."

After a hearty breakfast of boiled duck eggs and hot buttery bread, Nika and his friends ventured into the rain and made their way towards the market. The wind howled relentlessly around the narrow streets, whipping at Nika's cloak. He pulled it tighter as he dodged around a pile of refuse.

Despite the weather, there were still plenty of people haggling loudly over wares. Many of the stalls boasted brightly coloured canopies to protect their goods and customers from the rain. The smell of freshly cooked exotic meat wafted under Nika's nose and made his mouth water, even though he'd already eaten.

"Oh yum, bullbark balls," Gaitan said, sniffing the air.

"What's that?" Nika asked.

"They're considered a delicacy over in the East," Gaitan replied.

"Horrible." Priye scowled. "They take the testicles of the bullbark beast and marinate them for a whole day in garlic and herbs, then roast it slowly."

"What is a bullbark exactly?"

"It's larger and fatter than a cow, and much stronger. They roam wild in the savannahs to the west of here," Freyne offered. "Do you not have them in your world?"

"No." Nika shook his head.

Freyne paused under a canopy and squinted through the rain.

"We'll probably get this done quicker if we split up," he said, scratching his cheek. "We need to resupply our food stores, buy more waterskins, and find some desert robes. I think we should buy a wagon rather than another pack horse. What do you think?"

"Good idea," Gaitan nodded. "I need to sell my

breastplate and buy some better armour."

"I'll go with Freyne then," Priye offered. "I need to replenish my medical supplies too."

"Alright. We'll organise food and supplies. Nika and Gaitan can find us some desert robes, water skins, and whatever else you think we might need." Freyne dipped his hand into the purse of coins To'Rel gave them, and handed some to Gaitan. "Keep your ears open and see what news you can find from the west. We don't want any surprises. We'll meet back at the ship when done."

"Sounds good," Nika nodded. "See you soon."

Priye linked her arm with Freyne's and whisked him away into the crowd. Nika grinned and followed Gaitan in the other direction. After a while, Gaitan stopped at an armourer stall.

"Look at that chainmail shirt," he breathed.

The chainmail had long sleeves and looked to be thigh-length, only the links in the mail looked different to those in Chardi and Ur'Shad's. A large burly smith in a leather apron eyed them suspiciously.

"Whattaya lookin' at?" he demanded.

"I was admiring the ringwork of your chainmail, sir." Gaitan replied. "I have not seen such a weave before."

"Tis known as gracelock," he grunted. "The weave is much tighter than the usual, more protecting from arrows n'all."

"Can I try it on?"

"Like ye can afford it." The smith snorted derisively.

Gaitan dumped his pack loudly on the counter and fished out his bronze breastplate. Nika felt a little uneasy as he flashed back to being captured in Fraal by the militia wearing that very same uniform.

"I have this to sell, plus coin." Gaitan held the smith's glare, until finally the bigger man sighed and backed down.

"Ver' well. Comes with a maille coif 'swell. 75 gold."

Nika watched the exchange, fascinated. The smith undid the fastenings and helped Gaitan into it. The chainmail looked like a good fit; the coif covered his head, allowing only his face to be exposed.

"It's a bit loose in the arms. I'll have to pay to have it altered," Gaitan said thoughtfully, flexing his arms. "That will cost me at least 30 gold. How about I pay you 45 gold for it?"

"Don' be ridiculous," the smith grumped. "This weave takes much longer ter make than standard. I only use the finest o' materials. 60 gold would barely cover the steel ter make it."

"This breastplate is solid bronze, military grade. They cost 50 gold each over in the East. I'll pay you 30 gold plus the breastplate."

"Yer killin' me," the smith grumbled. "Tis been a slow week but. I'll accept, but yer can git someone else ter alter it."

"It's a deal then."

Gaitan fished out the last of the gold coins from his own purse, and a few from what Freyne gave him, and paid the smith. The big man reluctantly shook his hand to seal the deal.

"Tanks. Now be gone with yer."

Gaitan nodded and pulled Nika away from the stall.

"Where are you going to get it altered?" Nika asked.

"I'm not." Gaitan grinned. "I can alter it myself, and it won't cost me a thing. I already have all the tools I need."

"You sneaky mongrel."

"I doubt it cost more than 20 gold to make. Besides, Chardi told me I should switch to chainmail instead of the breastplate. It covers so much more, and protects my head," Gaitan said. "I just need to get used to wearing it while swinging a sword."

Nika's eyes landed on a stall loaded with musical instruments. The trader was playing a lute in an attempt to lure customers.

"Oh look," Gaitan said. "You should get another cittern."

The thought of playing music and indulging in his passion made his stomach turn. Nika sighed and shook his head.

"No. I will not play again until our mission is complete."

"But why?" Gaitan asked.

"I'm living on borrowed time." Nika shrugged. "I've been given a job to do. I will not relax until Khel is dead and the rifts are closed."

"Such a shame. Your music brings so much joy to people. The world needs as much joy as possible right now."

Nika didn't reply. He really didn't want to talk about it, though he knew his friend was just trying to be supportive. As they walked past a mystic begging to tell their fortune, he spotted a stall selling crocheted and knitted goods. Amongst the scarves and shawls was a crochet mouse the size of his hand.

"I need to get this for Arnie," he grinned. "He'll be so offended by it."

"Offended?" Gaitan looked confused. "It's just a cat. Come to think of it, why do you even bring it with us?"

"First of all, it's *he*, not *it*. And second, I really have no say in that," Nika replied. "Wherever I go, he follows. He gets mad if I leave him locked up in a room for the day."

"You act as though he can talk," Gaitan frowned.

"He never shuts up." Nika grinned. "Can you pay the lady? I don't have any money."

---

The rain slowed to a light drizzle by the time Nika and Gaitan made it back to the ship. Freyne was standing by a large wooden wagon talking to Bren and Rhill, and waved them over as they approached.

"We're almost loaded up," Freyne said. "We can't leave until early morning though. One of the straps on the harness broke, so the waggoneers are organising another."

"It's already lunch time anyway. We wouldn't get very far even if we did leave now," Nika said thoughtfully. "I guess another night in comfort won't hurt. We won't get much opportunity in the coming weeks."

"That's right. Let's load up what you've got there and make sure we have everything. Bren and Rhill have offered to guard it overnight."

"Thanks, guys." Nika nodded.

"Only happy to help. If it weren't for you, we wouldn't have a job," Rhill said. "Maple's the best captain I've ever worked for."

"Yeah." Bren nodded his agreement.

"Let's head back to the inn," Freyne said, scratching his cheek thoughtfully. "I'd like to go over the map and make sure we have everything we need for the journey. Lorendia is considered the anus of the mainland, as it's mostly dry and barren land. There's not much in the way of civilisation between here and Maikaden. Our jaunt across the Eastern Isles was a stroll down the garden path compared to what lies ahead."

That evening, the inn was packed with merchants and sailors from Kalissaden, who docked earlier in the afternoon. Maple tutted disapprovingly as the sailors quickly became rowdy.

"If my boys ever behaved like that, they wouldn't have a ship to return to," she growled. "Their captain has no control whatsoever."

"I'd like to see them try and last a day with you," Priye smirked.

Maple snorted.

"Maple, you old tart! It's about time you showed up!" Maretta pushed her way through the crowd and banged some pitchers of ale on the table.

"Nice to see you too," Maple said slyly. She stood up and pulled the innkeeper into a tight hug.

"Are you in port for long?" Maretta asked once they parted.

"I'll probably be in port for a few days, then head back to Al'Obrel," Maple replied. "I think it's time I spent a bit more time with my brother and sort out my affairs back home."

"That's fair. You know you always have a bed here though." Maretta winked.

"Only if you're in it," Maple winked back.

Maretta laughed.

"Of course. How about the rest of you?"

"We'll be heading west towards Maikaden," Freyne replied. "We have business over that way. My wealthy sister's wedding."

Nika's heart gave a lurch as Freyne's words sunk in. In all the craziness of the last few weeks, it hadn't occurred to him that Maple wouldn't be going with them. He'd become so used to her company, the thought of leaving her behind created a vast emptiness deep inside him.

"That's a long journey you face then," Maretta said. "Are you going the long way around Kalissaden Ranges, or braving the desert and going via Cadrinhal?"

"The desert," Freyne replied.

"Oh, be careful then," Maretta said. "I've heard some gruelling tales come out of the desert. You don't want to die just for a wedding."

"We'll be ok." Freyne assured her.

"Very well. I had better get back to work. I'll talk to you all later." Maretta winked again at Maple and disappeared into the crowd.

"Was she coming on to you?" Gaitan asked.

"She'd better be." Maple grinned. "She's amazing in bed. It's been too long since I've had some fun."

Gaitan's eyes turned sly, but before he could say anything, Priye clipped him over the back of his head.

"What was that for?" he demanded.

"Don't even think it," she warned.

"It's ok, sweetie." Maple laughed. "He couldn't handle the both of us."

Gaitan clammed up and sat glaring at Priye.

Nika wanted to laugh and enjoy their last evening together, but as he sat looking around the faces of his friends, the seriousness of his mission hit him like a block of wood in the back of the head. Freyne was right; their journey across the Isles was just a stroll, a warm-up for the real hike ahead. A part of him wondered if the prophecy was really just the first step of a much larger picture; surely those gifted with Sight would have seen Khel's ruse for what it was. Were the gods still playing them?

"Excuse me."

Nika's thoughts were interrupted by a large man in intricate scale mail standing by the table, his hand hovering over a wicked-looking sword strapped to his waist. His thinning black hair was combed to one side, and he was sporting a few days' growth on his cheeks.

"I overheard that you're heading west through the desert," the man said. His accent, paired with his deep voice, was exotic to Nika's ears. "To travel that way without a guide is suicide."

"We are hardly tourists," Gaitan said defensively.

"Perhaps, yes." The man leant down and placed his hands flat on the table. "The Lorendian Desert is home to many deadly scorpions, snakes, and other creatures that will kill you with one bite. And then there's the wyverns. But I'm sure you know how to kill them, yes?"

Nika frowned and stared at the big man.

"What's a wyvern?" he asked.

"That's what I thought. You're all as good as dead out there." The man stood up straight and turned to go.

"Wait," Freyne called. "What is your price?"

"Well. As luck would have it, I'm going that way anyway. I'll take you across for 50 gold if you provide my meals."

"What's your name?" Freyne asked.

"Joplin."

"Can you excuse us for a moment?"

Joplin nodded and pushed his way to the bar.

"What do you all think?" Freyne asked once he was out of earshot.

"It's a lot of money," Gaitan pointed out. "We'll be ok alone, won't we?"

"I don't know," Priye said thoughtfully. "He wasn't lying about the deadly creatures. I learnt about them while I was studying medicine. I think we should at least trust his warning."

"Weren't you saying earlier that we go across a causeway?" Nika asked finally.

"That's right. There's supposedly wells hidden along there with water and places for travellers to set up camp," Freyne replied.

"What if they're empty or we can't find them?" Nika continued. "Having someone with us who knows the land might be useful. He looks like a skilled fighter, so if something happens, we've at least got help. I think we should hire him."

"Do we have enough supplies for an extra person?" Gaitan asked.

"We have plenty," Freyne assured him. "We can also hunt along the way if needed."

"Alright, I'm in." Gaitan nodded.

"Me too," Priye agreed.

"I'll go and talk to him then. Back soon."

Nika was too emotional to sleep, and the next morning he had to fight to keep his feelings under control. They rose early, and met Joplin by the wagon. After packing his few supplies in with the rest, Nika and Freyne stepped aside to say a final farewell to Maple.

"I want you two to be careful," Maple said, pulling them both into a tight hug. "When all of this is over, I expect to be seeing you at Iryna's wedding."

"We'll do our best," Freyne replied. He freed himself from her arms and stepped back.

Nika tried to blink away his tears, but his efforts proved fruitless. He stood sobbing in Maple's arms for a few minutes until he finally got himself under control.

"It'll be ok, sweetie," she said gently. "We'll see each other again, I promise."

"I know." Nika sniffed. "I'm going to miss you."

"I'll miss you too. You're like family to me now, and I love you both dearly. Now get going before I lock you in the brig of my ship and never allow you to leave."

Nika gave her one more squeeze and wiped his eyes, then turned and leapt into the saddle behind Freyne. Freyne turned and passed him Arnie-Kyn, then nudged Streek into a walk. Nika took one last look at his dear friend and waved, then turned and buried his face in Freyne's back.

*"Even the larger packs need to leave one behind sometimes, young whelp,"* Arnie-Kyn said. *"Your pain is shared by all. Such a harsh land is no place for a being who lives their life at sea, though. Now pull yourself together, we have a long journey ahead."*

4

The plains of Lorendia stretched further than the eye could see. The dry summer wind sent shimmering waves through the long golden grass, and here and there tiny yellow flowers grew in patches, offering the rolling land an occasional splash of colour. Every now and then, a startled rabbit would dash from the grass and disappear behind a rock or into a burrow.

The ground was hard and parched, littered with jagged rocks hidden amongst the grass. Dry creek beds wove their way through the plains, accented by clusters of box and ironbark trees. A hint of green was starting to show, as fresh grass forced its way through after the recent heavy rains. The party followed a wide road that was carved into the land by slaves hundreds of years ago.

Although it was just a week into summer, the days were already hotter than Nika was used to. Even the nights were warmer than usual, making sleep difficult. Adding to Nika's discomfort was the strange whispering that he'd first heard at the University. Once they left Loren Point it began, and there was little respite from it. The constant whispers left him irritable and with a constant headache, and to make it worse, no one else could hear them. Even Arnie-Kyn had no idea what was causing it, leaving Nika to feel like he was going crazy.

After around three and a half weeks of steady riding,

Joplin steered the wagon off the road and led the party towards a cluster of trees some distance away.

"Where are we going?" Gaitan asked, shielding his eyes from the sun. He sat between Joplin and Priye on the long driver's seat under the shade canopy.

"You'll see," Joplin replied.

Nika nudged Streek to follow the wagon, curious as to where Joplin was leading them.

Beyond the trees was a rocky rise which looked impassable. Joplin steered them to the left, and eventually came to a narrow pass that led them into a dense wood. In the middle of the clearing was a pristine pond fed by a stream.

"I'm not sure that many others know about this place," Joplin said, climbing down from the wagon. "I call it the oasis. I usually stop here and rest for a day or two, rehydrate, and enjoy the serenity. From this point on, it's only going to get worse out there, yes."

"It will be good to bathe again." Priye shot a sideways glance at the two men. "You both need one."

"You don't exactly smell like roses," Gaitan hit back.

"No, but I don't smell like a week-old corpse either," Priye smirked.

"A small creek runs off from the pool over the other side." Joplin pointed as though he hadn't heard her comment. "We'll bathe in the creek so we don't murky up the main body of water. It's pure and is fed from a spring, so it's safe to drink."

Gaitan stumbled from the wagon and stalked off into the trees, mumbling to himself. Priye laughed and allowed Joplin to help her down.

"A bit sensitive, yes?" Joplin frowned.

"Oh, he's alright," Priye replied. "I just like to keep him on his toes. I need something to keep me entertained on these long journeys."

Nika dismounted and climbed into the back of the

wagon where Freyne was sleeping. He pressed his body against Freyne's and gently shook his shoulder.

"Wakey wakey," Nika said softly. "Joplin found us a nice spot to set up camp."

Freyne yawned and rolled over in Nika's arms.

"What time is it?" he asked.

"Early afternoon," Nika replied. "I can wake you when dinner's ready if you want more sleep."

"I just want to snuggle," Freyne grumbled. "I missed you last night."

"I'll have a nap before my watch tonight. We can snuggle then," Nika offered.

"I'm getting too old for this." Freyne sighed. "I guess I'd better get up and help."

Freyne's face lit up when he saw the pond and trees. It was much cooler beneath the canopy, and Nika could even hear birds chirping. Arnie's ears pricked up, and he disappeared towards the sounds to hunt his dinner.

Once they'd set up camp, Nika helped Gaitan to fill the waterskins, then gathered his towel, soap, and some fresh clothes and headed to the creek with Freyne. They found a spot where the banks widened a little, and they could see the pebbles on the bottom through the crystal-clear water. Nika stripped off eagerly and stepped carefully into the stream; it was cool and felt refreshing on his burnt skin.

"This reminds me of a stream I used to bathe in," Freyne said dreamily.

"Just think. Had I not come, you'd probably still be there enjoying life," Nika said. He sat down and let the cool water wash over him.

"I wouldn't change a thing," Freyne replied, joining him. "Not one thing. My life has led me to you, and for that I am grateful."

Nika rested his head on Freyne's shoulder, and felt the stress of the journey wash away in the stream. The whispering was quieter in the oasis, which made him feel much better.

"Are you ok, boo? You've been quiet and withdrawn lately," Freyne said, wrapping his arm around Nika's shoulder.

"I'm fine," Nika fibbed.

"No you're not. Usually whenever we get some privacy and in water, you're all over me. What's wrong, boo?"

"It's just…everything." Nika sighed. "The heat. What we have to do. That feeling that I need to do something, but I have no idea what it is. I guess I'm just overwhelmed. I'm sure there are people out there with bigger problems than mine, anyway."

"I doubt that. You have a huge weight on your shoulders, and if you don't share that load, it's going to weigh you down," Freyne said. "Come here."

He helped Nika to slide in between his legs, and started massaging his shoulders. Nika felt the tension easing as Freyne worked at his muscles.

"You've been working so hard on your training lately that you haven't given yourself time to relax," Freyne continued. "If you don't find some way to rest your mind, you'll burn yourself out."

"I try. I just can't." Nika admitted. "My mind never switches off, even when I try and sleep."

"You should try meditating like I taught you," Freyne suggested. "As you know, for me, I slip into the highest realm and just listen. I listen to the birds and the trees, the wind and the rain."

"I've tried it a few times, but it doesn't work for me," Nika said. He leaned forward so Freyne could reach his muscles further down. "If anything, I find it more stressful. I don't understand the languages like you do."

"You just need to take the time to find what works for you. If all else fails, I can make you a sleeping draught to help you get some sleep."

Nika leant back against Freyne's chest and pulled his arms around his waist.

"Or we can just stay here and hide for the rest of our lives," Nika suggested.

Freyne chuckled and kissed his neck.

"Don't tempt me. I don't want to upset Am and be stuck reading their laws again though. Hmm, I wonder if those fools have finished the first volume yet."

The night air was much cooler within the small oasis. After a hearty meal of rabbit stew, the small group sat around the fire with full bellies, watching as Priye and Gaitan bickered back and forth as was their norm. Nika felt refreshed after his bath and nap, and sat on a fallen log wrapped in Freyne's arms, with Arnie at their feet.

Joplin sat quietly, sharpening the blade of his sword. He stood up and gave it a few practise swings, filling the clearing with whooshing noises, then nodded his head in approval.

"Nice sword," Gaitan said.

Joplin wordlessly handed it over, and Gaitan's eyes widened as he tested the blade.

"It's adequate, yes. I have a smith crafting me a new one in Radik's City which will be better, more balanced," he replied. "That thing you wear, though, will be useless against a bigger foe."

"I was issued this when I was in the militia," Gaitan said defensively, handing Joplin's back. "It's kept me alive so far."

"The armour you purchased at Loren Point is good, but your sword is vastly inferior," Joplin continued. "Armour is useless if you have no weapon. You should have bought a decent sword instead. Regardless, the warrior must be skilled enough to handle any weapon he is handed. You can fight, yes?"

"Of course I can!"

"Ok. I give you lessons while we travel. It will give me something to do, yes." Joplin turned and pointed at Nika and Freyne. "You two need armour. It is dangerous to travel around these lands with nothing. You may as well be naked. I advise you to buy some when we get to Sepheren, yes."

"What's your story, Joplin?" Priye asked, changing the subject.

"Not much to tell," he shrugged. "I was a soldier in Cadrinhal for my five years mandatory service. Once I got out, I decided to be a mercenary. I make more money transporting travellers around the continent than I ever did in the military, and I enjoy the long journeys. I am a free man to do as I please."

"Do you ever tire from the travelling?" Nika asked.

"Sometimes," Joplin mused. "I have acquaintances and contacts in every city, though, so I always have a place to rest up wherever I am if I need a break, yes."

"You don't have a special person in your life then?" Priye asked.

"No, never really been interested," Joplin replied. "I have my dearest friends whom I will protect with my life, and I love them dearly. But romance is not for me, no."

"There's nothing wrong with that, dear." Priye said. "Now. Are we staying here another day, or leaving in the morning?"

"It's up to all of you." Joplin shrugged.

Nika and Freyne exchanged glances.

"Let's keep moving," Nika decided. "The sooner we get to Sepheren, the better."

"Very well," Joplin nodded. "Let's have an early night and try to get a good sleep then. Once we reach the turnoff for Linvia tomorrow afternoon, the journey only gets harder."

Nika sat on top of the rocky ledge, watching over the campsite while his friends slept peacefully. He'd come to enjoy his nights on watch. The quiet nights gave him time to think, and a break from the constant travel. He glanced up at the stars, drawing comfort from their twinkling. Although the constellations were different from his world, they had become familiar and reassuring.

Freyne's words came back to him, and with want of something to do, he slipped his mind into the darkest realm. Similar to the highest realm, Nika's vision was lit up with the bright and colourful swirls of life force and plain white unmoving sprites. Although the realm tinged his sight in darkness, he was able to see the land more clearly before him.

A single white sprite was moving towards him. Full of curiosity, Nika stepped from his body and ghosted towards it. As it drew closer, he heard more of the strange whispering, only this time it was growing louder, and sounded separate instead of inside his head. Nika stopped, and watched in surprise as the sprite paused and hovered in front of him.

*"Find Saramas,"* it whispered.

*"What?"*

*"Find Saramas. FIND SARAMAS!"* The sprite shook for a second, then shot back into the direction it came from.

*Well, that hasn't happened before,* Nika thought. *How strange. I wonder who or what Saramas is? I guess I'll ask Freyne and Arnie-Kyn about it in the morning.*

With a sigh, he turned and ghosted back towards the campsite. He floated above the trees, circling the clearing and keeping his eyes peeled for any movement. For the first time in weeks, Nika's mind finally felt at peace and relaxed; no more whispering inside his head, no external noises and chattering.

*Come to think of it, if I tell Freyne and Arnie about this, they probably won't believe me anyway,* Nika thought. *Maybe I should wait until I know more about this Saramas person. I don't want them to think I'm going crazy or overdoing things.*

Nika didn't mention the strange incident or the whispering for the rest of the journey to Sepheren. For the remainder of the long hot and dusty ride across the plains, he used the darkest realm for respite from his discomfort in the physical form.

For each day they spent travelling since leaving Loren Point, Nika carved a marker into the wagon to help him keep track of time. He had to remind himself that there were forty-two days in a month, unlike his world of thirty. After forty-nine days of travel, the grand city of Sepheren appeared on the horizon, a golden smudge that broke up the haze of the desert behind it. Even though Nika was excited to finally reach civilisation, he knew the worst of the journey was still yet to come. Beyond the city was the vast Lorendian Desert, home to many deadly creatures and beasts that Nika hadn't even heard of.

Although Joplin had proven to be trustworthy and was fast becoming a friend, Nika hoped that his stories were exaggerated. The thought of deadly snakes crawling into their tent made his skin crawl. It was going to be a nerve-wracking two weeks.

The majestic city of Sepheren was a sprawling metropolis of mustard-coloured buildings, similar to the bluestone terraces Nika had grown used to, only they were constructed from mud instead. The structures were all joined together in long rows which formed narrow passageways shrouded in shadows, just wide enough for four horses to walk through side by side. Within a few twists and turns of the road, Nika was lost.

The tops of the mud buildings were formed into battlements, and there was no shortage of suspicious guards eyeing them as they passed slowly through the labyrinth. Instead of armour, they wore desert robes that blended well with the colour of the mud. Apart from the guards, the streets were empty, giving Nika the feeling that the place had been abandoned long ago.

He couldn't tell where one house ended and the next began; the wooden doors all looked the same, and the windows high up in the walls were all narrow slits without glass. Occasionally a set of stairs led to the battlements, all moulded from the same smooth mud. Nika was fascinated by the strange city.

After riding for some time, the narrow streets began to widen, and Nika noticed a few people wandering about in the shade. They turned another corner, and found themselves in a dead end, with nothing but a large wooden door in front of them. Joplin halted the wagon and dismounted.

"We'll leave the horses here in the stables. We go the rest of the way on foot, yes."

Joplin pounded his heavy fist on the door, and shortly after it opened a crack. He spoke to someone and handed them some coins, then motioned to the others to join him. The door opened wide, revealing a large stable within. The attendant led the way down a long aisle with stalls either side, and stopped when they reached an exercise area for the horses.

"Take what you need with you," the attendant said. His accent was strange to Nika's ears, soft yet nasally at the same time. "I'll take good care of your horses and wagon."

"Thank you. We'll return in two days, yes."

Once they'd loaded up with their packs, Nika and his friends followed Joplin through the stable to the far end, and exited through another door. The street was much wider than those they'd passed through earlier, and showed signs that people had been there recently. Nika sat Arnie on the ground and walked between Freyne and Priye, trying to take in everything all at once.

"Does anyone actually live here?" Gaitan asked as they walked.

"Hundreds of thousands of people." Joplin nodded.

Towering above the buildings a good distance away were the spires of what looked like a palace. Whether it was mud or sandstone Nika couldn't tell, but a part of him wanted to run off and explore the city, and discover its secrets. He shook his head and tried to focus on where Joplin was taking them.

A loud shout behind them made Nika jump; he turned in time to see six guards chasing someone wearing white desert robes along the battlements. One of the guards managed to catch a handful of their robes, and tried to stop the runner. With a loud tearing noise, the robes tore free, revealing a woman dressed in black leather and with long flowing purple hair. She leapt over the battlements and landed catlike, not far from where Nika stood. A wicked looking crossbow was slung across her back, and she wore high boots with tall pointed heels. Before he could get a look at her face, she bolted back towards the stables and disappeared.

"You don't see that every day," Gaitan said, trying to catch another glimpse of the woman as the red-faced guards pushed past them. "I wonder why they're chasing her?"

"We don't want to find out," Joplin said. "This way."

They stopped at a plain wooden door much like every other door they'd passed. Joplin opened it and stood aside to let everyone inside. The room was empty, except for a dusty old rug on the floor. Joplin stamped his boot three times on the rug, and stepped back.

The rug rose into the air, revealing a set of stairs leading below. A man eyed them for a moment, then beckoned them to enter. The stairs were steep and lit by an occasional torch. Finally they reached a passage, and Joplin paused.

"What you see on the surface is nothing but a ruse. The people here live underground where the temperature is much cooler," he explained.

"Why go to all the trouble of building it then?" Nika asked.

"For defence," Freyne offered. "During one of the great wars, an army attempted to take the city. They invaded, and thought it was abandoned. It was hot and inhospitable, and there was no water, so the army moved on. Not one life was lost here. Meanwhile, the people live underground in comfort and rarely need to visit the surface."

"Wow," he breathed.

"Correct." Joplin nodded. "Come. I take you to the lodgings."

The passage opened into a large chamber filled with stalls and people as far as Nika could see. The people were dressed in brightly coloured fabrics and went about their business without paying any attention to the party. The chamber was lit up by natural light, though Nika couldn't see where it was coming from.

*"The light is reflected down here by a series of mirrors,"* Freyne explained. *"They even have a temple of Am down here somewhere, which I learnt about during my studies."*

*"Wow,"* Nika repeated. *"Is the underground city still a secret?"*

*"Not anymore,"* Freyne replied. *"It has been known about for years since the wars ended. An army did try to attack since, but they couldn't find the entrances, so they gave up."*

"This is the northern bazaar," Joplin said as they

walked. "Similar to the markets you would be familiar with. We can restock our supplies here later."

Nika reached down and picked up Arnie-Kyn, and followed Joplin through the bazaar and into a wide passage that had been carved roughly out of stone. The next chamber was a round dome, three levels high and with doors evenly spaced along each level. Nika glanced around, his mind boggling at the architecture.

"What you want?" A woman with a stern look shuffled across to them from one of the doors and stood with her hands on her hips. Her accent was thick, and she pronounced her w's as v's.

"Give us four pods, woman," Joplin said gruffly.

"We don't serve you kind here. Leave." She glowered at him.

"My kind? I am a soldier from Radik's City. Have you no manners, wench?" Joplin glared back at her, his hand resting on the hilt of his sword.

Nika swallowed hard; the tension in the air was thicker than the heat above ground. He looked uneasily at Freyne, then glanced back at Joplin and the woman.

The woman suddenly laughed and threw her arms open wide. Joplin swept her into a big hug, laughing heartily.

"You crazy woman, yes." Joplin let her go and turned to Nika and the others. "This is my friend, Arana."

Nika let out a deep breath.

"Welcome. I give you the lower pods next to the far passage. Much cooler," she smiled. "Come."

The pods were tiny. Each one had a moulded mud slab with a thin mattress on top, and a space to sit their packs. Freyne had to stoop so he didn't hit his head on the roof.

"This is different," Nika murmured.

"Even a neophyte's cell is bigger and more comfortable than this." Freyne nodded. "At least it's a private place to sleep though."

"Is there a place to bathe here?" Nika asked.

"There are no baths here," Freyne explained. "You're not going to like it."

"Not going to like what?" Nika frowned.

"These pods are the only privacy we get in this city," Freyne answered, somewhat delicately. "These people have little modesty. You'll see."

Nika felt his belly squirm from Freyne's words. A loud knock made him jump.

"I'm taking Gaitan to the amenities. Do you want to come so you know the way?" Joplin asked once Freyne opened the door.

"Now is as good a time as any," Freyne nodded. "Let's go."

After hiking through a maze of passages, they finally stepped through a door and into sunshine. Nika squinted his eyes closed, and paused to allow them to adjust. They were on a smooth stone platform with what looked like a stone bench seat running along the length of the wall opposite the entry. Evenly spaced along the bench were holes with grooves, and a number of barrels were strategically placed every few feet.

Nika turned and looked behind him; the platform was built out over the desert gorge that bordered the western wall of the city. As he turned back towards the bench seat, his stomach turned to lead as he realised with horror where he was standing. Unperturbed, Joplin took a rag from a stand by the door, and dropped his trousers. Hitching up his armour, he sat over one of the holes.

Mortified, Nika backed out of the door as fast as his feet could take him.

"Are you kidding me?" he demanded as Freyne joined him.

"I told you you wouldn't like it," Freyne said with the slightest hint of a grin.

"There is no way I'm…*doing that*…with an audience!"

"There's no plumbing here," Freyne explained. "Very little water. The people have adapted to desert life over thousands of years. It's a way of life for them."

"I don't care. That's something I need privacy for." Nika crossed his arms uncomfortably.

"It's ok, boo. We'll come back tonight and take turns. I don't fancy sharing, either."

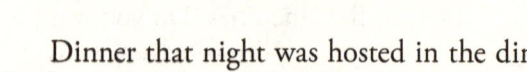

Dinner that night was hosted in the dining hall, not far from the bazaar. The chamber was square, and lined with rows and rows of moulded mud slabs to mimic tables and bench seats. It was lit up by oil lamps, and the walls were draped with soft fabrics which made it feel more homey and less like a mud hut. The chamber was filled with around a hundred people, all dining merrily. Nika sat quietly next to Freyne and picked at his meal of spiced rice and beans. His belly was sore, and rumbled rudely.

"This is the common area," Joplin was saying. "All those who don't wish to or are unable to cook can come here for a free meal. No one goes hungry."

"Who pays for it all?" Gaitan asked.

"The Marquess. The people can volunteer for guard duty to give back for the free meals if they wish. There are no homeless people here, yes."

Freyne rubbed his knee against Nika's.

*"Are you ok, boo?"* he asked.

*"Not really,"* Nika confessed. *"I don't feel so good. I think I'll go back to the pod."*

*"Want me to go with you?"*

*"I'll be alright. You enjoy your dinner."* Nika pushed his plate away and stood up. *"I'll see you soon."*

No one paid any attention as Nika left the chamber. He stuffed his hands in his pockets and walked through the underground passageways towards the amenities, hoping with every fibre in his body they were empty.

Lucky for Nika, he was able to relieve himself without interruption. The platform was lit by a single lantern; the night sky was dotted with countless twinkling stars, and in the distance, crickets chirped to one another. The desert night was bitterly cold, a stark contrast from the dry arid heat of the day.

After scrubbing his hands thoroughly with the supplied alcohol, Nika wandered back inside, glad that some of his pain was eased. He walked slowly back towards where he thought the pods were, his mind far away.

"Halt! Who dares to trespass on Marquess property?"

Nika froze and swept his surroundings; he was in a small unfamiliar chamber with an ornate gate in front of him, which hid a flight of mud steps. Two angry-looking guards were pointing long spears at his heart.

"Er, I'm sorry," Nika said quickly. "I think I'm lost…"

"Silence! You're under arrest for trespassing."

Nika's heart started beating faster, and the pain in his belly returned. The guards moved closer, the tips of the spears brushing against his desert robe. He bit his lip and instinctively reached his mind towards the lowest realm.

"Ah, a mancer, huh? That makes you a spy, too!"

Someone placed something heavy on Nika's head, and before he could do anything, he blacked out.

Freyne sat listening to Joplin talking about some of his great adventures. He caught Priye's gaze, and she rolled her eyes with a smirk.

"Where's lover-boy?" she asked quietly.

"He wasn't feeling too good. He's gone back to the pod." Freyne replied.

"I bet it's the food," she nodded. "I can mix something up to help him feel better when we get back there."

"Thank you. My own medicinal skills are minimal compared to yours. I only know a few remedies that I've picked up over the years. Hopefully he's feeling better after a lay-down." Freyne looked up as Arana approached the table with a big grin on her face. She'd changed into a loose flowing purple dress, and looked quite pretty with her hair cascading freely over her shoulders.

"Well, there you are, woman!" Joplin stood and ushered her to the table.

"Hello, everyone," Arana smiled.

A flush crept into Gaitan's cheeks as she sat on the slab next to him.

"I no see you for a while. What brings you this way?" she asked.

"My friends here are on the way to a wedding and needed a guide to cross the desert." Joplin paused and took a sip of his cactus juice. "What's news, yes?"

"We have a new marquess," she replied. "Rumour has it she's a woman. Not to be trifled with."

"A woman? The old timers will have trouble swallowing that," Joplin grinned.

"Apparently one of the elders was overheard complaining about her. We haven't seen him since." Arana looked around, then lowered her voice. "Last week, there was some drama in the southern quadrant. Someone caused one of the chambers to collapse. It killed around a hundred people, maybe more. There are people still missing."

Freyne frowned and leaned in closer.

"How did that happen?" He asked.

"No one knows," she shrugged. "Some people say it was a mancer, some say it was an earthquake. I didn't see it, so I can't say for sure. The marquess has issued more guards on the surface though, and they're pretty jumpy."

"Could it have collapsed by itself?" Gaitan asked.

Arana shot him an incredulous look.

"All of our structures are heavily reinforced, and moulded in such a way that they will never collapse. The engineers are constantly monitoring the chambers for stress lines."

A shiver travelled down Freyne's spine.

"Is there any way I could go and take a look?"

"I doubt it." Arana shrugged. "The section has been sealed off. No one is allowed in the area, and the guards will arrest anyone caught snooping. You're best to stay out of things like this. My people don't take kindly to foreigners sticking their noses where they don't belong."

"Understandable." Freyne stood up and stretched. "On that note, I think it's time for me to retire for the evening."

"I need to go, too. Early rise for me." Arana slid off the slab and smiled. "Sleep well, everyone."

The dining hall was slowly emptying as people finished their meals and left for their homes. Freyne walked back to the pods with Joplin, Gaitan, and Priye, his mind distracted by Arana's news. He had a bad feeling in the pit of his stomach, and found himself wondering if Khel had something to do with the collapse.

It was much cooler in the domed pod chamber, and the few people moving around spoke in hushed tones.

"Most people retire early here, and rise before sunrise," Joplin said softly. "They go to the surface first thing and collect water from the dew traps."

"This place is so strange," Gaitan stated.

"Indeed." Joplin stopped to unlock his door. "See you tomorrow, yes."

Gaitan let himself into his own pod, and Priye followed Freyne to the far door. Freyne turned the handle, but the door was locked. With a shrug, he took a small key from his pocket and jiggled it in the lock.

To his surprise, Nika wasn't there. Arnie-Kyn was perched on the bed next to the crochet mouse, and eyed

61

Freyne as he stepped inside.

"*Where's Nika?*" he asked the cat.

"*One thought he was with you?*" Arnie replied.

"*He left around an hour ago and said he was coming back here.*"

"What's wrong?" Priye asked from outside.

"He's not here," Freyne replied.

He sat on the bed and slipped into the realm. He projected himself from his body, and scanned the area for Nika's aura. There was no sign of him anywhere. Feeling a jolt of panic, Freyne checked the amenities, then double-backed through the bazaar to the stables.

Nika's aura was nowhere to be seen. He was gone.

## 5

A sharp pain stabbing into his head caused Nika to wake. He tried to open his eyes, but he couldn't; his head felt heavy, and his mind was numb, as though a heavy fog had taken up residence inside his brain. Nika tried to move, but his body wouldn't respond. He soon became aware of voices around him, and tried to focus on them. He knew he should feel scared and confused, but the fog was too thick, and thinking hurt.

"What are we going to do with him, Mistress?" a man asked.

"I haven't decided yet, Captain." A woman said. Her voice was warm and thick with an accent.

"May I suggest we execute him? He was found snooping around near the entrance to the palace, after all. He's probably the mancer that collapsed the cavern last week."

"He's too cute to be a menace," the woman purred. "I think I'll keep this one as my concubine. It's time I had a new pet."

"Do you think that is wise, Mistress?" the man sounded unsure. "He could be deadly."

"Don't you dare question my authority." Her voice turned to poison. "Now take him to my court and prepare him for me. I'll be along shortly."

Nika felt himself being lifted and carried, then

dropped onto something hard. Pain shot through his head, and once again his senses shut down into nothingness. He had no concept of time or space, only darkness and fog.

The smell of cologne jolted his senses awake. He was laying on something soft that brushed gently against his bare skin. The weight on his head lessened a little, and the slightest amount of fog dissipated. He managed to open his eyes a crack.

"Ah, hello, my pet. You're finally awake." A woman stepped into his vision and shoved her face in his. "Oh my, look at you. Even your eyes are pretty. If you're a good boy, I might even let you stay in my private chamber."

Her eyes were brown, but instead of the warmth that greeted him every time he looked into Freyne's, hers showed nothing but cunning and spite. Her long black hair glistened down her shoulders in stark contrast to her pale skin. She wore a flimsy black chemise that showed off more than Nika was comfortable seeing. She reminded him of a vampire.

Nika jammed his eyes shut. The woman sat next to him and began stroking his hair and chest, like he was a dog. A part of him wanted to recoil in horror, but still he could not move. He tried to reach out his mind to the realms to no avail; a sharp jolt of pain shot through his head, and his entire body shook.

"Now now, don't be like that," she chided him. "You *will* give me what I want. No man has ever been able to refuse my...charm. And if you don't play nicely, I will hand you over to my Lord, and you can do his bidding instead. I'm the only one protecting you from being enslaved into his service as a mancer."

A loud banging of fist on wood reached Nika's ears, and the woman's hand froze.

"Wait here, my pet. Mistress will be right back, and if you're really good, I'll lessen the halo just a little more so we can have some fun."

The woman pressed her lips to Nika's, then left. He had just enough sense of self to recognise his rising panic. Cautiously, he pushed his mind towards the realm again, but jerked it back just in time to avoid another jolt of pain. He was trapped.

On the edge of his hearing, he could hear raised voices in the next room. He turned his focus to trying to move his fingers and toes, when he felt a soft sensation tugging somewhere in his mind. Nika hesitated; his head was already pounding with pain, he didn't want more.

A stronger tugging sensation pulled at him again. It was foreign, strange, nothing like the gentle pull of Freyne's mind. Nika wearily relented, and felt his mind being pulled towards the darkest realm. Before he could snatch it back, he found himself safely within the realm. He pushed himself from his body and looked around at his surroundings; the fog was gone and he was finally able to think clearly.

His body lay on a pile of cushions next to a throne, naked except for a simple loincloth covering his most private of parts. A thin silver ring embedded with rubies sat atop his head; its aura was dark grey much like the fog it inflicted.

A single white sprite floated above his body and hovered.

"*You are in danger,*" it whispered.

"Huh? What – who are you?"

"*I am no one. You are in danger, and I don't have much time. You must find Saramas.*"

"Who or what is Saramas?" Nika demanded.

"*Listen. You must not allow yourself to remain captive of the Mistress. The silver halo on your head is a realm blocker which prevents access to the three realms. You are lucky that I was able to pull you into the darkest realm, but you will need to remove that halo if you are to have any chance to escape. The Mistress has several mancers in her service, and your lover won't be able to ward them off by himself."*

"Where's Freyne?"

*"Find Saramas. Head to the Fens. Now hurry. You don't have much time."* The sprite hovered for a second, then shot towards the door.

Nika followed the sprite with his eyes, and in the distance, he could see the faint outline of Freyne's familiar aura, though instead of his usual deep purple, it was outlined by a dark throbbing red. Nika turned back to his body and studied the halo. He hadn't tried to manipulate the darkest realm before; he hesitated as Freyne's teachings came back to him.

*"The darkest realm is unlike the others. We use it to manipulate life, not our surroundings."*

The sounds of metal on metal and yelling came closer. Five more auras became visible and were moving towards Freyne's. Nika bit his ethereal lip; he focused on his body until he could see his own life force flowing through his veins. He began to draw power from the realm and funnel it into his left arm. His physical body broke into a sweat as Nika used the dark forces to animate his arm. With a final burst of power, he jerked his arm and pushed the halo from his head. It fell to the ground with a clang. He was free.

Nika returned to his body just as the door burst open. The woman and around twenty guards, plus four others wearing long black robes, ran into the room and barricaded the door. No one paid any attention to Nika. He kept his eyes closed, and pushed himself half into the lowest realm.

"They're getting closer, Mistress! You need to flee." One of the mancers looked panicked.

"I'm not going anywhere," the Mistress hissed. "You will kill them all, or I will summon my Lord and you can deal with his wrath."

"Y-yes, Mistress."

The sounds of fighting grew louder, and the guards in the room readied themselves. Nika focused on keeping still and formulating his plan of attack. A loud scream echoed from the other room, then everything went silent.

After thirty agonising seconds, the door exploded inwards with a loud roar. Five guards were thrown backwards from the blast. Freyne stepped inside, flanked by Joplin and Gaitan, their swords dripping blood. A deep gash in Gaitan's left thigh trickled onto the floor. Freyne was glowing with pure energy from the realm; his look was pure murder.

"Release him now, and I'll let you live," he warned, his voice dripping with acid.

"Boys, why so hostile?" the Mistress purred. "Put away your swords. I'm sure we can solve this in a much friendlier fashion."

Gaitan faltered for a moment, and stood staring at her with a look of lust on his face. Joplin slapped him, rousing him from his reverie.

"Your powers of seduction are useless, woman." Joplin spat. "Release him."

"Who do you think you are? You are outnumbered, both in strength and power. Give it up now, and maybe I'll let *you* live."

The Mistress made a gesture and the guards rushed forward; Gaitan and Joplin moved to block their blows. Freyne downed two of them easily with blasts of energy. Nika sensed movement in the realm, and could see two of the mancers readying themselves.

One of the mancers was slowly drawing power from the realm. Nika instinctively drew a pocket of power also; once the mancer reached his limit, Nika pushed the pocket towards him. The mancer's face suddenly looked shocked as the extra surge flowed into his body, more power than he could control. With an ear-shattering scream, his body exploded from the inside, splattering everyone around him in gore.

The other three mancers faltered. As the guards froze in horror, Gaitan and Joplin cut them down easily. Freyne took care of the second mancer, as the remaining two snatched the Mistress and tried to drag her to safety.

Nika was ready. He sprang to his feet and blocked the door with his body. The Mistress screamed and stumbled backwards; she tripped over her own feet and fell roughly down the step of the dais. One of the mancers hurled a fireball at Nika, but he swept it easily to one side and sent his own ball of energy back. The mancer was hurled backwards and crashed into the heavy throne.

The final mancer fell to his knees and cowered with his hands over his head.

"Please don't kill me!" he cried.

"Give me one good reason why I shouldn't?" Nika growled.

"I-I saved you! You would have been dead had I not told the others that you're a mancer." The man was visibly shaking. "They were going to kill you for trespassing."

"So instead, you allowed them to think that I was responsible for collapsing your tunnels just to make yourself look good," Nika summarised. He looked at the halo on the floor, and reached out his hand. The halo flew into his grasp, and he glared at the mancer. "Let's see how you like it."

Nika jammed the halo on his head, and the mancer fell roughly to the floor, paralysed. He turned to the others just as Gaitan downed the final guard. Joplin already had the Mistress and was binding her hands behind her back. Freyne lowered his hands and released the last of the energy he was holding. Nika bent down and pulled a scimitar from one of the dead guards' hands. The room was filled with blood and gore.

"Are you ok?" Freyne demanded.

"I'm fine." Nika grimaced. "We need to get out of here."

"What are we going to do with the woman?" Joplin called.

"We'll bring her with us to the far edge of the causeway and let her find her own way back," Freyne grated. "That should keep the guards off our back and buy us some time."

"You'll never get away with this," she hissed.

Joplin slapped her in the face and dragged her to her feet.

"Come. We must go."

Gaitan wordlessly handed Nika a desert robe from one of the fallen guards, then helped Joplin force one onto the Mistress. They gagged her mouth and pulled the hood down so no one could see her face.

"This way." Joplin hoisted the Mistress over his shoulder and hurried back through the destroyed door.

Gaitan limped a few steps and collapsed to the ground, gasping in pain. Nika helped him to his feet, and slipped his arm around his friend's waist. Freyne took his other side, and together they helped him hobble from the room.

Nika's mind balked at the carnage in the next room. Bodies of palace guards lay strewn across the floor in pools of blood. The image of the mancer exploding forced itself into his mind, and a horrible feeling grew from his gut and into his throat. Before he could do anything, he threw up what little was in his stomach. To make matters worse, the whispering was back with a vengeance, almost shouting, and echoed loudly in his head.

"Are you alright?" Freyne demanded.

"Just go," Nika said shortly.

The palace was empty and eerily quiet. They stepped into an antechamber by the main entrance; the mud walls were covered by large tapestries, and a number of ornate wooden seats lined the walls, flanking a door on the left and right. Two dead guards were slumped in the corner, and a trail of blood showed they'd been dragged from outside.

"Hey, let us out! Somebody, please help us!" Someone banged on the door to left.

Joplin paused and shouldered the door. The latch broke easily and he stumbled into the room. A number of men and women were huddled together, their hands tied behind their backs. Joplin wordlessly cut their bonds and nodded towards the entrance.

"Thank you," one of the men blubbered.

"Get out of here, yes," Joplin said gruffly.

The man beckoned to the others, and they fled from the palace. Nika and Freyne followed cautiously. Opposite the entrance, Nika recognised the gates that he'd seen just before he was captured. Arana waved and hurried over to them.

"Thank goodness you're all ok," she said quickly. "Come. I must get you to the surface. It's no longer safe for you here."

"Where's Priye?" Nika demanded.

"She's with the wagon. Now come."

---

Arana guided the party up a flight of stairs which led to a plain empty house, much like the entrance to the bazaar. From the doorway, Nika could see they were right next to the palace; it towered above the city, casting them in shadow.

Priye climbed down from the wagon with another woman and hurried towards Gaitan. His face was pale and his head rolled around as though he were on the edge of consciousness.

"Put him in the back," she ordered briskly.

Nika and Freyne carefully lifted him into the wagon, then quickly got out of her way. Joplin wrestled the Mistress into the driver's seat and turned to Arana and her friend.

"Thanks for your help, yes." He hugged her tightly.

"Any time. Be careful out there. I see you soon, my friend."

"Thank you," Nika added.

Arana smiled at Nika and Freyne, then dragged her friend back into the house. Nika turned to Streek, and was surprised to see Arnie-Kyn perched on top, his tail flickering. Nika reached up and collected the cat, then hurled himself onto the saddle. Freyne wordlessly mounted behind him.

Joplin urged the horses into a walk and led the way through the abandoned city streets. Nika followed the wagon, deep in his own thoughts. The images of the mancer filled him with horror; the man was dead because of him. All those guards were dead because he wasn't watching where he was going.

*"Stop wallowing in pity, human."* Arnie-Kyn said.

*"I'm not wallowing,"* Nika said defensively. *"All of those deaths were unnecessary."*

*"They were necessary, boo,"* Freyne said gently. *"It wasn't easy for us to find you. One of Arana's friends is a palace guard, and he was the only way we were able to locate you. The marquess, or Mistress they call her, was already organising a party to come and round up the rest of us."*

*"But why?"* Nika asked.

*"Someone used mancery to collapse a section of the underground city,"* Freyne explained. *"The people from that quadrant were getting ready to rise up against her for not finding who was responsible. You just happened to be in the wrong place at the wrong time, and she realised she could blame it all on you to make herself look good again."*

Nika shuddered. He wanted desperately to wrap himself in Freyne's arms and forget his time at the palace, and hated having to wait. It was hot outside already, and he guessed it was around lunch time.

*"Wait a minute. How long was I gone for?"* Nika asked. *"It was evening when they captured me."*

*"Around fourteen hours,"* Freyne said. *"We had Arana and her friend asking around their circles to try and locate you. It was only around three hours ago that her guard friend found out that you'd been taken to the palace. I couldn't see your aura anywhere."*

*"They put some realm blocker thing on my head."* Nika shuddered again. *"I was only able to access the darkest realm. Luckily I was able to use it to get the halo off my head."*

*"How did you manage that?"* Freyne asked. *"The darkest realm cannot be manipulated like the others."*

*"You taught me how to manipulate someone's life force in order to kill them. I figured that if we can reduce life, we can also give life. So I poured the life force into my arm and made it push the halo off my head. After that I was able to return to my body and function properly again."*

Arnie sat up and turned his head to face Nika; his eyes bore into Nika's for a moment, like he were searching for something.

*"What?"* Nika demanded.

*"One has nothing constructive to add."* Arnie settled back down between Nika's legs. *"At least you avoided being the woman's concubine."*

*"Hey! How did you know about that?!"*

*"Concubine?"* Freyne asked.

*"Nothing happened."* Nika grumbled. *"Please, just drop it."*

---

Freyne was quiet as they rode through the abandoned streets of the city's surface. The events of the last few hours were still fresh in his mind, and the fear of losing Nika yet again was too real to ignore. He was exhausted; his eyelids felt heavy and it was a struggle to keep them open. The churning nausea from realm exposure made him want to throw up.

The rage he'd felt when he learned of Nika's capture left a sour taste in his mouth. Many guards were slain in their path to rescue Nika, and although Freyne knew it was them or him, he still felt the guilt stabbing at him. He was a man of his faith, not a cold-blooded murderer.

The city gates came into view, and a lone guard waved for them to stop. Joplin halted the wagon, and bent down to shake the guard's hand. Freyne recognised him as Arana's friend.

"Go quickly now. Remember the plan. Take care, my friend."

Joplin clasped his hand firmly, then urged the horses into a brisk walk.

"Halt! Close the gates!"

Freyne flinched and felt Nika tense. A number of guards swarmed from the guard hut and started turning the winches to close the heavy wooden gates. Behind them, the surviving mancer from the throne room emerged, red-faced and out of breath.

"That's them!" he wheezed. "They have the Mistress! Kill them all!"

Before Freyne could react, the mancer attacked with a sharp stab into his mind. He gasped and grasped at his head. For a split second it felt as through a white-hot knife was being pressed into his skull. The world spun so fast his vision blurred.

A sickening scream pierced his ears, and the pain lessened enough that he could open his eyes. Freyne spotted the mancer sprawled on the ground next to several bodies; the rest of the guards were running away in terror.

"GO! Let's get the fuck out of here!" Nika bellowed.

Joplin shoved the Mistress from the seat of the wagon and urged the horses into a gallop; Freyne clung onto Nika tightly as Streek leapt forward through the gates. He took one last look at the bodies strewn around the ground, then everything went black.

Freyne woke with a start; someone was shaking his shoulder. He opened his eyes to see Nika peering at him with a worried look on his face.

"Are you ok?" Nika demanded.

"I…think so." Freyne grimaced as the nausea returned. "Where are we?"

"We're in a smuggler's cave. Joplin said we'll be safe to rest here until nightfall."

Freyne glanced around the cave; a small fire crackled nearby, and Priye was stitching Gaitan's wound against his protests. The only light came from the fire and Nika's firestone.

"What did you do to the mancer and those guards?" Freyne asked.

Nika sat roughly on the ground and rested his head on Freyne's shoulder.

"I don't know exactly. I just – it was almost like instinct. I don't know how else to describe it." Nika sighed. "I don't think I'll ever get used to this."

*"We'll make a mancer out of the human yet."* Arnie-Kyn materialised into Freyne's view, and sat staring at Nika. *"As all young whelps must learn, trusting your instinct will keep you and the pack alive."*

*"What was all of that even about?"* Nika asked. *"According to Am, everything happens for a reason. I don't see any reason for that drama back there at all. It doesn't make sense."*

*"It is not our place to question the reason,"* Freyne replied automatically. *"I believe the quote is 'Trust in Am, for only they can see the bigger picture that is beyond the sight of any mortal –'"*

Freyne broke off as the sound of footsteps echoed through the cave. Joplin stepped from the passage and paused to let his eyes adjust.

"No one followed us," he said finally. "I covered up

our tracks just in case. We should be safe here until it gets dark, yes."

"Why didn't they follow us?" Gaitan demanded. "Are we heading into a trap?"

"Sepherites are notoriously superstitious and afraid of anything magical," Joplin replied, sitting on a flat rock by the fire. "On that note. Who are you people?"

Freyne glanced at Nika.

*"Do we tell him the truth?"* he asked quickly.

*"I think we can trust him."* Nika nodded.

"We are who we said we are," Freyne said, returning his gaze to Joplin.

"I guide people across these lands often enough to know that you aren't heading to a wedding," Joplin said pointedly. "I don't care what your business is, but I need to know if we are heading towards danger, yes."

"That's fair. There is no wedding," Freyne admitted. "We are looking for someone who is causing a lot of trouble. If you wish to part ways at Loralyon we'll completely understand."

"Who is the one you seek?"

"His name is Khel," Freyne said carefully. "I believe he has ties to the Black Ibis cult. Do you know of him?"

Joplin shook his head.

"No. I have heard of this cult, though. It was outlawed in Cadrinhal after someone tried to assassinate the king many years ago. Any cultist found in Cadrinhal is put straight to the death." Joplin narrowed his eyes in thought. "I will uphold my end of the agreement and take you to Maikaden City as agreed. Now get some rest. We leave at sundown, yes."

6

Ironstone Keep loomed threateningly in the distance, towering above the forest like a dark sentinel. The streaks of red iron veins visible in the black stone made it appear like the rock itself was bleeding. Surrounding the keep was a vast forest of death; what was once lush and green and teeming with life was now a wasteland of dead trees, and more recently, ghouls and other foul creatures.

Ashavan paused and removed his gauntlet so he could wipe the sweat from his brow. As he glanced up at the keep, a foreboding aura seemed to emanate from the building itself, a warning to all to stay away. A prickling sensation travelled from Ashavan's spine to the tips of his fingers; he looked down and noticed the exposed skin on his forearms were raised in little bumps and his hairs were standing on end.

As though the punctuate the moment, a sharp pain stabbed at his wrist. He turned his hand over and looked at the ibis symbol tattooed on his skin; the black ink was glowing a sickly orange colour. Without delay, he resumed his trek towards the keep with the howl of a ghoul on his tail.

There were no guards at the gates, nor the main entrance. Ashavan sheathed his sword and hurried inside, then strode purposefully towards the war room which was located in the highest tower. He groaned inwardly at the thought of having to climb all the way to the top; his bones were weary after his long journey, and his armour seemed to weigh heavier with each step he took.

Gone were the days of servants and members of the Brotherhood roaming the corridors, who would stop and give him a wide berth, sometimes cowering in fear. Like the forest, the people that once lived and worked within the walls of the keep were now dead.

Ashavan shuddered and forced the horror of the great purge from his mind. He couldn't afford to show any form of weakness while in his Lord's presence, or he too would be expunged. *The only way I can protect Tysion is by staying alive. I can't break my promise to him, not now, not ever,* he thought. As Ashavan approached the large doors that led to the war room, he spotted Ornas striding towards him, the usual frown upon his face.

"Ashavan." He nodded curtly.

"Ornas."

Ashavan hated the man, but knew better than to let it show. Without another word, he pushed open the doors and entered. The war room was really just a repurposed chamber, dominated by a large table in the middle covered with maps and scrolls, and overflowing bookcases which lined the round walls. An elegant armchair sat to one side, and at the far end of the chamber, a pair of ornate wooden doors opened onto a balcony, offering a view of the dying landscape. Lord Du'Rakis stood in the doorway, wrapped in his dark cloak as always.

Ashavan dropped to his knee and planted his fist on the ground as was expected of him. Ornas joined him, and together they stared at the floor, unmoving.

"Report?" Du'Rakis demanded.

"It is done, My Lord." Ashavan said formally. "Ivynhope is expunged."

"No survivors I trust?"

"None whatsoever, My Lord."

"Good. And you, Ornas?"

"I have the journal you requested, My Lord. Since earning the king's trust, he gave it to me willingly."

Du'Rakis turned and reached out his hand. Ornas pulled a small book from his robes and placed it in their Lord's hand.

"Come. We must go to Sepheren."

Ashavan dragged himself to his feet, his armour creaking in protest with every move. He followed Lord Du'Rakis onto the balcony, and into the swirling haze of energy they called a portal. Immediately, his body felt weightless, nothing but a passing breeze in time. His vision blurred and warped, and everything started to spin faster and faster, making him dizzy. Bright lights rushed past him, blinding his senses. Just as he thought he couldn't take the spinning any longer, his feet landed on solid land, and he stumbled, almost colliding with Lord Du'Rakis. Ashavan staggered to one side, and bent over with his hands on his tassets, fighting against the urge to throw up.

The room was lit by torches, and the few windows showed that it was dark outside. For a moment he was confused, then remembered the time difference compared to back home.

"I see the mighty General Ashavan still can't handle a wee portal," a voice purred.

Ashavan looked up to see Rissa smirking at him. He glared back, barely hiding his disgust for the youngest of Lord Du'Rakis' generals.

"Silence. What happened here?" Lord Du'Rakis snapped.

"Those mancers you sent me were useless, My Lord," Rissa replied. "We collapsed the section as you ordered, and rounded up the prisoners. The plan was going well, until the palace was attacked and the prisoners escaped."

"WHAT? How did they escape?" Lord Du'Rakis hissed.

"The guards captured someone snooping around, so they brought him to me for executing. He's a foreigner, so I decided to pin the collapse on him to silence the denizens." Rissa paused and gestured around the throne room; Ashavan noticed pools of blood and gore covering the floor. "His friends stormed the palace and killed all the guards to free him. So now the prisoners are back in the labyrinth hiding, or so they think. They're in the storage chamber in the Eastern quadrant. It will hardly be a challenge for Ashavan to cut them into pieces."

"Who were these people?" Lord Du'Rakis demanded.

"No one important, My Lord." Rissa shrugged. "I think they were just mercenaries looking for a fight."

"Let's get this over and done with," Ashavan said, drawing his sword impatiently.

"My, aren't you grumpy today," Rissa smirked.

Ashavan scowled.

Lord Du'Rakis held up his hand for silence. A cold shiver ran down Ashavan's spine as it always did when his Lord was using his powers. He licked his lips while gripping his sword tighter with both hands. He hated mancery and anything he couldn't kill with his sword; magic was the one thing his armour and strength were useless against and left him completely vulnerable.

A low rumble below the palace caused the floor to vibrate. Ashavan looked at Ornas and Rissa, who both seemed unbothered by whatever their lord was doing. After a few seconds, the shaking stopped. Lord Du'Rakis turned and faced them, though his expression was hidden by his hood.

"Sheathe your sword, Ashavan. You won't be needing it."

Ashavan did as he was told, puzzled. As the steel slid into the scabbard with a hiss, a deafening explosion beyond the palace shook the floor once more, and Ashavan lost his balance. A high-pitched ringing sounded in his ears as a wave of energy rippled from the explosion epicentre.

"What was that?!" he yelled.

"The prisoners are no more. We are done here." Lord Du'Rakis beckoned to Rissa. "Your mission here is complete. Come with us back to the keep, we have much to do."

---

The ancient causeway stretched across the gorge and disappeared into the desert far on the other side. Even with his enhanced vision, Nika couldn't make out the bottom of the chasm. His mind boggled at the thought of the massive pylons and the bridge itself being built by hand with no machinery or engineers. He wasn't even sure how it was possible that the structure was still standing after thousands of years.

Behind them, Sepheren glowed golden against the night sky. The gates were still closed, but no guards could be seen. Nika turned his back on the city and tried to push the memories from his mind.

"Let's go," Joplin called from the wagon. "We need to put as much distance as possible between us and Sepheren. I don't think they'll come after us, but we need to be careful just in case, yes."

Nika felt his eyes drooping and fought to stay awake as they rode across the causeway. He'd hardly slept that afternoon, and the fatigue of the incident at Sepheren still weighed heavily on him. The sound of the horse's hooves on the stones soon lulled him into a doze.

*He stood alone on a mountain path, a hint of snow on the ground, the sky a dark grey colour. He could sense a darkness, a being of pure evil. Nika started to run, but it followed him, hunting him, hungry for human flesh.*

*Nika looked over his shoulder; the beast was nowhere to be seen. He slowed to a walk, then turned his head back towards the path.*

*The beast lay before him, an enormous serpent, its long body thicker than that of a person. Its eyes were black and soulless; it drew back its head and hissed, a long pointed tongue protruding from between its sharp fangs.*

*The snake drew back its head, then paused; the snake's face blurred for a moment, then morphed into the face of the Mistress. Before Nika could react, a terrifying explosion ripped through the snake...*

Nika jolted awake in fright, just as a bright flash lit up the sky. Before he could wipe the sleepy confusion from his eyes, Streek reared up onto her hind legs, and Nika fell roughly onto the stone. A loud roar echoed around the gorge and the causeway shook; Streek bolted with Freyne still in the saddle. Behind them, an explosion ripped through Sepheren.

A strange dark energy emanated from the city and made his spine tingle; something powerful yet foreign, pulsating and swirling. Nika could feel each and every pulse deep within his bones. He stayed on the ground, staring into the distance with awe. He had no idea what the energy was, but somehow it felt familiar.

As quickly as he'd felt the strange energy, it disappeared, leaving him feeling momentarily empty. He shook his head, confused.

"Are you alright?"

Nika turned to see Freyne behind him, leading Streek by her reins.

"What was that?" Nika asked.

"What was what?" Freyne stopped and looked puzzled.

"You didn't feel it?"

"Boo, I have no idea what you're talking about," Freyne said with a frown. "Did you hit your head or something?"

"No." Nika pushed himself up off the ground, and accepted Freyne's proffered hand. His body hurt from the fall, but he was at least ok. "Thanks. Er, where's Joplin?"

"He's around a mile back that way," Freyne replied, pointing. "We're not far from the desert. Let's get going, I don't want any more near misses or whatever caused that explosion to catch up with us."

Freyne helped Nika back onto Streek, and sat behind him with his arms protectively around his waist.

"Where's Arnie-Kyn?" Nika asked, as a pang of worry shot through him.

"I put him in the back of the wagon with Priye. He's fine."

Nika breathed a sigh of relief, and leant back into Freyne's arms. So much had happened in the last two days that Nika's mind was too exhausted to even try and process anything. Feeling safe within Freyne's arms, he settled back and closed his eyes.

*"So, what's the story behind the causeway?"* Nika asked, trying to distract his thoughts. *"Why would anyone want to build a stone road across a desert?"*

*"The causeway was built thousands of years ago, long before I was born,"* Freyne said. *"It was considered impossible to cross the desert on foot. The leader of Loralyon wanted a shorter route to reach the rest of Lorendia, so he started building the causeway. He also built fifteen waystations spaced evenly along the way, so that each day travellers have a safe place to rest and recover.*

"He used slaves, of course, and many died from the extreme heat or cold. Building across the gorge was the hardest and took a hundred years alone. Sepheren was built soon after by the slaves whose indentures were over."

*"I honestly can't comprehend the amount of hard work that went into something like this,"* Nika admitted. *"Back where I came from, we had machines to do all the work for us. People were paid generously for their skills, and everything was done safely. It does my head in just how little life is regarded here."*

*"It's not all doom and gloom,"* Freyne said gently. *"Once*

*all of this is over, hopefully I'll get to show you the magic that this world has to offer."*

*"We'll see."*

Nika dozed on and off as they rode. The sound of the horse's hooves on the stones and the familiar creaking of the wagon was oddly soothing. Every so often, the mysterious whispering would return for a while, before fading into silence again. The occasional phrase he could make out was always the same: *find Saramas*.

Images of the Mistress and the carnage of the palace plagued Nika's dreams when he did manage to sleep. During one such dream, someone rubbed his thigh, and he jolted awake with a start, expecting to see the ghoulish face of the Mistress.

*"Sorry boo. I didn't mean to startle you."* Freyne removed his hand.

*"Where are we?"* Nika grumbled. His head was still sore from the previous day.

*"Not far from the waystation. The sun is starting to rise."*

Nika sat upright and stretched, then rubbed his eyes. In the dim light, he could make out the arid waste beyond the causeway. The land was covered in sharp jagged rocks and dotted with an occasional dried prickle bush.

Joplin halted the wagon outside a large stone building next to the causeway. He dismounted and pushed open the heavy wooden doors and stood aside to let them through. Priye shimmied across the seat and drove the wagon inside.

"Wait here a moment, yes." Joplin made his way across to the piles of hay and poked around with his sword. A single snake reared up and hissed, and he promptly sliced off its head. "Ok, all clear. First, we wipe down the horses and give them drink and food. Then we can set up camp."

Nika helped Gaitan down from the back of the wagon

and reached for a water skin. Arnie-Kyn leapt down and stalked towards the dead snake.

"How are you feeling?" Nika asked his friend.

"The pain is still there, but I slept well," Gaitan said. "Priye gave me some potion that helped me sleep. I haven't rested that good in a long time."

"I'm glad you're feeling better," Nika said sincerely. "Thanks for helping me back there."

"That woman was a looker," Gaitan grinned. "I was half tempted to offer myself in exchange for you."

"She's horrible." Nika said flatly.

"But you've been with women before," Gaitan pointed out. "I thought she was cute."

"She was nothing but a lowlife conniving troll, who was willing to take advantage of my body against my will. There was nothing cute about her. And besides, I care for Freyne too much to even think about straying."

"I didn't mean it like that." Gaitan said quickly. He pointed towards the well in the far corner. "Come on. Let's go and fill the water skins."

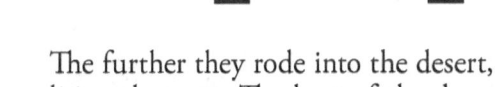

The further they rode into the desert, the harsher the conditions became. The heat of the day made it difficult to sleep, even within the well-constructed waystations. The nights were hardly an improvement; the air was so cold, they had no choice but to dress warmly. There was no respite. Nika was hot, tired, covered in rashes, and smelt disgusting. Even during his days on the oil rig, he couldn't remember ever smelling so bad. Priye soon stopped picking on Gaitan for his hygiene; the water in the wells was limited, and Joplin forbade them to waste so much as a drop.

The sight of the final waystation emerging from the darkness made Nika's heart soar. The last fifteen days of crossing the desert were perhaps the worst he'd experienced since waking up on the Isles. Deep down he knew there was worse to come, and he pushed that thought from his mind. *Just focus on one day at a time, or you'll overwhelm yourself,* he told himself.

"We keep going," Joplin announced. "Just a quick break here."

"What? Why?" Gaitan demanded.

"We are officially out of the desert now," he explained. "There is a better spot I like to camp at, yes. Then we can have a decent rest. We go back to day travel tomorrow."

Gaitan humphed and crossed his arms.

Nika was too happy to be out of the desert to care about where he slept. After a quick stop to relieve themselves and change from warm clothes into desert robes, Nika felt reinvigorated and ready for another few hours of riding. As they emerged from the waystation, the sun was shining and a dark patch of clouds looked ominous in the direction they were heading.

"Ahh, looks like we made it just before the wet season," Joplin mused. "We shouldn't have to worry too much about the wild animals. They'll be too busy migrating to the waterholes, yes."

Nika ignored him, and shifted his weight on the saddle. He could feel another rash forming from riding for too long, and grimaced.

After a mile, the causeway ended, and Nika felt a surge of relief as Freyne steered Streek off the stone path and onto the gravel highway that led to Loralyon. The rolling lands before them was covered in tall dry grasses, and here and there were small clusters of trees. Joplin turned the wagon off the highway and into the wild grassland. As they rode, the dark clouds swirled and grew. Every now and then Nika could see a flash of lightning. The air was thick and humid, and the whispers were replaced by the deafening chorus of cicadas.

It was mid-afternoon when they finally arrived at Joplin's camp site. A number of large boulders almost as tall as Nika formed a protective clearing, and was surrounded by trees which served as a wind break. A short distance away, a small creek meandered by, dry except for a single pool of stagnant water. Nika busied himself with gathering sticks and wood for a fire, as Gaitan and Joplin erected a shelter to protect them from the weather. Freyne disappeared, and soon returned with a small animal for their dinner.

By the time Nika had the fire roaring and Freyne's catch sizzling on the spit, the storm cracked overhead, filling the dark sky with long forked lightning. The air was still mild, and although the storm was loud, Nika felt at peace. It wasn't until they'd finished eating that a new sound caught his attention, and he strained his ears to hear it.

"It's raining!" Gaitan exclaimed.

"By the gods, you're right, yes!" Joplin stood and poked his head out from the shelter just as the sky opened with a steady downpour. With a big grin on his face, Joplin tore off his desert robes and under garments and stepped naked into the rain.

Freyne nudged Nika with his elbow and stood up, unfastening his desert robes. All thoughts of modesty left Nika's mind; he stripped off and followed Freyne into the rain. Nika closed his eyes as the cool water ran over his body, soothing his chafed skin and washing away weeks of travel. When he finally looked back, he spotted Priye stripping off, and Gaitan averting his eyes awkwardly, his face bright red.

"Don't be a prude, dear. I've seen more of those things than you can know," Priye laughed. "Come on!"

Gaitan reluctantly undressed and stepped into the rain, covering himself and clearly embarrassed. Priye handed him the soap, and one by one they washed themselves.

Joplin broke into song, and started dancing in the rain. Priye joined in, and soon they were all dancing except for Freyne. Even Gaitan relaxed and started having fun. Nika's jaw soon ached from laughing and grinning so much; good food, good friends, having a good time. He felt liberated and free, and for once comfortable in his own skin. Yes, he had a long and tiring journey ahead, and the fate of the world landed on his shoulders. *I'll worry about that tomorrow,* he thought as he linked arms with Joplin and skipped around. *My problems will still be there in the morning. I guess it's ok to have a little fun once in a while.*

**7**

The remainder of the journey through the savannah was much more bearable than the desert. Although the days were mostly warm and humid, the evening storms which brewed every few days brought with them welcoming relief. The further they rode, the greener the landscape became, and the temperatures slowly dropped. The distant peaks of the Kalissaden Ranges grew whiter by the day, as the snows covered everything as far as the eye could see.

Nika was sick of travelling. Two long months of constant riding, and he still had no idea where to find Khel. The thought of spending a week in an inn, with decent food and no riding, felt like a luxury he would never have. *Even just one night when we get to Loralyon will be nice,* Nika told himself. *A proper bath and a sink so I can shave this fucking beard off. And a haircut...I look like a bum.*

The sight of Loralyon from atop a small hill filled Nika with excitement. From their vantage point, he could see the city nestled between a roaring river and massive jungle. He could tell the others were excited too; Joplin spurred the horses into a fast trot, and Freyne urged Streek to keep up.

Nika's excitement soon waned, though. As they grew closer, he could see that the city itself was raised off the ground, and water from the river was already flooding under the boardwalks that acted like suspended roads.

"Ah, beautiful Loralyon," Joplin proclaimed as he steered the wagon across a bridge and into the city.

"I don't see what's beautiful about it," Gaitan snorted. "Looks like a good place to be eaten alive by mosquitoes."

"I was being sarcastic, yes."

Instead of being protected by stone walls, Loralyon was surrounded by a single row of vertical logs which had their tops sharpened like pencils. The logs snaked their way around the city, immersed in the rising waters. As far as Nika could see, everything was made of wood; the houses, boardwalks, shops, and even what he assumed was a garrison.

"Why would they build a place like this out of wood? Wouldn't stone be better?" Nika asked.

"I'd hate for a fire to break out," Priye agreed.

"The wood came from clearing this area when the city was built. It is resistant to fire, water damage, and rot," Joplin explained. "The city is only submerged during the wet season, after which everything dries out. The floodwaters are vital to the crops that grow nearby."

Brightly coloured boughs and decorations were wound around the safety rails of the boardwalks, as well as the doors and windows of the houses they passed. The colours added a vibrancy to the otherwise dull place.

"Of course!" Freyne blurted out. "It must be Kharung!"

"Are you sure?" Priye asked.

"Positive."

"Er. What's Kharung again?" Nika asked.

"The major mid-year festival," Freyne answered.

"This time last year I was still in the militia," Gaitan said thoughtfully. "I was stationed at the garrison at Fraal at the time. The feast was terrible, but we all got really drunk."

"I spent my last Kharung amputating some poor man's

leg," Priye mused. "He ended up dying from an infection anyway, but at least we tried."

"I think I was in Alvyre," Joplin nodded. "I was so drunk, I can't remember, yes."

"What about you?" Gaitan asked, looking at Nika.

"We don't do that where I'm from." Nika shrugged.

"This is the inn," Joplin announced, saving him from Gaitan's scandalous look. "Wait here a moment, yes."

Nika glanced around, taking in his surroundings. They were in a wide open square, the centre of which was a fancy rotunda with a pointed roof. All of the buildings in the square faced the rotunda, the grand focal point. Despite the misty rain, people went about their business as though everything was normal for them. Most of the people were dressed in furs or leather armour, equally as drab as the swamp forming beneath them.

A group of around twenty people wearing desert robes huddled together on the opposite side of the square. Nika eyed them suspiciously; they looked out of place, something wasn't quite right. Someone tall wearing black robes approached the group, and pointed towards an alleyway. The people hurried into the narrow passage and out of sight.

The tall person watched them leave, then looked around furtively. A lock of purple hair escaped from their hood, and a jolt of recognition shot through him. *The woman we saw in Sepheren!* He realised, watching as she too hurried into the alley. *What on Earth is she up to? Who is she?*

"Kharung is tomorrow night," Joplin confirmed, interrupting Nika's thoughts. "We've been invited to the city's celebration. I suggest we go and get settled in our rooms and have some lunch, then we can head to the market and buy gifts for each other."

"How many nights did you book?" Freyne asked.

"Three," Joplin replied. "We've been travelling nonstop

for almost three months. We all need a break. Besides, we'll need time to sleep off our hangovers. Tomorrow night will be wild, yes."

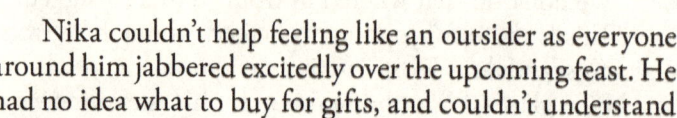

Nika couldn't help feeling like an outsider as everyone around him jabbered excitedly over the upcoming feast. He had no idea what to buy for gifts, and couldn't understand the need for gifts in the first place. Nevertheless, with Gaitan's help, he managed to pick out some things that his friends would hopefully like.

Throughout the day, the large square outside the inn was converted into a space for hundreds of people to dine. Wooden trestles and seats were soon set up, leaving a space around the rotunda for kegs of liquor. The smells of various types of foods wafted under Nika's nose, making his mouth water.

"Anyone would think we're about to meet with a king," he noted, gesturing at their new outfits. Even Priye had changed into a beautiful sapphire blue dress instead of her usual nurse's garb.

"This occasion is more important than meeting with royalty," Freyne grinned, taking a sip of his liquor.

"You seem really excited about tonight."

"I am," he admitted. "Kharung for me has always been centred around the religious side of things. It was up to me and the priests to deliver the sermons and prayers. I had to watch from the sidelines as everyone else got to feast and get drunk, then dance with their loved ones. This will be the first time I get to celebrate Kharung as a somewhat normal man, *and* I get to spend it with you. So yes, I am really excited."

"Well, I'm glad I get to share it with you," Nika said, rubbing his leg under the table.

Crowds of people were filing into the square and

seating themselves along the long tables. Others were wheeling more of the large kegs of liquor and placing them so revellers could help themselves. Nika took a sip of his liquor; it was sweet, yet strong, and he could feel it burn all the way into his stomach. It reminded him of the fruity port he would sometimes sip on snowy nights while on shore leave. A fleeting memory of spending Yule at one of his favourite bars, singing carols and dancing with cute women flashed before his eyes, and for a moment he felt homesick.

A woman, man, and three young children sat opposite Nika and his friends, bringing him back to the moment.

"Happy Kharung," the woman smiled. "I'm Minna, and this is Innis, my brother. Where are you all from?"

"We're from the Eastern Isles," Freyne replied politely. "Except for Joplin there."

"Oh wow, that's a long way away. What brings you here?"

"We're on our way to my sister's wedding," Freyne answered. "Do you live here?"

"I'm originally from Lisaden, but my husband was killed a few months ago. My brother offered for my children and I to stay with him, so here we are."

"I'm sorry to hear that," Gaitan offered.

"Don't be. The man was an idiot," Innis snorted. "I would have killed him myself had I got my hands on him."

"It was a blessing to be truthful." Minna nodded. "But enough about that. Let's get the gifts out of the way."

Nika watched as she handed the children a small soft bundle each. They squealed with delight as they unwrapped new shoes and cloaks each, and a small animal carved from wood. Straight away the eldest stood up and modelled his new attire, while the younger two played with their wooden toys.

"These are for you two. It's dangerous to travel around here without armour, so make sure you wear this when we leave, yes." Joplin handed Nika and Freyne a leather cuirass each. "They're only basic, but they cover your heart and vital organs, and should help to keep you alive should we get into any trouble."

"Thank you." Nika inspected the armour in his hands. It was a dark shade of brown, and felt quite heavy. He slipped it under the table and handed out the gifts he'd bought.

"Looks like I'll be able to adjust them for you if they don't fit right," Gaitan grinned, holding up some artisan tools he received from Freyne.

Gaitan handed everyone something small wrapped in a handkerchief. Nika unwrapped his slowly and found a shiny silver chain nestled inside.

"Did you make these?" Priye asked, holding hers so a small pendant caught the light and glinted.

"Of course I did." Gaitan shrugged. "I had to do something to keep me awake on my nights on watch."

"Thank you, dear. It's lovely." She reached up and fastened the necklace around her neck. "What did you two get for each other?"

Nika blushed as everyone looked at him expectantly. Freyne placed a square parcel in Nika's hands, and nodded to him to open it. Nika unwrapped it carefully, and a small leather-bound journal with a lock fell into his hands along with an unsharpened pencil and tiny key. He flipped it open; besides a short message from Freyne, the journal was blank.

"I know you've been struggling with a few things lately. Maybe it will help you to write it all down and get it off your chest," Freyne said gently. "Also, I know you're not interested in music at the moment. But if inspiration strikes, you've got something to write in. I hope you like it."

"I love it. Thank you." Nika said sincerely.

He sat the journal carefully with the soap and razor

he received from Priye, and fished through his pocket for a moment. He wanted badly to reach out and show Freyne his full appreciation, but knew better than to risk it in public. Instead, he took Freyne's right hand under the table, and slipped a ring onto his finger.

"I was hoping to give you this in private," he murmured. "Its meaning is similar to the wristband you gave me."

Freyne studied the ring on his finger, his face a mystery. The metal was woven in a similar pattern to the leather on Nika's band, and had a tiny magenta gemstone embedded in it.

"Thank you, everyone," Freyne said. "This –"

"FRIENDS! WELCOME!" A loud voice boomed. The crowd grew silent as a man wearing furs and a red sash stepped into the centre of the rotunda. "Thank you all for coming to such a special occasion. The gods have blessed us with all the food and drink we will ever need. Happiest of Kharung, everyone!"

The crowd cheered, and a wave of servers appeared pushing carts laden with roasted meats and vegetables. Nika had never seen so much food in his life. He eagerly loaded his plate with mostly cabbage, potatoes, and corn, and smothered them in rich gravy.

"I don't think I've ever seen someone look so excited about vegetables before," Minna smirked.

"What? Oh. All we've had to eat over the last few months is rice, beans, and occasionally meat. I'm not used to this kind of diet."

"Don't tell me you came through the desert?" Innis asked incredulously.

"Of course we did, yes." Joplin shrugged.

"Do you know what happened at Sepheren?"

"There was an explosion," Gaitan said. "We'd already left when it happened though. Any word on what caused it?"

Innis looked around quickly, then leant forward and lowered his voice.

"I'm one of the chieftain's personal hunters. When I was delivering some of the meat for tonight's feast, I overheard him talking to one of his advisors about a spy report he received by pigeon. Apparently, some unauthorised people were in the storage chamber where they keep the explosives used for excavating new sections of the city. The official statement from the palace is that they were the saboteurs who collapsed the other section. They were stealing explosives and accidentally set them off. The unofficial word is that the marquess was involved, and has disappeared. The city is in an uproar right now."

"I hope Arana is ok." Joplin frowned.

"Most of the eastern quadrant is gone," Innis said. "The rest is mostly ok, but the dust is so bad the engineers are sinking new shafts for ventilation. Teams are still trying to dig out the collapse and recover bodies. It's pretty grim."

"I'm curious as to why your chieftain feels the need to have a spy at Sepheren," Priye said with her usual smirk.

Innis looked at each of them in turn, and his face turned red.

"By the gods, I shouldn't have told you that! I'll get in so much trouble if anyone finds out I was listening. I was hoping to hear a report on the bullbark migration."

"It's ok. Your words are safe with us," Freyne assured him. "Thank you for the information, friend."

"The main herd was heading steadily east and should reach the breeding grounds any day now." Joplin said.

Somewhere to their right, music started to play. Nika focused on listening to the tune instead of the conversation, feeling each and every note as it was played. It was a happy tune, one that made him want to relax and enjoy himself. Deep down, the only thing he missed from his own world was music, and being free to sing and play whenever he liked. Gaitan was right; his music did bring joy to people.

Nika took a deep swig of liquor from his goblet, then passed a chunk of boar to Arnie-Kyn under his seat. *My decision not to play until Khel is dead still stands,* he thought. *But that doesn't mean I can't have a little fun here and there, maybe write some songs. Come to think of it, it's funny that we just happened to get here in time for Kharung. Maybe Am had a hand to play there. They probably did this as some kind of reward or something. Either way, tonight is special to Freyne and he deserves to have a great night. Who am I to deny him that?*

It was only much later, after the gifts were taken back to the safety of their rooms and the children were sent away to bed, that the celebrations were taken to a whole new level. The world spun a little whenever Nika moved his head too fast, and he knew he was slurring his words. Gaitan and Innis had swapped seats, and Gaitan had his arm around Minna's shoulders, talking to her animatedly. She had her hand on his chest, and seemed to be into whatever he was saying.

*"Tri tiero ve nethvia tri mahsan Kharung. Tri tiero ve forthrah tri tocwen sa annebras toso kiye hara casrah!"* the chieftain bellowed above the noise.

"What did he shay?" Nika asked.

"Tonight, we shelebrate the mighty Karren. Tonight, we shatter the shies and let the god shear our call," Freyne translated. "Native Thorington tongue."

"You can shpeak that?"

*"Yar, jo cusin e con."*

Everyone around them yelled and cheered loudly. Nika looked around and could see that the crowd had grown to at least double in size, maybe even more. The sound of heavy drums pierced the night, and a completely different kind of music began to play. The instruments produced deeper tones, complementing the beat of the many different drums that were being played.

Nika had never heard anything like it, but the music

resonated deeply in his core. He staggered to his feet, and dragged Freyne roughly towards the clearing around the rotunda. The space was packed with people grinding against each other, moving to the beat as though they were in a trance.

"Whaa—?" Freyne's face betrayed his confusion.

With a grin, Nika started dancing in time with the drums, allowing the music to consume him. Freyne stood rooted to the spot, a hint of fear on his face. His eyes swept the crowd dancing around him, everyone too drunk and oblivious to care about anyone but themselves. Almost reluctantly, Freyne too began to move awkwardly with the beat. At first his movements were stiff, but as he loosened up and the liquor quelled his inhibitions, he too began to flow with the music and enjoy himself.

Most of the men and some of the women around them were topless, the heat of the alcohol rushing through their veins and sweat dripping down their brazen chests. Nika helped himself to Freyne's waistcoat, and soon they too were topless. As the music thumped around them, they came closer together, their bodies touching. Nika slipped his arms around Freyne, and they danced together to the beat of the drums.

Around them, people had coupled up and were dancing somewhat erotically. As Nika glanced over Freyne's shoulder, a startling realisation dawned on him. The people around them were not just men and women couples, but a mix of people just like him and Freyne. There were no guards around waiting to arrest anyone; that night, they were free to love whoever they wanted, with no laws or consequences to deter them. A warm feeling grew in his gut and moved into his chest, and without further thought, he leant forward and found Freyne's lips with his own.

The freedom of that kiss was even more intoxicating than all of the alcohol he'd consumed that night. Freyne's arms tightened around him as he kissed Nika back roughly, fighting for control. Nika relented, and Freyne kissed him hungrily, sparking a fire of desire deep within his loins.

Out of nowhere, a strange sensation rocked Nika's body, plunging him into sudden silence. The world around him froze, and a strong mind forcibly joined with his before he could defend himself. He felt himself being dragged into the darkest realm.

*"Ah, there thou art, Nickolai. I have been looking for thee,"* a dry voice said.

Nika pushed himself from his body, and was standing face to face with another man's projection. The man was wearing dark robes, his face hidden by his hood, and several of the white sprites were encircling him protectively.

*"Who are you?"* Nika demanded. The haze from the alcohol was gone, and he could think clearly again.

*"I am Saramas."*

*"So, you're the one those whispers keep telling me to find. What do you want?"*

*"I need to see thee, face to face. I have vital information for thy quest,"* Saramas said. *"Take the track through the jungle that leads to the abandoned city. From there I will have a barge waiting for thee."*

*"Why should I trust you?"* Nika asked defiantly.

*"Because if I could infiltrate thy mind so easily like that, thou shalt have no chance when thou face Lord Du'Rakis. Only I can teach ye the forgotten mancery that even thy lover dost not know."*

*"Lord who?"*

*"We don't have time to talk right now. I grow weak. Come to me and I will tell thee everything."*

Saramas and the sprites disappeared in a flash, and the realm dissipated around him. Nika landed roughly in his body, and fell to his hands and knees, gasping for breath. The alcoholic haze returned, and he felt himself swaying from dizziness. A pair of strong arms lifted him to his feet and steadied him.

"What the hell jush happened?" Freyne demanded.

"I – I don't know," Nika stuttered. His body felt weak, as though Saramas had been drawing from his own energy. "We have to go to Saramas."

"What? Who's that?"

Nika rubbed his eyes and frowned.

"I'm too drunk to try and explain it right now. But I need to do this and you need to trusht me. Please?"

Freyne pulled Nika into a hug and held him tightly while people still danced wildly around them.

"Of course I trusht you. Whatever you need, I've got you. Ok?"

Nika nodded. Freyne's scent mixed with his sweat was slowly rekindling Nika's former desires. He found Freyne's lips and kissed him suggestively.

"Let's get out of here before I lose all of my self-control and embarrass us both in public," he said. "I still need to thank you for my gift, and that's going to require more than just words."

Joplin was wise for booking the inn for the extra night. Nika didn't wake until almost lunch time the next day, and was so seedy, he spent the majority of the afternoon in bed snuggled in Freyne's arms, passing a waterskin back and forth. Freyne's hangover cure didn't help, and to make things worse, Arnie-Kyn sat at the foot of the bed, silently judging them.

It wasn't until early evening that someone knocked on the door.

"Oh, fuck off." Nika grumbled to no one in particular.

Freyne went quiet, and Nika heard the faintest whisper from the realm, followed by the door opening a crack. Joplin, Gaitan, and Priye shuffled into the room followed by two maids carrying trays of food.

"Just pop them over on the table, dears," Priye instructed, rearranging the furniture so they could all sit.

"Sure, just come in and help yourselves," Freyne said.

Nika grunted his agreeance.

"We'll all eat in here," Joplin said. "We need to plan the next leg of our journey, yes."

"What a night," Gaitan grinned, helping himself to the couch. "That would have to be the best Kharung of my life."

"Let me guess. You spent the night making illegitimate children with poor Minna," Priye snorted.

"Of course not. We took precautions." Gaitan said defensively.

"Sure, sure." Priye put her hands on her hips and turned to face Nika. "Get up, you two!"

"Unless you want to catch an eye-full, you might want to pass us our trousers," Freyne said dryly.

Nika didn't realise how hungry he was until the covers were removed from the trays and the smells wafted under his nose. To his delight, the meal was a meat stew in rich gravy with a side of boiled cubes of potato.

"In the morning, we can take the main highway from here to Carida," Joplin said, turning serious. "It's a long trek, but the road is clear and safe. There is plenty of shade along the way, and game to hunt and eat. Since we don't have to cart water and as many supplies, I sold the wagon and bought some pack horses so we can pick up some speed."

"We need to make a side trip," Nika said quickly.

"Where to?" Joplin frowned.

"Er. There's an abandoned city not far from here. We need to go there and meet someone."

"No one goes to that city. It's haunted and out of bounds, yes."

"There will be a barge waiting for us." Nika ignored him and continued. "I think it will take us into the Fens.

I don't understand completely."

"The Fens? Are you still drunk?" Joplin asked.

"No?"

"The Fens is surrounded by swamp marsh for miles in every direction. It's fed by the Kalissaden River that flows from the mountains, and Radik's River that flows from the sea. The land is like a giant bath plug. It is believed that the water flows through the centre of the Earth and replenishes the oceans on the other side of the world. Some of the mightiest hunters have gone in there and never returned."

"You still haven't told me what this is all about," Freyne added, looking at Nika.

"I don't even know." Nika threw his hands up in exasperation. "All I know is that I'm going, even if it's by myself. Whatever lies in that swamp has the answers I need for finding Khel. We've had a few fun days, so now it's time to get serious again and focus on the task at hand."

"I don't like it," Joplin declared.

"You don't have to like it. You can wait for us with the horses if necessary," Nika said bluntly.

"I'll come," Gaitan offered.

"So will I," Priye nodded. "One of you are bound to hurt yourselves along the way."

"You know I won't leave your side," Freyne added quietly.

"Very well." Joplin sighed. "I guess we're heading north then. We'll leave at dawn."

8

The morning was icy and miserable. The steady drizzle of rain made the boardwalk slippery underfoot, and reduced visibility to a few feet. The chill seeped into Freyne's bones, and his joints ached. The leather armour dug into his armpit uncomfortably, souring his mood before the day even began. Only Nika seemed unperturbed by the chill, warmed no doubt by holding Arnie-Kyn under his cloak as he always did when it rained. The sound of footsteps floated from the darkness, and Freyne looked up in time to see Gaitan hurrying towards them, accompanied by Innis who was leading his horse.

"Sorry I'm late," Gaitan said. "I wanted to say a quick goodbye to Minna before we left."

Joplin wordlessly took his pack and buckled it to one of the horses. Freyne could tell the big man wasn't happy about the upcoming journey.

"Terrible morning." Innis yawned. "Gaitan mentioned that you're traveling north towards Macedon. I'm heading that way to hunt, so I can take you part of the way."

"Thank you." Freyne nodded. "Let's get moving."

The city was almost empty as they rode in silence towards the north gates. Even though the sun had risen, the sky was still a miserable grey. Freyne pressed himself closer to Nika's body for warmth, and tried to make sense of where they were going. He knew something happened to Nika that night they were dancing, but he was too drunk to remember. *That liquor was potent. I can't believe I lost my self-control and danced,* Freyne mused. *Who is this Saramas, though? How was he able to infiltrate Nika's mind so easily like that? Maybe that's why Nika is so worked up. He hasn't been himself since we got back to Al'Obrel. I just hope he isn't leading us into a trap.*

Beyond the city walls, the path narrowed into a single boardwalk and spanned a wide field that was rapidly filling with water. Dead trees rose from the swamp and looked ghostly in the gloom. The looming jungle ahead looked dark and foreboding through the rain. Freyne's senses prickled; an unwelcoming sensation floated to him on the wind, a warning to stay away.

They rode in silence, and soon reached the cover of the jungle. After a few miles, they came to a junction and the boardwalk branched into two directions. Innis reigned in his horse and turned to face the sodden group.

"This is where I leave you," he said. "Continue on the path for around an hour and you will come to the edge of the ruins. That's the outskirts of Macedon. Be careful. There are rumours that the place is haunted."

"Thank you for your help," Nika said.

"You're welcome, friends. If you pass through Loralyon again, please do drop in. Until then, farewell." Innis nodded politely, then turned his horse and disappeared down the western road.

"Let's go then, yes." Joplin said gruffly.

The northern path was covered in moss and overgrown with vegetation. The boards creaked under the horse's hooves, and occasionally something rustled in the bushes or splashed into the water. Freyne's unease grew; something wasn't right. Even the horses were looking a little spooked, as though they too could sense it. As they rounded a bend, Freyne spotted something white strewn across the path. Joplin reigned in sharply and swore under his breath.

"Gri'Ran's claws! I told you this would be a bad idea, yes."

Freyne dismounted and crouched down to examine the body.

"He's been dead for less than an hour," he said quietly as he searched the corpse. "Stabbed twice by a blade. No weapon or items –"

He broke off as the hairs stood up on the back of his neck, and instinctively pushed his mind into the highest realm. The usually serene realm was bubbling with obnoxiously loud voices, and immediately Freyne caught a warning. *Danger ahead! Beware!* In the distance he could just make out the outlines of several black auras.

"Trouble ahead," he hissed once he exited the realm.

He didn't wait for a response. Freyne discarded his heavy cloak on the boardwalk and drew one of his daggers. With his senses alight, he leapt over the safety rail and scrambled up a tree. As quickly and silently as he could, he passed through the dense jungle, leaping from branch to branch high up in the canopy.

A shout followed by a cruel laugh guided Freyne towards a wide clearing. Down below, he could see a number of ruined buildings slowly being reclaimed by nature. In the centre was around twenty people wearing filthy desert robes, surrounded by a ring of cloaked figures. A feeling of dread washed over him as he watched the scene below.

"Traitors!" one of the cloaked figures shook his fist in anger and stepped inside the ring. "Did you really think you could escape from Lord Du'Rakis?"

One of the captives lunged forward and attempted to punch it, but the figure evaporated into a transparent mist and effortlessly dodged the attack. The swirling mass solidified, and laughed again. The captive spun around, and for a split second Freyne could see the absolute terror in his eyes. Whatever the black figure was, Freyne knew it wasn't human.

"What's the matter, Erias? Not starting to regret your

life choices, are you?"

The man called Erias took another swing, and once again the figure turned into a mist and dodged his fist. From his hiding place in the tree, Freyne could finally see the face of the robed figure, and at once felt himself tremble in fear. The creature was unnatural, an abomination against nature, yet Freyne could sense a form of intelligence behind its lifeless eyes.

Erias fell to his knees in despair, and held his hands out pleadingly towards the figure.

"Please, lieutenant. I beg you. Let us go."

"I'm going to take one of your lives slowly and painfully at a time, until you give me that filth you call your leader," the figure hissed. "Starting with you, Erias."

"Noo! Please!" Erias whimpered and covered his head with his arms.

The lieutenant drew itself up, and began drawing what Freyne could only assume was life force from Erias. The man screamed and writhed about in agony. With his heart thumping in his chest, Freyne carefully sheathed his dagger, and summoned a ball of fire in his hand. Taking a deep breath, he drew his arm back, and hurled the fireball at the malevolent figure, willing it to burn.

His aim was perfect. The creature stopped what it was doing and let Erias fall to the ground, then turned its baleful glare on Freyne. Before he could shield himself, the figure conjured a dark ball of energy and hurled it back at him. Freyne's body was wracked with pain, and a high-pitched ringing sounded in his ears. He felt himself turn limp, and he fell into darkness.

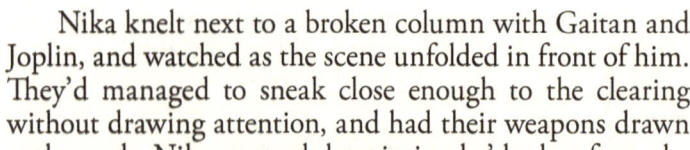

Nika knelt next to a broken column with Gaitan and Joplin, and watched as the scene unfolded in front of him. They'd managed to sneak close enough to the clearing without drawing attention, and had their weapons drawn at the ready. Nika grasped the scimitar he'd taken from the palace guards tightly, his knuckles white from the effort.

"What are those things?" Gaitan whispered nervously.

"Ghosts," Joplin hissed. "I told you this place was haunted. If we get out of this alive, our contract is null and void. I'm leaving, yes."

A surge from the realm snapped Nika's attention back to the clearing, and he watched in dismay as Freyne hurled a ball of fire towards the ghost. His stomach turned to lead as the robed figure retaliated with what looked like a much stronger attack; for a moment Freyne froze, then he tumbled lifelessly to the ground.

"Freyne!" Nika shouted, forgetting the danger they were in. He vaulted over the column, only to realise that everyone's attention was now on him.

The robed figures evaporated and swirled around him, until he was surrounded. He knew he should be terrified, yet a strange calm washed over him. The figures stared blankly at him, almost as though they were waiting for something.

"Leave this place! Begone!" Nika yelled defiantly.

The entities hovered for a second, then once again evaporated into the mist, and shot towards the sky and disappeared. Nika tensed, waiting for an attack, but nothing came.

"What was that?" Gaitan demanded, looking at Nika oddly.

"Only the gods know," Nika snapped. "Get Priye up here now!"

Freyne lay in a heap on the edge of the clearing, unmoving. Nika skidded to a stop and knelt down next to him. He held his breath as he carefully rolled Freyne onto his back with shaking hands. His face was scratched and bruised, and his skin was pale and felt clammy to touch. Nika searched for a pulse, and felt tears spring to his eyes. He was alive.

"Wrap him in your cloak," Priye ordered as she joined Nika by his side. "See if you can carefully drag him under that ledge so he's out of the rain, and then I'm going to need a fire. If he goes into shock he could die. Bring me my pack too, dear."

Nika did as he was told, and rummaged in his own pack for his firestone. He soon had a warm inviting fire, and sat holding Freyne's hand.

*"Is your mate alright?"* Arnie-Kyn asked.

Nika turned to see the cat seated nearby under some debris.

*"I – think so?"* Nika frowned. *"What were those things?"*

*"Perhaps the more pertinent question would be, who are those people?"*

Nika looked across to where they were huddled under a section of a ruined building, talking to Gaitan and Joplin. He'd forgotten all about them in his haste to tend to Freyne. Two of them broke away from the group, and followed Gaitan and Joplin towards the fire. Nika forced himself to stand up, torn between greeting the strangers and staying by Freyne's side.

As they drew closer, Nika recognised the one called Erias.

"Thank you for saving us. I am Erias, and this is Yger." Erias bowed.

The woman put out her hand, and Nika shook it. Her grip was firm, an extension of her physical strength.

"Er. I'm Nika. This is Freyne and Priye." He replied.

Yger pulled back her hood, and Nika felt his jaw drop as he recognised the woman with purple hair. Her choice of makeup highlighted the exotic beauty of her eyes, giving them a smouldering look. To Nika, she was beautiful, and after catching a glimpse of Gaitan's face, he could see that his opinion was shared.

"You're a damned fool. You are lucky you're alive," Yger said bluntly.

"What were those things?" Nika asked, ignoring her insult. He knew she was right.

"I don't know," she said, helping herself to a broken

pillar by the fire. Her accent was even thicker than Joplin's; clearly the main language was not her native tongue.

"We saw you being chased at Sepheren," Nika said, gesturing vaguely towards the city. "Then I saw you sneaking around Loralyon, and now you're here. Why do I get the feeling you had something to do with the collapse of the tunnels?"

"This is none of your business." Yger's face hardened. "Did that slut of a Mistress send you to try and kill me too?"

"No. She's lucky we even left her alive."

"What you mean?" Yger demanded.

"Perhaps we could stop dancing around and help each other by sharing information, yes?" Joplin interjected.

"All you need to know is that my people were being captured and murdered," she said. "We hid in what we thought was a safe place in the southern quadrant, and planned to leave the city that night. But there was an explosion. The chamber collapsed and killed many. We –" she gestured at the others "– were on the far side of the collapse, and managed to get away. A small group of survivors on the other side were rounded up and taken to the palace. Everyone else are dead.

"Once I got my group out, I went back to try and free the others. I couldn't even get close, so the rest of us fled. Your turn."

Nika gave her an abridged version of his kidnapping followed by the explosion. Her expression grew sad.

"The prisoners you released. They were my people," she said. "The rest of them would have perished in the explosion. We are the only survivors."

"Who is doing this?" Gaitan frowned.

"We don't speak of him," Yger replied, standing up. "And now, we must go. He will never stop hunting us."

"Where are you going?" Nika asked.

"Somewhere safe. Thank you again for saving our lives. All the best in your travels."

Yger stood up and strode towards her friends with Erias without looking back. The others had removed their desert robes and were collecting their confiscated weapons.

"That was strange," Priye noted.

"She's beautiful," Gaitan sighed, still watching Yger and her friends leaving the clearing.

"Rithvend native," Joplin grunted. "They are a strange race, yes."

Nika sat next to Freyne and took his hand. He was much warmer, and the colour was slowly returning to his cheeks. A soft groan escaped his lips.

"Will he be alright?" Nika asked, gently squeezing Freyne's hand.

"I think he'll be fine." Priye nodded. "Whatever hit him must have stunned him. His pulse is strong and his breathing is ok. I've treated the scratches so they don't get infected."

"Thanks," Nika said.

Freyne groaned again, and his eyes flickered open.

"I have never seen a Mack truck before, and I have no idea what they look like or do. But I believe I've just been hit by one," he murmured. "Help me up."

Nika breathed a sigh of relief, and helped him into the sitting position. He leant over and kissed Freyne on his cheek.

"You should rest," Priye argued. "We don't know the extent of your injuries yet."

"I'm ok, just sore." He grimaced. "What happened? Where did those people go?"

"They left," Nika replied.

Priye handed him a tin cup with one of her remedies in it, and Freyne sipped at it.

"So, what now?" Gaitan asked, squatting next to the firestone.

"We continue on," Nika said. "As soon as Freyne is ready, that is."

"And you?" Gaitan looked pointedly at Joplin.

Joplin glared at them all in turn, then threw his arms up in defeat.

"Fine. I'll come with you. Just keep those ghosts away from me, yes!" He turned and stomped back towards the horses, muttering to himself.

"What's wrong with him?" Freyne asked.

"He was scared of the ghosts." Nika shrugged. "He's a bloody scaredy-cat."

It was mid-afternoon by the time Freyne felt strong enough to continue. The rain finally tapered off and the sun peeked from behind a cloud, making the air grow humid. The party had a quick dry lunch, then Nika led them to where he knew the barge would be waiting. He could sense something guiding him in the right direction, and followed his instinct. There were no more signs of Joplin's ghosts, and it was clear that the city was truly abandoned.

The river was swollen and muddy-brown from the heavy rains further upstream. At the end of a small dock was a barge, complete with a livestock pen and a sheltered area in the aft for people to sit. Despite the fast-flowing river, the barge was eerily stationary.

"This is it," Nika announced. He dismounted and helped Freyne down from Streek's back. Freyne stumbled, and Nika caught him as his legs almost gave way beneath him.

"Sorry." Freyne winced.

"Don't apologise. I've got you."

Nika helped him across the gangplank, then swung open the gate of the livestock pen. The horses still looked nervous, but once Nika had Streek safely loaded, the others reluctantly followed.

"This is unnatural," Joplin grumbled.

"Everything we do tends to be unnatural," Priye smirked. She linked her arm into Joplin's and walked him across the gangplank. "Don't worry, dear. Those two will protect us, I'm sure. And should they fail, I can always stitch us up again."

"Leave me alone, woman."

Priye caught Nika's eye and grinned, concealing her sarcasm from the big man. Joplin sank onto a bench and sat pouting with his arms crossed. Gaitan rolled up the gangplank and stood with his hands on his hips.

"There's no oars or any way to control it," he said. "There's not even a guide rope tying us to the dock. With no oars or even a rudder, we'll be swept away in this current."

A soft almost inaudible whisper reached Nika's ears. With a jolt, the barge lurched forward and drifted towards the middle of the river.

"It's unnatural," Joplin repeated, scowling.

"Some barges are pulled along by a pulley and winch system though," Gaitan pointed out.

Nika ignored them, and made his way past the livestock pen to the bow. He leant over the rail and stared into the murky water, straining his ears to hear the whispering. The whispers he'd grown accustomed to since they reached Al'Obrel had been strangely quiet since Kharung, and Nika wasn't sure how he felt about the silence. A part of him felt empty, as though something was missing, but what and why, he had no idea.

He heard soft footsteps behind him, and knew it was Freyne without having to turn around.

"Want some company?"

"I always want your company." Nika sighed.

Freyne leant on the rail next to him, and for a while they travelled in silence. Nika could sense his mixed emotions.

"How did you get rid of those shadows?" Freyne asked finally.

"I don't know," Nika admitted. "They surrounded me. I just...told them to leave. And they did. Do you know what they are?"

Freyne shook his head.

"I have no idea. All I know is they are dark energy, something against nature. The voices of the highest realm were screaming. I've never heard them like that before."

Nika frowned and thought for a moment.

"Do you ever hear the voices while outside the realm?" he asked.

"Sometimes. I think because I've spent hundreds of years just listening and meditating, sometimes my mind is connected without even realising. Maybe it's my subconscious. I am well known to many forces of nature, and they have saved my life more than once."

"Maybe you can access that realm without leaving your body just like I can with the lowest realm," Nika mused.

"I never really thought about it," Freyne admitted. "All those years of intense studying and training taught me that this is impossible. I have read every book, journal, and piece of documented information that exists, and they all say that it can't be done."

"Maybe the mancers who wrote them didn't live past a thousand years like you."

"Maybe they weren't a part of some great prophecy that went wrong and needed the gods to intervene," Freyne said wryly.

"Yeah."

Nika shrugged off his cloak and wiped his brow. The further they drifted from the ruins, the wider the river became, and the air grew thicker and warmer. He could feel the leather armour digging into his sweaty skin, and he longed to be able to take it off.

"I thought I was dead when that thing attacked me," Freyne said after a while. "All that went through my mind was regret over doing something so stupid. To come so far just to die from an emotionally-charged attack. I had to do something, though. It was sucking the life force from that man's body."

"How are you feeling now?"

"Exhausted, and sore all over." Freyne sighed. "If I'm honest, I just want to sleep right now. For a week, with no interruptions, just peace and quiet. If anything happens when we meet this Saramas fellow, I don't think I'll be able to help you. I'm far too old for this."

The barge approached a junction in the river, and turned to the right into a smaller tributary. The further they drifted, the more the foliage thinned and the water cleared. The vines and ferns gave way to tall thin trees covered in moss, which widened towards the base of their trunks. The banks broke up into small grassy islands, until they were left drifting in a misty green swamp. Even the water was covered in green algae, leaving a trail of black water exposed as they floated deeper into the fens.

It was late afternoon when the barge finally slowed to a stop next to a grassy island. The sun was already sinking, and wispy tendrils of fog began snaking its way through the trees. Nika's belly squirmed from both nerves and anticipation. Somewhere up ahead lie the answers he so desperately needed.

A low drawn-out cry sounded from somewhere to their left, followed by a *whooshing* sound. Nika shivered and pulled on his cloak as Joplin lowered the gangway. Something felt different; he could sense many presences around him, and although he felt uneasy, he knew he and his friends were safe. He slipped his and Freyne's packs over his shoulder and helped Freyne onto the bank.

*"Leave...horses. Come."*

A chill ran up his spine, as though he were being watched. He scanned the shadows on the bank, until he finally spotted her. Nika blinked, unsure if he were imagining things or not. Joplin's choice of curses confirmed what he saw. A lone human skeleton stood in the shadows and beckoned, her eye sockets empty yet seeing everything.

*"No...weapons. Husband...this way."*

114

9

A gentle breeze rustled the leaves on the aged oak trees in the gardens. The autumn hues of yellow, orange, and red added a splash of colour to the usually pristine grounds. A lone peacock strutted through the flower beds, pausing now and then to forage and trample the king's flowers.

The view from the castle was dazzling in the mid-morning sun. Far below, the people moving along the spiralling roads of the city looked like ants, and in the distance, the ships bobbed gently against their tethers in the harbour. The sun glinted off the water, and just visible were the towers of the Great Monastery of Am.

Iryna leant over the rail of her balcony and sighed. Her adventure with Nika and the others felt like a lifetime ago, and she missed her freedom immeasurably. Being stuck in the castle and forbidden to leave without an entire security detachment bothered her, even though she knew deep down that it was for her own safety.

The gates of the courtyard below swung open, and King Lok's royal entourage rode through into the grounds, startling the peacock. Iryna's father walked down the steps with Chardi and greeted Lok with a firm handshake.

"Welcome, my friend. I trust your journey was smooth and uneventful?" To'Rel's voice floated to Iryna on the breeze.

"As well as it could. I trust you will tell me why your city gates are locked, and why we are not using the main entrance?"

"Of course. Come inside. We'll talk in my private office. We have much to discuss, and I'm sure you would like some refreshments."

Iryna pushed herself off the rail and turned to go back into her chamber as someone knocked on her door.

"Who is it?" she called.

"It's me."

Iryna opened the door, and the moment Ur'Shad stepped inside, she slammed it shut and threw herself into his arms.

"Any news?" she asked.

"None." Ur'Shad shook his head. "No word from our friends. Still no idea who your father has chosen for your husband."

"Blast." She sighed and untangled herself. "Maybe he'll announce it during Lok's visit. I just hope it's not his son. Biron is repulsive."

"We'll just have to wait and see."

Iryna checked her hair and tiara in the polished mirror next to her bed, then squared her shoulders.

"I guess we should get down there and greet our guest. I would hate to upset a potential future father in-law."

Lok, Nahal and To'Rel were already in the office next to the court. The guards waved Iryna and Ur'Shad into the room, and she curtseyed gracefully to the royal guest.

"Greetings, Your Majesty," she said formally.

"Ahh, hello Princess. It's good to see you again."

In Iryna's opinion, King Lok resembled a barbarian overlord more than a king. He wore leather armour and thick bear furs, and had a heavy bastard sword strapped to his waist. His helm, balanced precariously on his knee, had a golden crown inlaid into the design. His orange hair was long and parted into two braids, as was his big bushy beard. Despite his appearance, though, Iryna had always known him to be a gentle man.

"I didn't think you would join us." To'Rel nodded at her with a slight grin. "So, to business."

Iryna sat next to her mother and Ur'Shad stood in his usual position behind her.

"To business. You can start with your gates and all the extra guards patrolling the city."

"I've received some grave news from my allies on the mainland," To'Rel began. "According to King Dird of Drarlum, there have been attacks in several of the cities to the west..."

"There are attacks in cities every day," Lok snorted. "Just this last week I had to break up a skirmish with my own sword."

"Not like this. These are full scale attacks leading to hundreds of deaths at a time," To'Rel continued. "The Black Ibis cult is being wiped from the face of the world by Khel. While this is not necessarily a bad thing for us, the real concern is innocents getting caught in the crossfire. If any of these cultists have made it across the sea to our lands, having them try to hide in our cities could bring the trouble here. We don't want this."

"With the number of scholars and merchants that pass through our gates every day, we couldn't possibly screen each and every person," Lok pointed out. "How can you tell these crazies apart from the other crazies?"

"I'm not sure yet. I thought of individual passes, but paperwork can be easily forged. Inspect any of the merchants at the University market and you'll find six or seven different permits."

"We live on an island. The best line of defence would be to monitor all incoming ships into your ports. Everyone traveling from the mainland must give a valid reason for coming here. If not, send them back on the next ship," Lok suggested.

"I like that. But rather than send them back, maybe we could set up a quarantine camp instead." To'Rel said thoughtfully. "I can assure you there is mancery at play here. Khel destroyed his entire army at Rarn, so rest assured he would have no problem tearing apart our cities just to wipe out any defectors. I can have my service mancers monitor the new arrivals, and when we are sure they pose no risk to the state, we'll release them. What do you think?"

"Didn't Freyne mention that this cult was anti-god in nature?" Iryna asked thoughtfully.

"That's the gist of what he was saying, yes." To'Rel nodded. He gave her an odd look, clearly surprised that she was even paying attention to the conversation. "What are you thinking, daughter?"

"We have an entire monastery full of monks just across that bridge," she said, gesturing in the direction of the University. "We should get them involved. Set up a space for a field temple, and hold mandatory prayer to Am. Any cultists would surely look uncomfortable in doing so, which could help us weed some out."

"You know, that's a good idea." Lok nodded. "Religion has been on a steady decline for years now. I can't remember the last time a prayer was uttered in my court. The fact that Am showed themself to you in the Monastery, and you have several witnesses to back you up, shows that they need our support. The best way to fight an anti-god group would be with gods, right?"

"Right. The world has never been the same since the last holy war, and now we seem to be on the brink of another. If Nika doesn't get rid of Khel, we're in a lot of trouble. And if we don't show our gods the level of respect they deserve, why should they help us?"

"How many temples do we even have?" Iryna asked.

"The University, Se'Maan, and Ru'Amin," To'Rel replied.

"Qual-Eran is the only temple on my half," Lok added. "And what about Bar'Am?"

"Karatha and Riz'Hra are the only two standing, I believe," To'Rel replied. "Durham has been abandoned since Sa'Mel was killed, and Ner'Am was destroyed. There are none in the Independent District."

"I think we need to have a temple in every city," Iryna said. "Rebuild those that were destroyed, and build new ones where needed. Open the Monastery for recruitment to train new priests, and get them filled as quickly as possible."

"I never realised religion was a great concern to you," Nahal mused, speaking for the first time.

"You all seem to have forgotten. I was there when Nika gave himself for us. I personally saw Gri'Ran come to life, and Am in their physical form. Not to mention the gods from the other worlds, right here in our own world. The gods don't owe us anything. Humanity blew that the first time around, which is why Am and Gri'Ran left us in the first place. If anything, we as a people owe the gods for their protection, not the other way around."

"This is fair. To build these temples will take years and countless funds, though." Lok said.

"We don't have to build fancy bluestone temples to appease Am," Iryna said, feeling her patience wear thin. "We can start with an open space and a few logs cut as seats for all I care. The importance is reuniting our people with their god."

"She has a point," To'Rel said. "I've been touched by Am. I felt their love first-hand. We are not entitled to any of the help they have been giving us. Let's help Nika and the others by controlling what we can control. I'll write to Kaiton immediately and let him know of our plan. If we can get him on board too, we are just one step closer to protecting our people and our future."

"I will go to the Monastery and talk to the high

priests," Iryna declared, standing up. "I'll have Chardi organise an escort and we'll leave right away."

"Very well." Lok nodded. "I'll help with the letter and sign it so Kaiton knows I'm on board. We are now officially at war, ladies and gentlemen, so this afternoon we'll assemble a war council and start planning. Borders, religion, and contingency plans should our friends fail."

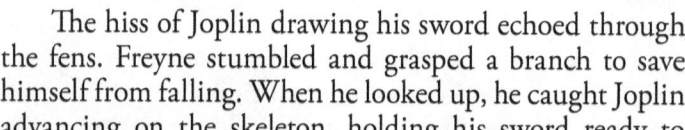

The hiss of Joplin drawing his sword echoed through the fens. Freyne stumbled and grasped a branch to save himself from falling. When he looked up, he caught Joplin advancing on the skeleton, holding his sword ready to strike.

"No, stop!" Nika yelled.

Joplin ignored him and continued towards the perceived threat. Freyne sensed a surge from the realm, and Joplin was flung backwards, his sword flying from his hand.

"What in the gods?" Joplin yelled from the ground.

"You heard what she said! No weapons!" Nika yelled back. "If you're going to jump at shadows, you can stay here with the horses."

"I didn't hear anything," Joplin growled, pushing himself off the ground. "You're delusional."

Nika stared down the bigger man in an act of defiance that Freyne had never seen from him before. He could feel the tension sizzling in the air, and was almost afraid one of them would do something stupid before he could intervene.

"Calm down the both of you," Priye snapped. "Don't make me pull your trousers down and spank you like children, because that's exactly how you're behaving."

"I never should have come," Joplin hissed.

"Don't, then." Nika spun around on his heel and

stalked angrily towards the offending skeleton. Together they disappeared into the fens.

"What was that all about?" Gaitan asked. "I didn't hear anyone say anything either."

"I don't know," Freyne replied. "I've never seen him like this."

"Do we follow or stay here?" Priye asked.

"Of course I'm going," Freyne said. "It's up to each of you if you come or stay."

Freyne made his way painfully in the direction Nika left. He could feel himself shaking, and a thin layer of sweat dampened his brow. His sides hurt, but he pushed on, following Nika's footprints in the soft ground. Without warning his legs gave way, and he fell roughly to his knees.

"Fuck," he whispered, choosing Nika's more colourful vocabulary.

A pair of hands grabbed him by the arm and helped him to his feet.

"Come on," Gaitan said. "Whatever is up ahead, Nika needs us."

"Thank you," Freyne said.

Priye slipped under his other arm, and together they followed Nika's trail deeper into the fens. Trailing behind was Joplin, carrying the rest of the packs and cursing quietly under his breath. The further they walked, the colder and gloomier it became. After around a half hour, Freyne spotted Nika up ahead. He reached out and joined their minds together.

*"Wait for us, boo."*

*"Where are you?"* Nika paused and looked around.

*"Right behind you."*

Nika turned and waited for them to catch up. Behind him was a narrow boardwalk that spanned a body of water and led to a dank cottage lit by oil lamps. The anger seemed gone from his face, replaced by something else altogether. Wordlessly, Nika moved and took Gaitan's place.

*"I'm sorry about earlier. I-"*

*"Shh. It's ok. Where's your guide?"*

Nika pointed towards the cottage. A lone person dressed in black robes with his hood up stood watching them, the skeleton by his side. An unfamiliar mind joined forcefully with his and Nika's.

*"Ah, there thou art, Nickolai and Christophe. Come and join us. We have much to discuss."*

―――――⌐‾‾‾⌐―――――

The clearing surrounding Saramas' cottage was decorated by skulls of all sorts of creatures, including human, Nika was sure. Despite all the signs of death, Nika could feel that there was some sort of life around him, too. Saramas dismissed the skeleton, then beckoned. Nika and his friends followed him behind the cottage to a set of stairs leading into a small underground grotto.

At the bottom of the stairs, they entered a small round chamber with a bench seat circling the room. The walls were mosaiced with shells and pieces of bone carved into delicate patterns, and a single beam of light shone from a small rounded vent directly above a fire pit. The glow of the flames dancing across the walls was dazzling, and in a way Nika was reminded of the Inner Sanctum of the Monastery. He removed Arnie from beneath his cloak and placed him gently on the ground.

"Be seated. We don't have time for pleasantries," Saramas said. His voice was deep yet scratchy, leading Nika to assume he hadn't spoken out loud for some time.

Nika and Freyne sat obediently. He couldn't help noticing that Joplin sat next to the door, fidgeting uncomfortably. The man seemed spooked, and a part of him felt bad for yelling at him earlier.

"Well, here we are," Nika said. "What is so important that you've felt the need to hound me all the way from

Lorendia?"

"Strong words for one so naive," Saramas said, a hint of amusement in his voice. "Surely thou hast figured it out by now?"

"I didn't at first," Nika admitted. "It wasn't until I met your wife that it all clicked."

"Wife? What are you talking about?" Freyne asked.

"Ever since we returned to Al'Obrel, I've been hearing whispers," Nika explained. "They were quiet at first. But when we were outside the catacombs under the monastery, and again crossing the Causeway, there were spots where they were much louder. I had no idea what it was, and at times I thought I was going crazy. Then there was the incident with those things at Macedon. They should have killed me, but no. I told them to leave and they did. Why? Why me?"

"I thought thou wouldst figure it out when thou were captured by the Mistress," Saramas said dryly.

"You know all of this is foreign to me," Nika said defensively.

Gaitan, Priye, and Freyne all looked at each other, the confusion clearly written on their faces.

"Does this have something to do with how you manipulated the forces of the darkest realm to escape from the realm blocker?" Freyne asked.

"It has everything to do with the darkest realm," Nika blurted out. The words rolled from his tongue; to speak them out loud finally after months of keeping silent somehow made everything feel so real, so true. "You like to visit the highest realm to meditate, listen to the voices of nature and communicate. When you suggested I try and find what works for me, I did. I found that within the darkest realm I could get the same relief that you do.

"You also taught me that when we enter a realm for the first time, there is a chance that we are altered. Whenever I'm within that realm, I see the sprites and yes,

I can understand them. They have spoken to me many times."

"I... I had no idea," Freyne stammered. "I'm so sorry. How, though?"

"What are you even talking about?" Gaitan asked.

"Nickolai hast experienced death, on more than one occasion. The moment he entered the darkest realm, he was clearly granted the gift. A rare gift, indeed." Saramas clasped his fingers together. "Necromancy is a forgotten art. It is so rare, we are lucky to have one born in a million people. There are around a hundred necromancers dotted around the world currently."

"How did you know, though?" Nika asked.

"I can read the whispers of death as fluently as Christophe can read the whispers of nature. When a necromancer comes into his birthright, the realm sings out in celebration. It is something you will come to enjoy. There was only one time where I felt fear at an awakening."

Nika covered his face with his hands for a moment and massaged his temples as the words sunk in. He didn't want to be able to talk to the dead at all, yet he knew deep down that he had been for some time. It was a part of him now, and no matter what, he wouldn't be able to free himself of it. The thought of raising skeletons and undead creatures grossed him out, though. He wanted no part of it.

"Animating the dead is just one of the many things we can do," Saramas continued. "As with any type of mancery or magick, there are rules we must obey, or we can bring about our own destruction. That is why thou art here. I need to teach ye how to not kill thyself permanently."

"I feel sick," Nika mumbled.

"If ye need to be sick, kindly do it outside."

Nika stood and hurried up the stairs, feeling his insides heaving. He bent over a clump of grass and threw up the contents of his stomach until there was nothing left. He stayed bent over for a while, dry retching and trying to control the nausea.

A twig snapped behind him, and a hand patted him on the shoulder.

"Are you alright?" Freyne asked gently.

"No. I don't think I'll ever be alright again."

"Why not? Talk to me, boo."

"Death goes against everything we do," Nika mumbled. "We're trying to save lives, not take them. Having to kill Khel is bad enough."

"No. Death is as much a part of nature as is life. Remember what we spoke about in the Monastery, about balance. Death is not something to be afraid of, and it's not evil or anything like that." Freyne rubbed Nika's back as he heaved again. "I don't know anything about necromancy, but the fact that you can do it means that Am approves and probably meant for this to happen. Either way, you need to listen to Saramas and learn as much as you can from him while we are here. You don't want to miss the one thing that could bring Khel down for good."

"You're right." Nika sighed and straightened up a little. Freyne handed him a piece of cloth to wipe his mouth, and a waterskin.

"Do you feel any better?" he asked.

"Not really," Nika admitted, taking a sip of water.

Nika could hear footsteps shuffling up the stairs. He turned to see Saramas staring at him.

"It will be dark in under an hour. Go set up thy camp over there, then come and join me. We will eat together, then Nickolai and I will begin his training."

The evening was cold and still. A thick fog rolled in to surround them, muffling the sounds of the bugs and creatures of the fens. They set up camp as instructed, and joined Saramas by a hot fire. The flames reflected off the polished skulls, which seemed to be watching them.

After a dinner of spicy stew, Joplin, Gaitan and Priye sat huddled together, chatting quietly. Freyne nudged Nika and nodded towards Saramas.

"Off you go," he said softly.

"Aren't you coming?" Nika hesitated.

"No. This is all about you now. I obviously don't experience the realm like you do, so this is something I cannot learn. Go on, it'll be ok."

Nika sighed and stood, then walked deliberately to where Saramas was seated.

"Art thou ready then?"

"I guess," Nika replied.

"When ye address me, thou shalt call me Master," Saramas said. "Understood?"

"Er. Yes, Master."

"Very good. Let us begin."

**10**

Nika quickly learnt that Freyne was a much kinder, patient, and caring teacher than Saramas. Where Freyne was gentle and allowed Nika to learn at his own pace, his new master was rough and forceful. Saramas demanded his attention at all times, and was not afraid to punish Nika should he slip up. After just an hour of learning the rules that first night, Nika was exhausted and his head ached.

It wasn't until the next day that Saramas pulled him into the darkest realm.

*"Thou art already familiar with this realm,"* he said once they'd eaten breakfast. *"The problem is, thou hast learnt it wrong. Everything ye think ye know must be unlearnt. Mancers cannot manipulate this realm, but necromancers can."*

Nika gazed around the realm. They were surrounded by the white sprites, and wherever Saramas moved, the sprites followed.

*"What exactly are those, Master?"* Nika asked.

*"For such a powerful mancer, thou aren't that bright."* Nika was pretty sure that Saramas was rolling his eyes beneath his hood. *"The sprites are what we call essence, remnants of life force. Those souls who are not taken to the afterlife are left in a plane between this world and the next. Essence occurs where people die."*

Nika thought back on his journey, remembering the sprites along the causeway. With a shiver, he realised without doubt that many of them would have been the slaves who built it all those years ago.

*"The quality in terms of usefulness depends on a few factors. Some are weak and have little to no use, merely a whisper of a memory long gone. Others are strong enough for us to use. Watch closely."*

Saramas locked onto a single loose sprite and captured the essence with ease. It hovered in front of him, awaiting orders.

*"Once thou hast captured it, thou can control it. It can be a powerful way to communicate with other necromancers or locate people. That is how I found thee. Simply fix the image of the person thou seek in thy mind, and release the essence. Try it."*

Nika fumbled, but eventually captured a sprite.

*"What do you want?"* it whispered.

*"Er. Show me where Freyne is."* Nika easily pictured Freyne in his mind's eye, and released the sprite as he was taught.

The sprite sped off towards Freyne and whizzed around him. Nika grinned as Freyne jolted upright and looked around, then pulled his cloak tighter around him. The sprite slowed, then drifted away.

*"Adequate first attempt."* Saramas grunted. *"Be sure to be specific in thine instruction, and order the sprite to return afterwards. Otherwise, thou hast no way of knowing if thy orders were carried out or not. Understood?"*

*"Yes, Master. I have a question though. When I was at the monastery, I heard the whispers coming from the catacombs. Those bodies would have been blessed by Am and taken to the afterlife. How was I able to hear them?"*

*"Essence likes to gather in such places in the hopes that they will taken to the afterlife too."*

*"Ok. Sorry, just one more question. How did you know what I look like?"*

*"Like I said, when a necromancer awakens, the realm celebrates. I, and every other necromancer out there who is attuned as I, have seen thy face. As such, I hast been watching thee for some time. Who did ye think sent the sprite to help thee whilst trapped by the Mistress?*

*"This brings us to the next lesson. Closing off thy mind from others who access that realm. Currently, thou art as visible as a bright beacon in a dark cave. I was able to track and watch thee with ease. It is dangerous to leave thy mind open and vulnerable. If I wanted to kill thee, I could have many times over."*

Nika watched as Saramas captured another sprite, and set it to orbiting his head like a halo. He finally understood why there were constantly sprites circling his body. He gritted his teeth and concentrated on capturing another. It took a few goes, but eventually Nika got the sprite to do his bidding.

*"There are different methods for procuring protection, but we do not have the time to go over them. Remember that the rules of realm exposure are still relevant. I hast a book thou can study during thy travels, and I expect thee to practice daily. Understood?"*

Nika nodded.

*"Yes, Master,"* he added quickly.

*"Good. Let us move on."*

Nika bit his lip, still uncomfortable with the idea of messing with the dead. Saramas drifted from the fire and led Nika inside the cottage to what looked like a ritual altar. On top was a pile of stark white human bones.

*"A corpse is just a corpse. An empty shell doomed to rot back into the earth. What ye do with it is entirely up to thee. We can reanimate and control it. Watch."*

Saramas gently scooped one of the sprites that orbited him into his hand, and fused it into the bones. Nika could feel him channelling some life force into both the skeleton and the sprite. The sprite grew and swirled, until the bones were surrounded by a glowing haze. Before his very eyes, the bones spun and rearranged themselves, until the skeleton stood in front of the altar.

The sight of the skeleton outside the realm was nothing compared to within. The bones glowed, held together by life force. Nika sensed nothing evil about it, just life shared with it by Saramas.

*"Ah... My love."* The skeleton whispered.

*"Nickolai. Meet Mira, my wife."*

*"Er. Hello,"* he said.

*"Welcome."* Mira took a step closer to Saramas and stood gazing up at him.

*"Reanimation is draining. As thou can see, I use my own life force to sustain the minion. Using this method, thou hast absolute control of it. I could send her to scare thy friend if I so willed it."* Saramas chuckled to himself, then grew serious again. *"We can raise more than one minion at a time, but be wary. The more ye raise, the more of thy life force thou use. Overdo it, and thou shalt die. Another thing to understand is thou can reanimate any corpse with any essence. These bones did not belong to Mira."*

*"Whose were they, Master?"* Nika asked.

*"Some foolish hunter who got lost in the fens,"* Saramas snorted. *"He got trapped in mud and couldn't dig himself out. I came across his corpse months after he died. His essence was furious and refused to believe that he was dead. Sometimes such confusion can lead to what common folk refer to as ghosts or hauntings."*

*"Is there something we can do in that case?"* Nika asked.

*"Yes. There are a few options. We can tame the spirit and help it come to terms with its death. Or, we can capture it and use it at will in summoning. Don't ever release an angry spirit from its place of haunting, though. Angry spirits can manifest into revenants, which can turn rather evil."*

Saramas looked at his wife; something seemed to pass between them, an unspoken word. He pulled the life force, and the bones spun back into their place on the altar.

*"Never use an angry sprite or spirit in reanimation. They*

can wrest control from thee and break free. Remember it is against our laws to release wights and revenants upon the physical realm. Now it is thy turn to reanimate those bones."

For Nika, the hardest part of anything so far was capturing the sprites. While they willingly allowed Saramas to use them, they did not want anything to do with Nika.

"*Be firm. Thou art the one in control, not them. This is not a place to be gentle!*" Saramas scolded him after another failed attempt. "*They will not respect a weakling. Assert thy dominance! Thou art their master, so bloody act like it.*"

Nika gasped as Saramas dealt him a sharp slap in the back of his mind. Tired and in pain, he drew himself up and tried again.

"*Much better.*" Saramas said once he finally captured one.

Nika managed to lock the essence onto the bones; reanimating it with life force was the easy part. Once again before his eyes, the skeleton swirled and came to life before him.

"*What do you want?*" it demanded.

"*Do not speak to me like that,*" Nika said firmly.

"*Sorry, Master.*" The skeleton bowed, though Nika could sense its insincerity.

"*Adequate. Now return it.*" Saramas ordered.

Nika did as he was told and sent the bones back to their resting place.

"*Good. Take a break.*"

Nika returned to his body and withdrew his mind from the realm. He took a deep breath of fresh air, surprised to find he was shaking and felt weak. Saramas left the fire and disappeared inside the cottage.

"You don't look so good," Freyne noted, joining him.

"I'll be fine. It has to be done." Nika shrugged.

Freyne handed him a piece of fruity damper.

"Eat this. Priye baked it for lunch for something different."

"Didn't we just have breakfast though?" Nika frowned.

"Don't forget we experience time differently in the realm," Freyne said.

"Where are the others?" Nika asked, only just noticing they were gone.

"They went to tend the horses," Freyne replied. "Arnie-Kyn is lurking around somewhere. Oh. Here he comes. I'll leave you two to it."

Saramas was holding a thick tome under his arm, and made his way purposefully back to where Nika sat. As Freyne stood, the necromancer motioned for him to sit.

"While I have ye both here alone, there is another matter we must discuss. Thou must find and destroy Lord Du'Rakis before he destroys this very world."

"Who is that, Master?" Nika asked, feeling his insides squirm at the thought of sidelining his mission. "You mentioned that name when you came to me on Kharung."

"I heard it at Macedon, too," Freyne added.

"Lord Du'Rakis is tearing across this continent even as we speak, stirring up chaos and disrupting the very fibre of our universe. He must be stopped, by whatever means necessary." Saramas tapped his fingers on the book sitting on his lap. "Rakis was a powerful necromancer who lived to the west of here. He and I kept in touch over the centuries. Last time we spoke, a few centuries ago, he mentioned that someone was propositioning him, demanding to be trained in necromancy. I never heard from him again since that night.

"When a necromancer dies, the realm goes through a short period of grieving. All necromancers feel the loss, and we bow our heads together. To lose one of our own is painful, beyond any grief a mortal can feel. As such, when Rakis died, we were thrown into a deep period of mourning.

"Around a year ago, there was talk of a new threat, one which was unwelcome to our community. We soon heard his name. Lord Du'Rakis. Du means *conqueror of* in one of the old languages. It was then clear to us that Rakis was murdered and his talents stolen."

"So this Du'Rakis is a necromancer too?" Freyne asked.

"No. There is a difference between an awakening and a theft of powers. Du'Rakis has illegally gained knowledge of necromancy, which makes him so incredibly dangerous. He kills without conscience, and raises his victims all while violating our laws."

Nika frowned, and stared into the flames. A cold shiver travelled down his spine.

"The Miscreant lives, and even now is wreaking havoc amongst the cities of the mainland." He quoted Am's warning slowly, remembering their words. "It has to be him. '...Purging his following, sweeping the cities to destroy the survivors.' How did I not see this sooner?"

"I don't quite follow," Freyne said.

"Sepheren. Macedon. Think about it. We're not chasing Ami'Khel any more. Khel is Du'Rakis!" Nika stood and paced up and down as he pieced everything together, then froze as a sickening thought dawned on him. "Fuck me. Khel – Du'Rakis – was the reason the tunnels collapsed in Sepheren. Yger and her people are ex-cultists, trying to escape! That – that means the Mistress works for him. He caused that explosion, and what I felt must have been a rift."

Freyne opened his mouth to speak, but Nika held up his finger for silence and resumed his pacing.

"Those things we saw at Macedon. Erias referred to one of them as Lieutenant. I think Khel – Du'Rakis, whatever his name is, reanimated his dead lieutenants. That's why they disappeared when I spoke to them. They were summoned by Khel. I was able to undo his summon."

"Very good, my young apprentice. It all becomes clear once thou focus thy mind and piece it all together. The signs were always there, thou was just too ignorant to see them."

Freyne chuckled, then laughed.

"I'm sorry," he said, wiping his eyes. "I guess Joplin's ghosts really were ghosts in a sense."

"Actually, they are known as revenants," Saramas corrected him. "They are intelligent and can think independently from their master, while still fulfilling their orders. They exhibit the memories and characteristics of their living form, but are able to be summoned and dismissed at will. Revenants are dangerous business."

"Where do we go from here?" Nika asked. Once more, the reality of what he had to do cut him deeply, and the magnitude of it all made him feel like an insignificant fly. He sat roughly on a seat and stared into the fire.

"I wilt continue to train thee as much as I can before thou must leave. This book contains step-by-step instruction on some of the finer uses of necromancy. Thou shalt need to study and practise hard. As for thee, Christophe. It is time for thee to discover thine own roots. Thou hast been shielded from the truth for too long. We are heading towards a great war, possibly the worst this world has ever faced."

"What are you talking about?" Freyne demanded.

Nika's heart quickened and he felt himself tremble as the words of Saramas sunk in.

"Thou must head far south, and venture deep into the forests of Llunn. Thou shalt find thine truth there."

"Out of the question. I am not leaving Nika." Freyne said, his expression turning dark.

"What's going on?" Gaitan asked.

Nika looked up to see his friends had returned.

"I really don't have the time nor patience to sit around repeating myself." Saramas crossed his arms, a hint of annoyance in his voice. "Let me say this in a simpler manner so that all of thee can understand. Humanity is on the brink of a catastrophic war. To fight a war, we need armies. In this case, we need more than just humanity to unite for a change and fight it together. Dost no one understand the gravity of this situation?"

"We need to warn Kaiton and To'Rel," Gaitan said immediately.

"Du'Rakis has several leaders of this land under his thumb. Thou must be careful who ye trust."

"Didn't To'Rel say his allies were in Drarlum and Rithvend?" Gaitan asked.

"I'm surprised you even remembered that," Priye noted.

"Drarlum is closest," Joplin said quietly.

All eyes turned to the big man. Nika hadn't heard him speak since their disagreement, and made a mental note to apologise to him as soon as he could.

"To travel to Rithvend is much more dangerous, yes. Cadrinhal is a cultist-free space, so it makes sense to go that way."

"How do you expect me to travel all that way?" Freyne demanded. "It would take me months to get there."

Saramas chuckled, though to Nika it sounded more like Arnie-Kyn coughing up a hairball.

"Thou dost forget who and what I am. I have a... friend who can take you there."

"Where are *we* going then?" Nika asked finally.

"Thee and thy friends will head north. Exactly where, we will figure out soon."

Freyne stood up abruptly and stomped off towards the grotto.

"What's wrong with lover boy?" Priye asked.

Nika ignored her and followed Freyne behind the cottage. When he stopped, Nika could see he was visibly shaking and red in the face.

"He can't be serious!" Freyne exploded. "I... I promised you I would never leave you again. I can't break that promise. Especially not now when so much is at stake!"

"Freyne..."

"Am sent us on this journey. Who is Saramas to go against the word of a god. *My* god?"

"But what if..."

"Joplin knows the land better than anyone. He can go." Freyne sank onto a mossy log and buried his face in his hands.

*"Are all humans like this then?"* Arnie-Kyn leapt down from a tree and sat at Freyne's feet.

Nika jumped, startled at the unexpected intrusion.

"Where have you been?" he demanded.

*"Exploring. Hunting. One is a cat, after all."*

A soft sob escaped from Freyne's lips. Nika sank next to him and pulled him against his chest.

"Shh. It's ok," he whispered.

*"Both of you have heard some unpleasant truths today,"* Arnie said, his tail twitching. *"You both need to pull yourselves together. 'Trust in Am, for only they can see the bigger picture that is beyond the sight of any mortal.' One can quote Gri'Ran's laws too, if you like."*

"Th... this is Am's doing?" Freyne sniffed.

*"They probably had a hand to play in this,"* Arnie-Kyn said. *"Think about it. Do you really think one would have allowed you to come here if Saramas was a threat to Nika's safety?"*

Nika rested his head on Freyne's and tried to soak in as much of him as he could. He scent, his warmth, his touch. Deep down he knew what had to happen, and the thought wrenched at his heart.

*"Logically, you are the only one who can get a message across to To'Rel and Kaiton. To send Joplin or the others would be too great a risk. They could be killed by bandits or captured and sent to work in the salt mines. Logic aside, though. You know you can't keep running from your own truth."*

"What are you talking about?" Freyne managed.

*"You know exactly what I'm talking about. 'It is time to find your people and bring them home.' See, one can quote the skies, too."*

"You're impossible." Freyne grumbled.

*"You are not being asked to leave forever, you know.
Once you have completed the task, you will find your way
back."*

"How will I find you?"

*"You will know."*

No one spoke over breakfast the next morning. Instead
of eating, Freyne busied himself with writing a letter each
to To'Rel and Kaiton. The thought of abandoning Nika in
his time of need crushed his very soul. *At least this time it's
agreed on and not an unexpected surprise. He needs me to do
this,* he told himself over and over.

The very idea of the long journey ahead was daunting,
and facing it alone even more so. Even more confusing was
Arnie-Kyn's rehashed message to find his people. What
people? His people were dead, murdered in his village all
those years ago. He had no people left, except for Nika
and his friends.

"Art thou ready?" Saramas asked.

"I will never be ready for this," Freyne murmured.

Saramas drew Nika aside, and they both grew quiet.
He felt a strong surge from the realm, followed by a low
drawn-out cry. A large beast swooped down from above,
and with a heavy flap, descended into the clearing.

"What in the gods?" Joplin turned pale and looked as
though he might faint.

"Meet my beloved Ruke." Saramas stepped forward
and stroked the beast on its bony nose. Its body was similar
to that of a dragon, but instead of four legs, it had just two.
Its wings were long and leathery, reminding Freyne of a
bat. "Ruke is a skeletal wyvern. He wilt take thee wherever
thou need to go, and wilt protect thee without question.
I'll set up the harness."

"I guess we'll be seeing you," Priye said. Her usual
smirk was replaced by an almost sad look.

"Hopefully sooner than later," Freyne replied.

Priye opened her arms, and Freyne hugged her. She squeezed him tight, and finally let go.

"Be careful. I can't stitch you up from the other side of the continent."

"I'll try."

Gaitan stepped forward and put out his hand. As Freyne reached out to shake it, Gaitan opened his arms instead and pulled him into a brief hug.

"We'll all miss you," he said simply.

Joplin shook his hand firmly, then stood back. Freyne turned and faced Nika.

*"I have no words left,"* Nika said, falling into Freyne's arms. *"You know I love you. I will see you soon enough."*

*"I love you too, boo."*

"It is time," Saramas called.

Freyne reluctantly let go, and paused to wipe a tear from Nika's eye. He picked up his pack off the ground and climbed carefully onto Ruke's back, then strapped himself into the harness.

"May thee forever hold Am in thy heart," Saramas called.

Freyne took one more look at Nika as Ruke flapped his giant wings. With a great thrust, they leapt forward and rose spiralling into the sky. Freyne's stomach lurched, and he clung on tighter to the harness around Ruke's neck. By the time he looked back towards the clearing, all that was left was a lone tendril of smoke in the distance. With another flap, they were gone.

---

Nika buckled the last pack to the saddle and stood back, unsure what to do next. Streek nuzzled his shoulder, and Nika reached up to scratch behind her ears. It had been an exhausting few days since Freyne left, and he was glad to be on the move again.

It hadn't been easy, and Freyne's abrupt departure left a wide gaping hole deep inside him. Although he was surrounded by his friends, the loneliness he felt during the voyage from Barthra returned with a vengeance. *Stop it,* he told himself. *Freyne's mission is just as important as mine. He hasn't abandoned us, he's just doing what needs to be done. To'Rel and the others need to know what's going on. I wonder who his people are, though?*

"I think that's everything," Gaitan said.

Nika let himself out of the livestock pen and turned back to Saramas, who was standing opposite the closed gang plank.

"Thank you for everything, Master," Nika said sincerely.

"Thou can thank me by studying and practising hard, my apprentice. What thou hast learnt is merely the basics, but given lots of practise, thou shalt soon master it. Thou hast done well, and I am proud of thee."

Saramas reached into his robes and held out a metal rod around a foot long. The tip was decorated with a gold five-pointed star with wings, its centre a golden cage dotted with tiny diamonds. Inside was a void of pure darkness, that swirled like farthest reaches of the universe. It looked suspiciously similar to his tattoo.

"This is what we call a focus. It allows us to channel the powers of the realm more precisely without fully leaving our physical realm. There is a chapter in the book that will show thee how to use it properly. Keep it safe, and don't let others touch it."

Saramas held it out, and Nika took it. Warmth radiated through his hands and spread to his arms.

"Oh good, it has bound itself to thee. Now go. Forever hold Am in thy hearts."

The barge jolted, and started to drift away. He heard a soft whisper from the realm, and turned back to see the skeletal Mira waving.

*"Farewell...Nickolai. God speed...on thy quest."*

# Part Two

# Maikaden

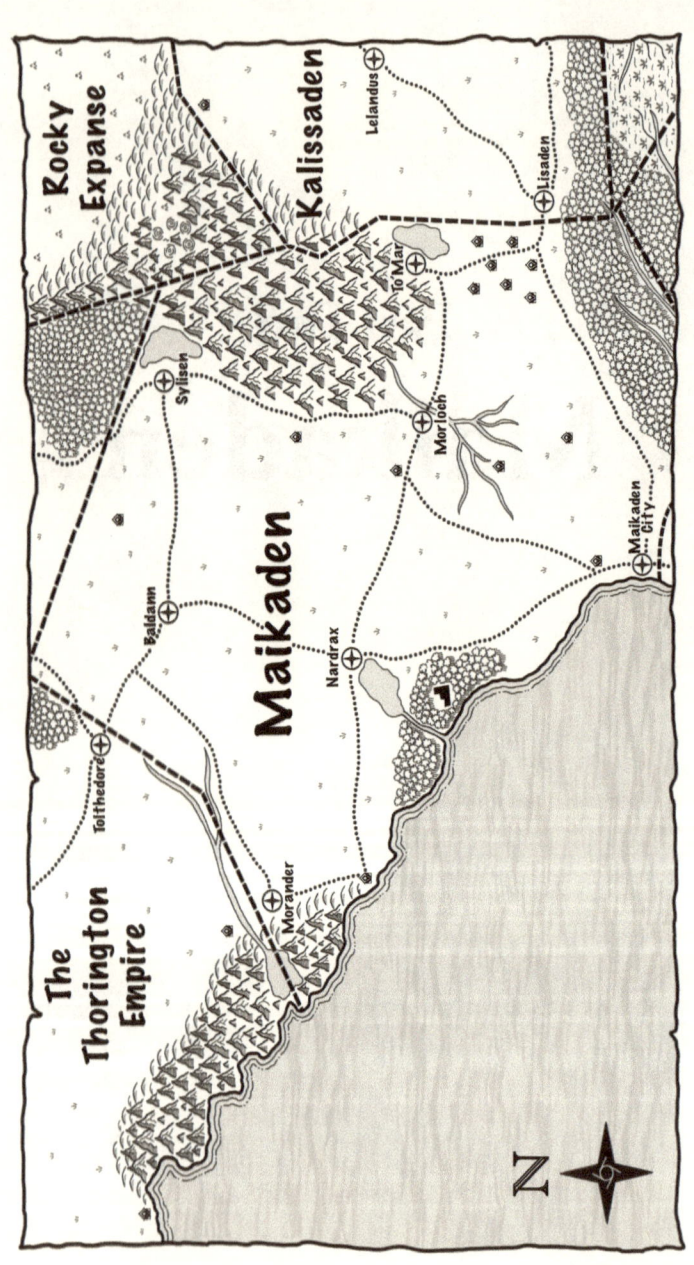

## 11

Emperor Thrul's court was furnished lavishly with expensive silks draped along the walls, and plush cushions strewn about the floor. The throne, candelabras, goblets, oil lanterns, and anything metal was plated in gold. In Ashavan's opinion, the place was gaudy and a waste of money.

The emperor sat on his throne, bouncing his young daughter on his knee, while his wife sat on the dais playing with their two boys. Standing close to Thrul's left shoulder was Belarüs, dressed in the horrid golden robes of an imperial advisor.

A few nobles lounged around on cushions, sipping wine and talking quietly to one another. No one paid any attention as Ashavan and his Lord strode towards the emperor. Ashavan maintained his position one step behind his Lord's right shoulder, his hand never straying from the hilt his sword. He locked eyes with Belarüs, who leant down and whispered something into the emperor's ear.

"What do you want, commoner?" Emperor Thrul asked, eyeing them disdainfully.

Ashavan tensed. Clearly the emperor had no idea who he was talking to.

"It has come to my attention that you have been harbouring known criminals within your city," Lord

Du'Rakis said. His voice was cold, sending a shiver down Ashavan's spine.

"Granting sanctuary to refugees is not a crime." Thrul waved his hand dismissively. "Leave, before I have you arrested.

"Where are they?" Lord Du'Rakis demanded.

"Who do you think you are?" Thrul snapped. "How dare you speak to me like that. GUARDS!"

"They won't come," Lord Du'Rakis spat. "You have one final chance."

Ashavan took his cue and drew his sword with a steely hiss. The emperor's eyes bulged from his head. He wrapped his arms protectively around his little girl.

"I strongly advise you to tell them where they are, Your Imperial Highness," Belarüs said smoothly.

"T... They're staying in the old concubine wing," Thrul stammered. "Behind the imperial suite."

"Ashavan, you know what to do. Kill them all." Lord Du'Rakis crossed his arms.

"*All* of them, My Lord?"

"What part of my sentence don't you understand? The brats, too."

Ashavan sucked in a deep breath and lowered his visor. He took a step forward, and the emperor began to whimper.

"Please! I told you what you wanted to know. I'll give you whatever you want. Just leave my family out of this."

Lord Du'Rakis raised his hand, and an audible click sounded from each of the doors of the court. Some of the nobles screamed and scurried to the exits. Try though they might, the doors wouldn't budge. Ashavan advanced on the cowering emperor and raised his sword to strike. He flexed, ready to commence the downward swing.

"No! Don't hurt my daddy!"

The little girl's crystal blue eyes were wide with fear, and bore into Ashavan's face. He faltered, feeling his heart shatter into a million pieces.

"What are you waiting for?" Lord Du'Rakis demanded.

Ashavan bit his lip. It was them or him. He strengthened his grip and plunged his sword into the little girl's heart, killing her instantly. The screams of her mother and the nobles echoed in his ears. He withdrew his blade and ran through the imperial family, one by one. The sweet little boys clung to their mother, tears in their eyes, too afraid to make any noise.

He turned to the nobles, and moved towards them purposefully, his sword dripping with the blood of the innocents he had just murdered. His mind felt disconnected from his body as it cut down the rest of the nobles without any mercy.

As the final noble woman slid from the end of Ashavan's sword, Du'Rakis finally spoke.

"Did you get it, Belarüs?"

"I did, My Lord."

Ashavan turned as Belarüs pulled a scroll from his pocket and walked down the steps of the dais. He bowed deeply, unperturbed by the carnage around them.

"The letter clearly states that in the event of the emperor's death, should he have no immediate heir, I am to be placed as regent until such time as a replacement is found. Thrul has seven brothers, so it will take some time for them to fight over the throne. By the time they kill each other and appoint a leader, we will be done here."

"Good. We'll go and take care of the rest of the scum."

Ashavan wiped his blade on one of the cushions, and sheathed his sword. He drew his wide double-edged dagger and walked across to where Belarüs stood.

"Where do you want it?" he asked shortly.

"Here."

Ashavan plunged his dagger roughly into the space between Belarüs' collarbone and shoulder. Belarüs hissed from the pain, and held his hand to the bloody wound. Ashavan tore a section of cloth from one of the bodies and tossed it to him. Belarüs pressed it to the wound and made his way back to the throne.

"I'll expect an update as soon as you're sworn in as regent." Du'Rakis held up his hand and unlocked the doors. "Let's go, Ashavan."

Ashavan fell into step with Du'Rakis and followed him from the court, leaving the doors wide open. The guards all stood frozen at their posts, unaware that their beloved emperor and his family were all dead.

Murdered.

It didn't take them long to find the quarters. A golden door led from the emperor's private suite directly into what was once the home of hundreds of concubines. They walked down a narrow wing with many doors completely coated in gold. Ashavan could hear the sound of laughter and chatter growing louder with each step.

The common room was filled with people lounging around on cushions, talking amongst themselves and laughing. Children chased each other while some women sewed and some crocheted. Ashavan blinked, then felt his stomach turn to lead. *The wives, lovers, and children of the men who fought in the battle of Rarn. These people aren't even a part of the Brotherhood. And he wants me to...*

The room grew deathly quiet as the occupants realised who was standing in the only entrance to the gilded room. There were no windows or doors other than the emperor's bedroom. Ashavan stared at the faces of his soon-to-be victims; they looked sad, tired, as though they'd been through a great ordeal already.

An infant let out a high-pitched wail, bringing Ashavan back to the moment.

"Your menfolk betrayed me. Therefore, you all must die," Du'Rakis said without any hint of remorse.

It was all over quickly. Ashavan felt numb as he swept through each of the golden dorms, expunging what was left of the families of the Brotherhood. And still, Du'Rakis showed no guilt or sadness for the hundred or so slaughtered innocent lives.

Du'Rakis turned and led the way back to the compound. Once they reached the gates, he paused and turned back to face the lavish palace. He raised his hand, and the guards all shook their heads and looked around, confused. It didn't take long for them to discover the massacre.

"You have pleased me today, Ashavan," Lord Du'Rakis said as a horn was blown from the palace. The guards on the gates gasped and bolted towards the imperial court. "Take this portal back to the keep. You have earned a few days' rest. I will return once I have finished with Enbarak and Ornas."

Ashavan sat on the edge of his bed, dressed in nothing but his undergarments. It felt strange to be out of his heavy armour. Each time he stood up or moved his arm, he lost his balance from over-compensating. He felt clean and fresh from his bath, no longer itchy from a weeks' worth of stubble. Ashavan stood awkwardly and studied his face in the polished metal he used as a mirror. His eyes were sunken and tinged with red, accompanied by dark patches of grey.

The man who looked back at him in the mirror was unrecognisable. He was a murderer, a monster; he'd crossed a line when he killed that sweet little girl, and there was no going back. The thought of having to clean the blood and gore off his armour turned his stomach. Tysion's gift, hours of love and skill poured into the one-of-a-kind set, was now contaminated by the blood of the innocent.

Ashavan unlocked the door to his balcony and stepped into the icy cold wind. The chill bit into his exposed skin as he leant on the rail and stared into the darkness. The face of the little girl flitted before him. *"Don't hurt my daddy!"*

He stared down at the black mark of the ibis on his wrist, remembering the day it was tattooed onto his skin. How he felt so proud that day, to serve for such a great cause that would truly change the world for better.

Everything he was taught to believe: the sermons, the teachings, were all lies. But he refused to believe that, refused to accept that he'd wasted so many years already just to be used and abused. Instead, he pushed himself harder, desperate to prove himself and be recognised. The taste of regret burned deep in the back of his throat; Tysion was right. He *was* brainwashed, ensnared by a master who cared not for him or any other life in existence.

Tysion, the only one he'd ever loved, and would love until he took his last breath. The one he swore to protect. The fear of being forced to cut him down while Du'Rakis watched was a living nightmare he couldn't escape from. *If only I knew how to pray,* he thought, glancing down at the ground far below. *No god would ever have me anyway. I am a monster. There is no forgiveness for what I have done.*

With a deep sigh, Ashavan returned to the warmth of his quarters. The blood-splattered armour sat eerily on its stand, a grim reminder of his earlier crimes. Feeling his deep shame, Ashavan took his cleaning cloth and gently dabbed at the embellishment on the front of his chest plate; an embossed Ŧ inlaid with gold and surrounded by a coppery sun. Tysion's mark.

An overwhelming wave of grief and remorse swept over him without warning, and before he could control himself, he felt the hot tears fall onto his cheeks. He dropped the cleaning cloth and sat weeping into his hands uncontrollably.

*I'm so sorry, Tysion. I have ruined everything. If there is a god out there listening, please just strike me down now. This world does not deserve the pain I have unleashed upon it, and I do not deserve to live after taking so many innocent lives. I can't do this anymore.*

## 12

The gates of Lisaden were closed and unwelcoming. The drawbridge was raised, exposing a wide pit of spikes surrounding the great walls. Guards were evenly spaced along the battlements, aiming their armed crossbows at all who neared.

"I don't think this is a good idea," Gaitan frowned. "Do you think we should just avoid the city and keep going?"

"They've seen us now. If we turn back, they will deem us suspicious and come after us, yes." Joplin said. Since leaving the Fens, he was almost back to his former self. "We're almost out of supplies since our hunter left."

"Let's just keep going. If they let us in, we might be able to find out what else Khel – Du'Rakis is up to." Nika scratched at the stubble on his cheek, trying not to think about Freyne's departure.

"Remember our new cover story," Joplin said, urging his horse forward.

Nika could feel every eye on them as they stopped at the edge of the pit.

"Halt! State your business!" a guard shouted from the gatehouse window.

"We are returning home to Maikaden City," Joplin yelled back. "We seek lodgings for the night and to replenish our supplies, yes."

"Where are you travelling from?" the guard demanded.

"Loralyon. We spent Kharung there with family."

The guard ducked away from the window, and soon reappeared.

"We will lower the bridge. You must submit to a search before we grant you entry."

The sound of heavy grinding gears echoed from the bridge, and it slowly descended into place. The gates rose up half way, and a detachment of mounted guards rode swiftly across, their weapons at the ready.

"Everyone dismount and place your weapons on the ground," the captain ordered.

Nika felt his stomach churn uneasily. He dismounted and stood to one side with his friends as the guards rummaged through their packs. Arnie-Kyn's claws dug into Nika's skin and his tail flickered; Nika was more concerned about the focus tucked into his trousers. He didn't need a necromancer to tell him it was valuable and should be protected at all costs.

"What is this?" One of the guards held up the heavy tome gifted by Saramas.

"It's called a book, you idiot," the captain snapped. "Put it back. You lot are cleared to enter. The western slums are off limit to everyone, and curfew is at sundown. Anyone found roaming the streets after dark will be arrested and hanged."

The captain waved to his men to remount, and they rode back across the drawbridge. Nika let out a deep breath and quickly remounted.

*"Can you please stop clawing me?"* he asked.

Arnie retracted his claws, but said nothing. As they rode slowly across the bridge, Nika felt the unmistakable probe of another mind. Ever so gently, he drew a shield around him and his friends, and hid his aura.

"They have a mancer," he said quietly. "Just act normal. I'm watching him."

The people in the streets eyed them with open hostility. Nika could sense their fear and mistrust, and even hatred from some. They rode slowly through the city until they finally reached an inn. As Joplin reigned in, the door flung open with a bang.

"Go away! You are not welcome here!" A burly innkeeper yelled, brandishing a mop.

"Fine. We'll spend our gold elsewhere." Joplin wheeled his horse around, leaving the innkeeper red in the face.

By the time they found an inn willing to host them for the night, the sun was already sinking towards the horizon. Nika stashed his packs and Arnie in the room he was to share with Gaitan, then made his way downstairs. The dining area was only half full, and most of the people sat talking quietly amongst themselves. Nika joined Joplin at the bar and ordered a round of stouts.

"Did you have any trouble getting into the city?" the innkeeper asked.

"We were searched, but that was about all," Joplin replied. "I've never seen Lisaden so edgy before. What's going on?"

The innkeeper placed three tankards on the bar and lowered his voice.

"The city was attacked by mercenaries not long ago. In one night, a few hundred people were stabbed by swords while sleeping. No one knows why. People are scared. No one wants to wake up to find their loved ones have been murdered."

"That's horrible," Nika said, taking a sip of his stout. "I hope none of your friends or family were harmed."

"I don't have any friends or family," the innkeeper grunted. "Will you be dining downstairs or in your rooms?"

"We'll eat down here. Oh, there you are, woman." Joplin slipped his arm around Priye's waist. "Let's go and get a table, yes."

151

"I'll take mine upstairs," Nika said quickly.

The innkeeper nodded and turned to serve another patron. Nika collected the spare tankard and followed Joplin and Priye to their table, just as Gaitan joined them.

"Remember. If you so much as put one hair over my side of the bed tonight, I will cut you with a blunt knife," Priye said under her breath. "Then, I will stitch you up with my thickest needle. Don't even snore or break wind in my direction."

Nika couldn't help but grin. The thought of sharing a room with Gaitan that night also had him feeling awkward, but at least they had a single bed each. He handed the spare tankard to Gaitan and lowered his voice.

"I'm going to eat in our room. I want to scout out the city and check a few things. Keep your ears open and see if you can pick up any news or information. These people are scared, and people act weird when they are scared. We don't want to stumble into any issues."

Joplin placed his arm around Priye's shoulder. Nika could tell he was enjoying playing his role as her husband, and was pretty sure he aimed to annoy her as much as he could. Priye slipped her hand onto his leg, a glint of mischief in her eyes.

"We'll come and see you afterwards," she said.

Nika nodded, and made his way back to his room with his stout in hand. The fire in the hearth was almost out, inviting the icy winter chill into the air. He knelt down and stirred up the coals, bringing it back to life. Once he was satisfied, Nika fetched the book and focus from their hiding place, and dragged the armchair next to the fire.

A knock on the door startled him. He opened it cautiously, but relaxed when he realised it was just a maid with his dinner. She handed him a tray and curtseyed.

"Is there anything else you would like, sir?" she asked.

"No. Thank you." Nika smiled and closed the door.

Dinner was roasted meat with a generous portion of

root vegetables and thick gravy. Once he finished eating, he sat his tray on the floor in the hallway, and settled into the armchair with his feet resting on the footstool. He flicked through the pages of the book until he found the section on how to use a focus.

*1.*

*A focus is a vital tool for necromancers. As much as a warrior values his sword, a necromancer should value his focus. Therefore, this tool should be treated as an extension of one's abilities. Imbue it with essence for protection and to prevent unauthorised access and theft.*

*2.*

*A focus may or may not bind itself to a necromancer. Only proficient masters worthy of respect will be able to wield such a powerful tool.*

*3.*

*Using a focus is straight forward. Instead of drawing power directly from the realm, one channels through the void instead. This allows for the master to aim their powers more precisely, and in some cases, can amplify those powers.*

*4.*

*The void can be useful for concealing small items should the necromancer have need. Alternatively, enchanted items such as crystals, gems, or rocks can be held in the void to imbue the focus with those properties. Only the necromancer who controls the focus may do so.*

*5.*

*Only the master of the focus should touch it. The necromancer should always dedicate a sprite to protect it from unauthorised use.*

Curious, Nika pulled the firestone from his pack next to the armchair and sat staring at it in his hand. It was slightly smaller than the void, albeit a rougher shape.

*"Can you try not to cause an explosion or fire this time?"* Arnie-Kyn asked wryly.

*"I'll try. I can't promise anything, though,"* Nika replied.

Arnie leapt onto Nika's lap and started kneading his legs with his claws. Nika sighed, then carefully inserted the firestone into the focus. The dark centre of the void glowed red and orange.

"That's handy," Nika said out loud. "At least I don't have to worry about losing the stone now."

He carefully tested the stone within the focus. The light was easy enough to adjust, and even the flames were more controlled, licking around the golden cage without burning anything.

*"You look entirely too comfortable for someone so worried about me burning things,"* Nika said, scratching Arnie behind his ears.

*"One is cold and you are warm."* Arnie closed his eyes, purring.

Nika re-read the page, then sat the book aside and readied himself. He reached out his mind towards the void, and sure enough he could see directly into the realm without disconnecting from his body. It felt different, detached. Usually while deep in the realm, he could feel it encompassing him. Using the focus, though, he could still hear what was going on around him; the crackle of the fire, doors slamming down the hall, and the occasional laughter or shouting downstairs.

*"Why do they call it a focus?"* Nika asked. *"I find it more distracting than anything."*

*"You're just not used to it,"* Arnie said. *"You have no trouble doing the same with the lowest realm."*

Nika closed his eyes and concentrated. After a while, the void opened up, allowing him to see further into the realm and with more clarity. It was almost as though his field of sight overlapped with the vision of the realm. He could see the colourful life force of the people downstairs, Arnie's aura, and down the hall, a lone white sprite hovered by a window.

Remembering his lessons, Nika reached out an invisible hand and captured the sprite. It felt a little easier using the focus.

*"Who are you?"* it demanded.

*"That is no way to speak to me. I will be asking the questions here."* Nika said firmly. He squeezed the essence as Saramas taught him, just enough to show that he meant business.

*"Ow. I apologise, Master."*

*"That's better. How did you die?"*

*"I was murdered,"* it said casually. *"It's not a good idea to take a married woman as a lover. Their husbands get insanely jealous."*

*"How unfortunate. Do you know the way to the slums to the west?"*

*"Yes."*

*"Yes what?"* Nika demanded.

*"Yes, Master."*

*"Better. Take me there at once."*

*"Yes, Master."*

Nika pushed himself from his body, only to find himself emerged fully in the realm. The sprite guided him through the city to a run-down area dotted with fresh essence. The deaths weren't concentrated to one area; rather they were scattered amongst random dwellings. To Nika, though, it was obvious. The killers weren't being random, they were targeting specific people. Somehow, they knew where each and every victim was located.

A few of the sprites drifted towards him and hovered.

*"Help us, please!"*

*"What happened here?"* Nika asked.

*"We don't know. We were sleeping, and then we were dead."*

155

A few more sprites drifted across and joined them.

"*Were you members of the Black Ibis cult?*"

"*At one time, yes. After what happened at the Battle of Rarn, though, we defected,*" one of the sprites answered. "*We heard that he killed the entire army. Then he sent General Ashavan to finish off the rest of us. How did he find us?*"

"*I don't know,*" Nika replied. "*Is there anything I can do to help you all rest in peace?*"

"*Avenge us. Protect those who are still hiding.*"

"*I'll do my best,*" Nika said sincerely. "*I must go now. Goodbye.*"

Nika nodded to his captured sprite, and together they sped back to the inn. As he drifted through the wall, he caught sight of Gaitan waving his hand in front of Nika's blank staring face. Joplin looked uneasy.

"*You have served me well. You have my thanks,*" Nika said.

"*You're welcome, Master. That was fun. May I serve you again?*"

"*Very well.*" Nika concentrated, and infused the sprite into his focus. "*You are to hide and disguise this focus from view until I need you again. Understood?*"

"*Yes, Master.*"

Nika slipped back into his body and blinked. Gaitan jumped at the sudden movement and stepped back.

"You scared me half to death," he grumbled.

"What did you expect?" Priye asked.

Gaitan mumbled something incoherently.

"What did you find out?" Nika asked, changing the subject.

"Not much." Joplin shook his head. "There was no mention of Du'Rakis. All we heard was that it was a group of foreign mercenaries. That's why everyone's so jumpy and scared of strangers, yes."

Nika sat down the focus and carefully pulled Arnie into his arms. His legs were stiff from sitting for so long.

He stood and stamped his feet to wake them up.

"Did you find anything?" Gaitan asked.

"Surprisingly, I did," Nika replied. "The mercenaries were led by a General Ashavan. The victims were all ex-cultists trying to hide from Du'Rakis. Somehow the cultists are traceable."

"You found all of that while sitting in this room?" Gaitan asked, a little surprised.

"That. Also, a man was murdered just up there in the hallway." Nika pointed. "He's learnt his lesson not to chase after married women. A little late, if you ask me. He'll be coming with me."

That night, Nika's sleep was plagued by nightmares. He dreamt about the snake in the mountains again, which always left him shaking and sweaty. The worst dreams were those of Freyne getting hurt while on his long journey; visions of him falling from the sky and being attacked by a wild beast in vivid detail. Nika missed him terribly, and the thought of him traveling in the opposite direction filled him with all sorts of emotions he didn't want to face. He'd shed more than enough tears already, though, and was determined to face the weeks ahead with a positive attitude.

Around two hours before dawn, he gave up on sleeping and tiptoed back to the armchair, being careful not to wake Gaitan. The inn was quiet and calm, the only noise coming from an occasional snore down the hall. Nika stared into the flames dancing lazily in the fireplace, reflecting on his life since waking up on the alter almost a year ago.

He cradled the focus in his arm and closed his eyes, slowly retracing his steps since that day. The library, being attacked in the slums, waking up and meeting

Freyne for the first time. King To'Rel and the urgency of the prophecy, and their journey with the princess. That night in the ruins, his first kiss with Freyne. He thought back to how nervous they both were, and how each night thereafter they explored each other's bodies a little bit more. The image of Freyne's naked body crept into his mind, and Nika reached out to run his fingers over his strong chest, all the way down to his manhood...

*"Danger! Wake up, Master!"*

Nika's eyes shot open with a start, and he glanced around the room in panic, almost forgetting where he was. The faintest hint of light peeked through the drapes and fell across Gaitan's face. Nika frowned and settled back in the chair, trying to remember what woke him. *I must have dreamt it,* he thought.

Just as his heart stopped racing and he grew calm, he heard it again.

*"Danger!"*

Nika scowled, and dragged his mind into the darkest realm. A lone sprite jittered in front of him, clearly agitated.

*"What is it?"* Nika asked.

*"More lives are in danger! Please, Master. You said you would help us."*

*"Calm down. What's going on?"* Nika yawned.

*"More of our people have been captured."*

*"Show me. Take me to them."*

Nika followed the sprite through the realm, street by street, until they came to a narrow alley crawling with guards. Nika drifted higher, and spotted three prisoners with their hands tied behind their backs. He followed slowly as the guards marched them through the alley and streets, until they finally came to a squat prison building.

"Throw 'em in the brig," one of the guards called. "We'll do a sweep and see if there are any more. Set up the gallows in the main square. We'll hang them at noon."

The prisoners were marched into the building and

thrown into a cell with two others inside. Nika felt his eyes widen as they fell on a familiar person, with just a hint of purple hair showing from under the hood of her cloak.

*"It's Yger!"* Nika said sharply.

*"She is one of the defectors who tried to save us,"* the sprite said. *"Please, help her."*

Nika scouted out the building, but from what he could see, there was no way to escape.

*"I'm going to go and wake my friends,"* he said. *"I can't free them alone. Even then, we're going to need a way to get them out of the city. I'll do what I can to free your friends."*

Nika's morning was nail-bitingly tense, but thankfully Joplin and Gaitan agreed to help free Yger and her friends without any arguments. Nika half expected Joplin to refuse, but surprisingly the big man sprung to action and helped to formulate a plan.

With under an hour left before the execution, they hid in the alley not far from the prison and waited. It felt almost strange to be using the lowest realm again; Nika realised he'd been so focused on his training since meeting Saramas that he hadn't even thought of the lowest since. He ghosted above the alley way, watching a small group of guards approaching. Once they drew close enough to the entrance, Nika returned to his body.

"Here they come," he whispered. "Now."

"HELP!" Priye shrieked.

"Shut your mouth, woman!" Joplin yelled.

"Keep your hands off me!"

The guards paused, then ran into the alley.

"Halt! Unhand her this instant!" one of the guards yelled.

From his hiding place, Nika focused his mind, and stunned the guards. They froze, unable to move. He felt himself break into a sweat from the effort of holding four minds all at once. Gaitan and Joplin moved quickly and stripped off their uniforms, then tied their hands and gagged them.

"Get changed. Hurry, yes." Joplin handed Nika one of the uniforms.

Nika quickly changed into the red doublet and hose, then pulled on the leather plate skirt and chest plate. He cringed as he buckled on the helm which smelt of the guard's sweat and probably contained fleas.

"Ok, let's move," Nika said, drawing one of the guard's swords. He released his hold on their prisoners, his heart thumping in his chest. "You WILL do what we say, or we WILL kill you."

The guards nodded. Nika felt terrible, seeing the fright in their eyes. But he wasn't going to stand by and allow them to execute innocent people.

Nika, Joplin and Gaitan marched their captives towards the prison building, leaving Priye to fetch their horses. There were eight guards lounging around as they entered. Nika could feel his palms sweating; *what if they recognise our prisoners? What it we get caught?*

"What have we got here?" a captain asked, only half interested.

"We found more of them, Captain," Joplin said.

"It's almost noon. The others should be here soon. Let's go and get the others shackled up." The captain stood and stretched, then strode into the back area where the cells were located.

Yger and her people sat against the far wall of the cell, a look of sadness and defeat etched into their faces. Nika's heart thumped in his chest; they were almost there. The captain fumbled for the keys on his belt, then reached to unlock the door.

"Mmmm. MMFFF!"

One of the captives tried to make a dash towards the

captain. Joplin hit him over the head and he sunk to the floor. The captain glared at the other captives before his expression changed to one of recognition.

"Wait a minute! *Ergal?!* What in the gods?"

Joplin shoved the closest captive towards the captain, knocking them both to the ground. The other guards quickly realised what was going on, and drew their swords in a steely hiss. Nika parried a blow with his sword, and repelled the guard with a well-timed ball of energy that sent him skidding across the floor. Nika managed to stun three more of the guards, then stood over the captain with the tip of his blade aimed right between his eyes. Joplin and Gaitan made short work of the others.

"Quick, get their uniforms," Gaitan said, panting.

"What...who are you?" Yger demanded.

Nika took the keys from the captain's belt and unlocked the cell, ignoring her question.

"Drag them inside. We'll lock them up," Nika said. "Yger. You and your people get changed into their uniforms. Hurry, we don't have much time."

He stood back and once again projected himself high above the prison. A few streets away, around fifty mounted soldiers were riding towards them. Nika scanned the streets and alleys, and finally spotted Priye at their rendezvous point.

"We have to go now," he barked as he re-joined his body.

The guards were all locked in the cell, and Yger and her people were ready to go. She snatched her heavy crossbow from the pile of confiscated property and slung it over her back, then quickly shoved her clothes into her pack.

"Which way?" she demanded.

"This way." Nika took the lead, and ran from the building. As they reached a narrow alley, he paused and checked behind them. The guards were dismounting and getting ready to enter the prison.

"Shit. Come on."

It didn't take them long to find Priye, who was dressed in the extra guard's uniform. The packs were all buckled to Streek, leaving the rest of the horses free to ride. Nika counted them; there were enough horses for everyone.

"Where did you get the extras?" Nika asked as he mounted.

"I stole them," she grinned.

"You?" Joplin looked surprised.

"Why not? We've already committed several crimes punishable by death today. What's one more?"

"You astound me, woman." Joplin shook his head, though the edge of his mouth curled into a hint of a grin. "Everyone into formation. Let's go, yes."

Joplin led the way towards the northern gates. No one paid much attention to nine guards riding through the city, though Nika was still sweating nervously. As they neared their target, Nika felt the unmistakable whisper from the realm, followed by a surge aimed towards them. He blocked the attack, then slipped his mind back into the realm.

It wasn't hard to locate the mancer; his aura was wide open, unshielded, and stood out easily. Nika could tell he wasn't very strong; his abilities were limited to the middle realm. Nika concentrated and lit a barrel of lamp oil on fire to draw the mancer's attention, then attacked with a sharp blow from behind, stunning him. The mancer faltered and collapsed.

The guards at the gates were much less trusting than Nika hoped. The sergeant on duty questioned Joplin, demanding to know his rank and barracks number. Nika looked over his shoulder to see the mounted guards from the brig galloping towards them. He sucked in a breath and looked around, thinking quickly. His eyes fell on the winch that held the gate in its upright position.

"What's going on?" the sergeant noticed the advancing

soldiers, then glared at Joplin and drew his sword.

"Oh, no you don't!" Joplin was faster, and swung his blade, sending the captain's head flying through the air.

Nika focused on the winch, and shattered it easily. The drawbridge fell and hit the earth with a loud bang. As the ground shook, he hurled a much stronger blast at the gates, blowing them to oblivion. Without waiting, he kicked his horse forward and galloped across the bridge, his friends close behind. Some of the guards on the battlements shot their crossbows, but missed. Nika risked a look over his shoulder; the soldiers were falling back behind them. They did it. They were free.

After around an hour of steady riding, they came to the edge of a small wood. Nika reigned in his horse, and immediately checked to see if they were being followed.

"It's all clear," he announced, dismounting.

He hurried across to Streek and opened one of the packs, and carefully lifted Arnie-Kyn into his arms.

*"Are you alright?"* he asked.

*"Don't talk to me. Put me down, human."*

Nika sat him on the ground and watched as he slunk off into the trees.

"I'll ask this again. Who are you people?" Yger demanded.

"It's us." Gaitan removed his helm and grinned.

"YOU!" Yger looked surprised. "I don't know what to say."

"Thank you is good enough, yes." Joplin nodded.

"Where's the rest of your people?" Nika asked.

"Most of them got away when our camp was attacked," Yger replied. "I have no idea if they made it out or not."

"Where are you heading?"

"It's a secret. I can't tell you," she said stubbornly.

"You do realise that Du'Rakis can track you, don't you?" Nika demanded.

"What...how did you know?" A hint of fear crept into her eyes.

"I know because I'm looking for him." Nika stared her down, feeling his nerves almost give way. "I've been sent to put a stop to this nonsense he's started. You can't run from him. He will find you and slaughter you all. Or send his general to slay you while you sleep."

The ex-cultists looked at each other nervously.

"Alright then. We're going to To'Mar. We have a secret camp there full of survivors." Yger relented. "If you try anything funny, we'll kill you."

Joplin caught Nika's eye.

"To'Mar is only a few weeks out of our way. We could escort them that far, replenish our supplies, then head to Maikaden City, yes."

"Alright," Nika agreed.

"We don't need your help," Yger argued.

"You and your people may not believe in the gods, but we do," Nika said pointedly. "I could have let those revenants kill you off one by one, or left you to be hanged at Lisaden. Given the history of your cult and what they did to Freyne's family, I should kill you all myself. But no. Am has some need to keep you alive, and I will not go against their will."

"Fine. We will go with you." Yger grunted.

"Get changed, everyone." Joplin ordered. "The soldiers will be on the hunt for nine people dressed in their uniforms. We need to move carefully, especially when we cross the border, yes."

---

In the days following the escape from Lisaden, Nika couldn't help feeling on edge. He knew Du'Rakis could track the cultists somehow, and the thought of having to face him so soon frightened him. Although his skills were improving daily, Nika knew deep down that he wasn't ready for a confrontation. Not yet. He busied himself with reading his book and writing in his journal as a way to keep grounded.

Late in the afternoon on the second day since fleeing the city, Joplin turned sharply north, and led them away from the road they'd been following. Eventually they found a shallow gully dotted with a few trees that was protected from the wind. A narrow stream made it a perfect spot to set up camp.

"This will do nicely," Joplin announced. "It should be safe enough to have a fire tonight, yes."

"Are any of you good at hunting?" Priye asked hopefully.

One of the cultists stepped forward.

"I am, my lady."

"I think we are beyond pleasantries, don't you?" she asked. "Please, call me Priye. This is Nika, Gaitan and Joplin."

"Um, ok. I'm Angar." The man looked shy.

"The others are Hari, Iphan, and Lashur," Yger offered.

"See? That wasn't so hard, was it?" Priye held her hands to her hips. "Nika and Gaitan, you two can go and get some wood and start the fire. Angar, go hunt us something decent to eat. Hari and Lashur, you two can go and fill the waterskins. The rest of you can set up the tents. Hop to it!"

Dinner that night was a succulent wild goat roasted over the fire. They didn't have much else to eat other than the meat, but Priye still had some seasoning in her supplies. The meat melted in Nika's mouth, and there was more than enough for everyone.

"A meal fit for a king," Nika murmured, holding his belly with both hands.

"I second that," Joplin nodded. "Perhaps you would make a good wife for real, yes."

"Been there, done that," Priye smirked. "Never again. That one night being *your* wife was bad enough."

"It wasn't that bad, was it?" Joplin asked. He looked

a little hurt.

"You snore, and when you're not snoring, you're producing noxious gas," she said.

"Women." Joplin threw up his hands. "Glad I was never interested in having one."

Nika laughed, but broke off as his thoughts turned to Freyne. His forays with numerous women in his old life were nothing compared to the intimacy he and Freyne shared. He felt a wave of loneliness dull his mood, and looked up at the stars. *I miss you. Hurry back. I need you.*

"So, Yger. Where are you from?" Gaitan asked. He got up and moved around the fire and sat next to her.

Yger scowled and shimmied across so he wasn't so close.

"That's none of your business, little man," she snapped.

"I was only trying to start a conversation," he said defensively.

"And I'm ending it."

Nika pushed himself up off the ground and brushed the dirt from his trousers, then walked quietly away from the fire. He gave his eyes a moment to adjust to the darkness, then climbed to the top of the gully. The night was cold, and the wind cut through his shirt to his skin. Nika pulled his cloak tighter, and wandered around until he found a smooth boulder. He climbed it and sat staring into the starry sky.

*"Nickolai..."* a soft whisper came to him on the breeze.

He slipped his hand into his cloak and withdrew the focus from the makeshift sheath Gaitan made for him. He closed his eyes and allowed himself to ease into the void. Before him was a sprite that felt familiar. He reached forward and joined his mind with it.

*"Hello, Master,"* Nika said.

*"How goes thy training?"* Saramas asked.

*"I think I'm doing alright,"* Nika replied. He quickly described the events of Lisaden.

"*Good. Thou art learning. There is one small thing we need to discuss though.*"

Nika shifted and made himself more comfortable.

"*Did I do something wrong, Master?*" he asked.

"*Nay. But the spirits of the realm are concerned. They are aware of thy activity, and some have already whispered thy name. We need to protect thy real identity, lest Lord Du'Rakis discover who thou art. Remember, if he knows thy face and name, he can attack thee from afar.*"

"*Wouldn't an alias be just as easy to identify me?*" Nika asked.

"*Nay. Thine real name is a part of who thou art. No one can take that from thee. An alias can be anything, though, and there is no way one can link that to thy real identity unless thou reveal it thyself.*"

"*What should I do then, Master?*" Nika asked. The thought of being exposed to Du'Rakis in any way scared him, though he didn't want to admit it.

"*The council of necromancers are aware that I have taken on a new apprentice, and demand to know who,*" he said. "*In mine old age, I overlooked the chance of them finding out. Now I must register thee.*"

Nika sat in silence for a moment, waiting for Saramas to speak again.

"*We do not use our birth names,*" he said finally. "*The word 'Sa' translates to 'pupil of'. My master was Ramas, hence my name. I shalt call thee Sarik. Lord Sarik, as thou art not a master yet.*"

"*I'm not a lord, either.*" Nika said.

"*Necromancers are worthy of such a title, should their master bestow it upon them. So yes, thou art a lord necromancer.*" Saramas said.

"*Er, ok. Thank you, Master.*"

"*Keep up thy training. I shalt contact thee again soon.*" Saramas sounded pleased with himself.

"*Wait! Before you go, I have a question,*" Nika said

quickly. *"Du'Rakis is somehow able to track those who were in his cult. Would you have any idea how he's doing that?"*

*"There are a number of ways,"* Saramas said after a pause. *"Tracking one person demands a lot of energy from the realm, and would not be an adequate method to control an entire cult. This leads me to believe he's used ancient blood magick. The only way to find out is by inspecting the body of a cultist. Look for any marks or brands that stick out."*

*"Thank you, Master."*

*"Be well, Nickolai. Lord Sarik. I shalt speak to ye soon."*

Nika felt the link sever between them, and the sprite sped away. He sighed and pulled his mind back from the void; there were so many questions he desperately wanted to ask, but the only two people who could help him were far, far, away.

## 13

The Maikaden border was swarming with soldiers, more than Nika expected to see. A crude wall constructed of logs marked the boundary; groups of twenty soldiers patrolled both sides of the wall, leaving little room to slip through. To make matters worse, Nika could make out the auras of two mancers actively sweeping the lowest realm. Being careful not to alert the mancers, Nika ghosted along the lines, hoping to find an easier place to cross.

"What did you see?" Joplin asked the moment Nika stepped back into his body.

"There's at least a hundred soldiers at the border," he replied. "The only place we can cross is further up that way. A small section of the wall is missing. It's guarded by another twenty soldiers, though."

"Can we not split up and pass through in pairs?" Hari asked.

"They have two mancers," Nika said, shaking his head. "They would be able to see through the ruse."

"Not only that," Yger added. "They know that nine people fled Lisaden. I daresay they would have locked down the city until they at least fix their drawbridge. They will know it's us."

"There are nine of us," Gaitan pointed out. "Well, eight fighters, and twenty of them. We are outnumbered, so either way it will be risky."

"The mancers will hear and alert the others if I use my particular talents," Nika said.

"Can't you just summon a skeleton and scare them away?" Priye murmured to Nika.

Nika shook his head.

"It doesn't work that way. I'd need an intact skeleton to do that, and I don't think any of these guys will want to lend me theirs. Besides, Joplin will get upset again. He's kind of annoying when he's pouting."

Priye laughed heartily, drawing an irritated look from the others.

"Sorry," she said quickly.

"Twenty soldiers is hardly a challenge," Yger snorted. "I have four bolts left. Let's go and get this over with."

No one talked as they slipped into position and got ready for the attack. Yger crawled to the top of a small mound and lay prone behind a rock, aiming her crossbow at the soldiers. Gaitan and Joplin crept as close as they could, moving slowly to avoid their armour making any noise. At Joplin's insistence, Gaitan ditched his old sword and replaced it with one they'd taken from the Lisaden guards. They crouched either side of the narrow path and waited in ambush.

Angar, Iphan, and Hari got into their positions not far away, spaced strategically along the path. Nika did one final check of their surrounds, then signalled to Yger. She signalled back to let him know she was ready, and Nika took a deep breath. He stood up, jammed his hands in his pockets, and strolled along the path towards the soldiers, singing a merry tune.

"Halt! Stay where you are!" One of the soldiers shouted.

Nika held up his hands and forced a smile.

"Lovely day for a walk," he called.

The captain pushed his way through his men and

glared at Nika.

"What business do you have here?" he shouted, waving his sword.

"I was just enjoying my walk," Nika called back. "I'll just be on my way, then."

He turned and strolled back towards where Priye was hidden, being careful not to walk too fast and ruin the ambush.

"Hey! I said halt! HALT!"

Nika kept walking, and heard the sounds of many feet running towards him. A strangled cry rang out, followed by more shouting. He quickly snatched his sword from its hiding place behind a rock, and turned back to the fray.

The fight was over already. Yger slung her crossbow over her back and chased after the one remaining soldier; with her long legs, she caught him in no time. The soldier tried swinging his blade at her, but a perfectly timed cartwheel took her out of harm's way and distracted him long enough to plant a firm kick to his chest. He doubled over, and Yger delivered a sharp uppercut to the chin, knocking him backwards. She knelt down and grasped his head firmly in both hands, and twisted with a sickening *crack*.

Nika's head filled with angry whispers from the freshly departed guards. They were confused and bewildered, and some were angry.

"*Silence!*" Nika ordered. "*This is what you get for mindlessly killing people. Now leave me be.*"

Gaitan was staring at Yger with awe written across his face.

"What you staring at, little man?" she demanded.

"I... nothing," he said quickly.

Joplin busied himself with rummaging through the soldier's pockets and collected as much gold and coins as he could find. From the captain he pulled a fresh piece of parchment and unfolded it.

"Uh oh. Time to get going, yes."

He held up the parchment; a charcoal sketch showed Yger's face in detail, with the words 'Wanted: 1,000 gold to the person who apprehends this man.' Yger snatched the parchment and tore it into shreds, then kicked the body of the captain with all her strength.

"Let's go, before I decide to go and kill the rest of them," she hissed.

―――

Ashavan stood on his balcony, watching the fog roll through the trees. The few days' rest he was granted by Lord Du'Rakis had him feeling well rested. The thought of slaughtering more people, though, left him with a sense of dread.

Someone knocked on his door, and he frowned.

"Enter," he called.

The door opened, and he held back a scowl as Rissa poked her head inside.

"What is it?" he asked shortly.

Rissa sashayed into the room with a smirk and helped herself to the corner of his bed. She was wearing skimpy negligee as usual, and although Ashavan knew most men would find her alluring and attractive, she did nothing for him. He crossed his arms and leant against the wall.

"What's wrong with you?" she asked.

"Nothing."

"Oh, come on. These are exciting times. Liven up a little." She crossed her arms and mimicked a pout. "Our Lord has found some survivors from Sepheren. If you're lucky he might let you go and take some of that pent-up anger out on them."

"How could anyone escape that blast?" Ashavan demanded.

"They snuck out the night before." She shrugged. "We've received word that they slipped through Lisaden as well. Our Lord is watching them as we speak. He will call us soon."

"Sepheren was your responsibility." Ashavan frowned. "He could have your head for this. Our Lord explicitly stated there were to be no survivors."

"He's left a few alive deliberately so they'll flush out those in hiding." She leant back on the bed seductively and caught his eye. "I'd offer you to come to my quarters for a different kind of...release. But you're not like the others, are you?"

"What the hell is that supposed to mean?" he snapped angrily. "Do you really think I'd want Belarüs and Enbarak's used goods?"

"No need to be so rude about it." She huffed and sat up. "Such a pity. You'd be a much better lay than the others."

Ashavan balled his hands into a fist and glared at her, no longer hiding his disgust. In two steps, he could have his hand around her throat and snap her neck. A deep gong reverberated somewhere in the lower reaches of the keep, pulling him back from his murderous thoughts. Without a word, Rissa stood and hurried from the room.

Ashavan sighed heavily and hurried after her, slamming his door behind him.

Lord Du'Rakis sat in his armchair with his hands clasped under his chin. As always, his face was hidden under his hood. Ashavan followed Rissa through the door and knelt next to her.

"Pull up a chair, both of you," Du'Rakis ordered. "I have news."

Ashavan did as he was told and sat next to Rissa.

"As of this morning, the Thorington Empire is under my control. Belarüs is now the acting regent, which means we are almost ready to move forward into stage three of my plan."

"How goes Enbarak, My Lord?" Rissa asked.

"He's finishing up at Maikaden City as we speak.

Once he returns, we'll all be taking a little trip. The defectors who escaped from my lieutenants are heading north towards To'Mar. The direction all of the scourge have been running points to To'Mar, so it's safe to guess the last of them are hiding there somewhere."

Ashavan's gut did a somersault, and once again the feeling of dread rose inside him. *What if my Tysion's there?*

"Is something wrong, Ashavan?" Du'Rakis asked.

"No, My Lord. I was just thinking we could do a sweep of the area and see if we can find them. Otherwise, it is safe to say that the Brotherhood is no more."

"This is correct. Once Ornas finds the final piece I need from Araneda's archives, there will be no stopping us."

As they rode further from the Kalissaden border, the landscape changed from gentle rolling plains into fertile farmland. Every few days they passed extensive homesteads, which resembled small self-sufficient towns. Of an evening, farmers occasionally invited them to their mess halls for a delicious hearty dinner and let them sleep in their barns for a reasonable price.

Nika soon got the hang of reading while riding without losing his balance, and spent most of the days with his nose in Saramas' book. The more he read, the more he realised that necromancy was not dark or evil like he first thought, but rather just another aspect of nature.

> *Necromancy is one of the most taboo practises that exists in our world. Necromancers are often frowned upon and cast out of society to live alone as hermits. People are afraid of death – to them, death is final, and they are entering the unknown. Death is, however, just another stage of life. Once we die, we are granted freedom from the physical restraints of our bodies, and are faced with a choice.*

*The first is a choice to rest in peace for an eternity, and allow our memories to fade slowly from this world. We choose to leave our ties to existence behind, and go peacefully.*

*The second option is to remain in a state of perpetual in-between. For those who are confused or not ready to rest, they may stay and attempt to tie up their loose ends, or seek to gain closure for their death. They become essence, which a necromancer may control or manipulate if he so desires.*

*In a rare instance, someone may choose to remain behind and offer their service to their chosen master. A necromancer may recruit one or more as a familiar, so long as the bond is mutual and served with respect.*

*The final option is the least understood. Those souls who worshipped a god may be granted entry to the afterlife. Many a master has attempted to discover what lies within the afterlife, but none has been successful. It is believed that they are taken to a place known as the Crystal Heavens and walk freely amongst the gods, but this has not yet been verified. Any attempts to contact those who have been taken to the afterlife have failed, so it is the current accepted theory that death within the afterlife is also peaceful and eternal.*

Nika scratched his goatee, and felt a shiver travel down his spine. He'd been so close to accepting Am's offer to enter the afterlife when he died; had he been selfish and chosen that route, there would be no way to stop Du'Rakis and his reign of terror. He would have doomed the world.

Joplin let out a low whistle and held up his hand to stop. Nika slammed the book closed and slid it back into his pack.

"We've got company," Joplin announced, pointing to a cloud of dust rising on the horizon.

Nika projected himself and flew towards the dust

cloud. Around thirty soldiers wearing green uniforms were galloping towards them, looking serious. Nika swallowed and returned to his body.

"Maikaden soldiers," Joplin grunted once Nika relayed what he saw. "They usually don't head out this far. Maybe it has something to do with the attack on Lisaden."

"We don't have time to run," Gaitan said, nodding towards the incoming soldiers.

"Get off the road and let them pass," Yger called. She pulled off the scarf she borrowed from Priye and rewrapped it, being careful to hide her face.

As the soldiers grew closer, Nika watched in dismay as they slowed, then stopped. A lieutenant broke away and nudged his horse to move closer to Joplin. Yger hid behind Hari and Angar, her hand on the hilt of a sword.

"Good day, traveller. Where are you coming from?" the lieutenant asked politely.

"We're returning home to Maikaden City after visiting family for Kharung," Joplin replied. "Lisaden was closed, so we are going to To'Mar to replenish our supplies. Has something happened?"

The lieutenant passed Joplin a scroll. He unrolled and read it out loud.

"On this day, the thirty-third of Jalie, I hereby order all borders of Maikaden closed and sealed. No one may pass in or out of the kingdom for any reason, and to do so shall incur the death penalty. Further orders will be sent shortly." Joplin rolled up the scroll and handed it back to the soldier.

"Word is that Maikaden City has been attacked," he said seriously. "We're on our way to seal the borders. For the moment, there are no restrictions of travelling throughout the kingdom, but keep your ears open. Be careful where you go, nowhere is safe at the moment."

"Thank you, sir. We'll be careful, yes." Joplin nodded.

"Very well. Good day." The lieutenant nodded, then

wheeled his horse and galloped away with his soldiers in formation.

"Phew. I thought they were going to put up a fight," Iphan said.

"Me too," Yger said. "Come on. We need to get to moving. We will not be safe until we reach our camp, and we are still two days away."

*"Well, that's interesting,"* Arnie noted.

*"What is?"*

*"The date. Do you not recognise the significance of today?"*

*"No."* Nika frowned.

*"You really should keep track of the days,"* Arnie scolded him. *"Our journey together began a year ago today."*

---

The Kingdom of Drarlum stretched out far below. From the sky, the terrain looked like a patchwork quilt made from different hues of greens and tan; the farming lands and pastures were a welcoming change from the never-ending plains that covered Cadrinhal.

Freyne held onto his stomach as Ruke tilted forward and began descending in a spiralling motion. At once, his nausea returned, and as the wyvern turned on his side, Freyne threw up for what felt like the hundredth time since leaving the Fens.

The journey was almost constant since leaving his Nika behind. Ruke landed once per day, and only long enough for Freyne to hunt, eat, and relieve himself. On the few occasions when he drank too much water, he had no choice but to hold it in or soil himself. There was no other way.

Sleeping was no better; Ruke continued his flight into the night, and Freyne was forced to try and sleep as best he could. Often, the only time he could sleep was when his body finally shut down from exhaustion. Overall, the three weeks of flying were miserable, and he hated every moment he was away from Nika.

They grew closer to the ground, and Ruke folded his wings, landing on his two legs. A number of screams rang out from around them. Ruke let out a terrifying roar; Freyne peeked from behind his wing and could see a number of people fleeing from a small homestead. Ruke roared again, then walked towards a large open barn.

*"Go... king. I... wait."*

Freyne unbuckled his pack and freed himself from the harness. He slid roughly down Ruke's back and stumbled as he landed. His legs were stiff and sore, and his entire body ached. Ruke clambered into the barn, and Freyne pushed the heavy doors closed behind him. He stood back and glanced around, eyeing the compound.

The silence following the farmers' screams was almost eerie. Freyne shivered and made his way towards the main residence; the door was wide open, and the smell of something delicious wafted out to greet him. He followed his nose and found a loaf of freshly baked bread sitting on the table with a pot of butter and some cheese. Freyne's belly grumbled rudely, and against his better judgement, he helped himself. Once he'd eaten more than his fill, he searched the house until he found the master bedroom. Freyne rummaged through the wardrobe and found some formal attire that would fit, then went in search of a place to bathe.

The bath house was hidden away in a building next to the barn, and Freyne cautiously snooped around until he found a large copper. The fire had gone out long ago, but the water was just warm enough to bathe in. He turned the tap, and watched impatiently as the water drained into the tub.

*It's roughly two hours to noon,* Freyne thought as he stripped off his putrid clothes. *Once I finish here, I'll find a horse and head into the city. I just hope King Dird agrees to see me.*

Freyne arrived at the King's court early in the afternoon, feeling better than he had for a long time. For the first time since Kharung, he was clean and refreshed, and free of the itchy beard that sprouted along the way. He was lucky enough to find some cologne, too, which he knew was a rarity. Whoever the farmers were, they were clearly a wealthy family.

The court was busy, and full of nobility trying to make themselves look more important than they were. Freyne wove his way through the groups of people, earning plenty of glares. The king sat with his leg over the arm of his throne, twirling his crown in his hands and looking bored. As Freyne drew closer, a guard stepped in front of him, blocking his path.

"Halt! State your business," he demanded.

"I am Christophe Saul Du Freyne, royal envoy from King To'Rel of Al'Obrel. I seek urgent council with His Majesty, King Dird." Freyne held up the letter from To'Rel so the guard could see.

The king leant over his throne and eyed Freyne up and down.

"Let him approach, Ealric," he ordered.

The guard stepped aside, and Freyne bowed as elegantly as he could.

"Since when does a royal envoy travel alone?" Dird asked.

"The news I bring is of utmost importance. Please, Your Majesty. I need to speak to you in private. The safety of your people is at stake."

King Dird eyed him for a moment, then nodded.

"Very well." The king stood and gestured to Ealric and three other guards.

Freyne was escorted through a door behind the throne, and along a narrow passage to a small office. King Dird entered from a different door and sat heavily on a fancy divan.

"Please, sit. I'm sorry, what was your *title*, exactly?" King Dird didn't look so friendly outside of his court.

"My name is Christophe Saul Du Freyne. I am a high priest from the Great Monastery of Am, and I am King To'Rel's personal envoy, Your Majesty." Freyne nodded, and sat as he was told.

"I had the fortune to visit that monastery a few years ago," Dird said, his eyes boring into Freyne's without blinking. "I don't recall seeing you there. Are you newly appointed, or are you lying to me?

"I would never lie to you, Your Majesty. I was not there at the time of your visit, as I was preparing for my role in fulfilling the great prophecy."

"I was told that the high priest known as Christophe went missing over seven-hundred years ago. So you are either a ghost, or an imposter." The king leaned forward. "You have thirty seconds to explain yourself, and why I shouldn't arrest you. Go."

Freyne sighed, and stood up. The guards behind him tensed.

"Perhaps you'd like my *full* title, then. I stand here before you as Am's one and only disciple. And you know Am's penalty for falsely claiming such a thing. *'None shall ever claim to be mine apostolate without mine express permission. It is no man's right to fraudulently claim their words speak through me. Any who so endangers the truth of my words will be rendered unto death and forbidden to rest within the afterlife.'* The words I speak are nothing but the truth, Your Majesty."

As Freyne spoke, he could feel Am's presence swirling softly inside him, encouraging him to continue. The warmth spread through his body from his toes all the way to his cheeks.

"This world is on the brink of the biggest war since the holy wars, and right now you can either listen to me, or help condemn your kingdom to doom. You, a king who is allied with King To'Rel, would know of Ami'Khel - the Miscreant - who brought about the original holy wars. And although the Isles are located far from here, you would be well aware of the importance of that story..."

"I —" the king protested, but Freyne held up his hand. It was glowing.

"Shut up and listen, Dird. Ami'Khel lives, and even now is causing bedlam in the cities to the north of here. The one who goes by the name of Lord Du'Rakis *is* Ami'Khel. He is cleansing his chapters of his Black Ibis cult, and in doing so is killing hundreds, if not thousands, of people. He flattened his entire army at the Battle of Rarn as witnessed by the King's Army. He's out of control."

Freyne paused, then glared at the guards behind him. He slipped his mind into the lowest realm and swept the swords easily from their hands, sending them sliding across the stone floor. King Dird sat staring at him, his mouth agape.

"W-what do you want from me?" he asked finally.

"I will need your help to send your fastest carrier bird to King To'Rel and Kaiton with these letters." Freyne opened the one addressed to Kaiton and handed it to the king to read.

Dird's eyes widened as he read the letter and the gravity of the situation sunk in. He finally looked up, a hint of fear in his eyes.

"I-I'm so sorry, Your Eminence," he stammered. "Please, forgive me. You have to understand, I get people in here all the time trying to scam me. I had to be sure."

"I completely understand, Your Majesty." Freyne sat back down, and leant forward with his elbows on his knees.

"These letters were written three weeks ago from Loralyon," King Dird said slowly. "How did you get here so quickly?"

"Trust me, Your Majesty. You wouldn't believe me if

I told you."

"Very well. I will assemble my war cabinet and advisors for emergency planning immediately." King Dird stood, and looked at his guards. "You will extend our friend here the same courtesy we reserve for our most highest-ranking nobles. Please notify the staff."

"Yes, My King." Ealric bowed, and hurried from the room.

"Thank you, Your Majesty. If I may, is the temple of Am still in operation here?"

"Our temple was closed a few years ago. The priests now reside here and work from within the castle's chapel," Dird replied.

"Very well. Once we are done at the aviary, I will need to meet with the priests. The war we are about to face extends beyond the mortal physical plane, so we must start preparing now before it's too late."

# 14

To'Mar was a small open city with no walls or defences, nestled at the base of the Eloran Ranges. The air was thick with the refreshing scent of pine needles, mixed with the smell of freshly baked bread. A short walk from the last row of dwellings was an immense lake, dotted with a few small fishing boats. The sun glinted off the swells as it slowly met with the horizon.

"This reminds me of...where I'm from," Nika said dreamily to Gaitan and Priye. "Sometimes I'd go camping to a place like this for a week with some people I worked with. Fishing, more booze than we could drink, and singing around the fire of a night. Those were the days."

"Do you miss it?" Priye asked.

"I miss a few things, like faster travel options and coffee. But apart from that, not really." He shrugged. "It doesn't really matter, though. I can't go back."

"This way," Yger called. "Hurry up. It will soon be dark."

She spurred her horse forward and led them away from the city and into the mountains. They travelled along a winding path for a while, then turned off abruptly and rode through a patch of pine and fir trees. They emerged in a rocky ravine between two mountains, seemingly untouched by humans. Yger led the way towards a pile of large boulders, and held up her hand to stop.

"Why are we stopping here?" Joplin asked.

Yger swept her arm in a curve, pointing along the ridgeline. Nika followed her finger, and saw that they were surrounded by around thirty rough-looking people with bows trained on them. He sucked in a deep breath.

"Password?" someone demanded.

"Vengeance." Yger called.

"Welcome home. Come on through."

The archers disappeared as quickly as they showed, and Yger dismounted. She led them behind a large rock and through a narrow pass, then paused as another large boulder was rolled to one side, revealing an opening to a cave.

"Hey, it's Yger!" a little girl called excitedly from inside. "Yger's back, everyone!"

The child ran deeper into the cave, her happy shouts ringing through the passage.

They walked through the opening in single file, leading the horses one by one. A group of people rolled the heavy stone back into its place, and someone unshuttered a lantern, granting them enough light to see. The passage sloped downwards, and somewhere ahead, Nika could make out the sound of flowing water. The air smelt musty, damp earth mingled with rust and a hint of smoke from a fire.

The passage turned sharply to the left, and opened into a wide-open cavern that stretched further than Nika could see. Spread out before them were rows and rows of huts and small stone dwellings. Men, women, and children milled around, chatting to each other and going about their business. Over the dull chatter, the sound of hammer on steel echoed off the walls of the cavern.

To their right, a flight of wooden steps led to a mezzanine that disappeared into the darkness. The only light came from patches of yellow toadstools that seemed to grow everywhere.

"You—" Yger pointed at a young lady walking by. "Take these horses to the new arrival area, then notify the kitchens of our return. We will feast tonight."

"Yes, ma'am." The lady nodded and obediently took each of the reigns from their hands.

"This way," Yger said briskly.

Nika shifted Arnie slightly under his cloak and followed everyone up the stairs. From the mezzanine, he could see just how far the subterranean village stretched. It was much larger than he ever could have imagined.

Yger stopped and pushed open a heavy steel door. Inside, a number of people lounged around on comfortable looking couches which all faced the centre of the room. A few of them stood, startled at the intrusion.

"I have returned," Yger announced.

One of the men rushed forward and pulled her into a rough hug. Yger froze, and the man quickly unhanded her.

"I'm sorry," he said quickly. "I didn't think you were going to make it back."

"Do that again and I'll kill you myself," Yger said in a deadly voice.

The man stepped back, and as he turned, Nika recognised him immediately.

"Play nicely, you two," somebody snapped. "Erias has been worried sick about you. Now, are you going to introduce us?"

"Kajiran, Saeda, Osoric, Naldyn, Garoad, and some of you know Erias already." Yger introduced each of the leaders in turn, then gestured for everyone to sit down. Nika sat next to Priye with Arnie on his lap.

"Welcome, everyone." Kajiran was a short man, no taller than Nika's shoulder. He stood on a wooden crate, unashamed of his height difference. "As Yger said, my name is Kajiran. I was a captain in the Brotherhood before we defected. We are the founders of Endveraugh, which translates to *survivor's cave*. We are no longer affiliated with Du'Rakis in any way, nor do we observe any of the rituals and practises. We're renegades, and our only cause now is our very survival. Now tell me, which chapter are you all from?"

"We're from Sepheren." Hari pointed to himself and Iphan. "Did the others make it?"

"Some did," Kajiran nodded. "You will be reunited with them shortly. We like to debrief all of our new arrivals first. Now, how about you?" Kajiran looked intently at Nika.

"Er. Actually, we're not a part of this," he said.

"What? Yger, why did you bring them here?" Saeda hissed.

"They saved our lives. Twice." Yger said in a deadly tone. "First, they saved us from Du'Rakis' minions near Loralyon. And then they freed us when we were captured at Lisaden. We did not ask them for help, yet they put their own lives on the line to do so. Plus, they helped us cross the border and kindly escorted us here. We owe them our gratitude."

"That's good and all, but you know we can't risk being discovered," Osoric snapped.

"Do you all want to live in fear for the rest of your lives and hide in a stinking cave until you're old and grey, or do you want to be able to return to your homeland and live a free life?" Yger demanded.

"What's that got to do with anything?" Kajiran asked.

"He's going to help us." She pointed at Nika.

Nika shivered; he could feel the tension sizzling in the air around them, and wasn't overly keen on being involved in their internal politics. He sat Arnie on the couch next to him, then cleared his throat and stood up.

"It is my mission to find Du'Rakis and put an end to his madness," he said, sweeping the faces of his audience. "I don't know what lies you've been fed, but the truth is we're heading towards a great war. The Battle of Rarn was nothing compared to what is coming."

"How could you possibly know that?" Saeda demanded, crossing her arms.

"Tell me. What exactly were your orders for that battle?" Nika countered.

"We were to push through the King's Army and capture a group of criminals who stole from Lord Du'Rakis," Yger offered. "We were to dress in the uniform of the militia and capture the criminals, or die. We were not given a choice. Du'Rakis' generals killed all those who refused the orders."

"Did he tell you what those stolen items were?"

"No one questions Du'Rakis," Kajiran said. "He is powerful beyond words. He murdered an entire army. How can a mere commoner like yourself expect to beat him?"

Nika steeled himself, and looked Kajiran in the eye.

"We are the people the army was sent to capture. My name is Lord Sarik, and I am a direct blood descendant of Du'Rakis. I have been sent by the Kingdoms of the East to kill him."

The room grew silent, and everyone stared at Nika open-mouthed. He paused for dramatic effect, then continued.

"Whatever you've learnt about the gods, and the reasons you hate them, is all based on lies. I am living proof of that. But I'm not here to preach or demand that you all start following Am. The only reason we came here was to protect your friends and prevent them from being wiped out with the rest of your cult. We are not here to ask anything of you nor to impose. If you bring us our horses, we will happily go on our way and leave you in peace."

Nika sat back on the couch and crossed his arms. Kajiran and his people huddled together and spoke in hushed tones amongst themselves.

"Nice speech," Priye whispered. "Who's Lord Sarik?"

"It's an alias. Saramas picked it." Nika whispered back. "I hope I won't regret telling them the truth of who I am."

Kajiran cleared his throat, and the other leaders took their seats.

"Du'Rakis has killed thousands of our people. Not

just the Brotherhood, but our families, friends, lovers, and innocent people who were in the wrong place at the wrong time. After being controlled for most of our lives, we will never again bow down to any god or dictator. However, if you truly think you can kill Du'Rakis and set us free, we are happy to form an alliance with you." Kajiran held out his hand.

Nika stepped forward and shook it firmly.

"Ok. I accept."

A bell rung out somewhere in the town below them, echoing off the walls in brassy tones.

"That means the meal will be served within an hour. Let us retire to the dining area," Saeda suggested. "Tonight is a celebration of those who have been found and returned to us. Let's give our people the hope they desperately need. Not all of us want to hide in this cave until the day we die. We can discuss the upcoming war tomorrow."

Nika and his friends walked slowly through the centre of town with the founders of Endveraugh, passing all sorts of tradespeople and shops as they went. Kajiran pointed out the various fletchers, smiths, armourers, and tailors, who were packing away their stores and closing for the night.

To their left, a large wooden wheel laden with buckets turned slowly, driven by the flowing water that Nika heard when they first entered the cave. Next to it, a series of cogs powered a heavy chain that disappeared into the darkness above.

"What exactly is this place?" Joplin asked.

"It used to be a copper mine," Kajiran explained. "Many years ago, a section of tunnels further down collapsed and killed around fifty workers. The miners believed it was haunted so they abandoned it. When we came here, we were able to repair some of the equipment left behind. That wheel over there, for example, powers the bellows that circulates the air that we're breathing. There was a lot of tools and resources left behind that allowed us build what we now have."

"How did you find it?" Gaitan asked.

"Back when Du'Rakis started building his army for Rarn, his generals and lieutenants marched us all the way to the far side of Lake To'Mar," Yger explained. "We camped there for weeks and months, until Du'Rakis finally came. He opened some sort of portal, and demanded everyone march through it. We had no idea where it led or what would happen if we stepped through it; it could kill us for all we knew. Some of us were too terrified to go anywhere near it.

"Only two people could pass through at once, so it was taking a long time to move two thousand or so troops. That night, a group of us decided we'd had enough, and we snuck away and hid in the mountains. They came looking for us, of course. We ran around for days, and eventually found the opening to the mine. We managed to seal the entrance, and after a while they gave up looking for us. They never did find us. Ever since, we've been rescuing anyone we can and bringing them here."

"How many generals does Du'Rakis have?" Nika asked.

"Before the purge, there was Rissa, Ashavan, Belarüs, Ornas, and Enbarak," Kajiran said darkly. "We don't know if they too were killed or not."

"Ashavan. That's the one who killed your people at Lisaden with the help of mercenaries, so obviously he's still alive," Nika said thoughtfully. "I'm guessing Du'Rakis is forcing his generals to do his dirty work for him. Either way, it looks like we're going to need to kill them, too."

Kajiran stopped abruptly and turned to face Nika, his face serious.

"Only the most loyal and trusted few became Du'Rakis' generals, and even then, only if they had some sort of skill or power that was useful to him. They kill without question, follow his orders blindly, and show absolutely no remorse. Du'Rakis hasn't forced them to do anything they don't already enjoy. There is no shred of decency in these people whatsoever. They shed their humanity many moons ago."

Nika swallowed hard and nodded. Over Kajiran's shoulder, a man carrying a bucket and spade stopped walking, and was watching them with a frown, listening to what was being said. His eyes locked with Nika's for a split second, then he turned and hurried away. Nika shrugged it off, and Kajiran resumed his tour.

"This is the new arrival's area. Those are your horses and your lodgings over there," he pointed towards a cluster of small huts, then swept his hand across to a clearing filled with rows and rows of long trestle tables facing a fire pit. "The dining area is just over there. We eat together as a community. Feel free to go and freshen up first if you wish, then come and join us as our guests of honour. The feast will be served shortly."

The new arrival huts were tiny, a temporary living arrangement to house the new arrivals until they could build their own home. The small sitting area was empty except for four arm chairs. There were just three other rooms; two single quarters, and one double. There were no beds, just low stone slabs roughly the same size. Nika was so used to sleeping on the ground on nothing but his bedroll, another night didn't bother him.

"Who gets the double?" Gaitan asked.

"I've already had my turn sharing," Priye said, shaking her head.

"Me too," Joplin said quickly.

"That answers that then." Nika shrugged and picked up his things. "My rules are the same as Priye's. If so much as one hair touches me, you're sleeping outside. I'm going to get changed."

"I'll get changed out here then." Gaitan sighed.

Nika quickly made his bed, then sorted through his clothes. Most were smelly except for the finery he wore for Kharung. He poured some water into a small bowl and washed his stinky areas as best he could, then pulled on a pair of thick black hose. *These things remind me of stockings,* he thought ruefully. *Why can't they just wear trousers over here like back on the Isles? They're much warmer and look better.*

He eyed the light blue undershirt that he wore to Kharung, then shoved it back into his pack. He slipped on his long black waistcoat instead, leaving his arms and shoulders bare. As he buttoned it up, he paused, and gazed at the leather wristband Freyne gave him. He traced the pattern with his finger, reliving the treasured memory for a moment and forgetting where he was.

"Are you done?" Priye called through the door.

"Almost." Nika jumped, startled. He turned his belt so the focus wasn't too noticeable, then looked at Arnie-Kyn. "Are you coming, flea bag?"

*"One does not have fleas,"* Arnie said indignantly. *"While you are feeding your face, one will scout around. Don't forget, these people are against our gods. Be wary in trusting them."*

*"Am I doing the right thing here?"*

*"What do you mean?"* Arnie asked.

*"This cult killed Freyne's family, and now we have an alliance with them. Am I allowing myself to get side-tracked, or will this somehow help us in our quest?"*

*"Knowledge is power,"* Arnie-Kyn said, his tail flicking. *"These people once lived and breathed Khel's teachings and propaganda. They have been under his thumb for years, so they know better than anyone how the cult functions. They have also been betrayed by their leader, so they are vulnerable and would probably like to avenge their loved ones. We can gain valuable information from them, so long as you ask the right questions."*

*"I have absolutely no idea what I'm doing,"* Nika admitted.

*"Just keep faking it like you have been. You'll be fine."*

The dining area was almost full by the time Nika, Gaitan, Joplin, and Priye made their way to the head table.

People chattered quietly amongst themselves as the cooks delivered platters of food to the tables. There was a sense of sadness in the air, and as he passed, Nika caught snippets of conversation. Some spoke of missing their loved ones, while others complained of being stuck in the perpetual darkness. A young child cried in her mother's arms, begging to know when Daddy would be back. Nika's heart broke.

"Thank you for joining us. Please sit." Saeda gestured to four empty seats.

Gaitan brushed past Nika and helped himself to the chair next to Yger. She'd changed into tight leather trousers and corset-style leather chest armour. Her boots reached her knees, accented by long pointed heels. The purple shade of her hair and matching eye shadow reminded Nika of Freyne's aura, and another wave of sadness washed over him.

Kajiran stood on his chair and cleared his throat. The cavern grew quiet as all eyes landed on him.

"My dearest friends. Today we welcome two new survivors to our number." He paused as a round of applause echoed throughout the cavern. "Unfortunately, I also have some sad news. We received word that our chapter in Maikaden City is the latest to have fallen. At this stage we don't have any numbers nor know if there's any survivors. When we know more, we will let you know..."

"What are we going to do about it?" a woman yelled. She stood up and shook her fist angrily. "We can't just hide in here for the rest of our lives. We have to do something!"

"We're safe here, and free. What's your problem?" another woman argued.

"What kind of a life do you call this? We're stuck in a stinking cave in the dark. We can't even go outside or risk being found!"

"Ladies, please. Calm down," Osoric called sharply.

"They have a point." A large man with a bushy beard stood up and crossed his arms. "You can't expect us to just sit here and do nothing for the rest of our days. We are just as imprisoned now as we were when we were under *his* thumb. You need to let us fight back, give us something to live for. At least give us the option to try and avenge those we have lost."

Kajiran held up his hands, and the cavern grew silent once more.

"We hear you. We have all lost so many who are dear to us," he said. "And you are all within your rights to want justice. I do too! But you all know that Du'Rakis is powerful beyond our physical limitations. You know what he did at Rarn, and what he continues to do to us.

"But you're right! We do need to fight back, and fight back we will do! It's time for us to start preparing. My friends; Du'Rakis is pushing the world into a war. While we do not have the means to fight him alone, we now have friends who can help us take him down.

"Fighting will be voluntary. No-one will be forced to give their lives for this. All I ask is that you help those who do, whether it's making armour, cooking meals, or caring for the children. We are all in this together.

"Now. Who wants to fight back and bring down that scumbag Du'Rakis?"

A loud cheer erupted and most of the survivors leapt from their seats, jumping and clapping their hands excitedly. Kajiran waved his hands, and the people settled back down.

"We don't have a strategy just yet. But we will be meeting over the next few days to put together a plan of action. For now, let's enjoy our evening and this wonderful feast."

The babble turned to talk of war and revenge, the former sadness replaced by excitement. Nika loaded up his plate with meat and vegetables from the platter and drowned it in gravy.

"Where do you get the food from?" Priye asked.

"Some of our people brought friends with them who

were not a part of the Brotherhood," Kajiran replied. "It seems that they are able to leave the safety of the cave without drawing attention to us. As such, it is safe for them to travel down to To'Mar and exchange precious gems and metals that we mine in exchange for food and supplies."

Yger reached out to take her tankard.

"What's that?" Gaitan asked, pointing at a piece of cloth wrapped around her wrist.

A section of the cloth was unravelled, revealing the corner of what looked like a tattoo. Yger quickly retied it and shot him a baleful glare.

"It's nothing. Keep your eyes to yourself, little man."

Once they finished eating, some of the founders drifted off to the trestles and sat talking with their friends. Naldyn sat next to Nika, his face serious.

"Are you sure you possess the strength to face him?" he asked.

"I do. I know you and your people don't care for the gods, but right now they are on my – our – side. This will be a fight to the death, so I assure you I will do all that I can to end this."

"Thank you. Is there anything I can do to help?"

"If possible, I would like to see the place where the army was camped and sent through that portal," Nika said. "Is there anyone who can take me there?"

"I will," Yger interrupted.

"You're one of our best fighters. I don't want to risk you," Naldyn frowned.

"I am not afraid of Du'Rakis. Besides, we are safe if we stay with Nika."

"I can't promise anything," Nika said uneasily.

"You said your mission is to kill Du'Rakis," she said, standing up. "If he can track us like you say, then let him come. You can kill him and his generals, and then we can get on with our lives."

## 15

Nika woke to the sound of the bell ringing through the depths of the cave. With no way to see the sun from inside, the bell was the only way the people of Endveraugh could tell when it was morning, noon, and evening. Much to Nika's relief, the flowing water was adapted to provide plumbed latrines, and there was constantly fresh water available to wash his clothes and bathe.

Once he'd hung his clothes out to dry, he made his way to the dining area, dressed in the same clothes he wore the night before. Priye, Joplin, and Gaitan were already eating their breakfast. Nika sat with them and Priye pushed a bowl of runny oats towards him.

"We saved you some," she said.

"Thanks. Where's Yger and Kajiran and all them?" he asked.

"I think they have their breakfast in their homes," Gaitan offered.

"Oh. I guess we should go and see them after we eat."

The oats were cold and bland, in need of sugar. Nika ate them without complaint, knowing it was probably all they had to offer. The few people still sitting at the trestles spoke excitedly to one another, and every so often looked over in his direction and pointed. As he glanced around, his eyes locked with a man who had wavy brown hair and a goatee, his green eyes tinged in sadness. The man sat alone, and he quickly looked away. Nika realised it was the same man who was listening to their conversation the day before.

"Kajiran will see you at noon." Yger stood behind them, her crossbow strapped across her back.

"Good morning," Gaitan said, a hint of sarcasm in his tone.

Yger glared at him and adjusted the strap slightly around her chest. Nika looked back at the man, but he was gone.

"What should we do before then?" Joplin asked.

"Now would be a good time to visit our smiths and upgrade your gear," she said. "Kajiran has granted you whatever you need."

"That's very generous of him," Joplin nodded. "I have a few holes in my armour that needs to be fixed, yes."

Yger turned and levelled her gaze at Priye.

"You said you're a healer, did you not?"

"I am." Priye nodded. "Is someone sick or injured?"

"Yes. We would appreciate your help if you don't mind."

"Let me go and get my bag." Priye stood and headed back to the hut with Yger in tow.

Nika pushed away his empty bowl and stood up.

"Come on. Let's go and get this over and done with."

The subterranean town was buzzing as Nika and his friends walked slowly through the streets, looking for shops of interest. People stopped and stared, whispering and pointing as they passed; he tried not to take notice, but couldn't help blushing from the unwanted attention.

Joplin hustled Nika and Gaitan into a small stone building lit by oil lamps. As his eyes adjusted to the brighter light, Nika could see that the walls were covered with all kinds of swords and weapons. Towards the rear of the shop, a smith hammered on a glowing red lump of metal.

"One moment." The smith plunged the rod into a bucket of water with a loud hiss, then hurried over. "Sorry about that. Welcome, my friends."

While Joplin and Gaitan discussed swords with the smith, Nika drifted around the room, eyeing the evil-looking weapons. He ran his finger across the spikes on a mace, and shuddered at the thought of being on the receiving end of it; they were created for pain and maiming instead of a quick clean death.

"What sort of weapon do you prefer, sir?"

Nika turned to see the smith watching him intently.

"I don't need one," he said quickly. "I already have one."

"Oh yeah? Let me see."

Nika looked at Gaitan, then reluctantly drew the focus. The smith's eyes widened as he ogled the thin rod and the glowing void.

"Wow. I've heard of those, but this is the first time I've ever seen one," he breathed. "Where did you get it?"

"It was a gift from my Master." Nika sheathed it.

"And...you can use it?" the smith asked.

"I wouldn't have it otherwise." Nika shrugged.

"Is it true then?"

"Is what true?" Nika groaned inwardly.

"The talk of the town is that you're here to kill Du'Rakis," he said, his excitement building. "Word is that you're a powerful mancer who is going to get revenge for us."

"I wouldn't go quite that far." Nika grimaced. "Like I keep saying. I will do my best, but I can't promise anything. Only time will tell."

"You will do us proud, I know it." The smith paused, then reached out and plucked one of the weapons off the wall. "It always pays to have a backup, just in case. This is what we call a morning star. It's similar to a club, but better-balanced and will do more damage."

The morning star was longer than the focus, a thin shaft with a comfortable handle and a spiked ball on the end. Nika gave it a test swing and nodded his approval.

"Alright. I'll give it a go," he said. "How much gold do we owe you?"

"We don't use money here." The smith shook his head. "Our supplies, resources, everything belongs to all of us. The miners gather the metal, and we forge them better and stronger tools. The gems are used to buy food and cloth so our tailors can make us clothes. There is no greed or hoarding here."

"If only the rest of society was like that," Gaitan said.

"The world would be a much better place," the smith agreed. "Is there anything else you need?"

"Where can we find an armourer?" Joplin asked.

"There are a few," he replied. "Just keep walking straight along this road and you will find them."

"Thank you," Joplin said.

They left the weapon smith and wondered further down the road.

"What did you two get?" Nika asked.

Joplin paused and drew his shiny new sword. It was only slightly longer than his old one, and featured an ornate hilt.

"This one is more balanced than my other one," he said proudly. "Gaitan finally has a decent sword to match his armour, yes."

"I have to admit, you're right," Gaitan nodded. "Hopefully there's a place we can practice later."

"I think you should have asked for a sword, too," Joplin said to Nika. "That wand you carry will be useless in a fight, yes."

"I'll be fine." Nika grinned wickedly. "There's plenty of ghosts around to protect me."

Joplin sighed and shook his head, muttering under his breath.

Someone tapped Nika on his shoulder, and he spun around, startled. The man with brown hair dropped his eyes to the ground and was trembling slightly.

"E-excuse me, sir. I'm sorry to trouble you. Please, I-I need to speak with you."

Nika could sense his nervousness mixed with a deep sadness.

"Ok. What can we do for you?" he asked.

The man beckoned, and led them into another squat stone building. This one was lined with different types of armour on stands around the front half of the room. Similar to the weapons hut, a forge and workbench occupied the rear.

"My name is Sashin Tonavay," he said, still looking at the floor. "I-I couldn't help overhearing that you're planning to kill Du'Rakis."

Nika nodded, silently dreading the thought of having that same conversation again. To his surprise, Sashin instead pulled something from his pocket and handed it to Nika with shaking hands.

"I know I have no right to ask anything of you. But please, please wear this symbol. If General Ashavan is still alive, it may protect you from him."

Nika held up the symbol in the light. It was as big as his hand, a round disc with a bronze sun, the centre gold with an embossed Ŧ. The fine details were exquisite, the work of a master craftsman.

"Did you know him?" Nika asked.

"I don't want to talk about it," Sashin replied. "While you're here, do you need some armour?"

"My armour is adequate, but it does need repair," Joplin said. He pointed to a few gaps missing their scales.

Sashin turned serious, and inspected Joplin's armour.

"It's well made. These shoulders are terrible, though. They leave your neck vulnerable." He slid his finger through the shoulder scales and poked him in the neck. "I think I have some pauldrons that I can modify for you."

Once he was done with Joplin, Sashin turned to Gaitan.

"Your shoulders, neck, and head are also vulnerable. Instead of that coif, try this helm." He handed Gaitan a full helm with a mail skirt that flared out just enough to protect his shoulders without limiting his movement. "This weave goes in a different direction compared to your gracelock, so even if a sword does manage to slip through the chain, the second layer will stop it."

Once Sashin was done fitting Gaitan with tassets and greaves, he helped Joplin remove his armour and carried it back to his workbench. He removed the thick pair of leather gloves he was wearing and wiped his brow. As he did, Nika noticed a mark on his left wrist.

"What's that?" he asked, pointing.

Sashin froze, then slowly held out his hand. There on his wrist was a tattoo of an ibis with its wings spread.

"It's a reminder of my life's mistakes," he said sadly. "Anyone who joined that cult was branded. I was only a member for a year before I left. To this day I regret ever stepping foot in that place."

"I'm sorry," Nika said. "I'll do what I can to help."

"Some of these people were once the most loving and caring people I've known. Unfortunately, they were so brainwashed they didn't realise they were doing evil. The only way to free us is by destroying that scum Du'Rakis. May the gods help you take him down once and for all."

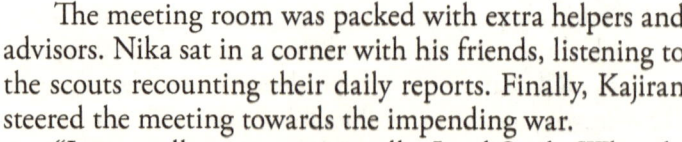

The meeting room was packed with extra helpers and advisors. Nika sat in a corner with his friends, listening to the scouts recounting their daily reports. Finally, Kajiran steered the meeting towards the impending war.

"I now call upon our new ally, Lord Sarik. What do

you have in mind for this upcoming war?" he asked.

"Please, call me Nika." He stood and cleared his throat. "In all honesty, I don't know. There are still some things we need to figure out. Like, what Du'Rakis is planning once he's finished killing your people, which kingdoms we can ally ourselves with, and so on. We have someone visiting King Dird of Drarlum right now, and while he's there he'll send word back to the Eastern Isles. I think the important thing to focus on right now will be preparing your people. Armour, weapons, and training for those who want to fight."

"I agree," Osoric nodded. "We're not ready for war yet. We can't even leave this cave without the risk of being found. Until we can solve that issue, we're useless. At least preparing for war will give our people hope and something to focus on until we know more."

"You said he can track us," Yger said abruptly. "How can he do this?"

Nika frowned and chewed his lip for a moment.

"Tell me more about your tattoos," he said, the words of Saramas echoing in his head.

"They're just tattoos." Saeda unwrapped hers, revealing an identical mark to Sashin Tonavay's. "All members were branded when they became initiated. It's a small iron device made from needles that's used to press the ink into the skin. That's it."

Someone at the back of the room cleared his throat and stood up, drawing everyone's attention.

"I overheard someone talking about this when I received mine. The ink is a special dye mixed with a drop of Du'Rakis and the general's blood to bond us all together as brothers."

Nika's own blood turned to ice.

"Does every single tattoo have that same mix?" he asked, his stomach churning.

The man nodded. Nika started pacing, deep in thought.

"The archers you have on watch," Joplin asked, he too standing up. "How is it they can leave the cave? Do they have these tattoos too?"

"Yes, of course they do," a woman to their left called.

Nika stopped pacing and scanned the room.

"What are those things they wear on their arms?" he asked.

"They're just leather guards to protect their arm when they fire the bow," Yger shrugged. "The armourer adds in a thin sheet of bronze to help steady their aim. What of it?"

Nika inhaled deeply, and placed his hand on the rough wall of the cavern.

"How didn't I think of this earlier?" he mumbled.

"What are you talking about?" Osoric asked.

"We're in a mine, surrounded by ores and metals," he said as everything clicked together. "Du'Rakis is tracking your tattoos with blood magick. That's why you're safe in this cave; the metal is blocking the trace."

Everyone started talking amongst themselves, discussing Nika's theory. He sat down, the pressure of his part in the war weighing heavily on his shoulders. Knowing he was responsible for so many lives left him feeling mentally exhausted. The perpetual darkness and warmth of the cave made him drowsy, and he longed to get back outside into the fresh air. Finally, Kajiran stood and raised his hand for silence.

"We'll have to test this theory to make sure it's safe," he said. "We can't gamble on people's lives without knowing for sure."

"How can we test them?" Saeda asked.

"Have Sashin make us some metal cuffs," Yger said. "I will take thirty volunteers to the surface. We will split into two groups of fifteen. When we are far enough away from Endveraugh, one of the groups will remove their cuff. If Du'Rakis comes, but doesn't attack the other group, we will know our theory is correct."

"It's very risky," Saeda frowned. "We don't want to lose any more of our people."

"I guess I'll get to test out my abilities too," Nika said wryly. "I'm going to have to face him sooner or later."

"Very well." Kajiran nodded. "We will call for volunteers tonight. Yger and Erias, I'll let you two organise this. In the meantime, let's take a break. I'll go and talk to our smiths and see what they can do."

Nika's sleep was once again plagued by nightmares. His fear of facing Khel manifested into twisted dreams of watching his loved ones die over and over. After a few hours of tossing and turning, Nika tiptoed from the hut and walked slowly through the cave. It was silent except for the constant splash of the water wheel.

He came across the large pen where the horses were kept, and leant on the rail. A soft whinny followed by a snort came from his right, and Streek moved to shove her face into Nika's.

"Hello, Streek. Have you missed me?" he asked softly.

He stroked her face and neck and scratched the spot she loved behind the ears. Nika could feel the bond between them, formed during their long journey together. He could almost feel the affection she had for her two riders, and once again he felt a deep longing for Freyne. Streek snorted and lowered her head, allowing Nika to reach out and hug her.

"I know. I miss him too," he said gently as the image of Freyne welled in his mind. "He will be back soon, I hope."

The faintest hint of calm radiated from Streek and brushed against his senses. Nika had grown used to sensing the emotions of people, but never had he felt them from animals. He stood with her in silence for a while, then finally yawned.

"I guess I should get back to bed." He sighed. "There's no point in facing my nemesis if I'm tired, is there?"

Streek whinnied softly in agreeance. Nika kissed her gently on the bridge of her nose, then slowly made his way back to bed.

The midday sun was warm on Nika's face, despite the wintery chill in the air. He pulled his hood up over his face, and walked with his new friends in silence. He felt over dressed in his new black leather armour. It fit him much better than the one Joplin gifted him, and left his arms bare at his insistence. His new sleeveless cloak was pinned together with Sashin's disc; paired with the black leather bottoms and new boots, he felt formal enough to visit a king.

He thought of the words of the leather maker and felt the corner of his mouth curl slightly: "If you're going to look your enemy in the face, you need to be dressed for the occasion. First impressions count, even when they're an evil bastard."

Gaitan and Joplin flanked him, their modified armour glinting in the sunlight. Sashin Tonavay added a few ornamental pieces to their gear, then took the liberty of cleaning and polishing it for them. Nika was quietly impressed with his work.

*"Are you ready for this, human?"* Arnie-Kyn asked from behind.

*"I have to face him some time. It may as well be today."* Nika shrugged. Deep down his heart was racing and his palms were sweating. He felt on edge, his senses capturing every noise and smell around him.

"At least it's a nice day for it," Priye said cheerily.

"You should have stayed in the cave. If Du'Rakis does

show, I don't want you harmed," Nika scolded her.

"Don't be ridiculous. I've seen more battles and fights than you could know. I'm more help to you here than if I was hiding in the dark. Besides, I didn't leave my home and come all this way just to miss the main show."

"That's fair." Nika sighed. "I have to admit that having you guys here is all that's keeping me from running and hiding."

"You'll be fine, dear."

Yger led them along the edge of the lake, and finally brought them to an extensive area of flat grassland dotted with fire pits and litter. It was clear that humans had populated the area for an extended length of time.

"This is it," she said, opening her arms to indicate the area. "The portal was roughly over there near that wood pile."

Nika nodded and turned back towards the mountain where he knew Erias and the other group were hiding. He slipped into the realm and swept around for auras; they were far enough away that surely Du'Rakis wouldn't see them. Nika held up his focus and willed the firestone to burst into flame, visible only to him and Erias. Once he was satisfied that he received the signal, Nika turned back towards the camp grounds.

"Now what?" Yger asked.

Nika wordlessly walked around the area where the portal once was. He closed his eyes and relaxed, feeling around him with his senses. It was soft, almost non-existent at first, but once he felt and recognised it, it grew stronger. He pushed his mind towards the void, and immediately saw the sprites spread out across the campgrounds. At once, they ghosted towards him.

*"Were you killed by Du'Rakis and his people?"* Nika asked them.

*"Yes. We didn't want to go to war,"* some replied.

*"We were scared. We tried to run, but they murdered*

*us,"* another said.

*"I am Lord Sarik. If you serve me, I can help avenge your deaths."*

*"How may we serve, Master?"*

*"Protect me at all cost."*

Nika concentrated and withdrew the single essence protecting his focus, and replaced it with one of the cultists. With great care, he formed the rest of the essence around him into glowing impenetrable spirit armour.

*"What do you require, My Lord?"* the essence from Lisaden enquired.

*"What was your name?"* Nika asked.

*"My name was Finomere, My Lord. Friends called me Fin."*

*"Ok, Fin. If my nemesis does show today, I may need your help to protect these people. And should I fall, you must go to Saramas and inform him. Understood?"*

*"Yes, My Lord."*

Nika watched as Fin zoomed along the line of Yger's people and Priye. Satisfied, he withdrew from the void and took a deep breath.

"I'm ready. Remove the cuffs."

---

Freyne sat alone in the abandoned temple of Am, taking in the damage and desecration around him. Vandals, bored youths, and those who never cared for the sanctity of the religion had all worked together to trash the once beautiful place. How anyone could damage something so holy and sacred was beyond him.

Despite the desecration, he could still feel the faintest hint of Am's presence. He lowered his head in prayer, the silent contemplation he'd spent many years practicing. Even with the obnoxious noises from the city around him, he felt himself enter the comforting trance, and soon nothing else mattered.

It had been a week since he'd arrived in Drarlum, and in that week they'd achieved so much. Dird's enchanted albatrosses were on their way to To'Rel and Kaiton and would arrive in just eight more days. Freyne wanted badly to stay and await a message back from his friends to the East, but deep down he knew his time there was up.

Dird's army was growing by the day, and was about to start the long march north to meet with Cadrinhal's forces. Where to after that, Freyne had no idea. No one knew where Du'Rakis would strike next, or what his next move would be.

Something new was bothering him, something he'd never felt in all his long life. A gentle pull to the south, a deep yearning for something mysterious yet familiar at the same time. A part of him was scared to take that step, but he knew he must trust the direction Am was guiding him. Even as Nika had to trust Saramas to find out that hidden part of himself, Freyne too had to have faith. Somewhere to the south lay the answers to questions about his family and his heritage that he knew nothing about.

His thoughts turned to Ruke and the displaced family from the farm. Several reports were delivered to the King's court over the past week regarding a horrifying beast in the barn, but at Freyne's insistence, they were ignored. The family were safe, that was all that mattered.

Freyne finally allowed himself to think of his Nika. The stranger from another world who turned into his dearest friend and the love of his life. He missed Nika with every beat of his heart, and longed to squeeze him in his arms again. While he didn't want to admit it at first, he knew it was for the best that they were separated for a while. Nika couldn't grow and test his powers, become the powerful mancer he was destined to be, with Freyne there to distract him. He'd taught Nika everything he knew; it was Saramas' turn to take over and guide him until he was ready to face Du'Rakis.

*I miss you so much, boo. Don't you worry. I'll be back with you soon enough. When you are ready to face Du'Rakis, I WILL be there by your side. I promise.*

**16**

Freyne rode cautiously into the farm, ensuring no one was around. Once he was certain it was clear, he tied the horse to a post and pushed open the heavy barn doors. The carnage greeting him made his insides feel queasy; a number of cow carcases were strewn about the floor, torn apart by Ruke's razor-sharp teeth.

"Did you have to?" Freyne demanded.

*"Was... hungry. Let's... go."*

Freyne sighed and climbed onto Ruke's back. He dreaded the upcoming flight, but steeled himself and quickly strapped into the harness.

"Ok, I'm ready," he announced.

Ruke clambered from the barn and into the daylight, then unfolded his wings. With a single flap, they rose steadily into the air. Freyne closed his eyes and concentrated on not throwing up his lavish farewell breakfast. After the long horrible journey to get to Drarlum, he at least learnt his lesson and brought a jar with him for the next leg of his flight.

To the south of Cadrinhal, the season was transitioning into autumn. The reds, yellows, and orange leaves of the trees below added a splash of colour to the patchwork landscape. He figured to the north, Nika would probably be experiencing winter, the seasons offset by one of the world's dividing lines. Freyne felt his face crease into a frown, as the thought of Nika nudged a niggling feeling in the back of his mind. He felt as though he'd forgotten something important, and with a start, he began retracing his steps.

"What have I forgotten?" he asked himself out loud. "I sent the letters. Lit a firecracker under the priests' arses. Talked Dird into rallying his army. I've done everything I had to do."

No matter how hard he tried, the niggling sensation would not leave him alone. To distract himself, he pulled his journal from his pack and flicked through his notes. It wasn't until he opened to his hand-drawn calendar that his stomach dropped.

*Oh, boo. You came to this world one year ago today,* he thought, staring sadly at the date. *I wonder if you even know? You've been in my life for four hundred and twenty days now. I just wish you were here so we could celebrate together.*

Ruke adjusted his path, and they started heading south across the sea. Freyne slipped his journal back into his pack and pulled on a warm pair of mittens, then settled back in his harness and stared into the clouds. He could feel the forces of nature tensing themselves for the upcoming war. They were scared, frightened. Whatever Du'Rakis was planning even caused the rocks deep in the earth's crust to tremble in fear. *Am, give us strength. This storm that's brewing will be the worst this world has ever faced, and could even be the end for us. Nika is our only hope.*

---

Yger's people lined up in a semi-circle behind Nika, Joplin, and Gaitan. With a steely hiss, they drew their swords as one, then removed the bronze cuffs. Yger cocked her crossbow and stepped forward next to Gaitan. Nika's heart was almost bursting from his chest, but he bit his lip and pretended to be fine.

"Maybe he's done killing cultists," Gaitan mused after a while.

"He will not rest until we're all dead," Yger spat. "It is my goal to stay alive long enough to piss on his rotting corpse. That coward deserves nothing more."

"It's completely possible that he's not looking for us right at this very moment," Nika pointed out. "He could be sleeping for all we know. Then again, maybe he knows he'd be walking into a trap. Let's wait a bit longer."

Nika and his friends waited and waited. He could tell some of the renegades were getting frustrated and impatient. The thought of reporting a no-show to the founders would surely be a devastating blow.

"I guess we could try again tomorrow," Nika said after a while. He squinted at the sun; they'd been waiting for almost two hours. "We should head back and report to the others."

"Why do I feel both relieved and disappointed at the same time?" Gaitan murmured.

"Don't worry, little man. You can die tomorrow instead." Yger made a gesture with her hand, and her people sheathed their weapon's. "Maybe if you're lucky, I can do it for you."

Yger strode towards her people, her long hair tussling in the breeze.

"She hates me, doesn't she?" he mumbled.

"Probably." Joplin sheathed his sword and patted him on the shoulder. "If you're lucky, maybe she kill you instantly, rather than make you suffer for a week, yes."

"Hey! You're supposed to be on my side," Gaitan complained.

Joplin laughed and walked across to where Priye stood with the renegades.

Nika took a step towards them, then paused. Something didn't feel right; it was almost as if the very atmosphere around him was beginning to tear, fighting against an unknown force. He turned slowly, and stared in disbelief as a small swirling anomaly formed before his very eyes just ten feet away. He stumbled backwards as it shifted and grew, sucking the moisture from the air.

And then he felt it; that same sensation he sensed at Sepheren, but magnified a hundred-fold. He drew his focus once more, and planted his feet firmly on the ground to steady himself. A deadly calm settled over him like a cloud, and he stood facing the growing rift with renewed determination.

Somewhere behind him, he heard a gasp, and once again his friends drew their weapons. The portal stopped growing, and shimmered as the connection between the two ends solidified.

"Get back!" Nika hissed.

A dark shadow formed in the centre of the rift, and two people stepped into the daylight. On the left, an armoured warrior, much larger than Joplin, drew a heavy two-handed sword that glinted in the sun's rays. Nika had never seen such an exquisitely-made set of armour before; the shoulders and bracers were decorated with spines, matching the two horns on his helm. As the warrior moved, the embossed pattern in the metal gave the illusion of dragon skin moving with his body.

Next to the warrior was a man dressed in a thick black cloak, his hood covering his face from view. Nika needed no introduction, and gripped his focus tighter.

"What have we here?" Du'Rakis threw back his head and laughed, a chilling cackle that sent shivers of revulsion down Nika's spine. "Looks like we've walked into a trap, Ashavan."

The unmistakable *twang* of Yger's crossbow broke the silence as she fired her bolt towards him, but Du'Rakis swept it aside with the slightest hint of amusement. He raised his hand ever-so-slightly; Nika could sense him drawing from the realm, readying his attack.

"Did you really think your pitiful group of not even twenty plebs could beat me?" Du'Rakis taunted. "You will all pay for this."

Du'Rakis raised his hand above his head and seemingly plucked a forked bolt of lightning from the cloudless sky, then hurled it towards the renegades. Time jolted to a standstill, and Nika watched in slow motion as a jagged lightning bolt streaked towards his friends. The tick tick ticking of time itself grew louder in the back of his mind. Nika threw himself into the path of the incoming strike. He deflected the lightning clumsily and sent it hissing towards a tree to his left. The tree cracked into two halves with a roar of thunder, and burst into flames.

He could feel himself shaking, but squared himself, ready. Du'Rakis looked Nika up and down, as though noticing him for the first time. Without warning, he summoned another bolt of lightning and aimed it squarely at Nika's chest. The attack was much stronger than the first. Nika blocked just in time and sent the bolt sizzling into the sky, followed by an ear-splitting crack of thunder directly above them. He could feel his hair standing up from the electricity in the air.

"Who are you?" Du'Rakis demanded.

The portal swirled again, and a woman stepped forward to stand at her master's right. It was Nika's turn to be caught off-guard. The woman wore a long black gown that hugged her frame and matched her black hair. Her pale skin was almost white, still as ghoulish as Nika remembered her.

"What did I miss?" she asked with a twisted grin.

"You!" Nika gasped.

"Yes, it's me," she said brightly. "And who might you be? Have we met already?"

Nika could feel some sort of energy radiating from her, but whatever it was did nothing to him. In his mind's eye, he visualised Joplin holding Gaitan back. Nika cleared his throat and focused.

"Maybe if you took the time to talk with your prisoners, and not force them to be your sex slave, you would know my name," he said, disgusted. "If I knew who you were back then, I would have killed you while I had the chance."

Du'Rakis turned his head slightly in her direction. The Mistress Rissa recoiled slightly from her master's glare.

"I have no idea what you're talking about," she scoffed, though Nika could sense her panic.

He reached up and pulled back his hood, allowing her to see exactly who he was.

"I. Am. Lord. Sarik. You should have killed *me* while *you* had the chance."

Rissa gaped at him like a fish out of water, her mouth opening and closing as she realised her deadly mistake.

Du'Rakis spun and clamped his fist around Rissa's throat, and squeezed.

"I will deal with you shortly." He hurled her through the portal, her screams echoing across the clearing. "As for you, *Sarik*. If I knew it was you on the hills above Rarn that day, I would have killed you that instant. Make no mistake, I will destroy you, and all your little friends too. But today is not the day."

With a flick of his cloak, Du'Rakis disappeared through the portal. General Ashavan turned to follow, then paused mid-step. He looked directly at Nika, then at the symbol around his neck. The General looked hesitant for a split second, then hurried through the portal. It flickered and swirled for a moment, before closing in on itself. As quickly as it formed, it was gone.

The cloud in Nika's mind slowly lifted, and he shook his head, blinking. He was sweating and shaking profusely, and his belly squirmed from nausea. Without warning, his legs gave way, and he fell roughly to his knees. A cheer erupted from behind, and the renegades surrounded him excitedly.

"You did it!"

"You were amazing!"

"Did you see that? We sure showed them!"

The world spun, and Nika felt himself sway. His belly heaved, and he threw up his lunch unceremoniously, barely missing Yger's boots.

"Stand back, everyone," Priye ordered brusquely. She knelt down next to him and rested her hand gently on his back. "We need to work on you not throwing up and passing out every time you do this."

"I know."

"I had a feeling this would come in handy," she said, wiggling a small vial in front of his nose.

Priye held the vial to his lips and helped him drink. He was so used to the horrid taste of her concoctions that the taste didn't even make him shudder. Nika raised his arm defiantly, and Joplin helped him to his feet. Gaitan quickly took his other side and supported him.

"Ugh. Thanks, guys." Nika paused to catch his breath and settle his belly. "Give me a minute."

A soft whisper reached him from the realm. He instinctively reached out his mind towards the void.

*"You did it, Master! You bested Du'Rakis!"* the sprites cheered.

*"It's not over yet,"* Nika said truthfully. *"Thank you all. I release you."*

*"May we serve you, Master?"*

*"You already served a master while you were alive. In death, you should enjoy your freedom,"* Nika said wearily.

*"We will follow you, Master. We will not rest until Du'Rakis is dead."*

*"Very well. It's your choice."*

The sprites unravelled from their shield of protection and started orbiting his body. Fin floated closer and hovered in front of Nika expectantly.

*"Fin. I want you to take a message to Master Saramas. Inform him of the events that have unfolded here today, and ask if he has any news for me."*

*"Yes, My Lord. You were great!"* Fin looped around Nika excitedly, then whizzed away towards the Fens.

Nika withdrew his mind and took a shuddering breath. The renegades were still talking excitedly to one another. In the distance, Erias' group was hurrying towards them.

"Let's head back," Nika said finally. "Kajiran and the others will be waiting for news."

***

The celebrations that evening ran well into the night. Nika was swamped by people praising and thanking him, and trying to give him gifts as a token of their appreciation. The constant attention was overwhelming, and yet he was stuck until the formalities were over. Speech after speech, toast after toast; he could feel himself growing light-headed from the strong wine that was being passed around freely.

"You don't look so good," Priye said quietly.

"I'd rather face Du'Rakis again than this." Nika sighed. "I'm just waiting for the chance to escape."

A flute started to play, joined by a collection of instruments. The survivors left their seats and started dancing merrily in the cleared space next to the tables. Yger stood to one side, her arms crossed and frowning. Nika and Priye both watched as Gaitan approached her and said a few words. Without warning, Yger pulled back her fist and punched him sharply in the face and sent him hurling backwards. She spun on her heel and stormed off.

"There's our exit," Priye smirked, pushing back her chair. "Remind me to thank him later."

"Where's Joplin?" Nika asked as they helped Gaitan to his feet and guided him towards the hut.

"I don't know," Priye said. "At least we know he isn't out there trying to woo women who aren't interested in him."

"That's not fair," Gaitan grumbled.

"'No' is a complete sentence," Priye scolded him. "Now back off, or knowing what we know of her, she *will* kill you."

"You'd be happy if that happened, wouldn't you?" he snapped.

"Don't be childish."

Nika pushed open the door and helped Gaitan into one of the chairs. His cheek and eye were both swollen, and a trickle of blood dribbled from his nose.

"How can she hit so hard?" Gaitan complained. "I've never met such a strong woman before."

The bedroom door opened, and Joplin leaned on the frame, his arms crossed. He'd taken off his armour and was dressed in plain linens, a sight Nika rarely saw.

"Ah, you been chasing that woman again, yes?"

"Oh shut up." Gaitan grumped.

"What came over you today? Walking towards the Mistress like that?" Joplin frowned.

"I don't know! Just drop it."

"How did you manage to escape so early?" Nika asked, trying to change the subject.

"Easy. Everyone was so focused on you, I just walked away, yes." Joplin grinned. "I had an early bath and was napping until you came back."

"OW!"

"Stop moving while I'm fixing it then." Priye slapped Gaitan's hand away and continued dabbing at his nose. "You're lucky it isn't broken."

Nika's mind was racing; there was so much he needed to sort through and process, but as much as he loved his friends, he knew the only one he could talk to was Arnie. He checked in his room, but Arnie-Kyn wasn't there. Nika slipped half of his mind into the lowest realm and searched for his aura; the cat was towards the rear of the cavern by one of the flowing streams.

"I'll be back later," Nika said.

He stuffed his hands in his pockets and walked purposefully to where he knew Arnie would be. Someone giggled to his left, followed by a *shush!* Out of the corner of his eye, he spotted two teenage boys with a stolen bottle of wine huddled behind a pile of stone, clearly drunk. He pretended to not hear them and kept walking, eager for his own space.

Arnie was seated on a low ledge, his tail flickering. Nika wordlessly sat next to him and stared at the water. The echoes of the celebrating renegades bounced eerily off the walls around them, almost ghostly in the darkness.

"*You did well today, human,*" Arnie said after a long silence.

"*Did I?*"

"*You're alive, aren't you?*"

Nika glanced at his feet, unable to find the words he needed.

"*Let's unpack this piece by piece,*" Arnie-Kyn suggested. "*Your spirit armour was strong. Your practise is paying off.*"

Nika nodded, still staring at his feet.

"*You blocked both of the attacks well,*" Arnie continued. "*You were a little clumsy, but it's hard to practise when someone isn't hurling lightning against you. How did it feel for you?*"

"*It was like time itself slowed down.*" Nika opened his hands in his lap, trying to describe it. "*I could hear that ticking sound again. When the bolts came at me, it was slow enough that I had time to react. I don't know how I blocked or what realm I used, I just did it. Does that even make sense?*"

"*It makes a lot of sense,*" Arnie said.

"*His powers are strong. Just blocking those two attacks*"

was draining, and that's without any attacks of my own. I think it will take more than strength to kill him; it's going to take a lot of luck, too."

"Even after what you did today, one can sense you are still holding back. What are you afraid of?"

"Nothing."

"You're a terrible liar, human. I think I know your problem."

"Ok then. Tell me if you're that smart."

"You're scared you'll become like him. An evil dictator who uses his powers to control everything around him. You are worried that you will learn to enjoy it. So instead of accepting who and what you are, you are trying to resist it."

Arnie leapt down from the ledge and sat at Nika's feet, staring up at him.

"What if I do, though?" Nika asked. "One person should not possess so much power. Would you really want me to kill off one bad guy, only to become a worse bad guy who can't be killed?"

"There is a difference, though." Arnie's tail whipped about. "You are a good person. You know love and compassion, and you care about people. You do not hold yourself above others, and you respect the gods, even though they're not your own. You are nothing like Khel, the very opposite in fact, so get that rubbish out of your mind quick-smart."

Arnie's words hit Nika like a ton of bricks. He could feel his eyes burning, and bit his lip to take the sting away. To have his fears validated, albeit by a cat, brought his emotions bubbling to the surface.

"What did Du'Rakis mean about the mountains above Rarn?" he asked, changing the subject. He wiped his eyes and hoped Arnie didn't notice. "He said he saw me there. How, though? We only saw Priye and the militia. Was he there, too?"

"Maybe? Either way, he has seen your face now, so I think it's safe to assume that he knows who you are."

Nika bent down and lifted Arnie onto his lap and scratched behind his ears.

*"I wonder if he'll kill Rissa,"* Nika wondered.

*"Du'Rakis' own general had his nemesis in her control, incapacitated and vulnerable. She could have saved him a whole world of trouble, but she underestimated your abilities. One is certain she will be heavily punished for this."*

*"Yeah."*

Nika sat with Arnie for some time, staring at the flowing water and replaying the day over and over in his mind until his head grew sore. He was missing a key piece of information, but in his exhaustion he could not remember.

*"I guess I should head back,"* he said finally.

*"Yes, we should. You need your rest."*

Nika stood and carried Arnie back towards the huts. The cavern was quiet and strangely calm. The two teens were sprawled out on the ground holding hands, passed out from drinking too much wine. Nika paused and rolled them onto their sides, and took the empty bottle with him.

*"One would have thought their parents would be looking for them,"* Arnie mused.

*"For all we know, their parents could be dead. Today, we gave them the hope they needed so much, the knowledge that soon they can leave this cave and live a somewhat normal life. These kids deserved to celebrate too. Underage drinking is a rite of passage for humans. So long as it's done safely, of course. Those two are going to be so hungover when they wake up tomorrow, they will learn their lesson."*

Nika woke to someone shaking his shoulder. The stage, crowd, and band members of his dream vanished with a *poof*, and he begrudgingly opened his eyes a crack. He was sprawled out across the slab, an arm and a leg both on Gaitan's side, and his face was pressed into a wet patch of drool. Priye stood on the far side of the slab, her face lit up with a mischievous smirk.

"What?" he grumbled, not wanting to move.

"It's almost lunch time. I think it's time you got up."

Nika blinked as his brain slowly kicked into gear, and soon became aware that he was almost naked except for his undergarments. At some point he'd kicked off his blankets, and to make matters worse, Arnie was curled up against his back.

"Big tough guy warning *me* not to touch. I woke up as little spoon," Gaitan laughed.

"Ugh. Sorry. You should have woken me." Nika yawned.

"Maybe you should try wooing a man next time, yes." Joplin said to Gaitan.

"I'll stick to women, thanks." He scowled.

Nika dragged himself into sitting position and covered himself with his pillow. His friends all sat on the slab and looked at him expectantly. Half of Gaitan's face was bruised and his eye was black and swollen.

"So... did I miss something?" Nika asked.

"Yes. Breakfast, and if you don't get your backside moving, you'll miss lunch too," Priye said.

"You weren't joking then?"

"She's telling the truth for once." Joplin nodded. "We were all wondering what our plans are now. Are we staying longer, or heading on our way, yes?"

Nika scratched his goatee thoughtfully. It already needed another trim.

"I think it's time we got moving," he said finally. "We've set the wheels in motion here. Kajiran and the others know what they're doing, so we're best to leave them to get on with it."

"Where to next?" Gaitan asked.

"I'm not too sure," Nika admitted. "I'm waiting for

word back from Saramas. Until then, I guess we should continue on our way towards Maikaden City."

"Let's pack our things first, then head on over for lunch," Priye suggested. "We can inform Kajiran of our intentions to leave. I don't know about you, but I'll be happy to get out there in the fresh air again. Even if we head down to To'Mar and buy some supplies, and stay the night there."

"Alright," Nika agreed. "Now if you don't mind, I need to get dressed. I know you've all seen it before, but that doesn't mean it's open to public exhibition."

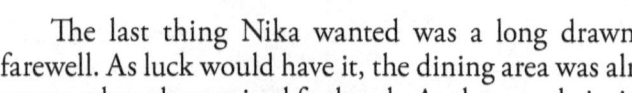

The last thing Nika wanted was a long drawn-out farewell. As luck would have it, the dining area was almost empty when they arrived for lunch. As they ate their simple meal of bread and ham, Nika looked up to see Yger and Erias strolling towards them. Gaitan slid down low in his seat, trying to hide from her.

"It looks like you have a fan club." Yger pointed.

A group was gathered outside their hut, waiting for Nika to make his appearance.

"Ugh." Nika held up his hand to hide his face. "It's a good thing we packed and loaded the horses already."

"You're leaving then?" Erias asked.

Nika nodded.

"When you finish eating, walk over that way and stay behind the houses." Erias pointed. "We'll go and get your horses for you."

"Thanks," Nika said.

"It's the least we can do." Erias smiled. "The way you lot have come into our lives, saved us, saved our people and helped us move forward, I'm starting to think the gods really do exist."

"For what it's worth, I've met them." Nika pushed

back his empty plate. "They're as real as you and I. Are you three ready to go?"

Joplin, Priye and Gaitan nodded.

"Alright, let's go."

Kajiran and the rest of the founders all stood when Nika entered, their smiles brightening the room. Sitting next to Saeda were the two boys Nika saw the night before, both with their heads hung and looking extremely unwell.

"How are you today?" Saeda asked.

"Drained," Nika admitted. "I'll be fine. How's your war preparations going?"

"We have the armourers making cuffs for everyone as we speak," Kajiran replied. "We decided that we'll still require our people to reside here in the cave, but they can leave for short amounts of time with an escort and a pass. We're not entirely free until Du'Rakis is dead."

"That's fair." Nika nodded.

"Our smiths are working hard to make enough armour and weapons for our fighters. We'll be building some extra forges and allowing the apprentices to help. Meanwhile, we have some of our more experienced fighters training the younger recruits. There's no point in surviving, then going to war and dying in the first wave." Osoric added.

The door opened, and Yger and Erias strolled inside.

"Your horses are ready," she said.

Gaitan shied away from her, his face hidden under his helm.

"Are you leaving us?" Saeda asked.

"Yes. We still have to track down Du'Rakis and finish him off. After our little encounter, I don't think he'll bother with tracking down any more of your people for a while. He'll probably watch from afar and try to find this place, so don't drop your guard."

"Thank you, all of you," Kajiran said warmly, holding out his hand. "You have given us hope when there was none. You have led us back to the light. Maybe the gods really are on your side. Stay safe, my friends. We will meet again."

Nika shook all their hands, then made his way towards the door. Yger followed them, and took the reins of a pure black horse.

"Where are *you* going?" Joplin asked.

"I'm going with you," she replied.

"WHAT?" Gaitan sounded as though he were about to faint.

"I will not rest until Du'Rakis is dead. I want to be there when he takes his last shuddering breath, and when he does, I will be the one to sever his head from his neck to make sure. In case you haven't figured it out yet, this fight is personal. So we can either stand around talking about it and waste more time, or we can head off and get started. Is that ok with you, little man?"

## 17

Rissa's screams reverberated throughout the walls of Ironstone Keep, blood curdling shrieks that scattered even the ghouls from the surrounding forest. Ashavan paced up and down the entire length of the war room, his heart palpitating in his chest. He could feel himself shaking and the sweat dripped off his forehead despite the freezing chill of the night. His breath came in short gasping gulps, and for a moment he thought he would burst into tears.

That man, who so brazenly defied Du'Rakis; his Master's sworn enemy, the one who fulfilled that ridiculous prophecy. That man, who Ashavan and the rest of the Brotherhood were taught to believe was worse than the gods themselves. That man bore Tysion's mark.

Ashavan sat his helm and gauntlets on the table. He could feel his adrenaline firing, urging him to do something, to go back to To'Mar and find Tysion, maybe hide from Du'Rakis. Surely the symbol was a message from Tysion to let Ashavan know he was still alive.

A muffled grunt followed by footsteps startled him; Ashavan drew his sword and swung his arm, stopping his swing an inch from Enbarak's nose.

"What in the gods is going on here?" Enbarak demanded, reaching for his battleaxe.

"Sorry." Ashavan quickly sheathed his sword.

Enbarak was the only one of Du'Rakis' generals whom Ashavan held a shred of respect for. He was short, little more than five feet tall, and wore a long bushy beard. For such a short man, he was built solid, a thick slab of muscle for a chest, shown off by minimal leather armour. Enbarak was the one man he could count on to have his back in battle.

"Who's screaming? Is it Rissa?"

Ashavan nodded, and quickly filled him in on the encounter.

"He's going to kill her!" Enbarak's face darkened, and he reached again for his axe.

"And if you go running down there, he'll kill you too," Ashavan snapped. "Wake up to yourself. She had her orders. Instead of killing any stray mancers like she was supposed to, she tried to shag one of them instead, and he escaped. That mancer was Lord Sarik, the one our Master has been hunting down since all of this began. He is angry. No, furious. Much worse than after Rarn. So if you want to die a horrible death, go ahead."

Enbarak swore and balled his hands into fists and glared menacingly into Ashavan's face. As he drew back his arm, the door blew apart with a loud *bang*.

Du'Rakis stormed into the war room, his cloak billowing behind him. Before they could get out of his way, Du'Rakis waved his hand. Ashavan flew backwards and crashed roughly into a bookcase before falling to the floor. Pain shot from his side and stomach, and he gasped for air, unable to breathe. Books tumbled and fell on his exposed head, followed by the heavy case itself. He reached up to try and shield himself, but the bookcase slammed onto his battered body.

For a moment he blacked out, but as he opened one eye, he spied Du'Rakis' feet disappearing through a fresh portal. He lay gasping painfully, winded, unable to breathe. Finally he managed to draw a deep shuddering breath.

"Are you ok?" Enbarak asked sharply.

Ashavan couldn't answer. Enbarak stood up the bookcase and freed him from the pile of books.

"Argh. I... don't know. Help me out of my armour," he managed.

Enbarak helped him out of his heavy chest armour. A sharp pain shot up his side, leaving him gasping for breath. Ashavan pulled up his undershirt; a deep bruise on his side was already forming. He could feel blood dripping from his face and neck. He pushed himself up and stumbled as the room spun around him.

"Let's go find Rissa and see if she's still alive," Ashavan groaned. "It will be a miracle if she is."

They found Rissa's body on the landing three flights below the tower. She was laying in a pool of her own blood, naked but alive. Every inch of her skin was covered in sharp bleeding cuts. Her shoulders were shaking from her silent sobbing.

"What has he done to you?" Enbarak demanded.

"What does it look like?" she snapped. "I stuffed up, didn't I? Now I must wear my punishment."

Rissa tried to push herself into sitting position, but slipped on her own blood.

"We need to get to the infirmary," Ashavan grated.

Enbarak lifted her carefully and carried her towards the infirmary on the lower floor. Ashavan staggered behind, wincing every step. His mind was in disbelief; Du'Rakis had never harmed him before, nor had Ashavan ever given him reason to. A part of him felt betrayed. How could his Master do that to him, when he, Ashavan, obeyed his every word and whim without question?

Once they reached the infirmary, Ashavan removed his bloodied undershirt and busied himself with treating his own wounds. He closed his eyes and poured medicinal alcohol over the cuts on his head and neck, grimacing at the pain. Behind him, he could hear Rissa hissing as Enbarak treated her cuts.

"What should we do?" Enbarak asked once he was done.

"We do what we always do," Rissa said weakly. "We wait until we are called, and then we go to him. We obey his every word without question."

Ashavan finished wrapping a bandage around his bruised ribs, and turned to face them. He almost recoiled from Rissa; her once beautiful face was also covered in cuts, shallow enough not to bleed too much, but deep enough to cause pain and scarring.

"Did he say where he was going or how long he'll be?" he asked.

"He said something about Ornas, so he's probably gone to Araneda," Rissa replied.

"Given his current state, we can assume he's going to tear through the archives and find those letters himself," Ashavan grunted. "We should go and rest up. I can only imagine what he'll do if he calls us and we're not in a fit state, even if it is by his own hand."

———

The weather turned sour as Nika and his friends left To'Mar. Icy cold wind blew from the Eloran ranges, where it was snowing at the higher altitudes. After spending the afternoon in the city to restock their supplies, they spent the night in a cosy inn before leaving early the next day.

Nika was glad to be on the move again. As much as he was grateful for the break in traveling, he still had much to do. He pulled his cloak tighter around him and Arnie and glanced around the little group; Yger rode at the front alone, followed by Joplin and Priye who were chatting quietly, and Gaitan rode next to Nika, pouting.

He wasn't sure that having Yger invite herself along

was a good idea. Although she was a great fighter, Nika couldn't tell if her threats to kill Gaitan were serious or not, and he didn't want to put his friends in harm's way. His main concern was the fact that even despite all they'd been through, Yger was still at one point a member of the Black Ibis cult, who were known for breaking their word and killing their allies. Could he ever truly trust someone who was once aligned with those who killed Freyne's family?

*"I am back, My Lord."* Fin's unmistakable whisper made Nika jump, scattering his thoughts to the wind.

*"What did my Master say?"* Nika asked quickly.

*"Master Saramas is conversing with the Council even as we speak. He said he was concerned that Du'Rakis didn't stay and fight, which leads him to think that Du'Rakis is waiting for some reason. He said he will contact you when he is ready."*

*"Thanks,"* Nika said.

*"You're welcome, Master."*

Fin busied himself with zooming around Nika protectively.

Up ahead, Yger held up her hand to slow down. Nika pulled gently on Streek's reigns, preparing to stop, when Yger pulled sharply to the left and galloped off the road towards a copse of trees. Streek turned and followed her without any prompting from Nika.

"What's going on?" Joplin demanded once they were safe in the cover of the trees.

"Shh!" Yger held her finger to her lips, then pointed.

Nika squinted and saw what she was pointing at. A group of soldiers flying the Maikaden crest were marching through the farmstead, rounding up the farmers and workers. Without waiting for an explanation, Nika slipped from his body and sped towards the commotion.

"Anyone else?" a burly captain called towards his troops.

"Got 'em all, Cap," a sergeant nodded.

"Wait!" a young boy who was surely no older than thirteen ran towards the soldiers, waving his arm excitedly. "I can fight too."

"How old are you, boy?" the captain asked.

"Nineteen, sir."

The captain and some of the soldiers laughed heartily, causing the boy to blush.

"If you are nineteen, then I am a hundred," the captain said. "Come back to me when your balls have dropped, son."

The boy's face dropped, and he hurried back towards his home with the men's laughter following him.

"You could have let him down a little gentler, don't you think?" one of the soldiers asked.

"Not at all. We don't want him sneaking back when no one's looking," the captain replied.

"If he wants to fight, why not let him?"

"I'm here to recruit men and women who can fight, not kids who still wet the bed and cry for Mummy," he said, crossing his arms. "The king is dead. When Braidor's successor is chosen and sworn in, they're going to want swift action against whoever levelled half of Maikaden City. The regent ordered us to raise an army, so that's what we're doing.

"The reports coming in all point towards a full-scale war. If we recruit the younger people too, who will grow up to replace all those lives that are about to be lost? Who will look after the younger children if their parents die in the war? So no, I am not taking anyone that young."

Nika ghosted past the troops to inspect a much larger group of people who were stationed a short distance away. A few hundred new recruits stood chattering to one another, some excited and some who were terrified. Nika doubled back to his body, and quickly filled everyone in.

"The king is dead?" Joplin frowned.

"It sounded like it." Nika nodded.

"This is bad," Yger said grimly. "When a king is murdered, the entire kingdom is locked down until the culprit is found. Most able-bodied folk are conscripted and forced to fight should it be found that the culprit be from an opposing kingdom. That's what's happening. If we get caught roaming around, we could be captured and forced to fight."

"So that's why those guys were heading to the border," Gaitan mused, avoiding Yger's glare. "Wherever we're going next, we won't be able to leave Maikaden any time soon."

"King Braidor was popular," Joplin added. "His people are going to be grieving. Watch what you say here. Also, Yger's right. We'll need to stay off the roads and travel across the rough country. Avoid the farms and take all the usual precautions, yes."

"Do you know the way?" Priye asked.

"This isn't my first time avoiding patrols, woman."

"Oh, now the truth comes out," Priye smirked. "Is this where you suddenly announce you're the head of a smuggling ring or something exciting like that?"

"A man has to make money somehow." Joplin shrugged. "Fifty gold to escort foreigners across the desert hardly covers my expenses. Sometimes I opt for more exciting bounties, yes."

The thought of him engaging in illegal activities shocked Nika in a way. Although he'd only known Joplin since Lorendia, it felt like he'd known him for much longer, to the extent that he'd forgotten that his new friend had his own life outside of their quest. Nika eyed the big man with renewed respect, keen to hear more about his more illicit journeys.

"Where to, then?" Yger asked impatiently.

Joplin thought for a moment as he got his bearings.

"We're around two hours away from sunset. The best hidden place to camp is around three hours from here.

Follow me, yes."

The campsite was hidden away in a deep ravine, the walls riddled with erosion which formed natural shallow caves. Nika rode with Joplin, his firestone lighting the way just for the little group. After a while, the ravine narrowed, forming a natural overhang to shelter them from the rain. A small creek wove its way along through the cut, flowing from the downpour.

Everyone got stuck into setting up camp, and soon they had a nice hot fire roaring in one of the caves. Yger brandished her crossbow and disappeared to hunt, while Nika focused on warming some water for a wash. Once he was done, Nika sat back next to Gaitan, watching Priye cooking. His belly rumbled as the smells of the stew wafted across to them. He soon became aware of a soft, almost inaudible buzzing sound on the edge of his hearing. He tried to ignore it, but it started growing louder.

"Can you hear that?" he asked.

"Hear what?" Gaitan frowned.

"Shh."

Nika focused on the sound, and soon realised it was coming from within the darkest realm. As he reached his mind towards the focus, the flames of the fire flared and flickered, sending sparks towards the roof of the cave. Priye jumped back and swore, startled.

There in the fire was Saramas, and five more hooded faces whom Nika did not recognise. He blinked, then sat up straight. Judging by the looks on their faces, the others could see the visitors too.

"Lord Sarik. We need to talk to thee," Saramas said.

"Of course, Master." Nika nodded.

"We are the Council of Necromancers, and I am Master Tharak. Hast thou received news of King Braidor's death?"

"Yes, My Lord," Nika replied.

"We hast investigated the death. There is little surprise

that it was orchestrated by Du'Rakis," Tharak said. "I personally spoke with Braidor's essence before his priests sent him to the afterlife. He was expecting his murder, and as such, made time to prepare his orders for when it happened. His alliance with Dird and Faadar of Cadrinhal is to hold firm, and even now his regent is amassing an army."

"We witnessed the soldiers recruiting farmers earlier today," Nika nodded.

"Whilst I was talking with Braidor, I discovered something else." Tharak paused and cleared his throat. "The essence of King Radik remains in the lowest depths of Gri'Ran's Gate. He refuses to speak with any of us."

"He won't have a clue who Radik was," Saramas said dryly.

"*The* King Radik?" Joplin asked incredulously.

"The one and only." Tharak nodded. "Thou canst fill Sarik in on that story later. Anyway, myself, Saramas, Sadia, and Finwen joined minds to try and get Radik to speak. Still, he refuses."

"I don't entirely understand," Nika admitted, blushing.

"The desire for essence to serve and obey a master is great," Saramas explained. "To be left to roam alone forever is something many essence fear. That is why it can be so easy to capture willing sprites. Whilst an essence may refuse one necromancer, they cannot refuse the combined will of four of us together."

"Why won't it talk to you then, Master?" Nika asked.

"Because, Lord Sarik, the only person the king will speak to is thee." Tharak replied.

"Me? Why me?" Nika demanded.

"I told ye he is like this," Saramas sighed. "Sadia, perhaps thou shouldst try."

"Fine." She moved forward so Nika could see her hooded outline clearer in the fire. "King Radik was more than just a mortal king. He lived and ruled for four hundred years until he grew ill. His people loved him, and still do. He achieved many great things in his life, and his death triggered the beginning of our modern-day calendar, which he and his astrologers invented.

"Radik was no mancer. Many wondered why he was able to live such a long life, with no apparent talent in any of the realms. Well, it wasn't discovered until after his death that he held the gift of Sight. Around a year after he left for Gri'Ran's Gate, one of his former advisors ventured down there to find his body and maybe lay it to rest.

"Groll broke into his chamber, and found hundreds of pages of writings and scribbles, along with the letters from Radik's brother. He picked up a journal and a letter, before Radik manifested into a wraith and chased him away. Groll fled with the two items, and ordered the gate to be sealed behind him. While we can only speculate on what was written in those two items, we believe that's what Du'Rakis is searching for. Whatever it is, it was worth killing Braidor and levelling half of Maikaden City to try and obtain it."

"What makes King Radik so important to Du'Rakis, though?" Nika asked.

"Radik was Rakis' brother," Saramas said pointedly. "Radik had a vision that someone was going to kill Rakis for his powers, and so he warned him to go into hiding for the rest of his days. Whatever it is that Radik has or knows, Du'Rakis wants it desperately. Therefore, I don't think thou needs me to tell thee to go to Gri'Ran's Gate with haste. If Du'Rakis finds that book and letter, we may be powerless to stop whatever he is planning next."

"Yes, Master. Am did tell us to head west, so that makes sense."

"We shalt be in touch." Tharak nodded. "Also, thou didst well defending thyself against Du'Rakis. Farewell, Lord Sarik."

The flames flared up once more, and when they

settled, the faces of the necromancers were gone. Nika let out a deep breath as he tried to make sense of the Council's words.

"What's this story Master Tharak mentioned?" Nika asked Joplin.

"King Radik was, and still is, a legend. As you heard, he ruled for four hundred years before he finally fell ill. Where to start though." Joplin thought for a moment, then clicked his fingers. "Most kings were expected to have many children back then, so there were enough heirs to carry on the bloodline. The king before him only had two sons, Radik and Rakis, who were twins. Rakis was first in line to be king, as he was the first born of the two, but when their father died, he refused to step up and handed all power to Radik.

"Radik was obsessed with Gri'Ran's Gate. From the moment he stepped into power, he went there with an escort to explore its depths. He was gone for several weeks before finally returning. He announced that it was time to put aside the ancient decrees regarding savages, and venture forth into the wild and explore. He ordered a new crossing to be built where the original land bridge once was, which took almost fifteen years to complete, yes."

"Savages?" Nika asked.

"Non-human races. There were quite a few, but now the pygmies are the only ones who still exist. For years, the giants and other beasts invaded using the natural land bridge that is now Radik's Crossing, and many wars ensued. Previous kings made it their mission to wipe any uncivilised races from the world. Gri'Ran's Gate was eventually built to prevent them from invading, and once complete, the land bridge was destroyed for good measure.

"Anyway. Once the crossing was complete, Radik sent one hundred soldiers plus support staff to explore the unknown lands and chart a map, then return and brief him with what they saw. Only three people made it back with a tiny amount mapped, and they spoke of savage beasts and unspeakable horrors beyond the mountains and volcanic wastelands.

"Prince Rakis heard of his brother's attempts to explore the lands, and offered to go himself. Radik refused, but of course his twin ignored him, yes. Rakis slipped away after dark and disappeared towards the crossing, never to be seen again.

"When Radik heard this, he was furious that his brother would disobey and put his own life at risk. He sent soldiers to look for him, and for over ten years there was no sign of Rakis. Overwhelmed with grief, Radik once again descended into the depths of Gri'Ran's Gate, where he remained for five months. No one knows what he did there or why, yes; he forbade his guards from entering, and made them camp outside the Gate. It is well documented that Radik had no food or water with him, so how he survived all that time is still a mystery, yes.

"Eventually, King Radik returned to the surface. He had changed considerably and was quite emaciated. He was rushed back to the castle where he received care and was fed back to good health. The king wasn't himself. Once he regained his health, he ordered his best horse to be readied, and set out across Radik's Crossing, alone.

"He found his brother on top of a large peak, content with living alone in solitude. They spoke, and Radik begged Rakis to return home to the safety of his kingdom. His brother refused, and argued that he had a higher purpose now, that he was studying some phenomenon on top of the peak. He promised they would write letters and stay in touch, so that's exactly what they did, yes. For the next three hundred years.

"Radik sent one final letter to his brother, and that was the last they spoke. He sent a detachment of his best soldiers to take all of Rakis' research to Araneda for safekeeping in the archives. Only reigning monarchs can access those archives, yes.

"Shortly after, a small army of the Brotherhood of the Black Ibis stormed Radik's City and attempted to kill King Radik. His own army was on high alert, and managed to slay each and every cultist who invaded. That's when he outlawed the cult in Cadrinhal, and drove those remaining from his lands.

"Radik never heard from his brother again. No one knows what happened to Rakis. The king soon grew ill, and no longer fit to rule the kingdom. Neither Radik nor Rakis had any children, so there was no heir to carry on the bloodline. He legally adopted his favourite cousin's son who he deemed worthy to rule Cadrinhal, and after a few weeks of inducting him into the role, King Radik passed over his crown. His final wishes were to be escorted one final time to Gri'Ran's Gate, and have it sealed for good. He made his way to his chamber where he lived out the remainder of his life, alone."

Joplin went quiet, and Nika mulled over his words. Everything clicked into place.

"It all makes sense!" he blurted out, standing up. "That Gate is the key, and I'm willing to bet there's a rift on that peak. We need to get there before Du'Rakis does. Not even the gods would know what he is planning next. How long will it take us to get there?"

"Eight weeks at normal riding pace," Joplin answered. "We can do it in six if we travel military style. We ride until midnight, and leave at sunrise. That gives us six hours to sleep, and we have three short breaks during the day. It's up to you all, yes."

"It can't be worse than riding with the King's Army that time," Priye said, handing out bowls of hot steaming stew. "I'm in."

Everyone nodded their agreement. Nika accepted his bowl from Priye and sat back down.

"Alright, let's do it," he said, giving the final nod.

"I know you won't like this, Joplin, but I'll set up some helpers to keep watch for us while we sleep. The long days will take too much of a toll on us if we have to rotate watch. If something does happen, we'll need to be able to fight."

To Nika's surprise, Joplin's face formed into a wicked grin.

"So long as we're safe, do what you must. You've proven you can protect us. The journey ahead is about to get fun and exciting, yes."

**18**

The steely ring of sword on sword bounced around the castle walls, accompanied by grunting and shouting. Iryna walked along the battlements with Ur'Shad and Chardi, inspecting the newest wave of elite guards sparring in the training grounds below. Iryna rarely had the opportunity to spend time with Chardi and Ur'Shad without anyone else around, and treasured those moments dearly.

"How are you holding up, Princess?" Chardi asked quietly.

"I'm just taking each day as it comes." Iryna shrugged. "I might get to meet my future husband some day. Hopefully before I die."

"I've never known To'Rel to be so secretive," Ur'Shad grunted.

"Me either," Chardi agreed. "Who knows. Maybe To'Rel was bluffing. Or maybe he changed his mind. You never know."

"I think the border issues are his main focus right now," Iryna said. "I just wish I could choose whoever I wanted like normal people do."

"If you could pick any husband on the Isles, who would it be?" Ur'Shad smirked.

Iryna held her chin and pretended to think about it.

"You know what? I think I'll pass on a husband. I

might run away with Maple and travel the seas with her. Maybe we could become pirates, and I'll take her to be my wife instead."

"Hey! That's not fair!" Ur'Shad spun around and tickled the princess until she squealed.

"Stop it!" she snorted between her laughter.

"I don't blame her," Chardi laughed. "Maple's much better looking than you."

"This is mutiny," Ur'Shad declared.

Iryna reached up and grasped his ear, and pulled his face down to her height. She planted a single kiss on his freshly-shaved head.

"You know I'm joking," she grinned.

Chardi leant over the battlement and watched one of his captains shouting at the recruits.

"See that idiot down there?" he asked.

Iryna and Ur'Shad nodded.

"That's Captain Rin. To'Rel almost promoted him to my old Chief role. I had to threaten to defect before To'Rel took me seriously and withdrew his recommendation. Thank the gods he promoted my guy instead."

"I still can't believe you're leaving us," Ur'Shad grumbled.

"It's not forever. Like I said, To'Rel wants someone he trusts to oversee the quarantine station and ensure the guests are treated humanely. When the threat is over, I'll be back."

"You know as well as we do that the threat will be far from over until Nika kills Khel." Iryna patted Chardi on the shoulder gently. "You still miss her, don't you?"

"With every beat of my heart," Chardi said sadly, staring into the distance. "I think the time away from Al'Obrel will be good for me. Every day that I'm here, I see something that reminds me of her. Some mornings when I wake up, I can almost smell her freshly washed hair in my arms, but when I open my eyes, she's gone. I don't think I can take this much longer, to be honest."

"Oh, Chardi."

Iryna pulled him into a tight hug and Ur'Shad joined in. They held each other tightly for a while, then reluctantly let go. As she turned back towards Ur'Shad, a movement in the sky caught her eye. A large white bird was circling the aviary, then descended gracefully and glided through the opening.

"A letter!" she gasped. "It *has* to be from Nika! Come on, I'll race you."

Iryna hitched up her gown and ran unceremoniously towards the aviary as fast as she could with the two large men in tow. A few of the patrolling guards eyed them suspiciously, but shrugged as they heard her laughs. She reached the tower and bent over, gasping for breath as Ur'Shad and Chardi clambered behind. Ur'Shad grabbed at Chardi's arm in an attempt to beat him, but tripped and slid across the stones. Iryna couldn't help but laugh as Ur'Shad picked himself up sheepishly and walked the rest of the way.

"That'll teach you for trying to cheat," Chardi laughed between breaths.

"Not fair," Ur'Shad grumbled.

Iryna hurried up the spiralling staircase, past the startled flock attendant and into the stinky aviary. Her father's pigeons fluttered and cooed in their boxes, eager to fly and stretch their wings. She walked past the boxes and found a lone white albatross perched on the windowsill with a scroll attached to its leg. Iryna picked it up carefully and removed the scroll, then placed the bird inside one of the empty boxes.

"Who's it from?" Ur'Shad asked.

Iryna unrolled the scroll and read it slowly, with Ur'Shad and Chardi leaning over her shoulders. As she read Freyne's immaculate handwriting, her heart dropped at the news.

*...and now, Nika is heading north to pursue Du'Rakis, while I'm heading south, in hopes that I can get these letters to you and Kaiton. I will write again within a few days to inform you of the outcome of my meeting with Dird.*

*Stay safe, my friends. May you forever hold Am in your hearts.*

*Your friend,*
*Freyne*

"So Khel is Du'Rakis?" Chardi asked, scratching his beard.

"Yes, it says so right here," Iryna nodded. "We need to go and see my father right away. Forget our borders and that camp. We're heading to war."

Iryna sat at the oval map table, listening to her father's generals and advisors bickering amongst themselves. It was late and she was tired, but she refused to miss any step of the planning.

"All we're doing is going around in circles," To'Rel said wearily. "I guess we should..."

The door slammed open, startling everyone in the room. Chardi half drew his sword, when they realised it was just a messenger.

"Your Majesty! Pardon the intrusion, but we've received a letter under King Dird's seal!" the messenger pushed his way through the room and handed To'Rel the letter.

Iryna hurried across to her father and tried to read the letter over his shoulder. He shot her an irritated glance, and she stood back quickly, knowing better than to push her luck. To'Rel cleared his throat and read the letter out loud.

*To my dearest friends of the East,*

*I hope this letter finds you and your family well. By now you should have received the letter sent from your envoy Christophe Saul Du Freyne. In response, as of today the 28<sup>th</sup> of Jalie, I have declared war against the scourge Du'Rakis and all those who are aligned with him. I, King Dird of Drarlum, hereby request your aid in this war as our allies.*

*My brothers to the north, Braidor of Maikaden and Faadar of Cadrinhal have agreed to fight with us. I am still awaiting word from Kalissaden and Lorendia, though I'm sure we can count on Lorendia remaining neutral.*

*We will be marching with Cadrinhal towards Kalissaden via Loralyon, and Maikaden will rendezvous with us there. If you accept my call to arms, it will be best for you to direct your army to the port of Khymas.*

*I shall await your response most keenly.*
*From your brother,*
*Dird.*

The generals erupted, talking loudly amongst themselves. To'Rel rubbed his eyes and looked sideways at Iryna.

"I should have learnt to have my mail taken directly to my quarters by now." He sighed. "Why don't you go and get some rest?"

"My friends are over there in the thick of this mess, and they aren't laying around resting," Iryna said stubbornly. "I'm not leaving until this meeting is adjourned. We're all in this together."

"Very well." To'Rel cleared his throat. "Listen up, gentlemen."

The room grew silent and everyone gave the king their full attention.

"There is nothing further for us to debate. We will be

accepting Dird's request for aid. Therefore, I hereby declare that as of this day, the 42$^{nd}$ of Jalie, I accept King Dird of Drarlum's request for aid in the war against Du'Rakis. We are officially at war."

"If that is the case, My King, are we to proceed with the quarantine station?" General Thoma asked. "We will probably need all the fighters we can get over on the front lines."

"I think the bigger concern will be refugees," Chardi replied.

"I think you should butt out and leave this to the generals, *Master Chief*," General Rauk'i said snidely.

"That's enough from you, Rauk'i!" To'Rel snapped. "As of right now, I'm promoting Chardi to general. He's had more world-wide experience than most of you put together."

The generals murmured amongst each other for a moment, and Rauk'i hung his head.

"Sorry, Your Majesty. Welcome aboard, Chardi."

Iryna glanced at the map on the table and moved the painted wooden pieces around thoughtfully.

"Chardi is right," she said, pointing at the blue allied blocks. "We will have control of these kingdoms along here, so we can expect possibly thousands of refugees to come over, especially if the fighting pushes us south."

"In that case, let's just call it a refugee camp and be done with it," Thoma nodded.

"We'd better prepare for that first thing tomorrow," To'Rel agreed.

He pulled on one of the cords on the wall, ringing the bell designated for his servants. The side door opened immediately, and a servant entered and bowed deeply. To'Rel quickly penned his orders on a sheet of parchment and added his seal to the bottom.

"At noon tomorrow, I require all our quartermasters, tent-makers, artisans, cooks, and anyone relevant to gather in my court for a meeting. Also, send my fastest birds to Lok and Kaiton." He rolled up the scroll and handed it to the servant.

"Yes, Your Majesty," he bowed.

"The high priests too," Iryna added quickly. "I will speak with them after tomorrow's meeting."

"Yes, Your Royal Highness. Will that be all?"

To'Rel eyed her with a raised eyebrow, but Iryna ignored him and smiled at the servant.

"That will be all for now. Thank you."

"Who are you and where's my daughter?" he asked, still looking at her funny.

"Aww, does Daddy miss his precious little brat?" she pinched his cheek and smirked.

"You're impossible." To'Rel sighed and rubbed his tired eyes. "I know some of you will want to stay here all night and start planning this now, but we all need to sleep so we can think clearly in the morning. Therefore, let us retire for the evening, and start afresh at sunrise. Dismissed, everyone."

Iryna stayed back until it was just her, To'Rel, Ur'Shad and Chardi. Once the door closed, she turned back to him.

"Did the letter say anything else, Father?" she asked quickly.

"Yes. Your idea for reintroducing religion back into our cities was the right thing to do. Freyne must have really impressed Dird, or threatened him, as he will be rebuilding his temple and putting his priests to work. Apart from that, he said that Nika, Priye and Gaitan were all ok and they miss you, Chardi and Ur'Shad. They all send their love."

---

The expanse of the Llunn Forest stretched further than Freyne could see. He knew not what existed beyond the forest, be it more rolling landscape or the edge of the continent. His mind boggled at the sheer size of it, broken up occasionally by a few mountains or a lake here and there. The further they flew, the more the forest changed. The birch, spruce and pines soon blended into maples and oaks, and sometimes Freyne caught sight of beautiful coloured parrots flying over the canopy.

Since leaving Drarlum, Freyne eventually grew to enjoy flying with Ruke. He learnt to control his stomach so he didn't feel ill while taking off and landing, and he even got used to sleeping while flying. Each and every mile they flew, the calling to the south grew stronger, filling him with a deep longing.

The forest finally ended, opening to a wide lush green field. In the distance, yet another forest loomed, though Freyne could sense something else emanating from the trees. Beautiful mahogany and teak trees, dotted with oaks, untouched by human hand. Ruke tilted and aimed towards the edge of the trees.

A cold shiver tingled down his spine, a sense of warning. A loud cry came from behind them, chilling Freyne's blood. Ruke turned sharply and folded his wings, dropping suddenly and leaving Freyne's stomach in the air. As Ruke spun, he flapped his wings and shot back up, narrowly avoiding something large and scaly.

Freyne's heart pounded in his chest, and he clung onto the harness, terrified of falling out. As Ruke spiralled again, he saw it; a majestic bronzed dragon much larger than Ruke was in pursuit, attempting to claw them from the sky.

Ruke tried to dodge the dragon, and descended towards the tree line. The dragon swooped, its sharp talons slicing through Ruke's wing. The wyvern shrieked and tilted dangerously to one side.

*"Cut... harness. Jump!"*

Freyne could feel his own panic as the dragon flew around for another attack. Ruke narrowly dodged a stream of fiery breath; Freyne could feel the intense heat barely miss his body. He took a deep breath and slipped his pack onto his back. He drew his dagger, then ducked as the dragon flapped above him.

*"Thank you."* Freyne rested his hand on Ruke's neck to show his gratitude, then cut at the straps to the harness.

*"We'll... meet. Again. Go now."*

Ruke banked once more to their right, and Freyne fell towards the canopy far below. He tumbled through the air, dizzy and disoriented, certain he was about to die. Of all the things that could have killed him over the years, he was to die from falling off the back of a wyvern. Am's presence flooded into his body.

*"Not today, my son! Pull yourself out!"*

Freyne felt himself slow down, just enough to allow him to steady himself and stop tumbling. He blinked as the treetops drew closer, and slipped his mind into the lowest realm. With all his strength, he pushed away from the ground below him, slowing his descent, though not nearly enough. He crashed roughly through the canopy and slammed into the ground. His body bounced and rolled to a painful stop.

He felt himself sliding in and out of consciousness, Am's presence slowly fading away. His entire body was numb, and for a moment he thought he was dead or dying. He couldn't feel anything, he couldn't even move.

A low grunt and growl came from somewhere nearby, increasing his terror. More grunts and hisses surrounded him, and something sharp poked him in his chest. Freyne's eyes flew open; eight hostile faces stared down at him, growling and hissing at one another. Their faces were tinged with green, their hair messy and entwined with twigs and leaves. The one holding the spear had bright coppery hair and vibrant green eyes. She stared deeply into Freyne's, then pulled back her spear in surprise. She said something in their guttural language, and one of the others forced something into Freyne's mouth. Everything spun, and he drifted off into oblivion.

The weeks following Du'Rakis' outburst and abrupt departure were perhaps the hardest Ashavan had ever had to endure. The uncertainty of his future loomed heavily on him. Was Du'Rakis planning to kill them when he returned, or was he merely punishing them? He hated not knowing the answers almost as much as he hated the fact that his life was in the hands of his deranged Master.

For Ashavan, the weeks of sitting around doing nothing led to his mind having freedom to dwell on things he'd usually push aside. His longing for Tysion, his deep remorse for slaughtering all those innocent people, and most of all, regret for not leaving the Brotherhood much sooner when he had the chance. Tysion was right; his heart *was* ensnared, and as far as Ashavan was concerned, he would never be free.

With a miserable sigh, he finished sharpening his sword and slid it back into its sheath. He'd finally finished working out the dents in his armour, and polished it all so it shone like new. He stood up from his stool and pulled on his thick cloak, then let himself out of his room.

Ashavan walked aimlessly through the long halls of the keep, feeling more alone than ever. Enbarak and Rissa couldn't care less about him, and he knew with certainty that he couldn't risk speaking openly with them. He absentmindedly climbed a grand staircase and let himself into the library.

The library was dark, dusty, and littered with cobwebs. Ashavan backtracked to the door and took one of the lanterns from the wall so he could see. Rows and rows of old books and scrolls filled the room; the shadows from the light flickered across the shelves, sending spiders fleeing into the cracks in the shelves.

Ashavan found a private alcove tucked away by the window, with a large desk littered with candles, parchment and quills. He sat down his lantern and carefully lit some of the candles, then glanced around. Next to the desk was a lush red arm chair which looked comfortable and inviting.

A single book glinted in the light of the candles, filling him with curiosity. He plucked it from the shelf and helped himself to the chair, then opened the book to the first page.

*My Experience with Forgiveness – Mr Jokar*

*I was raised on a small farm in Maikaden. We were poor, and rarely had coin to spare. We could not hire farm hands like some of the larger farms, so as soon as I was old enough to manage even the most simplest of chores, I was put to work. From simple tasks such as collecting eggs from the chickens and ducks, to later on toiling in the field. I learnt as much as I could from my father and uncles, but when I was just nineteen, my father died suddenly.*

*My mother decided to leave the farm and return to her family in Kalissaden. I, of course, didn't want to leave. I was actively wooing a young lass from another farm, and I didn't want to leave her behind. And so I stayed by myself, alone.*

*Of course I was unable to maintain the crops, except for a small vegetable patch for myself. Instead, I focused on my ducks and chickens. I built more pens, and concentrated on breeding them. Over the next few years, I made enough coin from selling fresh eggs, and became popular within the area. I finally plucked up enough courage to ask the lass for her hand in marriage, but to my utter despair, she turned me down. Unbeknownst to me, she was already betrothed to another man who was much richer than I.*

*I was devastated, and retreated to my farm. The only times I left after that were to visit the market to sell my eggs and buy what I needed. I had my chickens for company, I was content. One day, however, I returned home to find that foxes had ravished almost half of my birds. My poor chickens, gone.*

*Something wasn't right, though. I'd dealt with foxes before, and they only took enough for their fill. To make matters more confusing, there were no holes in the fences to* allow a fox to enter. And so I set a trap. I took my wagon and headed towards the markets again, but this time I hid in the nearby woods, and waited.

Sure enough, my sweetheart's betrothed came into my farm with several foxes on leashes, and let them into one of my pens. What happened next, I am not proud of. I took the scythe that I once used to harvest the wheat, and I harvested him and his foxes instead. Killed them all.

Once the rage subsided and I realised what I had done, I was mortified. I hurried back to my horse and rode towards Maikaden City in a daze. Still to this day, I have no idea how I went all that way without eating or drinking much. Once I got there, I rode straight to the temple of Am and walked inside.

I took myself up to the altar and fell to my knees and wept. I had never been a praying man, but that day I prayed and prayed. I begged for Am to come and smite me down, for what I did was beyond wrong and I did not deserve to live.

To my surprise, Am appeared before me. They told me that everything happens for a reason, and although my experience was harsh, it had to happen for the good of mankind. Only Am can see the bigger picture, I guess.

Am told me I could either go back to my farm with their forgiveness, or I could stay and become a priest. At first I shied away from the offer to be a priest; I had no desire to live in a temple and pray all day. But once I returned to the farm, to the rotting carcass in my pen, I knew I couldn't live with my guilt. And so I gave my life to Am. With their forgiveness and understanding, I lived many years serving my god. My message to anyone who reads this: people commit atrocities every single day, and sometimes those with no ill intent are caught up in things outside their control. If you feel guilt and remorse, there is still a chance for forgiveness. Hold Am in your heart, always, for they will be there with open arms when you are ready.

Ashavan slammed the book shut and hurled it with all of his might against the wall. Instead of breaking apart like he'd hoped, the book bounced quietly to the floor and landed open. He buried his face in his hand, then dared a peek at the page. The story of Mr Jokar and his chickens glared up at him in defiance. At once he saw red, and his pent-up emotions spilled free.

"You killed one pitiful man that deserved it! You didn't have to stare into the eyes of innocent children and murder them in cold blood! No one will ever forgive me for what I have done!" he shouted, losing it.

With another burst of anger, Ashavan threw the book on the ground and kicked it. It flew through the air and knocked a small vase off a shelf, which shattered into a hundred pieces. This time it landed open but face-down. He glared at it, then stalked across to where it lay innocently on the floor. He bent down and picked it up with shaking hands; once again, it was open at that same page.

"STOP IT!! I'M A MONSTER!" he screamed towards the roof, tearing the page from the book and ripping it into shreds. "I don't deserve forgiveness! If anything, I'm the one who should be rotting in some pen or field somewhere! So, unless you're going to kill me, leave me alone!"

# Part Three
# Gri'Ran's Gate

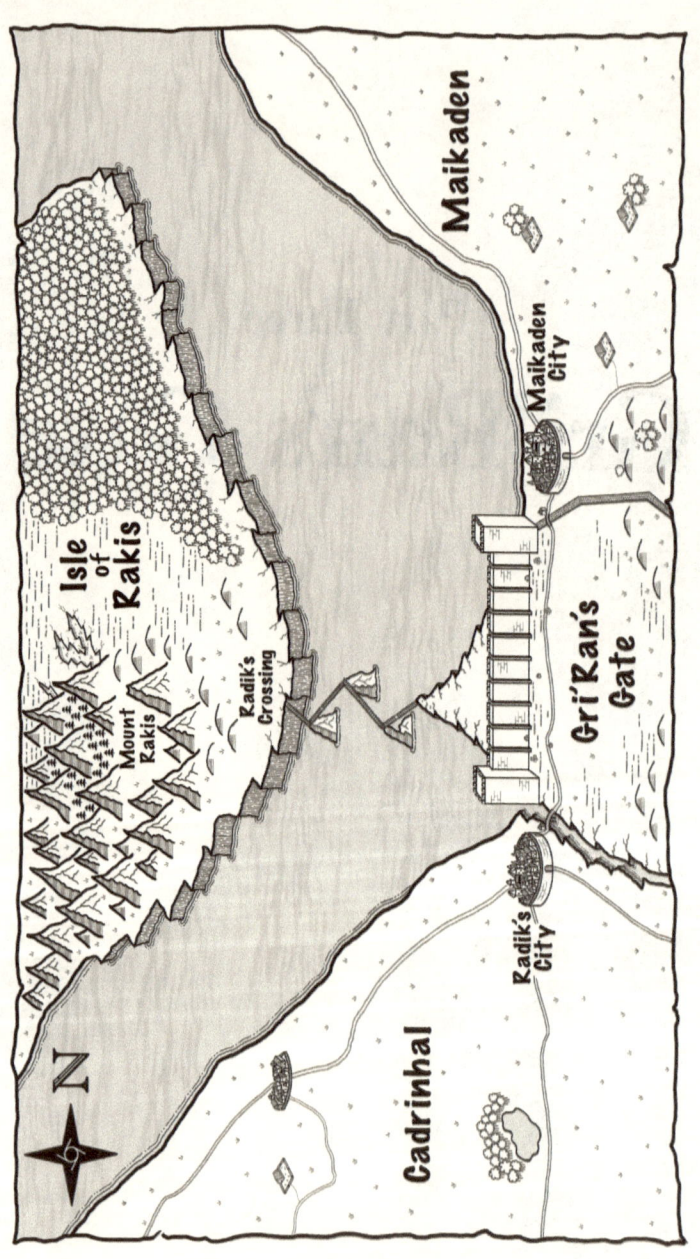

## 19

The sky above Maikaden City was marred by a cloud of low-hanging smoke that drifted lazily inland, swept along by the icy south-easterly breeze. From their hiding place on a small hill, Nika could smell the burnt-out city and shuddered. Everywhere they looked, mounted patrols were sweeping along the length of the border, roads, and the entirety of the city's walls.

"That line you can see along there is the border," Joplin explained, pointing. "It is a wide ditch filled with sharp spikes that is impossible to cross. There is only one way through, and that's via the checkpoint that connects to the main road, yes."

"Can we go back through the forest and go around it?" Gaitan asked.

"No. It's patrolled all the way to Radik's River, which marks Cadrinhal's border. That river is too dangerous to try and cross."

"Is that not Cadrinhal right there?" Nika asked, pointing at the wide expanse of flat grassland that stretched along the length of Gri'Ran's Gate and disappeared into the distance.

"That area is neutral ground," Joplin replied, shaking his head. "Radik's treaty demands it be kept neutral at all times."

"How do we cross then?" Gaitan asked.

Joplin grinned and pointed at Nika.

"We have a mancer, so we may as well use him, yes? There is a portable bridge that smugglers use to cross the fortifications. Now usually, we have half the team cross down at the checkpoint during the day. They ride along the road until they are out of sight from the border patrols, then double back and meet us up here, yes. While they're doing that, the rest of us move the bridge into position. When they get here, we throw the guide ropes across, and they help pull while we push so we don't damage the spikes. This allows us to ride across safely without leaving a trace, yes." He paused and scratched his hairy cheek. "There's one small problem, though. The bridge is currently on the other side of the border from when we used it last, and obviously we can't send someone across since the checkpoint is closed."

"And you want me to move it into position, don't you?" Nika guessed.

"That's right, yes. Can you do it?"

"I think so," Nika nodded. "I mean, I've lifted things before, just not that big."

"We could just fight our way across," Yger suggested hopefully.

"No." Nika shook his head firmly. "I don't know what we're looking at once we get inside the Gate. The last thing we need is guards chasing us through there. Fighting is our last option."

"Don't worry, woman. If we get caught, *then* you can kill someone, yes."

To Nika's surprise, Yger's face twisted into a rare grin.

"I like you," she declared. Without another word, she slid back down the hill and made her way back to Priye.

"What?!" Gaitan exploded. "How can she like you but hate me so much?"

"Do you really want me to answer that?" Joplin asked.

"No, I guess not." Gaitan grumbled.

"Come. We hide here until dark, then we cross, yes."

Nika slid down the hill and rejoined the others inside the hidden cave. He picked up Arnie-Kyn and sat on a sawn-off tree stump, warming himself by the fire.

"Are you sure it's safe having the fire?" he asked. The closeness of some of the patrols left him feeling uneasy.

"Of course. I've used this spot many times, yes." Joplin nodded.

"You owe us a story," Priye said, her hands on her hips. "Just what have you been getting up to?"

"It doesn't matter." Joplin waved his hand dismissively.

Yger exchanged glances with Priye, then stood up and crossed her arms.

"You will speak, or I'll force it out of you," she warned. "I can break any man."

"Fine." Joplin gave in and leaned back against the cave wall. "Back when I was a soldier in the Cadrinhal army, I was part of a unit who was sent to guard the shipments from the salt mines. Most of the kingdom's income comes from salt exports, so it's guarded very closely.

"I soon found out that there's no trade agreement between Cadrinhal and Sepheren. The previous marquess had a fight with Faadar and their contract was torn up. They believed that the salt should be free since it comes from the ground, yes.

"Faadar went as far as to restrict the other kingdoms from forward selling to Sepheren, effectively cutting them off from an essential nutrient. Over time, the people were starting to become sick. Some of the others in my unit had family there, so you can see where this is going.

"The head of the mine attempted to make an agreement with the marquess, but their price was four times the regular price. And so we decided to take matters into our own hands. Once or twice a year, I meet up with my friends, we steal some salt, and smuggle it to Sepheren."

"Why do you go the long way around?" Gaitan asked.

"Sometimes we hijack one of the caravans and steal a wagon or two. Other times we're forced to sneak into the mine itself and steal some from there. We go a different way every time so we're not predictable, yes."

"That's actually quite noble of you," Priye said. "Here I was thinking you were smuggling something terrible like slaves or weapons."

"We've all done things we're not proud of," Joplin growled. "I'm going to check the border."

Nika moved further into the cave and settled himself on the hard ground with Arnie. His body was stiff and sore from the constant riding, and with his regular monitoring of their surrounds during the long days, he was exhausted.

"Wake me up when it's time to go," he yawned.

---

The night was cold and windy; the moon hid behind the clouds, plunging them into darkness. At Joplin's insistence, Nika, Gaitan and Yger pulled on their armour and checked their weapons. Nika had never seen Joplin so serious before; the big man took charge, and no one dared to question him. After one more quick check for patrols, Nika nodded that he was ready to go.

"Alright, move it out," Joplin said shortly.

They crept quietly towards the edge of the pit and crouched down, their weapons drawn. The pit was much wider than he'd anticipated, and the spikes were deadly sharp. A short distance away, the body of a decaying animal showed exactly what would happen should they fall in. The sounds of laughter and swearing floated eerily to them on the wind from a patrol camped several miles away. Nika gritted his teeth, his nerves on edge, and forced himself to focus on the task at hand.

"Where is it?" he whispered.

"Under those three rocks over there," Joplin whispered back. "It's camouflaged to look like the ground. This section is where it needs to go, as it's the narrowest part of the entire border, yes."

"Ok. Get back, everyone."

It took him a few minutes to make out the faint outline

of the bridge. It was more of a ramp than anything, barely visible to the naked eye. With his mind half in the lowest realm, Nika carefully lifted the rocks off one by one, and soon broke into a sweat. The rocks were heavy, and as he dropped the last one, he began to doubt being able to move the bridge at all.

Nika wiped his brow, and attempted to lift the bridge. It rose a few inches off the ground, then fell back down noisily in a cloud of dust. Pain stabbed at his head, and for a moment little coloured lights swirled in front of his eyes.

"Fuck me," Nika hissed, holding his hand to his head. "I don't think..."

*"You will never be able to do anything if you don't believe that you can."*

Nika spun around. Arnie's eyes bore into his, watching his every move.

*"Remember what we spoke about back at Endveraugh. Stop holding back! We need to cross this border tonight, and quickly too. Pull yourself together, human!"*

"What's wrong? Can't you do it?" Joplin demanded.

Nika evaded Arnie's look and glared back at the bridge. He stood up and drew his focus, more for encouragement than for usefulness, then held out his left hand towards the bridge. Nika focused his mind until he saw nothing but the bridge, and began to draw from the lowest realm. He could feel the forces growing inside him, swirling through his body waiting to be released. His entire body tingled from the power flowing through him.

With deadly precision, Nika directed the forces towards the bridge, and lifted it evenly from all four corners. It rose into the air, and without so much as a shudder, he guided it across the ditch and into position. He lowered it carefully, and it fell into place with a thud.

Nika bent forward and rested his hands on his thighs, catching his breath. The bridge had a layer of dirt and grass growing across it, to disguise it while not in use. He was quietly impressed.

"Ah, there we go." Joplin waved to Yger and Priye to bring the horses, and gestured to them to cross.

*"One told you so,"* Arnie-Kyn said, dashing across the bridge behind the horses.

Nika didn't reply. Out of the corner of his eye, he saw movement, and spun to face it. A raggedy group of soldiers were creeping towards them, their weapons at the ready. Although they wore the uniforms of Maikaden soldiers, their armour was mismatched and inconsistent. Most were missing helms, and others wore pieces that didn't fit properly. Nika heard the *twang* of Yger's crossbow, and one of them tumbled to the ground, clutching at his throat.

Joplin dashed forward and met with the closest soldier. He swung his sword and buried his blade deep into his unprotected neck, almost severing it from the soldier's body. He pulled back in time to parry a blow, then cut off his attacker's arm. Yger picked them off one by one, her bolts hitting with deadly accuracy. One of the soldiers rushed at Nika, but before he could do anything, the soldier doubled over and fell roughly onto the ground. Nika drew his morning star and busied himself with another soldier. As Nika grappled with him, he heard a curse and a shout behind him.

"Hey, it's that wanted man!" one of the men yelled.

Nika swung his star and connected it with his opponent's head. A sickening *crunch* made his blood curdle, but he had no time to feel sorry for him. He turned back to see Yger fumbling with her crossbow, trying to unjam it. Two soldiers rushed towards her with their swords ready to strike. With an angry shout, she hurled the crossbow at her incoming attackers and cartwheeled out of the way. She crouched cat-like, then leapt at the closest soldier and tackled him easily. Yger pulled a small dagger from her boot and sliced into his throat, then spun and caught the wrist of the other soldier who was about to strike. Almost with ease, she knocked the rusty sword from his hand, then punched him in his face. Blood spurted from his shattered nose, and as he staggered back, she spun on her heel and delivered a sweeping kick to his head, sending him sprawling.

Gaitan was locked in an intense one-on-one fight with a larger man, the clash of their swords ringing loudly in the night. With a grunt, Gaitan dodged and buried his sword to the hilt into his opponent's armpit. He tried to pull out, but it was stuck. Another soldier rushed him from behind; he grabbed Gaitan around the neck and tried to pull him back, but instead of falling backwards, Gaitan's helm slipped off. The soldier discarded the helm and drew his mace, taking a clumsy swing. Gaitan let go of his hilt and elbowed the soldier in the face. He snatched the soldier's mace and tried to swing, but there wasn't enough room. He staggered back, then drove his boot into the tender region between the soldier's legs. The man squealed and collapsed in a heap.

Nika quickly disposed of two more soldiers, and turned just in time to see Yger overwhelmed by three men. Gaitan screamed bloody murder and charged; he caught them off-guard and slammed the mace into the first soldier's head, shattering his skull and sending blood and brains in every direction. The second man had Yger in a hold on the ground, her arms held tightly behind her back, while the third prepared to run her through. Nika ran towards them, but he was too late.

Yger's eyes widened as the blade sped towards her chest. Gaitan threw himself between her and the tip of the sword. Nika watched helplessly as the blade pierced his friend's shoulder. Gaitan landed roughly, but sprang to his feet and tackled the surprised guard. Yger threw her head back and stunned her captor, then scrambled from his hold. She pinned him down and drew another dagger, then made several long cuts in his face.

Joplin finished off a final opponent, then swept their surroundings for any last soldiers. They were all dead or dying. He and Gaitan swiftly finished off the few soldiers who were rolling about, writhing in pain. In keeping with Joplin's instructions, Nika rummaged through the bodies numbly and helped himself to any money and valuables he could find. As deplorable as it was, they needed the coins more than the dead people.

A sharp scream followed by a slap made Nika jump and look up. Yger was bent over her captive, still carving deep gashes into any exposed skin she could find and growling words at him in her own language.

"Stop playing with your food, woman! Kill him now, we don't have time for this, yes!"

Yger shot Joplin a deadly look, then sliced her victim's throat and spat on him. She stood up, her eyes blazing with anger. Wordlessly, Gaitan handed her her crossbow, and hurried back to Nika, avoiding her glare.

"What are we going to do with the bodies?" Nika asked.

"Leave them," Joplin grunted. "They're not real soldiers, they're a raiding party. They don't deserve anything. Once we cross, we hide the bridge and get as far away from here as we can, yes. We have to get to the next hiding place as quickly as possible."

Gaitan collected his helm, then pressed his boot against the dead soldier and wrenched his sword free, gasping from pain. Together, they hurried across the bridge. Nika turned back, and once again he lifted the bridge and returned it to its hiding spot, being sure that it couldn't be seen. It was much easier the second time, and the rocks felt much lighter in comparison.

"You're bleeding," Priye said sharply, pointing at both Nika and Gaitan.

Nika looked down, puzzled, and realised he'd been cut on his arm. He tore off the rest of his sleeve and held it to the cut.

"We'll worry about it after," Gaitan said, swinging into his saddle. "Let's get out of here."

The moon peeked out from behind the clouds, and together they galloped through the darkness with just enough light to see. Nika was too hyped up and on edge to feel the pain of his injury. He followed Joplin blindly until he finally held up his hand to stop. Joplin dismounted and poked around on the ground for a moment and fished out a piece of rope, then pulled on it. A panel disguised in dirt slid back revealing a deep dark ditch. Joplin dropped his rope and pointed inside.

"We'll need a light. Watch your step, yes."

Nika lit the way using his focus and led the others inside. They were in a roomy man-made dugout that had plenty of food and water for the horses. It smelt musty and damp, with the slightest hint of mouse or rat. Arnie's ears pricked up, and he stalked off into the darkness.

"We'll stay here for a day or two," Joplin said once he'd slid the panel back in place. "We'll be safe here, so long as we stay quiet, yes."

"Did you and your friends build this?" Nika asked.

"No. I heard about it from another smuggler," Joplin said. "It's used and maintained by a few different smuggling rings."

Nika opened his mouth to ask another question, but Priye caught his eye and pointed to a long bench seat. He sat obediently, not game to argue with her.

"You. Out of that armour, now," Priye barked.

Gaitan tried to remove his chainmail, but his rapidly diminishing strength left him panting. To Nika's surprise, Yger stepped forward and helped peel the gore-splattered armour from his body. His undershirt was a bloody mess. Yger drew one of her daggers, and Gaitan shied away from her. Wordlessly, she cut away his undershirt and pressed a wad of it to his wound, then guided him to the seat next to Nika.

Priye took one look at the hole in Gaitan's shoulder, then rummaged around in her bag. She mixed a few ingredients together into a potion, then helped him down it in one gulp.

"There you go, dear. This is going to dull the pain and make you sleepy."

Gaitan's eyes drooped and he swayed. Yger caught him and helped to lay him across the seat. Priye rolled up her sleeves and got to work.

"What a damned fool," Yger said, shaking her head. "At least he's a decent fighter. I expected far less from him."

"He might be a pain sometimes, but he's a good man," Priye said sternly.

"Whatever." Yger stalked off towards the horses.

Joplin moved about the dugout and lit several oil lanterns, and busied himself with lighting a fire. Nika extinguished the firestone, then carefully pulled back the blood-soaked cloth on his arm. Almost immediately, more blood oozed from the wound.

"Look at the butterflies," Gaitan slurred.

"Yes dear, they're pretty," Priye murmured as she sewed him up.

"Butterflies? I don't see any butterflies." Joplin frowned.

"He's just hallucinating." She shrugged.

"What did you give him?" Nika asked.

"Just a little something I borrowed from the infirmary at Endveraugh."

"You astound me, woman. First you steal horses, and now you're stealing medicine?"

"Hardly. Those glowing mushrooms grow wild in that cave. I just helped myself to some that were already dried and ready for use." She grinned. "Gaitan will just feel a little happy for a while and maybe see things. He's very lucky. Thanks to the mail, the blade missed the shoulder joint and didn't get in too deep. He should heal up ok.

As always, the main risk is infection, but I have plenty of medicinal alcohol to keep the wounds clean. All I need is for you lot to stop getting injured. There we go."

Joplin helped him sit up. Gaitan stared around with a goofy grin, reaching for things that weren't there with his good arm. As Yger stepped back into the light, he froze and gawked at her. Her hair was no longer long and purple; she'd changed it to a dark vibrant red that reached her shoulders, and her makeup was different, too.

"What?" she demanded.

"You're so beautiful," Gaitan said dreamily.

Yger's face hardened and her hand balled into a fist. Nika froze, half expecting her to draw a knife and stab him.

"Please don't kill him," Priye said with a sigh. "I've only just fixed him. He's still drugged up and isn't thinking clearly. Or maybe he is; you *are* beautiful. He's just telling the truth, so settle down."

Yger unclenched her fist, though she still looked peeved.

"Nika, your turn."

---

Gri'Ran's Gate was a massive structure that dwarfed even the spires of the Great Monastery of Am. Nika expected a simple wall no more than three or four storeys high, but in reality, it easily reached around twenty storeys, maybe more. His mind boggled at the sheer size of the ancient fortifications and how it could have possibly been built by hand. He couldn't imagine anyone trying to attack it; to breach such a thing would surely be impossible.

"Why did they build it so high?" Gaitan whispered in awe. He was almost back to his usual self, though he often winced in pain.

"To keep the giants out," Joplin replied. "Shh."

265

A mounted patrol trotted past, hardly paying attention to their surroundings. They laughed amongst themselves, and didn't notice anyone lurking behind an old storage shed. Once it was safe, Nika nodded to Joplin, and they crept towards the wall leading the horses. The large double-doors were sealed by a series of complex locks.

"The next challenge is unlocking this," Joplin whispered. "We can't break down the door because someone might notice and come after us. I can't pick it, either. I've tried in the past."

Gaitan pushed forward and helped himself. He picked the mechanism in no time.

"I thought you said it was a challenge," he whispered as he swung open the doors.

Joplin shook his head in disbelief and waved for everyone to go in. Inside was pitch black. Nika lit his firestone, enough for him and his friends to see. Just as they got the horses inside and closed the doors, he could hear another patrol galloping towards them. Joplin slid a heavy piece of wood across the back to reinforce them, then nodded.

If Nika was surprised about the outside, then he was gobsmacked by the inside. Directly in front of them was a large fenced-in platform with a gate, attached to an intricate pulley system; instead of a wheel or lever to activate it, though, there was an odd mechanism that looked out of place. Nika held up his focus and brightened it so he could see more. A flight of stairs to their right zig-zagged to the upper levels, and to their left, another flight led downstairs.

"Wow," Priye whispered.

"What's that?" Gaitan pointed at the platform.

"It's called an elevator," Joplin replied. "Troops, horses, weapons, anything can be loaded into it and hoisted to the top. They have them at the salt mines. Fascinating, yes."

"Ingenious," Yger agreed.

"Will it be safe to leave the horses here?" Nika asked.

"I think so." Joplin nodded. "Bring anything that is important just in case."

Nika unbuckled his pack then patted Streek on her nose.

"Don't worry. We'll be back soon," he said softly. He turned back to Joplin. "Are you sure you're comfortable with this? We'll be talking with a ghost, you know."

"You know how to handle them, and I trust you," he said simply.

Nika joined his mind with the focus almost subconsciously, and called Fin to him.

*"Yes, Master?"*

*"We're looking for King Radik. Please scout out a safe route for us."*

*"Yes, Master!"* Fin zoomed down the stairs and out of sight.

"This way."

Nika beckoned and led his friends in the direction that Fin went. The stairs were steep and narrow, with no safety rail to save them if they slipped over the edge. Nika put his hand on the wall to steady himself, and walked carefully, deep in thought. According to Joplin, it was a two week ride from one end of the gate to the other. Nika couldn't help but worry; what if Radik was all the way over on the Cadrinhal side?

They finally reached the bottom of the stairs, and once again Nika was blown away by the size and scale of Gri'Ran's Gate. They were in a cavern that stretched high above them, supported by thick arches. It led into a smaller tunnel with arches every few feet.

*"Master! I have found His Majesty. Ride the transporter to the bottom, and I can guide you from there,"* Fin said excitedly.

*"Transporter?"* Nika asked.

*"Follow this passage. You will see, My Lord."*

They came to another cavern, and there at the far side

was what Nika could only describe as a tram, though it was clear that it was anything but. It was constructed of thick wood, reinforced with steel and sheets of metal. The front and back were curved and had thick glass windows, built for speed. It had eight metal wheels and was affixed to rail-like tracks.

"What in the gods is that?" Joplin asked.

Nika ignored him and drifted towards it, a mix of fear and excitement tingling through him. He opened the door cautiously, and examined the dash. It had a mechanism similar to that of the elevator upstairs, but no controls or wheel for steering. He could feel the faintest trace of the realm, and instinctively probed at it with his mind. At once, he found a crystal mounted inside. He gently nudged it awake, and the tram lit up; a bright crystal in the ceiling shone light into the interior, and another mounted on the outside lit up the tracks in front. Nika grinned and looked back at the others.

"What are you smirking at?" Yger asked suspiciously.

"We're going for a ride. Get in, everyone. I'm in the front!"

Nika settled himself in the driver's seat, and looked behind. There were four passenger seats and a small space to sit their packs. Joplin and Priye sat behind him, leaving Yger and Gaitan to sit together.

"Strap yourselves in," Nika warned. He buckled the leather strap around his waist, being careful not to crush Arnie. "Is the door locked?"

"Yes. But what is this thing?" Joplin sounded scared.

"This is what I would call fun," Nika grinned. "Hold on. I think we're going to go really fast."

He looked down at the dash and concentrated on the crystal. In his mind's eye, he could make out three options for controlling the tram. The power from the crystal was flowing into the lights, but was yet to be connected to the main circuitry. Ever so gently, Nika rotated the crystal, and at once the tram vibrated to life. He rotated it once more, and it lurched into a gentle roll.

It moved slowly forward towards a narrow tunnel, where the tracks angled sharply downwards and disappeared into the darkness.

"Hold on," Nika warned. "Here we go."

The tram tilted forward, and then it was free; they coasted down a steep decline and deep into the bowels of the earth. Priye shrieked; Joplin swore at the top of his lungs, Gaitan screamed, and Yger clung onto him for dear life. Arnie's claws ripped new holes into Nika's flesh and growled.

Nika leaned back and rested his arms behind his head. The ride was smooth, and every so often the decline flattened out to help control the speed. A tang of homesickness hit him as he thought of the trains and rollercoasters he rode with his foster family, then shifted to his car that he would never drive again. The long drives through the countryside, with no care in the world.

His thoughts turned to Streek and the untouched countryside he'd passed through in the last year; the nights of sleeping under the twinkling sky with his friends, talking around the fire and sharing their stories. A warm feeling crept into his heart. The moments he'd spent in his new world were priceless, and he wouldn't trade them for anything.

*"Are you ok?"* Nika asked once Arnie stopped clawing him.

*"One does not like this one bit,"* Arnie hissed.

*"Relax. We're safe. I had no idea things could be powered by the realm, though. Did you know that?"*

*"One has heard of it, but before today, one had never experienced it,"* Arnie replied.

*"How does it work?"*

*"I am a cat, not an engineer. Ask your mate about it when we see him next. One is sure he will know."*

*"I wish he was here to experience this,"* Nika said, feeling his mood drop a little.

*"One would gladly swap with him."*

Nika wasn't sure which was worse: a sulking Joplin or a sulking cat. He glanced back at the others; they all looked terrified.

"You ok back there?"

"Shut it, yes." Joplin growled.

Yger quickly let go of Gaitan and crossed her arms. Nika could sense her embarrassment. He leaned back and relaxed. It was impossible to tell how fast they were traveling or how far they'd gone, let alone how long. Eventually Nika could feel the tram starting to slow, and soon they rolled to a stop. The light in the crystals flickered and died. Nika relit his firestone and held it up so they could see.

Joplin reefed open the door and everyone piled out. It was hot and stuffy, and Nika felt as though the earth was pressing in on him. Eerie noises echoed around them. In contrast to the wide open spaces above, the chamber they were in was narrow and had a low ceiling. In front of the tram was an empty track that disappeared in the opposite direction from which they came.

*"This way, Master."*

Nika turned and followed Fin's glowing orb through a narrow passage with the others shuffling nervously behind him. They passed several open offices and alcoves, then paused when the hall came to an abrupt end. Nika held up his focus to see better; to their left and right, wide arches led to sprawling dungeons on each side, lined with gruesome cells filled with nasty torture equipment. Nika's gut filled with dread. He could feel the torment and agony of those who suffered there thousands of years ago. In front of them was another flight of stairs. Fin shot ahead, and waited at the foot of the steps.

*"This is it, Master."* Fin said. *"His Majesty is through*

*there."*

Nika sat Arnie on the ground and steeled himself, then knocked lightly and opened the door. It was a small office with a few chairs scattered around, all of them facing a large, cluttered desk. The walls were lined with book cases, and some of the books lay on the floor as though dropped in a hurry. Nika stepped inside and beckoned to the others to join him.

Behind the desk, a shimmering mist appeared and swirled, and slowly morphed into the shape of King Radik. Besides the revenants they saw at Loralyon, Nika had never seen a real ghost before. The ethereal king stood up, and Nika bowed deeply.

"Your Majesty..."

"Spare me the formalities. I know who thou art, Nickolai. I hast only been waiting three thousand years to talk to thee. Or was it four? Sit down, yes."

King Radik's voice was just as gruff as Joplin's, only his accent was much thicker. Nika did as he was told, and lifted Arnie-Kyn onto his lap. King Radik drifted through the desk, seemingly oblivious to the solid object in his path, and began floating backwards and forwards along the front of them. Joplin was staring it him with a mixture of fear and awe. Finally, the king stopped and faced them again.

"Where's thy lover?" he asked abruptly. "Don't tell me thou hast had a fight already."

"What? No!" Nika felt his cheeks grow hot. "Freyne had other business to attend to."

"What business? He should be here with thee."

"He went to Drarlum so we could get word to the kings of the Isles," Nika replied. "Then he was heading south to the Forest of Llunn. Saramas told him to go there and I have no idea why."

"Ah, I see. Those bloody necromancers are always sticking their noses into things." Radik crossed his ghostly arms and leant against his desk. "The problem with humans is they always think they can cheat their fate. They will try anything, no matter how irrational their ideas are. Fear of death, fear of not being in control. We can always count on humanity to be selfish and hold themselves above the rest of their race."

"You're talking about Khel, aren't you?" Nika asked.

"The Miscreant is one of those, yes. But there were countless others, too. Long before the gods we know came here, long before the time of the ancients. Our history is as ripe with iniquitous rabble, as is thine. He is not the first, nor wilt he be the last, yes."

"Did you know Du'Rakis lied – "

"DO NOT SPEAK THAT NAME BEFORE ME!" Radik roared; he shifted and transformed into a terrifying dark wraith with glowing red eyes and sharp teeth, and brought his face an inch from Nika's. Nika held Radik's glare, unwilling to show even the tiniest hint of weakness. He could feel Radik's anger mixed with a deep pain of loss and longing to be free. Arnie hissed and growled, and took a swipe with his sharp claws at the dead king.

King Radik looked down at Arnie, and for a moment something passed between them, silent words or understanding. Radik turned abruptly and faced his desk, his shoulders shuddering from silent ghostly sobs. Nika stole a glance at the others; they were staring wide-eyed at the king, clearly frightened. Joplin's arm was around Priye protectively, and Yger had a fresh bolt loaded in her crossbow, ready to fire.

After several awkward minutes, Radik returned to his former size, and turned to face them again. He sighed and shook his head.

"Forgive me. I hast spent the last thousand and more years roaming this fortress, alone, watching the world pass by around me. To witness the horrors of my visions play out one after another, powerless to reach out and stop them. My dear brother, my only friend and companion, was murdered by that sack of excrement. Rakis held me as I took my last shuddering breath and died right here in his arms.

"I stayed in this forsaken place for a year until that idiot biblioklept busted in and helped himself to my work. For I knew those fools wouldn't obey mine orders to stay away, oh no. Another foolish mortal pawn who played into this mess and made everything much worse than it had to be. One can never count on people to do the right thing."

Radik resumed his pacing. Nika shifted slightly on his chair, a question hovering on the tip of his tongue. He steeled himself and took a deep breath.

"That prophecy was just one tiny piece of a much larger one, wasn't it?" he asked pointedly.

"Thou art more intuitive than I gave thee credit for." Radik stroked his ethereal beard and leant back on his desk. "Critical thinking and analysis are a rare thing indeed, and worth rewarding. I shalt tell thee how it all works, though I doubt thou wilt like it. Let me begin with the basic building blocks of the world: nature.

"For all her beauty and grace, nature is quite flawed. Rather than focusing on improving that which already exists, she is constantly creating new life in an attempt to achieve her one and only goal, which as thou knowest, is balance. The juxtaposition between life and death, day and night, right and wrong. It's an unending cycle.

"Humans are probably her greatest flaw, yes. We lie, cheat, bend the rules, we're selfish and flat out refuse to do the right thing. Each and every one of us is, or has the potential to be, the next Ami'Khel. It's these idiots who are blunderous and set off a chain of events that can take thousands of years to fix, yes.

"My research led me to discover that many civilisations have risen and collapsed over the millennia, and we have indeed had gods here long before Am and Gri'Ran agreed to come. For instance, the war against the savages, the very reason this gate was built, was caused by one man who refused to see other races as equals. These cells were overflowing with all sorts of non-human species who suffered unspeakable horrors. Once beautiful peaceful races who survived for eons, all tortured and murdered, all due to one man's prejudice."

Radik paused, and his face grew sad.

"Rakis spent many years down here in secret, attempting to placate the thousands of miserable souls who were left behind. One by one, he helped them to move on and finally rest in peace. After my death, he would sit here with me and keep me company in between his research. Occasionally when he was to travel, he would bind me to him just so I didn't have to stay here alone. He kept me hidden from the other necromancers so I could have peace from their meddling.

"Back to my story about nature, and thy question. The gift, or curse, of sight was another of nature's creations to cover her mistake, yes. She gifted it to a select few in hopes that we could stop bad things from happening. Predictably, she trusted people to do the right thing, and of course they abused it. Some claimed they held the gift and wrote false prophecies just for financial gain, and others went so far as to use their visions for political advantage. Things got ugly.

"The gods met with one another and decided they needed to take things into their own hands. Those folk with sight were forced to make an oath to use their gift ethically and within a strict set of rules. Any deviation of those rules would lead to death and banishment from the afterlife.

"After Am and Gri'Ran left this world and returned to the Crystal Heavens, their control over their people lessened, and once again things slowly got out of hand, yes. Well, at the tender age of fourteen I had my first vision. Shortly after, I was visited by Gri'Ran in spiritual form. I was told that I had a great task ahead of me, and that my life would be complicated and long. And thus I too became a pawn in this story."

Radik drifted towards one of the book cases, passing directly through Gaitan.

"Hey!" Gaitan sprang to his feet and wrapped himself in his arms.

The king ignored him, and reached out to take an innocent-looking scroll wedged into one of the shelves. His hand passed through it, and he sighed.

"Take that scroll when we are done. It contains my entire vision up until this very point in time. I cannot see what happens beyond this moment."

Nika lifted Arnie into his arms and joined Radik at the case. The scroll was thick and tightly bound.

"What about the copy Freyne studied for all those years?" Nika asked.

"That, and the other copies written by the seers, are all abridged versions of this one main vision. No one could be trusted with the entire thing, so it was broken up into sections, and pawns were selected along the way to ensure things went smoothly."

"You talk about this as though we are all pieces in a chess game," Nika said pointedly.

"Ahh, chess. That's an adequate analogy, yes. We are all living in a giant game of chess, and right now we are down to the last crucial players. On one hand, we have the Miscreant, his generals, and his armies. On the other, we have thee and Christophe, and thy friends. The only difference is that the gods have been moving thy pieces up until now. The Miscreant controls his own pieces, yes. So from here on, it's up to thee which way this goes. Sooner or later, either Khel or thee will be forced into check mate. For the hope of humanity, we must hope it is not thee."

Nika sank back into his chair, his mind numb. He

really was just another pawn in someone's sick game. *Always trust Am, for only they can see the bigger picture,* he frowned.

"So you're telling me that once we leave here, we're on our own?" he asked.

"Nay, I did not say that. What I meant was that now, thou art in charge of making the next move. This game is now between Khel and thee, no one else. Everything going forward will be about thee and he meeting at the right time for the final confrontation. And *that,* my dear Nickolai, is why I hast waited four thousand years for thee."

"Four thousand years to tell me I'm just another token in a game that ultimately doesn't matter," Nika grated, his frustration getting the better of him. "I have no idea where to find Khel. We've come all this way based on the mere assumption that we'll find him and put a stop to all this shit he's causing. Everyone seems to know what the fuck is going on except for me, and all I keep getting fed is pissy little scraps here and there. I'm sick of it! I'm sick of the riddles and the subtle little clues. This isn't even my world *or* my problem! If everyone would just stop dancing around and tell me what I need to know, maybe I can get this over and done with so we can all go back to our damn lives!"

"Ah, there it is. I was worried that thou wert born without a backbone, yes. Listen closely, for what I have to say next will guide thee towards the next step of thy journey, yes."

Nika crossed his arms and listened, doing his best to absorb as much of Radik's story as possible. The king repeated the story that Joplin told him, only with much greater detail.

"And now, onto thy problem with the rifts. Tell me, dost thou knowest what a tendril is?"

"No." Nika shook his head.

"A tendril is a natural phenomenon which occurs in just a few places around the world. They are places where the forces of the realms converge and gather. Some believed it was a leak in the realm, but Rakis thought they were places where once-great structures stood as gateways to other worlds. Tendrils allow mancers to draw much more from the realm with less consequence, which means they can perform much greater magic.

"There is a tendril on Mount Rakis, and thou guessed correctly that there is also a rift there. It's not an ordinary rift, though. It's powerful, and while it remains open, it allows him to use smaller portals across the world without any effort. Once thou close that rift, Khel's ability to travel will be greatly hindered."

"And then what?" Nika asked.

"What happens then will be up to thee, yes. But I reiterate; thou shalt not be alone. Thou hast thy friends, thy lover, the kings and their armies, the necromancers as painful as they art, and of course thy god. Each and everyone in this room – and those who aren't here with us – were chosen to help thee along the way. Keep thy friends close, for there is no way thou can face him alone."

"Ok. Anything else I should know before I walk out that door?" Nika frowned.

"Yes. I have seen a number of alternative endings play out in my dreams. Some of them pleasant, some of them not so. While different, they all have one thing in common, yes. We are on the eve of the birth of a new god, and the outcome of this war shalt determine if they are benign or evil. For the love of all mankind, we all must pray for the former."

"One final question," Nika said. "What is so important in your brother's research that Khel is looking for?"

"My brother studied many things, so his research covers different areas and disciplines. It is impossible to know which one Khel is planning to use for his next move."

"Ok. Consider this my next move then. I want a list of each and every topic your brother was researching plus context. From this point on, I'm not blundering along blindly anymore!"

Radik grinned and clapped his hands, though they made no sound.

"Very good. Thou art learning, see? Take the third book on the fourth shelf down from that bookcase. It contains a summary of his projects to help keep his work organised. Thou hast made thy move, so now it's Khel's turn, yes."

*20*

*H*e walked through the forest, surrounded by narrow teaks that shot straight towards the sky, the canopy high above. There was no underbrush, just a thin layer of soft green grass and moss. Somewhere up ahead, it called to him, drawing him ever closer.

The deeper into the forest he walked, the closer together the trees became, until the canopy grew thicker and shrouded him in darkness. The teaks were soon joined by beautiful ancient mahoganies and oaks, and lemon myrtles with their soft white blossoms released their citrusy tang into the pure air. He paused to inhale the crisp scent of the leaves, then continued along his path.

A gentle whisper reached him as the breeze ruffled the canopy, and left a soft humming noise in his ears. He walked deeper and deeper, the hum growing louder and the trees growing more ancient. When he thought he could walk no more, he stepped into a clearing, and stopped.

There in front of him was an enormous tree, wider than a house and as old as the earth itself. The humming sound was louder and coming from the ancient wonder. He walked closer and laid his hand on the bark, feeling a deep love pulsating in his heart.

"My dear child, I have found you." The humming turned into words, words spoken by the tree itself. "I thought you were lost forever. Rest easy, child. You are home now."

*"I don't understand. Who and what are you? Where am I? Am I dead?"*

*"You are far from dead, my child. It is time for you to awaken fully and take the first breath of your life as it should be. But first, you need to wake up."*

*"Huh?"*

*"Wake up, Freyne. It's time."*

Freyne's eyes shot open, and at once a dull pain radiated from his back and made him groan. He was staring up at the leaves of an oak tree, the gentle hint of lemon myrtle still on the edge of his senses. His entire body was stiff, as though he'd been sleeping for a long time. He tried to move his hand, but his fingers hurt. Freyne felt himself starting to panic, and tried frantically to look around and see where he was.

A face appeared above him, one tinged with green and a gentle expression. Her hair was long and golden, a leafy twig woven into her locks. She studied him for a moment, then smiled and rested the back of her hand on his forehead. She said something, a series of clicks and growls, but all Freyne could do was look at her helplessly. She then frowned and pointed upwards, signalling something he couldn't understand.

The woman's expression showed her frustration, and she pointed instead at the trees and skies, and then to her mouth. She wriggled her fingers above her head, then sighed and dropped her arms to her side, shaking her head. Freyne scrunched his eyes closed. The humming noise was grating on him, and the pain in his back was growing worse.

A gentle tugging pulled at his exhausted mind, and before he could resist, he felt himself pulled half-into the highest realm. At once, the humming cleared and turned into voices. It felt different, but for the first time he was able to use the realm without leaving his body. He opened his eyes once more, his vision lightly overlayed with the realm. The woman's smile returned and she patted him gently on the shoulder.

"This is better, no?"

"Who are you? Where am I?" Freyne demanded.

"I am Ak-Naar. I am healer. When you can stand, I take you to chifa."

"What happened to me?"

"Battle in sky. Dragon and wyvern fought, you fell." She pointed to the sky and made hand gestures to demonstrate her words.

Freyne grimaced and tried to think. For a moment he was blank, but then the memories of Ruke and the dragon slowly trickled back. He felt his heart quicken, and he tried to sit up. She rested her hand on his chest and held him down.

"Not yet. Your body still broken."

"Is Ruke ok?" Freyne asked.

"Ruke?"

"The wyvern. Is he ok?"

"I think so." She shrugged and disappeared from his view, then returned holding an earthen mortar and pestle. "Drink this, and then you sit up."

Ak-Naar held the bowl to his lips and helped him sip the liquid. It was as vile as one of Priye's concoctions. He frowned, certain there was more he was forgetting. The medicine burnt all the way to his belly, and the heat radiated to the rest of his body, numbing the pain almost instantly. Ak-Naar moved silently around him, massaging his limbs gently one at a time until he could move them on his own. It wasn't until she lifted his leg that he realised he was naked.

"Where are my clothes?" he asked.

"Had to cut them off," she replied, moving to massage his neck and shoulders. "Healing powers don't work through human fabrics. Try and sit up. Slowly."

Freyne planted his hands and attempted to push himself up. His arms were surprisingly weak, and almost collapsed under his weight. Ak-Naar caught him and guided him upright. His head spun and his stomach heaved.

"Wait here. I return soon."

Ak-Naar grasped a thick vine and swung away. It was only then that Freyne glanced around, and realised he was perched on a thick branch of a tree high above the ground. He wiped a thin veil of sweat from his forehead and noticed his hands were shaking. All around him in the trees and moving between the trunks far below, were more of the scantily-clad green people, going about their business with no care in the world.

A scratchy sound drew his attention, and he turned just as one of the strange folk climbed onto his branch and crouched, eyeing Freyne with the curiosity of a child. His hair was blacker than night, and the lack of hair on his chest had Freyne guessing he was barely fifteen.

"Can I help you?" Freyne asked.

The boy edged closer and tentatively reached out and poked Freyne's foot, then scrambled out of reach. Freyne couldn't help but grin at his innocence.

"Ip-Tok! Go away!" Ak-Naar landed on the branch and scolded him.

The boy's eyes bulged, and he scurried down the trunk as fast as he could move.

"What's his problem?" Freyne asked.

Ak-Naar tossed Freyne a flimsy garment woven of fine leaves and grasses, and gestured for him to put it on.

"Very few of us have seen a living human," she said. "Usually intruders are killed long before they reach A'Llun'bar. Now come. The chifa demands to meet you."

Freyne pulled on the garment and stood slowly, holding onto the tree for support as his head spun again. It fit him snug, and was just enough to cover his nether regions and backside. He reached up to scratch his cheek, and was surprised that he was freshly shaven. As he pulled his hand away, he paused and stared at his fingers. The image of Nika flooded into his mind, and he felt a pang of guilt as he realised he'd forgotten all about him.

"Where's my ring?" he demanded. "I swear to my god, if you have lost it..."

"Calm yourself. It's right there." She pointed to where it hung on a twig. "You are lucky. It came off when you landed. The warriors found it."

Freyne snatched it and inspected it. The ring was undamaged; he slipped it back into place on his finger and gathered himself.

"I'm sorry. I guess we should go then?"

Ak-Naar smiled and pointed at a swinging seat on the end of a vine, connected to a winch.

"You too weak to climb. Sit, I lower you."

Freyne did as he was told, and Ak-Naar lowered him carefully to the ground. The grass that carpeted the forest floor was soft underfoot and tingled his senses. Ak-Naar swung down the vine and landed silently next to him. She was slightly taller than him, and wore nothing other than a covering across her breasts and a short leafy sarong. Freyne marvelled at her beauty. She wordlessly took his hand and led him through the trees. Her hand felt warm and comforting in his, and filled him with the encouragement he needed.

As he glanced around, he recalled his dream; everything looked almost the same, except for the green people stopping to stare at him, some in fright and some in wonder. They were roughly his height, some slightly taller, and all dressed in the woven garments of their culture.

For each step he took, pain shot into the middle of his back. Freyne gritted his teeth and willed himself to keep going, one step after another. He needed answers, and he wasn't going to give up until he had them. The path widened, and there in front of them was the enormous tree of his dream in all its glory. The Ancient One. Freyne gazed up at it, feeling the power radiating from deep within its core. He longed to step forward and touch it, talk to it, learn its secrets.

"Halt!"

Around a dozen warriors pointed their spears at his neck, breaking his reverie. Freyne glanced around slowly and realised he was surrounded by warriors.

"Bring it to me," a man's voice ordered.

The warriors lowered their spears, and two of them linked their arms with Freyne's and escorted him through a crowd. They stopped in front of their chifa, a hunched over old man leaning on a gnarled cane, his hair and beard whiter than the purest snow. Freyne was forced to his knees, and he gasped as the pain became almost unbearable. Ak-Naar hissed something in their language and slapped one of the warriors in the face.

"I am Tog-Ur. Humans are not welcome here. You killed our people and drove us from our land." The chifa glared at him, then turned to a group of warriors who stood to one side. "Ikk, why did you bring it here? And more importantly, why did you use healing powers on it, Ak-Naar? Explain yourselves!"

"Look at it closer, Tog-Ur." Ikk grunted.

"I don't *want* to look at it," Tog-Ur said angrily.

"He, not it!" Ak-Naar stalked closer to the chifa and pointed back at Freyne. "Look into his eyes! We cannot kill one of our own, you know the laws. LOOK AT HIM!"

Tog-Ur glared at her, and raised his hand to strike her. The warriors standing with Ikk raised their spears and pointed them at the chifa.

"Do it, or we will send you for trial," Ikk hissed. "Don't make us summon the elders!"

They held each other's glare for a moment, then Tog-Ur threw up his hand in defeat. He stomped across the clearing to where Freyne knelt, and bent over, scrutinising his face. As their eyes locked, the chifa's expression changed to one of shock, and he stumbled backwards.

"No. It can't be!" he gasped.

"Will someone tell me what in the gods is going on?" Freyne snapped.

"Bring him." Tog-Ur said abruptly. "There is only one way to verify this."

"Gently!" Ak-Naar added.

Freyne was helped to his feet and guided deeper into the forest with Tog-Ur leading the way. They walked in silence for a while, then stopped in a seemingly random stretch of forest. The chifa turned to Freyne and stared at him expectantly, though Freyne had no idea what he was expected to do or say. A soft whisper reached him from the realm, and instinctively he reached his mind out to join with it. The voice belonged to a presence that filled his heart with the purest joy he'd ever felt.

*"Freyne, my fina. Welcome home."*

He turned to his left, and was met by a twisted mahogany tree. Freyne took a painful step so he could see behind it, and his eyes fell on a thick majestic oak with sprawling branches. She was the most beautiful tree he'd ever seen, and without a doubt he knew she was a part of him. He walked towards her, ignoring the hisses and grunts from the green people, and stared up at her in awe. The tree's leaves were shaking, even though there was no breeze. He rested his hand on her bark, and warmth immediately radiated into the rest of his body.

*"Perhaps you can tell me what all of this is about?"* Freyne asked hopefully.

*"You have been lost to us for over a thousand years,"* the tree whispered. *"Every other tree had their guardian except for me. At last we are one as we should be."*

"It is true," Tog-Ur said behind him. "I apologise for my rudeness. Welcome home."

Freyne reluctantly removed his hand from the tree and turned to the red-faced chifa.

"Can someone *please* tell me what this is all about?" he pleaded.

Tog-Ur motioned to everyone to sit. Freyne sat with his back against the tree and crossed his arms, waiting. The warmth of their contact flowed into his back, easing his pain and filling him with something else he couldn't identify.

"We are the last of the A'Llun'bar dryads. We once numbered millions, and our forests spread across what is now Cadrinhal and Drarlum. Our people once lived in harmony with humans and shared our forests with them. We allowed them to hunt in our territory, and they allowed us to have a say in some of the laws and treaties that would impact us. We lived in perfect balance for generations.

"One day, a new king took charge, and decided to start clearing the land. He murdered large areas of our once beautiful rainforests, and then ordered us to leave. That king declared us savages, and in just a few years, overturned most of the laws protecting us. There was a war, and many of us were slaughtered."

"I've studied that war," Freyne said quietly. "It was horrendous, even from the human perspective. I'm so sorry."

"Our stories are passed on from generation to generation. It hurts as much for us as it did for our ancestors. Our pain will never truly heal." Tog-Ur paused and wiped his eyes. "To my knowledge, there are but three tribes remaining. Us, the U'Dav'lar who reside within the borders of pygmy territory, and the O'Gant'tok who's location is unknown. Our once great race now numbers under one hundred thousand."

"Have any of your people ever gone in search of the other tribes?" Freyne asked.

Tog-Ur shook his head.

"No. We are too scared to leave our boundaries. If humans discover that we still live, they may try and wipe us out for good. But enough about that. I must know. What happened to your mother?"

"My mother? She was killed over seven hundred years ago," Freyne said bitterly. "Why?"

"Do you not know about your heritage?" Tog-Ur asked incredulously.

Freyne shook his head. He could feel his frustration growing, but resisted the urge to snap.

"I have no idea what you are talking about. I don't even know why I was brought here."

"Your mother was a dryad, one of us. She ran away when she was young, and never returned. For many years her tree flourished, and yours soon sprouted. When hers died, we wondered if we would ever find you. Us younger dryads always scoffed and believed it was just a story, but no, it was true all along. You are dryad. You are the Lost Child."

The words hit him hard, and Freyne stared around him in disbelief.

"Dryad?" he asked, his head spinning. "I think you have me confused with someone else. Sorry to disappoint you."

"No. We are not mistaken." Tog-Ur shook his head. "You are a man of faith, as was your father."

"How could you possibly know that?"

"The story goes that a missionary of Am ventured close to our forest. Your mother saw him and they fell instantly in love. She brought him back here, but he was shunned and sent away. They only spared his life because she threatened to take her own if they killed him. He was escorted to the edge of our territory and banished. Your mother snuck out through our sentries that night and followed him, and she never returned."

"My father was a monk from the Monastery of Am

on a tiny isle to the East," Freyne said quietly. "They were some of the founders who built our village away from the hustle of the University. It was a beautiful village, too, hidden deep in a forest, until it was destroyed. But what's so important about me? And why would my parents keep this from me?"

"One of the legends passed down through our oral histories speaks of a lost child, a child who Am chose as their own, who will one day return to us. And when he does, he will be the one who reunites the lost tribes and brings them back together. Half human, half dryad. He will save us from extinction, and his name is known to all voices of nature. His name is Freyne."

Freyne's head was pounding, and he massaged his temples in an attempt to think clearly.

"That's enough," Ak-Naar barked. "He needs rest. Give him time to adjust."

"Very well." Tog-Ur stood and motioned to his warriors to do the same. "When you are ready, come and find me at the Ancient One. We will talk then."

Freyne nodded wearily and waited for the dryads to leave. Ak-Naar smiled and reached out her hand to help him up.

"There's just so much I don't understand."

"Like I said, you need time to adjust. Get to know your tree and explore who you really are. I go now. I will come and get you when it is time to eat."

"Wait. What happened to my pack?" he frowned.

"I'll have someone bring it to you. Rest up, now."

Ak-Naar glided away before he could ask any more questions, leaving Freyne alone with his racing thoughts. He turned back to his tree, and was once again struck by her beauty.

*"What now?"* he asked blankly.

*"Come and join with me. We have much to discuss."*

Freyne glanced around, feeling foolish. He was no

dryad; surely the chifa had him confused with someone else. And yet, as he reached out and touched the tree once more, he felt that same warmth envelop him, the sense of belonging. His curiosity got the better of him, and before he could change his mind, he climbed cautiously up the trunk to the lowest branch.

He stood on the limb, feeling the warmth spread through his bare feet and into the rest of him. Instead of pain in his back, he felt an odd tingling sensation. He stretched, feeling his strength returning, and scrambled higher up the tree to a wide fork. Freyne nestled in and leaned back against the bark. He closed his eyes, listening to the sounds around him.

*"Is it all true?"* He asked after a while.

*"Of course it is. Surely you realise that your affinity with the highest realm is far beyond the abilities of a human, mancer or not. Haven't you wondered why you can climb trees so easily where others would surely struggle?"*

*"I just thought everyone could do it."* Freyne thought back to his childhood for a moment, the short period where he was allowed to play with the other children in his village before he was sent to the Monastery. With a start, he recalled that none of the other children could climb like he could.

*"See? It is all true, fina. You are definitely a dryad or we wouldn't be having this conversation."*

*"Do you have a name?"*

*"I am one with you, so we share your name. Your dryad name, that is"*

Freyne thought for a moment, then frowned.

*"Wait a minute. Saramas said that Du means 'conqueror of.' I have Du in my name, too."*

*"Different languages have different meanings. Yours is a mix of human and dryad, that's all. It probably means something like 'beloved Freyne.' You could call me Lau which means tree in one of the ancient languages."*

"*Lau also means old or aged in native Thorington tongue,*" Freyne mused. "*Can I call you Lau?*"

"*Of course.*"

Freyne let out a deep breath.

"*Ok. Am obviously wanted me to come here for a reason,*" he said slowly, speaking his thoughts in an attempt to piece them all together. "*Why now, though? The world is on the brink of war. I need to get back to Nika, but instead I am here. There has to be a reason for this.*"

"*It will all come clearer when the time is right,*" Lau said wisely. "*You have been listening to the voices of nature your entire life. You know how cryptic they are, and you know how important it is to be patient. You have done well all these years, so a little longer won't hurt.*"

"*How does all this work?*" Freyne asked as another thought came to him. "*Have you been watching me from afar for all this time, or do we share my knowledge and experiences?*"

"*From afar. The bond of a dryad and their tree is absolute. I have watched you grow even as I grow, and I've felt your pain as deeply as you do. I feel your love for Nickolai and your deep longing to return to him.*"

"*How will I get back to him? Ruke is gone, and if I have to walk, it will take me months and months. I can't wait that long.*" Worry stirred inside him; the thought of being sidelined while Nika faced Du'Rakis alone struck fear in his heart. He'd already been away for too long.

"*Come on, my fina. You know to trust in Am, so calm your fears and your mind. You will be back with Nickolai soon enough. For now, sit back and rest. I think tonight will be a little wild and you will need your strength.*"

---

The clearing surrounding the Ancient One was packed with thousands of dryads, all eager to catch a look at their half-human guest. Freyne sat with his head bowed, already uncomfortable from all of the attention he was receiving. The dryads chattered noisily, their excitement ringing through the trees. One after another they walked up to Freyne just to touch or poke him. He grimaced, already wishing the evening was over.

"Are you ok, fina?" Ak-Naar asked.

"What's fina?" Freyne scowled.

"It means cherished one," she said simply. "You haven't touched your food."

"It's a bit hard with everyone staring and poking me," he grumbled. "Are dryads always so touchy-feely?"

"It's just the way we are. We feel through our skin, so to touch someone is to be one with their spirit. They're all excited and want to know you. We don't get to celebrate often. Only when new trees sprout."

Seven older dryads picked their way through the seated crowd, and at once the dryads grew quiet. Freyne dared himself to look up, and was relieved that the focus was no longer on him. Tog-Ur stood, and greeted each of them by gently touching his forehead to theirs in turn.

"Those are our elders, our guiding fathers," Ak-Naar whispered. "Chifa handles all minor issues of the tribe. Elders make big important decisions."

"Ok," he whispered back.

The elders turned and gazed at Freyne, and one of them held out his hands. Ak-Naar nudged him to stand up. Once again, all eyes were on him, and he stood up awkwardly, worried that he'd do something to embarrass himself. With a start, he suddenly understood why Nika was so shy and awkward at times. Not knowing how to behave in a foreign situation was nerve-wracking for sure.

"Welcome home, Freyne," the kindly old man smiled at him warmly. "I knew it was you the moment I saw you. I am Cayne."

One by one, the elders stepped forward and greeted him the same way they greeted Tog-Ur, and introduced themselves. Once the introductions were out of the way, Cayne pointed to the ground and they all sat in a circle.

"We know you have been through a lot these last few days," Cayne said softly. "We also acknowledge that our ways may be strange to you. Do not be shy, fina."

"Thank you." Freyne nodded politely. "It has been overwhelming to be honest."

"I know." Cayne rested his hands on his knees and shot Freyne a warm smile. "You have been told about the legend of the Lost Child I presume?"

"Yes. Tog-Ur told me about it earlier."

"I'm sure you are wondering how you are expected to reunite our tribes when it is something we ourselves have not been able to do. Sadly, there is nothing we can do. It cannot be done."

Freyne nodded.

"By now you have come to learn that we use the nature realm to communicate," Cayne continued. "We were once able to talk to the other tribes from afar. Something happened, though, and we were no longer able to join our minds with them. The rest of the tribes have since been lost to us. But not only that. For the longest time, it was possible to pass between the sacred trees of our tribes. The Ancient One could teleport us to her siblings, saving us from risky travel through human territory. As you can guess, this is no longer possible."

"What happened?" Freyne asked.

"Something unnatural blocks the power that the Ancient One draws from," Cayne said sadly. "Until that thing is sent away, we cannot travel."

"Are you talking about Ami'Khel and a rift?"

Cayne looked deep into Freyne's eyes, and at once he felt their minds join. Images of a mountain peak flashed in his mind, and he watched as a man wearing black robes opened what could only be a large rift. He felt his jaw drop open, and Cayne severed their connection.

"We do not know those words. Do these images help?"

"Where is that?" Freyne choked.

"It lies to the north-west of here, beyond the death wall," Cayne replied.

"I wonder if Nika knows about it yet," Freyne said, feeling his heart start beating a little faster. "He and our friends are hopefully on their way there to close – send it away. I just hope he's figured it out already."

"This is wonderful news!" Bog-Ur, another of the elders, threw his hands into the air. "If your friend can indeed fix this, we might be able to reunite with the other tribes after all."

The elders and some of the dryads around them who were listening started talking excitedly amongst each other. Freyne held up his hand.

"Not so fast. There is something else you should know."

The clearing fell silent, and all eyes were once again glued to Freyne.

"What is it, fina?" Cayne asked.

"This world is once again on the brink of war. The humans are gathering their forces and marching to the far north." The elders' faces grew stern. Freyne held up his hand again, and continued. "I am not asking you to fight in this war. I would never do that after how humanity has treated you. I'm just saying that I wish we could warn U'Dav'lar and O'Gant'tok to start preparing to defend themselves should the war spill into their territory. Are we allied with the pygmies?"

"The pygmies are our friends and have sworn to protect U'Dav'lar. They defend their borders against humans and kill any trespassers on sight," Bog-Ur replied. "Let's not discuss this now. We don't want to scare the youngers."

"Agreed," Cayne nodded. "We shall meet tomorrow. Tonight is about celebrating. Let us pour the myrtle wine and dance!"

# 21

Nika was quiet as the tram sped back towards the upper reaches of Gri'Ran's Gate. A part of him felt used, manipulated like a puppet, and he wasn't sure how to feel about it. His life somehow felt like a lie; had he ever truly been in control, or was that a lie, too?

"*We need to talk,*" he said to Arnie, ignoring the claws digging into him once more.

"*What ails you, human?*"

"*I feel so… lost. The gods, necromancers, seers, everyone saw this coming and knew what would happen up until this point. So why would Am give me the choice to come back to life if they already knew I'd say yes?*"

"*You may have noticed that nature often has trouble recognising her flaws. She puts a lot of love and care into her creations, but in doing so she trusts blindly. She has never been able to understand the unpredictable behaviour of humanity, and this has constantly been the cause of problems since she created them.*

"*The vision we see is not absolute, and can be altered as we have seen time and time again. The pawns as Radik calls them are chosen long before they are born, and although they are assigned their destiny, they do not always choose that path. Just like Khel. He didn't want to go through with the pact of his bloodline, so he chose to walk away from that path. Am* knows this, and so they were giving you the chance to decide your fate. One of Am's teachings is that each and every person should have control over their choices in life, as their body is their own and no one has a right to interfere.

"Those pawns are chosen, yes, but they also get to choose whether or not to go along with it. Look at Priye, for instance. She made her decision at Riz'Hra to stay with us when she could have returned to her normal life. Lana chose to come with us, even though one would assume that she was ordered to by Iryna. Each of our friends could have easily said no and walked away."

Arnie retracted his claws and poked his head through Nika's cloak. Nika scratched behind his ears as he mulled over Arnie's words.

"Why couldn't Am just tell me directly what to do? Why did I have to stumble along blindly all this time just to be told by a necromancer and a ghost? I just don't understand."

"Simple. You were not ready to confront Khel yet. There were still too many pieces on the board for you to be successful." Arnie repositioned himself and looked up into Nika's eyes. "Assuming the chess of your world is the same as this world, Saramas and Radik are two of the important pieces, as are all your friends and your mate. Each move must be executed at the right time and in the right way, lest Khel take more of our pieces. The difference to this game, though, is you can add more pieces to the board, as can he. You've already taken his remaining cultists and turned them to your side, and you've added in the kings and their armies. Remember, it is now up to you to add the pieces you need, and capture or kill those from Khel's side of the board."

"I'm so scared," Nika admitted, biting his lip. "One wrong move and it's all over. How can anyone trust me to hold so many lives in the palm of my hand? I suck at chess."

"Who would you rather trust, then? Joplin perhaps?"

"Hell no," Nika said quickly. He paused and thought hard, before it dawned on him. "There is no one else, is there?"

*"No. Not even Freyne would be suited for that decision. You need to trust in yourself, believe in who you are. Am wouldn't have chosen you to be their champion piece were you not up to the task."*

Nika pulled Arnie from his cloak and cradled him in his arms. The cat's tail whipped around irritably, though Nika could hear him purring softly. The tram climbed and climbed, and soon it reached the top of the incline and slowed to a stop. He wordlessly followed the others out of the tram and slipped his pack over his shoulder, being careful not to drop Arnie or knock the cut on his arm.

With one final glance at the transporter, Nika summoned a small ball of fire to light their way and set it to hover above them. He beckoned to his friends, and together they made the long trek back up the stairs to the horses.

Streek snorted and shook her head as Nika made it to the top step. He immediately went to her and patted her neck. A soft trickle of light filtered through the cracks in the door and from somewhere high above them. Nika yawned and sat Arnie down on the ground.

"Is anyone hungry?" Priye asked.

"Starved." Joplin nodded. "Where do we go next?"

"We go across Radik's Crossing and head to the peak," Nika answered. "Do you know how to get to the other side of the gate?"

"No. From my understanding, the gate is solid stone. There are no doors or tunnels through so it cannot be breached. My guess would be up, yes."

Nika nodded, and called Fin to him.

*"Yes, Master?"*

*"We need a way to get to the other side of this wall. Follow that elevator to the top and see if there's a safe way to get across."*

*"Sure thing, My Lord."*

"Let's rest up and have a bite to eat while Fin finds us

a safe path," Nika said, yawning again.

Priye handed everyone a thick slice of fruity damper each, then sat with Nika against the wall and ate in silence. He closed his eyes, feeling the fatigue from the last few days catching up to him.

*"If'gur!"* Yger swore loudly.

"What's wrong?" Joplin and Priye asked at the same time.

"My crossbow is jammed," Yger grumbled. "Usually I can fix it myself, but I think it's broken this time."

"Show me." Gaitan put out his hand and waited expectantly.

She glared at him, but for once Gaitan didn't shy away. After an awkward moment, she sighed and handed it to him. Yger crossed her arms and sat watching him, her face twisted into her perpetual frown.

"I need some light," Gaitan said.

Nika guided his fireball across to his friend and brightened it so he could see better.

*"I found a way, Master."* Fin announced. *"We go up the elevator and ride along the top for a bit. There is another elevator we can swing around to take us down on the other side."*

*"Good. Were you able to see what time it is?"*

*"It's almost noon, My Lord."*

*"How far is it to Radik's Crossing?"*

*"It's hard to say. Maybe around five days?"*

*"Ok. Thank you."*

*"Um. Do you want me to guard your focus again?"* Fin asked.

*"Come to think of it, no. I want you to stay close to me, keep an eye out for us. There's no need to have two of you guarding it,"* Nika replied.

*"Good. The grumpy king was being mean to me."*

*"Radik wasn't as willing as you were to come along with us,"* Nika admitted. *"I probably should have left him alone*

*down there, but I feel more comfortable having him here with me, just in case."*

*"That's fair."*

*"Thanks again. Wake me up when the sun's going down."*

*"Yes, My Lord."*

"Fin's found us a way to get through to the other side," Nika announced, pointing towards the roof. "I don't know about you, but I need some sleep. Let's continue when it gets dark again."

It was cold and raining when Nika woke, and the wind howled through the gate, shaking and rattling things he couldn't see. Yawning but eager to get moving, he shook everyone awake then loaded the horses onto the elevator one by one. By the time he was done, the others were up and ready to go. As they stepped onto the platform, a light sprinkling of rain dripped around them from the opening far above.

"Looks like we're in for a miserable night," Joplin said to no one in particular.

"The rain will give us cover and hide any noise we make," Yger said.

"Anyone want a sip?" Priye held out her flask. "This will keep you warm down to your toes."

"It also melts your insides," Nika warned.

"You're no fun," she smirked, taking a sip.

Yger accepted the flask and took a deep swig. Nika watched her, waiting for a reaction, but to his surprise she licked her lips and passed it back.

"Not bad. It could do with a splash of lemon," she said.

"She's crazy," Gaitan whispered to Nika.

"All women are," Nika grinned.

"What was that?" Yger demanded.

"I said hold on. I don't know how fast this thing will go," he said quickly.

"Smooth," Gaitan murmured.

Nika teased the elevator's crystal to life and turned it into the up position. At once, the heavy cogs groaned into submission and turned, raising the platform steadily into the air. Nika's knees almost buckled under him, and he clung onto the rail for dear life. The horses whinnied and shook their heads nervously.

The higher they rose, the more Nika could make out the enormity of the megastructure. Level after level, they passed weapon stores, boulders for catapults, large vats of oil, and all sorts of wartime paraphernalia. Long halls lined with sleeping cells for the soldiers, and towards the top, rows of wooden catapults, ready to be raised to attack anyone who dared to storm the fortress.

A strong wind whipped at their cloaks as the elevator thudded to a stand-still. Nika threw open the gate and stepped onto the solid landing. They were on the top of Gri'Ran's Gate, safely behind a ledge that faced the battlefield. Nika took Streek's reigns and led the way up a stone ramp to the top of the battlements, and looked across the field where so many non-human beings were slaughtered cruelly. In the gathering darkness Nika could just make out Radik's Crossing in the distance.

"So many unnecessary deaths happened here all because of one man," Nika said, feeling the sadness of so many souls surround him. "I only hope that I can stop Du'Rakis before so many more have to die. Innocent people should never have to shed their blood or give their lives for a leader who doesn't care for them. It's your move, Du'Rakis. Make it wisely, for I'm coming for you. And this time, I won't be holding back."

Life with the A'Llun'bar dryads was far different than anything Freyne had ever experienced. It didn't take him long to settle in and get to know some of the dryads and make plenty of new friends. They were a peaceful race, loving and caring, and they quickly helped him to feel welcome. Whenever he wasn't meeting with the elders to discuss the rift and their plans with the other tribes, Freyne was free to do as he pleased.

Ak-Naar quickly became his closest friend, and they walked hand in hand for hours each day, exploring the forest together and bathing in the icy streams. He felt a bond forming between them, unlike any other. There was something that drew him to her, and made him want to spend every waking minute by her side.

"You never told me what your ring is for," Ak-Naar said one day, holding up his hand so she could see it better.

"It was given to me by the love of my life," Freyne replied.

At once his heart filled with a deep longing and sadness. He sat down in the fresh grass next to the stream and laid on his back. Ak-Naar was quick to join him, and he held up his hand so she could continue her inspection.

"Who is the love of your life?" she asked.

"His name is Nika and he means everything to me. I feel so empty without him."

"Does this mean you are married?"

"Not married, but committed to one another," Freyne answered. "Marriage is illegal for two men in the human cities."

"That's horrible," she said fiercely. "There are no such rules here. In A'Llun'bar, love is above all else."

"Sometimes I think humans are the most savage of any race." Freyne sighed.

Ak-Naar pushed Freyne's arm out of her way and used his shoulder as a pillow.

"Don't tell anyone. I want to marry Naz-Arg, but I

don't think he's interested in me."

"The warrior with orange hair and freckles?" Freyne asked, raising his eyebrow.

"Yes. I think he's cute. Don't you?"

"Oh, he's handsome alright. It's what's inside that matters though. He doesn't look a day over nineteen though. How old are you?"

"Nineteen? I'm 236, and he is 187. What's wrong with that?"

"Nothing at all." Freyne turned his head so he could look at her face. "You don't look any older than 230."

Ak-Naar giggled and blushed.

"How old are you and Nika?" she countered.

"Nika will be 29 in around two months. That means I'll be 1005 in a few weeks."

"You so old!" she giggled. "Most dryads live to between five and six hundred years old."

"And you're as bad as Nika."

Freyne reached down and tickled her side. Ak-Naar squealed and leapt to her feet.

"I bet you're too old to catch me!" she dashed away thru the trees, giggling.

Freyne chased her all the way back to her tree, and caught her just as she was about to leap onto the lowest branch. He tackled her to the ground.

"How's that for an old man?" he panted. His sides hurt, and he wheezed for breath in between laughing.

"I let you win!" she gasped.

Freyne let her go and sat up, still laughing. Ak-Naar abruptly stopped and scurried to her feet, her face turning serious. Two older dryads were walking towards them wearing the disapproving frowns which could only belong to parents.

"Imu. Aba." Ak-Naar greeted them the usual dryad way of touching their foreheads together.

"We thought you would have brought him to meet

302

us sooner," her father tutted, nodding towards Freyne. "We've been waiting for an introduction."

"Sorry, Aba." Ak-Naar hung her head.

"Have you forgotten our history so soon?" Imu stepped forward and rested her hands on Freyne's shoulders, gazing intently into his eyes. "I never thought I would see this day. Did you know your Imu had a sister?"

"No?" Freyne shook his head, once again feeling confused. "She said she had no family outside of my father and I."

"This is heart breaking," Imu said sadly. "Rayne had a sister, Layne. Layne's dana was Nains, who was my Imu."

Freyne's heart skipped a beat and he felt his jaw drop. He looked at Ak-Naar, who was staring at him with as much surprise on her face.

"You told me we lost your great-aunt," Ak-Naar said, glancing from Imu to Freyne. "I thought you meant she died, not *lost* lost. This means we are cousins!"

"Freyne is my Imu's cousin, but that works." She smiled warmly at Freyne. "You call us Aba and Imu too. We are family."

Freyne's breath caught in his throat, and he felt tears spring to his eyes. Imu pulled him into a tight hug and squeezed him, crying tears of joy. As soon as she released him, Aba moved forward and hugged him too. Freyne could feel their love, so different from human love but special nonetheless. Once Aba let go, Freyne turned to Ak-Naar. Instead of hugging her, he snaked his arm around her neck and messed up her hair.

"Hey! That's no fair!"

Freyne laughed and wiped away his tears, then pulled her into a tight embrace. The pain of losing his family hundreds of years ago eased somewhat, and his heart swelled with newfound joy. As he held his beautiful cousin he silently thanked Am and Saramas. Nika, Lau, and family; for the first time ever in his life, he was complete.

The plateau beyond Gri'Ran's Gate was cold and barren, a place of pain, torment, and death. Nika tried not to think about all the dead bodies beneath them as they road across the uneven ground. He knew he wasn't the only one who felt that way; everyone was in a sombre mood, and they hardly spoke during the four nights of steady riding that it took to cross.

Radik's Crossing was a wooden bridge which spanned several natural-formed rocks in a zig-zagging fashion. Years of exposure to the elements left it rickety and dangerous. Nika peeked over the edge of the cliff; they were high above the sea, which crashed loudly against the land pillars. He gritted his teeth, and turned back to his friends.

"I don't trust it," Gaitan said uneasily.

"It's the only way across," Nika pointed out. "I don't like it either, but we don't have a choice."

"I think we should lead the horses across, yes," Joplin said. He too looked scared.

"We'll go across one at a time," Nika decided. "I'll take Streek and the pack horse across first to test it. One person on each section at a time. Ok?"

Everyone nodded, though he could tell they weren't too keen on the idea. He took a rein in each hand and cautiously stepped on the rickety bridge. It felt sturdy enough, though every now and then he was forced to step over a rotted board. Once he made it to the first pillar, he turned back and waved.

It took Nika just over an hour to cross. He tied the horses to a dead tree, and carefully stood at the edge of the crossing, waiting for the others. Joplin, Yger, and then Priye were the next to make it across to safety, and Gaitan edged slowly along at the rear, his fear of heights evident on his face.

"Almost there," Nika called. "You've got this."

Gaitan looked over the edge at the jagged rocks far below, and swallowed.

"Remind me again why I agreed to come with you?" he shouted back.

"Because I was going to kill you otherwise, remember?"

Gaitan laughed weakly, and finally made it to safety. He hurried away from the edge, and let out a big sigh of relief.

"I swear –" his words were cut off by a terrible groaning sound.

Nika turned back and watched in horror as the final two sections of the crossing broke apart and tumbled into the sea below. Gaitan's face turned white, and he staggered further away from the edge of the cliff. Priye wordlessly offered Gaitan her flask, and he took a deep gulp, screwing up his face as the firewater burned its way through his body.

"Don't EVER ask me to do that again!" he gasped.

Joplin clasped him on his good shoulder and shot Nika a grin.

"The sad thing is, if you did fall, we'd still have to put up with your ghost, yes."

Gaitan scowled and stormed off towards the base of the mountains. Nika covered his mouth to try and suppress his laugh, but failed. He laughed, and soon Priye and Yger joined in.

"Oh dear. Now we have a sulking Gaitan to put up with," Priye chuckled.

"Don't worry. I'll go and hunt him a rabbit or two. They can't complain while their mouth is full." Yger sniggered.

"Be nice, you lot," Nika said. "Let's go and find some place to camp. We have a long hike ahead of us in the mountains, so we're going to need all our strength. Come on."

The first snow of the winter drifted softly from the sky, adding a tinge of white to the surfaces of Ironstone Keep. Ashavan paused to wipe the sweat from his face, the icy wind burning with each heavy breath. He quickly reset the heavy practice dummies, then resumed his practice.

Ashavan was proud of his swordsmanship and strength. He'd spent most of his early years training under his sword master to try and better himself. He learnt the importance of conditioning his body and training in different climates and seasons. Never in his life did he think it would lead him to kill innocent people.

A familiar burning sensation stabbed at the tattoo on his wrist. He turned over his hand; the ornamental hole in his gauntlet framed the ibis, allowing him to see what colour it was glowing. It was a dark, angry red.

Ashavan sheathed his sword and ran back inside as fast as his feet could take him. He took the stairs three at a time and raced towards the war room. For Ashavan knew, red meant his master needed him immediately, no matter what he was doing. Even if he were naked, there was no time to spare.

By the time he reached the tower, he felt his lungs ready to burst. He took a few deep gasping breaths, then hurried inside. Rissa and Enbarak were already there, kneeling on the floor. Ashavan quickly joined them and tried to hide his raspy breathing. Their Lord had his back to them, facing the balcony, his hands clasped behind his back.

"I have found what I needed from the archives," he said quietly. "Enbarak. You're to go to Araneda and stay with Ornas and Belarüs until I give you further orders. I'm directing my armies to the northern-most edge of the Rithvend border, where we will march towards the fortress city that guards the mountain pass. The City of the Clouds is where the next stage of my plan will be enacted.

"Rissa and Ashavan. You two will come with me. You have one hour to prepare yourselves. Should we meet that insidious Sarik and his cretins again, I expect you to be ready to fight. Now go!"

Ashavan hurried to his quarters and locked his door, his heart thudding in his chest. Sarik was the only one who could tell him if Tysion was alive, and if Ashavan was to die that day, he needed to know first. He quickly got himself ready, then spotted the quill and parchment he'd taken from the library. He looked at the door, then back at the quill.

*I'm going to die anyway. What have I to lose?*

Enbarak was gone by the time Ashavan made it back, and Rissa joined him shortly after. Without a word, they followed Du'Rakis through the portal. The ride was rougher than usual, and as he staggered into frigid mountain air, he collided with Rissa.

"Ow! Watch it, you big oaf!" she snapped.

"Get out of the way then," he snapped back.

"Silence!" Du'Rakis hissed.

Ashavan shook his head and glanced around. They were standing on top of a massive mountain peak that soared high above the rest. It wasn't snowing, but it was bitterly cold. The summit was flat, albeit rocky, and shaped a little like a jagged crescent moon. To their right was a massive swirling portal, larger than he'd ever seen, and behind that was the crumbling remains of a small stone cottage He took a step towards the edge and looked down, then quickly retreated. It was a deadly drop all the way to the bottom of the peak should anyone fall.

"Ashavan. Stay here and guard the portals. Do not leave for any reason, and if our friends show up, kill them immediately." Du'Rakis swept past him.

"Yes, My Lord," he said automatically.

"Rissa, you're with me." Du'Rakis snatched her by the

wrist and dragged her into the largest portal.

*Does he want me dead?* Ashavan thought, a feeling of dread welling up inside him. *If I were to attack Lord Sarik, I'd be dead in an instant. Does my life and all I've done mean nothing to him?*

Ashavan cautiously made his way around the summit, scouting out his best position for defence should they be attacked. The far side of the crack was dotted with thorny bushes and a small, jagged rise near the edge of the peak. The other side was flatter, and around twenty feet away was a small flight of stairs that led down to the mountain path. As he walked back towards the portal, the unmistakable sound of laughter ghosted to him on the wind. He froze and listened, straining to hear it again, but as quickly as it came, it was gone. *It must have been the wind,* he thought.

The hours dragged by, and Ashavan quickly grew bored. He was cold and hungry, and his side was still slightly tender from his injury. He sat on a flat rock and tossed small pebbles at a stick on the ground. Out of nowhere, someone laughed and Ashavan jumped, dropping his handful of pebbles. He peeked over the edge of the summit, and his heart froze in his chest.

Less than an hour's walk down the side of the peak was none other than Lord Sarik and his friends, seated in a circle around a small fire. Their voices and laughter carried to him on the wind.

"Leave him alone," an older woman said with her hands on her hips. "I'd much rather have a sulking Gaitan than a clicky skeleton for company."

"I almost die, and this is how you treat me?" the man wearing chainmail argued.

"Come on, settle down you lot," Lord Sarik said. "If you did fall, you know I would have caught you. You'd be much lighter than the smuggler's bridge. You're alive and that's what matters."

"Knowing my luck you'd drop me."

Lord Sarik pulled something from his belt and twirled it in his fingers.

"Enough talk about death, ghosts, and skeletons," he said firmly. "If *any* of you die from here on, I'll reanimate your corpse and make you carry me the rest of the way up that hill. Got it?"

Sarik's friends all burst into laughter. Ashavan sighed; there was no way *his* lord would joke around like that, nor tolerate such banter. Lord Sarik clearly cared for his friends and would protect them no matter what. He watched them eat their lunch and rest, until Sarik stood and stretched.

"That mountain isn't going to climb itself," he said. "Let's get going when you're all ready."

Ashavan crept back from the ledge and tiptoed back to his post by the portal, his heart lodged in his throat. All of Du'Rakis' laws and teachings spoke about how evil Sarik was, how he was nasty and must be killed for the sake of the world. And yet, Ashavan could see with his own eyes that that simply was not true. Lord Sarik looked like someone he might've been friends with some day, had he not turned to the Brotherhood instead.

The sound of horse's hooves reached his ears, and he sucked in a deep breath. He quietly drew his sword, and poked the tip in the ground before him.

*This is it,* he thought, his insides churning. *Please don't force me to try and kill these people.*

## 22

The port of Se'Khel was full of war ships, bobbing on the water in the gentle swells. Iryna stood next to her father on the city wall, watching on as the thousands of soldiers milled around, awaiting their orders to board. Iryna turned back towards the city where the stone masons were working hard on the new temple, the *click click click* of their tools harmonising with the noises of the street.

"It looks like they'll be complete in another two or three weeks," she said, deeply impressed by the progress the masons were making.

"What?" To'Rel turned around, then noticed what she was talking about. "Oh. Yes, the masons are doing well. I think I'll pay them a little extra gold for their hard work. They deserve it."

"Mhmm."

"Are you alright, daughter?" To'Rel asked.

"I'm alright." She sighed and leant on the battlement. "Just a bit preoccupied, I guess. It's hard to believe that this started over a year ago when we snuck out of Al'Obrel, and now we are sending our army to war. Everything seems to have escalated so suddenly. I never thought I would see a war in my lifetime."

"This started long before Nika and Freyne showed up in my court that day. But I know what you mean." To'Rel nodded. "No king – or queen, for that matter – willingly sends their people to war without good reason. Disputes should be settled with diplomacy, not bloodshed. I have turned down a number of calls to arms in my time as king. But this? There was no way I was going to sit back idly while our friends are over there busting their backsides and risking their lives for us."

"It's not every day the world teeters on the edge of destruction," Iryna said sadly. "A part of me wishes I could go with the army and do my part. I feel so useless here."

"You've already helped immensely with your temple project," To'Rel said. "I'm so proud of what you've achieved. I don't think we would be this far along had it not been for your help."

"Don't get all mushy on me, father," Iryna scoffed, though a warmth grew in her heart from his words. "How long will it take for the soldiers to finish boarding?"

"A few more hours at least," To'Rel replied. "I can only imagine how they're feeling. Once upon a time it was expected for the king to ride into battle with his army. Now, we lead from afar."

Iryna pursed her lips, then linked her arm with her father's.

"Come on, then. Let's go and talk to them. Ask how they're *really* feeling, and give them some encouragement." She pulled him towards the stairs that led to the gates below.

"Wait! Are you sure about this? It'll only make them nervous if I'm there."

"Everyone thinks leaders or heroes are these great almighty people who can do no wrong," Iryna said fiercely. "Deep down, they are just normal people like you, me, and even that peasant over there. I would much rather follow someone I can relate to into war than some impersonal twat like Khel."

Iryna marched him down the road and into the throng of soldiers. At once, some of the men's eyes bugged out of their heads and they scrambled to attention.

"Rest easy, men," Iryna said, glancing at her father out of the corner of her eye. "Today, we are not royalty. We are here to fight the war just as you are, albeit in a different way. Is there anything *we* can do for *you?*"

The men looked at each other, a hint of fear and confusion on their faces. To'Rel shifted uneasily. Finally, one of them plucked up the courage and stepped forward.

"Please, Your Highness. What is this war about? No one will tell us."

"Of course, you have a right to know what you are fighting for!" Iryna climbed on top of a storage create and drew herself up, drawing the interest of a larger crowd. "You all know the story of Ami'Khel and how he broke his pact with the gods, right?"

The soldiers nodded, watching her intently.

"Ami'Khel lives, and is terrorising the mainland, killing thousands of innocent men, women, and children. He is raising an army and fighting for what we believe to be utmost control. You all heard the story of the Battle of Rarn, how he killed his army in the heat of anger..."

"So you're sending us over there where he can kill us all with the wave of his hand?" a soldier called out angrily. A murmur of agreeance rippled through the crowd.

"I would never send you into a war that was so poorly balanced," Iryna said, holding up her hand for quiet. "Khel may be his own champion and a law unto himself. But over there right now are our own champions, equally as powerful and racing to stop Khel in his tracks. Unlike Khel, our heroes are blessed by the gods themselves."

"How do you know this?" someone else called out.

"I know because all of those rumours about what happened at Gri'Ran's Rest are true. Our champion is Nika, who sacrificed himself to give us back the protection of the gods. I was there and saw it with my own eyes. You will not be fighting alone. You will be fighting with

Nika and even the gods themselves! Do you want to live in peace and safety like you're used to, or do you want your families to suffer under the rule of a tyrant? Because if he wins, we can kiss this world goodbye!"

The crowd erupted in chatter as the soldiers talked amongst each other. To'Rel cleared his throat.

"This war is not a petty call for arms from our allies to the west. It is a call for arms from the gods themselves, and we will be fighting in Nika's name, for ultimately he will be the one to vanquish Khel in the end. Are you willing to fight the War of the Gods and save our world?"

A loud cheer greeted To'Rel's words, and the soldiers all raised their weapons in salute.

"For Nika!" They shouted as one.

"I, General Chardi, will fight to the death in Nika's name! I too was there when he gave himself for us, and I will be there to fight for him to the very end!"

The soldiers roared deafeningly. Iryna spun around to see Chardi and Ur'Shad behind them.

"I need to speak to you two," Chardi said quietly.

Ur'Shad reached up and helped Iryna down from the crate, then drew her and To'Rel away from the cheering soldiers. Iryna followed her friends down to the docks. The soldiers parted to let them through, and all around them she could hear Nika's name being chanted as the story spread to the furthest reaches of the army faster than wildfire. They stopped next to a large warship that was loaded full of soldiers and ready to set sail.

"This is my ship," Chardi said, looking at the ground. "I was just coming to find you when I heard the commotion you were stirring up. I think they needed the morale boost."

"It was Iryna's idea," To'Rel said. "Do you have the comms crystal?"

Chardi nodded and flashed the crystal affixed to the cuff on his wrist.

"Good. We'll be in touch as soon as we get to the Fort. Take care, my friend. We'll be waiting for you to return." To'Rel clasped Chardi's hand firmly.

"Thanks, My King."

Chardi turned to Ur'Shad, and the two men hugged tightly.

"Be careful out there, brother," Ur'Shad said, patting Chardi's back. "I wish I could come and fight by your side, but you know the real war is keeping the princess in order."

Chardi laughed and pulled away. Iryna slapped Ur'Shad playfully.

"When I get back, we're going to go sail a lap of Kia-Mor with my sister and get drunk for the entire voyage. I promise."

"I'll hold you to that." Chardi grinned, then turned to Iryna. "As for you, Princess. Behave and stay safe, alright?"

"Can you excuse us for a moment, father?" Iryna asked.

To'Rel frowned, but walked back along the dock out of earshot. Iryna made sure he wasn't being nosey, then reached up and unclasped a necklace she was wearing. She pressed it into Chardi's hand.

"This was Lana's. She would have wanted you to have it. I hope it brings you luck and keeps you safe." Iryna felt tears spring to her eyes, and she pulled Chardi into a tight hug. "Please be careful over there, and if you see Nika and our friends, give them our love."

Chardi's eyes misted over. He bent down and planted a wet kiss on Iryna's cheek, then hurried up the gangplank and out of sight. The sailors pulled it closed behind him, and the order to raise anchor was given. The mighty sails bearing To'Rel's crest dropped with a mighty *boom*, and the ship drifted out to sea.

Mount Rakis soared above the rest of the mountains in the range, though it wasn't nearly as tall as some of the peaks they'd traversed above Rarn. The narrow path they followed was steep, which made it harder for the horses. Each step they took, Nika could feel the pulsating rhythm of the rift. He could sense its power, and could only guess what else was waiting for him on top of that peak.

Something made a *click* beside him, jolting him out of his reverie.

"I fixed it!" Gaitan said excitedly. He handed Yger back her crossbow proudly. "Sorry it took me so long to put back together."

Yger took it and examined it.

"I am impressed," she said. "Don't think this means I like you though."

"I know." Gaitan sighed and hung his head, though Nika spotted the hint of a grin on his cheek.

He turned his gaze to Priye, who was once again sipping at her flask.

"If you keep drinking all that fire water, there will be none left for when we get stabbed again," he said.

"Well, stop getting stabbed then." She smirked. "Why do you think I keep telling you to be careful? It's not that I care, it's because I don't want to waste it on cuts."

"You're a crazy woman, yes," Joplin laughed.

Nika finished the simple damper that Priye cooked for lunch, then stood up and stretched.

"That mountain isn't going to climb itself," he announced. "Let's get going when you're all ready."

Gaitan put out their fire, and Nika helped pack away their things from lunch.

"I think we should lead the horses up this next part," Joplin said, pointing. "It's steep, and we don't want to risk any accidents, yes."

Nika nodded his agreement, and tucked Arnie under his cloak. He led the way up the peak, the cold air burning his lungs with each breath. It took them a little under the hour on foot. The path widened and levelled out near the top, and to their right was a shallow depression that offered cover from the wind. The path stopped abruptly at a short flight of narrow steps leading to the plateau above.

"Let's leave the horses here then," Nika said quietly. "Tie them to that log and take a quick breather while I get ready."

He slipped into the darkest realm and ensured his sprites were protecting him and his friends, and sent Fin on ahead to scout out for him.

*"There is a man waiting for you, Master,"* Fin said once he returned.

*"Is it Du'Rakis?"* Nika asked.

*"No."*

*"Alright then. Stay close to me."*

He sat Arnie on the ground and drew his focus. Whatever was waiting on the summit, he was ready for. After one final glance around at his friends to make sure they too were ready, he nodded his head and walked purposefully towards the stairs. In between pulses from the rift, he could feel the power of the tendril swirling around him, raw untapped power. Should Du'Rakis choose to fight, Nika was sure the magnitude of their attacks could very well level the mountains. He gritted his teeth, and climbed the stairs.

Nika stepped onto the pinnacle of Mount Rakis, and was immediately in awe. The rift was enormous and took up the entire path between the two halves of the summit. He almost didn't notice the smaller portal next to it, nor the armoured warrior who could only be General Ashavan just twenty feet away. Nika froze, and held up his hand to warn the others behind him.

General Ashavan was standing with the tip of his mighty sword buried in the ground, his hands resting on the pommel, a sign that Nika knew meant neutrality. His aura was also neutral, and to Nika's surprise, he sensed raw fear from the general. Ashavan's stance was not what Nika was expecting, and he paused, unsure what to make of his next move.

"That's General Ashavan," Yger hissed. "Kill him!"

Before Nika could tell her to stop, she'd already loaded her crossbow and fired.

"No!" he swept the bolt out of the air and sent it flying over the edge of the mountain. "Keep out of this!"

Ashavan let go of his sword and slowly removed his helm. To Nika's continued surprise, the general was younger than he expected, around his forties. His dark blonde hair was tied back, and he was sporting a few days' growth. Nika could sense his inner torment, so many emotions that were overwhelming, and his eyes echoed that pain.

"Please. Before you kill me, I must know. The man who gave you that mark –" Ashavan pointed at the disc Nika still wore on his cloak. "–Tysion. Is he alive?"

"Sashin Tonavay gave it to me," Nika answered. "I don't know a Tysion."

Ashavan closed his eyes, then looked towards the rift. He removed a folded piece of parchment from inside his helm and held it out.

"Take this, before he comes. If you find Tysion, please tell him that I'm sorry."

Nika reached out using the realm and called the parchment to him, then tucked it safely into his pocket.

"Where's Du'Rakis?" he demanded.

Ashavan looked again at the portal, then replaced his helm.

"He's coming. Prepare yourself." Ashavan retrieved his sword and took up his battle stance.

Nika swallowed, and planted his feet firmly. The rift swirled and eddied, and Rissa stepped onto the peak followed by Du'Rakis. Nika's nemesis froze when he saw

Ashavan's stance, and spun around, clearly caught off-guard. In his arms was a young child, crying her heart out. Nika's stomach turned; how low would Du'Rakis go if he was willing to put an innocent child in harm's way?

"This ends now, Khel! Release the child!" Nika yelled.

"Now why should I do that? Don't you want to have a little family reunion? This brat is an orphan now, just as you were when *your* mother died. Oh yes, I know who you are, *Nickolai*, just as I know who you were before you came to this world."

"You know nothing about me!" he yelled back.

The child was screaming and trying to get out of Du'Rakis' arms. Nika felt sick to his gut.

"I bred you for my own use, nothing else. A tool for my plan. But when I read that prophecy, I knew I had to get rid of you. I sent an entire army to capture you, but those meddling gods ruined that. Since you were taken from me, I will take something from you instead, and end this filthy bloodline once and for all!"

Du'Rakis turned towards the smaller portal. Nika sent a ball of energy towards Ashavan and knocked him backwards, his body blocking Khel's escape.

"I'll say it one last time, Khel. Release the child!" Nika shouted. He could feel the tendril enveloping him and he allowed it to flow into his body.

"If you want her so bad, then take her!" Du'Rakis spun abruptly and threw the child high into the air over the edge of the peak, propelling her by the forces of the realm.

Nika gasped, and watched in slow motion as the child flew through the frigid sky to certain death. He felt himself running, and as he neared the edge, he leapt into the air, pushing behind him with the power of the tendril. Invisible strands lifted him through in the air, allowing him to snatch the child just in time. He clutched her tightly to his chest, and as he fell back towards the peak, he pushed against the ground on the opposite side to slow and cushion his fall.

An almighty roar from the darkest realm thundered painfully in Nika's head. His ears rang, and he lost his grip on the realm. He felt himself starting to fall, too disoriented to regain his grasp of the tendril. He fell roughly onto the far side of the peak and landed hard on his back. The momentum sent him sliding along the rocky ground, coming to a stop just in time before hitting his head on a rocky ledge. As he sat up shakily, he saw Du'Rakis with his arms in the air, directing a massive surge of power into the sky. He shielded the wailing child in his arms protectively as the sky above them turned a dark red, and the mountain started to shake.

Du'Rakis dropped his arms and fell to his knees. Rissa pulled him up and half-dragged him through the smaller portal, Ashavan limping behind. The portal shimmered and closed. After a few minutes the ground stopped shaking, though the sky remained tarnished with blood-like red.

The child's wails calmed to hiccuppy sobs. Nika looked down at the treasure in his arms; she had dark hair tied in two cute little pigtails, and steely grey eyes. She was wearing pink pyjamas dotted with unicorns and fluffy pink slippers.

"Mummy!" she sniffed. "I want Mummy!"

"Shh, it's ok bubba. Don't cry," Nika said as soothingly as he could. He could feel the pain in her cries, her lack of understanding for what had just happened. An image floated to him of a woman sprawled across her bed, dead. That same bed that Nika recognised all too well. "Come on, please don't cry."

He felt tears of his own coursing down his cheeks, and he sobbed quietly with her. Her pain, which she was too young to understand, was somehow his pain, too. He rocked her gently in his arms, a thousand emotions raging through him at once.

"It's ok. I've got you. I'm here," he said, over and over.

The little girl's thoughts were scattered, but in her sadness, she somehow projected them to Nika. Her mother's body, her favourite toy, a donkey she saw on a farm. And then he saw it: Du'Rakis' uncovered face, his hair just as black and his eyes that same steely grey. Nika felt the nausea rising, and he flashed back to the mountains above Rarn. The enraged hermit wasn't a hermit, but Du'Rakis himself.

"Nika!"

He looked up through his tears to see his friends running towards him, terror written all over their faces. They gathered around him, poking and prodding him and asking so many questions that he just couldn't hear. He held the child closer; no one could take her from him. She was far too precious.

A sharp slap in the face made him blink, and roused him enough to focus on what was being said.

"Can you hear me?" Priye demanded.

Nika nodded vaguely.

"Hand me the child," she ordered, holding out her arms.

"No! I have to protect her," he sobbed.

"I just want to check that she's ok," Priye said, exasperated. "I'm not going to hurt her. Hand her over, *please.*"

Nika reluctantly released his grip, and Priye plucked her from his arms.

"Can you stand?" Gaitan asked.

Nika stared at him blankly. Gaitan and Joplin each linked their arms with his and lifted him to his feet. Nika's head spun, and his legs almost collapsed under him.

"Pull yourself together, man!" Joplin growled. "We need you, yes!"

Nika steadied himself and waited for everything

to stop spinning. All around the mountains, ominous shadows were shooting towards the red sky in droves. He took a step, but faltered. Gaitan wrapped Nika's arm around his shoulder and helped him limp past the swirling rift and towards the stairs. The previously calm tendril was scattered and uneven, almost angry; whatever Du'Rakis used it for had drawn a lot of power.

"Wait," Nika managed. "I-I have to close the rift first. It's growing unstable."

Gaitan stopped and helped Nika face the portal. Instinctively, he pushed his mind into the heart of the rift, and followed it through time and space itself. When he broke through to the other side, he was staring at the place where his childhood home once stood, before it burnt down all those years ago. His own world was right there in front of him; all he had to take was a single step inside the portal, and he could leave the nightmare behind and return to life as it once was. No more Du'Rakis or war or gods; his life could go back to the way it was before, just hard work and music.

"Mummy!"

Nika turned and looked back towards Mount Rakis. All he had to do was rejoin with his body, and step through the rift, and then it would be all over. He would easily get his job back on the rig and pick up where he left off, the night when... Nika frowned as the reality sunk in once more. He was already dead in that world. His rig lay at the bottom of the ocean, and his colleagues' bodies were probably picked clean to the bone by fish and other sea creatures. He couldn't go back, even if he decided to. As though to convince him to stay, the memories of him and Freyne flooded to the front of his mind, and at once he faltered.

"Mummy!"

The child's haunting cries echoed in Nika's ears, rousing him. He wondered if he should at least return her to her home, maybe try and find her father, but the thought froze as something terrifying dawned on him. A thought that was too painful and horrible to deal with. He pushed it away, even as the image of the little girl's mother once again flashed before his eyes.

"I want my Mummy!"

Nika gritted his teeth and brought himself back to his senses. He latched onto the edges of the rift, and flew back towards his body, sealing it as he went, closing the portal to his world for good. As soon as he landed, he let go of the rift and fell roughly to his hands and knees; the air where the rift stood open for so many centuries stopped swirling and soon dissipated.

Nika staggered to his feet, and at once reached for the child. Priye's eyes were wide, and she wordlessly allowed him to take the precious bundle back into his arms. The tendril was slowly returning to calm, though Nika could tell it was still not right.

"Nickolai!" Saramas' ghostly apparition appeared in front of him.

"Master! What the fuck did Du'Rakis just do?" Nika demanded.

"He's just reanimated most of the dead that inhabits this land, that's what!" Saramas replied.

"Can I undo it?"

"Nay. The effort would kill thee." Saramas shook his head. "Thou must use the tendril to get word through to our allies. It's not men they'll be fighting. Du'Rakis now has an army of undead in his command. The Council are gathering the necromancers as we speak. We too shalt fight by thy side."

"Thank you, Master. What now?"

"The rest is up to thee, Nickolai. I grow weak. We'll be in touch." Saramas disappeared, leaving Nika alone with his friends on the peak.

"I n-need to sit," Nika stammered.

He staggered across to a large flat rock and sat on it, still clutching the child close to him. Priye immediately removed Nika's cloak and inspected his back for any injuries. Nika ignored her and numbly pulled the piece of parchment from his pocket.

*Lord Sarik,*

*My Master is planning complete annihilation of not only humanity, but the gods, too. He will be marching his army north to Rythasbar, where he plans to storm the fortress and open another portal of power. He is taking this war to the heavens, and I doubt anyone can stop him, not even you.*

*I know you have no reason to trust me. But if I were to trust humanity's fate to one man, it would be you, not Du'Rakis. Each and every day, we are faced with decisions that aren't easy to make, and should we make the wrong choice, we must live with the consequences. I have made many wrong choices in my life, so I hope this one will lead to lives being saved and not taken for once.*

*Ashavan*

"What does it say?" Yger demanded.

Nika handed her the note. In his mind's eye, he visualised Du'Rakis adding his army to the giant game board. It was Nika's move, and he had no idea which piece to move next.

"Rythasbar?" Gaitan asked, reading over her shoulder.

"It's an ancient fort deep in the mountains between Araneda and Rithvend," Yger said. "No one knows what's there. It's said to be virtually impenetrable."

"I'll bet it's another tendril," Nika said darkly. "That's where we're going next."

"How?" Priye asked. "The crossing's broken. We're

pretty much trapped."

"Everyone keeps telling me to trust in Am, so that's exactly what I'm going to do," Nika said. "As soon as I get my strength back, I'm going to reach out and warn our allies, and see if I can find Freyne. After that, we head back down the mountain and see where Am guides us."

"And just what are you planning to do with the little girl?" she asked.

"She's coming with us," Nika said flatly. "Du'Rakis obviously wants her for something and might try to get her back. Until I can wrap my head around all of this, I'm not letting her out of my sight."

Freyne sat with Ak-Naar, Aba, and Imu not far from the elders, eating his breakfast of nuts and dried fruit that was the staple diet of A'Llun'bar. Only the faintest light of sunrise trickled through the leaves above, and the gathered dryads spoke in hushed whispers.

Something felt different that morning, almost as though the forces of nature were holding their breath, waiting in anticipation. For what, Freyne had no idea. He shifted uneasily, but couldn't shake the feeling.

"What's wrong, fina?" Ak-Naar asked.

"Can you feel that?" Freyne glanced at Aba and Imu, then back at Ak-Naar.

"Feel what?" Aba asked.

"The forces of nature. They've never felt like this before."

Aba and Imu frowned and concentrated, then shook their heads.

"No. Remember, our senses are different to yours. You are magic, we are not." Aba said.

Freyne's skin prickled with warning, and he pushed himself half-off the ground, his senses on high alert. The sky filled with sounds of birds screeching, and in a flurry they took off all at once. The trees themselves shook and creaked, lowering their limbs to protect the forest from whatever danger was above them. The dryads all stopped talking and glanced up in fright.

"What's happening?" Freyne asked, pointing at the trees.

"Something *is* wrong," Ak-Naar said. She stood and pulled Freyne to his feet. "They only ever do this when we are in danger."

The ground shook suddenly, and Freyne fell painfully onto his back. A loud surge rumbled in his head from what could only be the darkest realm. A stabbing pain in his mind caused him to cry out and clutch at his head. When he finally dared to open his eyes, the one patch of sky still visible above the Ancient One turned a sickly red. Some of the dryads screamed, and clung to their loved ones in fright.

Freyne moved his mind into the darkest realm and scanned their surroundings. His limited view showed him the life force of the dryads and trees around him. As he looked up, he felt absolute terror stab into his heart. He didn't need to be a necromancer to know that the dark shadows flying towards the sky were souls of the dead flocking to Du'Rakis.

"Freyne! What is happening?" Cayne demanded, hobbling over to him.

Around them, the dryads were panicking. More and more were swelling into the clearing around the Ancient One, finding their loved ones and holding them tightly.

"Oh my God. Nika!" A feeling of dread washed over him all the way to his toes, and he started shaking uncontrollably. "I think Nika just faced Du'Rakis! Whatever just happened was not by Nika's hand. It was definitely Du'Rakis. By the gods, I can't lose him again!"

Freyne felt his panic worsen as he imagined all the different ways Du'Rakis could have killed him. He couldn't breathe, and he sat gasping and sobbing uncontrollably.

"Fina!" Ak-Naar shook him, and when that didn't work, she wrapped her arms around him and held him tightly. "Calm yourself. It's ok."

Imu rose to her knees and shimmied over to Freyne and hugged him too. The gentle scent of the sprig of lemon myrtle in her hair wafted under his nose, and he focused on it until he finally grounded himself from the panic. He drew a shuddering breath and wriggled out of their holds so he could wipe his nose. He wanted to say something, but the words wouldn't come. Freyne sat with his eyes closed, feeling the love of his family surrounding him.

His pounding heart soon slowed, leaving him shaking and barely able to hold himself upright. He craved the warmth and comfort of Lau. No sooner had he stopped shaking, another surge came, this time from the highest realm. Freyne weakly joined with the realm and listened.

*"I am healed...but still in pain. The rift has been closed..."*

Freyne's heart leapt into his throat as a warmth washed over him. Fresh tears welled in his eyes as he realised what it was.

"I felt and heard *that*," Ak-Naar said, looking at Freyne in wonder. "What was it?"

"He did it," Freyne wept. "Nika's alive."

A loud creaking noise came from behind them, and a new presence joined with the gathered dryads. A gasp reverberated around the clearing, and the creaking grew louder. Ak-Naar sat back and gazed over Freyne's shoulder at something, her mouth open in awe. Freyne turned around slowly and was instantly amazed at what he saw.

The Ancient One was moving its limbs slowly, reminding Freyne of someone waking after being asleep for a long time. Its leaves shook as the ancient tree came to life before them. Two giant eyes opened, and a knot formed into a mouth.

"My children." The Ancient One's words echoed triumphantly in Freyne's head. "I have been freed! I live again!"

The dryads all leapt to their feet and cheered. Freyne sat numbly on the ground, too drained to comprehend what was happening. The Ancient One smiled, then its expression turned serious. It turned and looked directly into Freyne's eyes.

"My children. The Miscreant has just unleashed new horrors upon this already pained world. While a war between humans does not concern us, a war against nature and the gods does. We must reconnect with the other Ancient Ones and tribes, and join together to defend ourselves. No matter how far we are from humanity, we will never be safe so long as the Miscreant runs free. Freyne, it is time for you to help us reunite with the lost tribes. Step forward and join with me."

## 23

Iryna felt herself being shaken roughly. She jolted upright in bed; Ur'Shad was standing over her still in his bedclothes, a look of panic on his face.

"What's wrong?" she asked, wiping the sleep from her eyes.

"Something's happened. Get dressed as quick as you can and pack a few clothes. Wait here for me. I'll be back in a minute." Ur'Shad disappeared through the door, leaving her to her confusion.

Iryna stumbled from her bed and started packing. She pulled on a pair of trousers and her traveling boots, a warm over-shirt, and her thick fur cloak. Confused shouts came from up the hall; Iryna snatched her journal and a few books, leaving her jewellery and expensive gowns.

"Are you ready?" Ur'Shad asked, returning without knocking.

Iryna nodded blankly. He too was carrying a loaded pack, and he'd pulled on his armour. Ur'Shad pulled her into a quick hug, then led her from her room.

"Where are we going?" Iryna asked, half-running to keep up with his long strides.

Ur'Shad ignored her question and picked up his pace. He hustled her to the small courtyard by the stables, where Nahal and To'Rel were surrounded by a small crowd of staff. She frowned, noticing a strange red tint to everything. A movement caught her eye, and when she looked up, she gasped in fright.

"Iryna! Are you ready to go?" Nahal demanded.

"Yes, Mother," she answered. "What's going on? What *are* those?"

"They're undead," To'Rel grimaced. "I've already received reports of dead bodies coming back to life. We're leaving for Fort Carn immediately so we can reach the generals. Are you sure you have everything you need?"

Iryna nodded and patted her pack. She sucked in a deep breath and put on a brave face, determined not to show her fear.

"Really? Just one pack?" Nahal asked.

"We're going to fight a war, not a beauty pageant," Iryna retorted. "Where's my horse?"

"The servants are preparing the carriage," To'Rel said. "The regent is sitting with my advisors right now and is getting ready to take care of the city."

"We don't need a stinking carriage!" Iryna exploded, stamping her foot. "Just saddle up the horses and be quick about it. We don't have time to be precious!"

To'Rel turned to walk away, but stopped and jumped back with a startled yelp. Nika materialised before them, a grim look on his face.

"Nika!" Iryna gasped. She ran towards him, but as she reached out to hug him, she passed right through him. "Huh?"

"What's going on, lad? Where are you?" To'Rel demanded.

"I'm on top of Mount Rakis," Nika replied, frowning. "Is the sky red where you are?"

"Yes, and there's ghosts everywhere," Iryna nodded.

"Ok, listen up. Du'Rakis has just raised an army of undead, and I've been told they are marching north to a place called Rythasbar. My allies, the renegades of Endveraugh, will join with your army at Kalan. Then you can go up through Kalissaden towards Rithvend. We're heading that way too, though we still have a long way to go to get there."

"We're leaving for Fort Carn right now. Once we're there, I'll be able to contact Chardi and my other generals and let them know." To'Rel said.

"You've sent Chardi over?" Nika asked incredulously.

"He wanted this," Iryna said sadly.

"He'd better not do anything stupid," Nika said. "How will you be contacting him?"

"Each general has been issued a special crystal. When we get to Fort Carn, I'll be able to talk with them directly and watch what's going on. Why?"

"Because once I leave here, I won't be able to contact you again," Nika replied. "Take your strongest mancers with you and see if they can figure out a way to link me with your crystal thing. But now, I have to go. Stay safe, all of you."

"Wait!" Iryna called, but it was too late. Nika's projection flickered and disappeared.

"That lad is full of surprises," To'Rel said, shaking his head. "Alright, everyone! Forget the carriage, we'll ride horseback. Let's move it out. We have a long way to go!"

---

Nika was shaking and his forehead was dripping with sweat. He wiped his brow and took a deep shuddering breath.

"It's happening in Endveraugh and Al'Obrel, too," he reported. "It's just past midnight in Al'Obrel. I caught Iryna and her family as they were evacuating to Fort Carn."

"How is she?" Priye asked.

"She looked ready for war, come to think of it," Nika said. "We didn't get to chat. I am worried, though. Chardi is heading over to fight in the war too."

"Chardi is a great fighter. He'll be fine," Gaitan said.

"Yeah, I know. I'm allowed to worry about my friends,

though."

"Did you find Freyne?" Priye asked.

Nika shook his head.

"I looked everywhere, but I couldn't find him," he said sadly. "Oh, I asked Kajiran about Tysion, the one Ashavan mentioned. He's not there."

"Of course not. I would say he's wound up dead somewhere long before this happened. And if not, he would have surely perished in the purge," Yger said. "If he were ever at Endveraugh, I would have known about it. Either way, if we do find him, I'll kill him myself. He's clearly in league with Ashavan."

"No. I think there is more to this," Nika said, shaking his head. "There's something different about Ashavan. I have a gut feeling that if we can find Tysion, we can get Ashavan out of the picture and focus on the Mistress and the other generals."

"Ashavan would already be out of the picture if you let me kill him when we had the chance," Yger snapped. She stood up and stormed down the mountain path.

"Oh, here we go again." Priye rolled her eyes.

Gaitan stood up and went after her. Nika was too tired and sore to even think about trying to talk him out of his death wish. He looked at Priye and sighed.

"I guess it will be his corpse to carry me down this mountain," he said.

No sooner had Nika finished his sentence, Gaitan reappeared and hurried back to where he was sitting before. His cheeks were bright red and his eyes were wide.

"What's wrong?" Nika asked.

"Nothing," Gaitan said quickly.

"Did she pull a knife on you again?" Priye asked.

"No!"

Priye crossed her arms and fixed him with a look.

"We're not leaving until you tell us."

Gaitan looked around furtively then lowered his voice.

"She…she was standing up to…you know." He made a gesture with his hands to demonstrate. "She has a…a peen."

Joplin roared with laughter and slapped his knees. The little girl woke and immediately started crying. Priye rocked her gently and soon had her calm once more.

"What's so funny?" Gaitan snapped.

"That'll teach you for being nosey and not respecting her privacy," Joplin said, wiping his eyes.

"Gaitan, dear." Priye's face grew serious. "Yger is in every way a woman. She was born in the wrong body, that's all. Do not disrespect her in any way, or *I* will be the one to stab *you*. Got it?"

"I would never! But…she's gorgeous. Did you know?" Gaitan shot towards Nika.

"If someone refers to themselves as a man, woman, or otherwise, that's good enough for me." He shrugged. "Who cares what's in their pants? That's just creepy."

Gaitan stared at his feet, his cheeks burning. Nika reached out and patted him on the shoulder.

"If you ever wish to be intimate with someone who has a peen, I'm happy to give you some tips and advice."

"Oh, shut up." Gaitan mumbled.

The little girl squirmed, suddenly full of life, and tried to wriggle out of Priye's grasp.

"Just when I got her settled." She sighed.

Nika put out his hands, and Priye passed her back to him. Nika once again got lost in her perfect innocence. She reached up and yanked on his goatee and giggled.

"Ow!" he winced.

"Spikey!"

"Who is she?" Priye asked.

"I have no idea." Nika wasn't ready for *that* conversation, and tried to end it before it started.

"Let's see. She has your eyes, nose, and hair. I doubt she's your sister," Joplin said.

"Don't tell me you were also one to leave a trail of illegitimate children in your wake," Priye said with a raised eyebrow.

Gaitan glared at her, but said nothing.

"I'm not going to answer that," Nika growled. "End of conversation!"

"If you say so," Priye smirked.

Nika ignored her and looked down at the girl.

"What's your name?" he asked gently.

"Lilla-Belle!" she squealed happily, still playing with Nika's goatee.

"Hello, Lilla-Belle. That's a pretty name."

"Are we done here, or are we camping the night?" Yger asked abruptly, rejoining them.

Gaitan stared at his feet, avoiding her gaze.

"Let's get off this mountain," Nika decided. "We still have a few hours light left. Hopefully we'll get to have a decent meal and sleep tonight. We'll worry about finding a way off this island tomorrow."

***

That night, Nika's sleep was anything but decent. Each time he dozed off he was either plagued by gruesome nightmares, or bothered by the grazes in his back stinging as he rolled over. Around an hour before sunrise, Nika finally gave up on getting any sleep, and sat up in his bedroll. Lilla-Belle was sprawled out beside him, sleeping in an odd angle, with Arnie curled up in a ball between them. On the other side of the partition, Priye slept peacefully.

Nika fumbled in the darkness for his pack, and withdrew the journal written by Prince Rakis. Being careful not to wake Lilla-Belle and Priye, Nika lit his firestone so that only he could see the light, and flicked through the journal. It was written in a language he didn't understand, and swore silently to himself.

He tossed the book back in his pack and sat watching over Lilla as she slept. He guessed she was aged around three, and wracked his brain trying to remember what he'd been up to three, maybe four years ago. The mere thought that he might be her father filled him with a mix of different emotions, but mostly fear and self-loathing. For if that was the case, it meant that he'd used her mother for a night of pleasure, and abandoned her to raise Lilla-Belle all alone.

Nika felt the deep stirrings of regret, regret for being so irresponsible and careless. Sure, he took all the proper precautions, but it wasn't unheard of for them to sometimes fail. He frowned as he tried to remember the faces of the long string of women from his drunken pub nights, but most of them were just a blur from all the alcohol he'd consumed.

A gut-wrenching thought occurred to him. Nika wrapped his arms around his knees as a sharp pain stabbed at his gut. What would Freyne think about it? Would he still accept Nika with open arms, knowing how he'd treated Lilla-Belle's mother, or would he be disgusted and walk away? The idea of losing him over a mistake made years ago left him wanting to throw up.

*Stop it,* he scolded himself. *You don't even know if it's true or not. This could all be some plot to unravel me by Du-Rakis. Spiralling into self-pity isn't going to do me any good. I need to pull myself together and focus on getting us out of here. I'll worry about her paternity after Du'Rakis is dead and this war is over.*

Nika was quiet the next morning. He sipped his tea in silence, staring into the fire and feeling his fatigue weighing heavily on his shoulders. The sky was that same red, and the sight of it made everything feel so much more overwhelming. He had no idea how they were supposed to get back to the mainland, nor how they were meant to get all the way north of Araneda in time for whatever

Du'Rakis was planning.

He opened his journal and recounted the events of the last few days. On another page, he copied Ashavan's note, then sat pondering over it. Could Tysion be the key to stopping Du'Rakis? Nika helped himself to another strong tea and sipped it slowly. The world felt different that morning, as though something else had awoken. Whatever it was had great power, though he couldn't tell if it was friend or foe. He wished Freyne was there to ask; he was much more attuned to nature than Nika would ever be.

"What's the plan?" Joplin asked.

"I'm sensing something over that way," Nika replied, pointing. "I have no idea what it is, but it's a start."

"Let's get moving then, yes."

Nika forced himself to get up and busied himself with striking camp. It didn't take long to pack away the tents, and soon they were ready to leave. He took one final look at Mount Rakis, then took Lilla-Belle from Priye's arms. He carefully sat her on Streek's saddle, then passed Arnie up too.

"Kitty!" she said excitedly.

"Be gentle," Nika warned. "Kitty's sharp."

*"You're obnoxious, human."*

*"I'm more worried that she'll hurt you,"* Nika admitted.

He swung himself into the saddle behind her, and wrapped his arms around her so she couldn't fall. Arnie-Kyn perched in front of her, his tail twitching as Lilla-Belle gently stroked his fur.

*"Are you ok?"* Nika asked as Streek broke into a walk. *"You've been quiet."*

*"One is fine,"* Arnie replied. *"Sometimes, much can be learned just from listening."*

They rode in the opposite direction of the crossing for a while, then turned sharply north, crossing a rocky waste that was ravished by volcanos. Ahead of them, Nika could see a sprawling forest that seemed almost out of place. The power he was feeling came from directly in front of them.

Curious, Nika joined with the highest realm. At once, his head was filled with loud voices, like all the creatures using it to communicate were shouting to hear each other. As beautiful as that realm was, Nika still could not understand what the voices were saying. There was just one word he could understand, spoken loudly by many different voices, and it filled Nika with longing.

*"...Freyne..."*

Nika pulled his mind back and sighed deeply to himself. He started to wonder if he would ever see Freyne again. What if he was dead somewhere, marching in Du'Rakis' undead army?

"Bunny!" Lilla-Belle squealed in delight, pulling Nika back from his spiralling.

She pointed as a rabbit ran across their path and disappeared into its burrow.

"Our dinner, yes," Joplin said.

"No." Lilla-Belle frowned and crossed her arms. "Big meanie!"

"You tell him, dear." Priye smirked.

"Maybe I should take her hunting," Yger said thoughtfully. "I was around that age when I started attending tribal hunts."

"It wouldn't hurt, yes." Joplin offered.

"Out of the question," Nika said flatly. "I'm pretty sure when I was that age, I was learning to use the potty, not how to kill animals. I'm glad she's already mastered *that* particular stage."

It was around noon when they reached the edge of the forest. The trees were gnarled and twisted, and a low dark fog wove forebodingly through the trunks. Nika felt uneasy, and the closer they got, the stronger the urge to turn around and leave became. Gaitan stopped abruptly and half-turned his horse.

"I'm not going in there," he declared.

"Me either," Joplin agreed.

Nika hesitated, then thought back to the ruins north of Al'Obrel

"It's an illusion," he said. "I've seen one of these before. Keep going."

He steeled himself and urged Streek forward, leading the way through the darkness. Sure enough, the fog shimmered and disappeared, revealing a lush green forest. That strange power felt stronger, and some of it radiated from the trees themselves. It felt like he was being watched. One by one his friends passed through the illusion, and stood marvelling at their surrounds.

"Wow," Gaitan breathed. "I wasn't expecting this."

Nika beckoned and turned Streek towards the power, keen to discover the source. Birds fluttered in the leaves high above, and every now and then Lilla pointed at small animals as they passed. The forest was teeming with wildlife, all unafraid of the humans passing through. Nika felt himself relaxing a little, when a grunting hiss made him jump.

A tall man leapt from a tree and landed catlike in front of them, hissing and clicking his tongue angrily. Nika reined in sharply as the man drew his bow and aimed an arrow at his heart.

"What do we do?" Priye whispered.

"I don't know," Nika admitted.

"You'd better do something quickly. There's more of them, yes," Joplin muttered.

Nika glanced around slowly, and his heart leapt into his throat. They were surrounded by around fifty of the tall, scantily-clad people, all heavily armed with bows and spears. Their skin was light brown, and Nika couldn't tell if it was a trick of the light or not, but their hair had a faint green tinge. A strange humming noise reached him from the realm, and instinctively he joined with it.

At once, Nika heard angry voices surrounding him, channelled through the highest realm.

*"Evil White! You kind not welcome here!"* The voice

belonged to the man in front of them, who pulled his arrow back further.

*"We mean you no harm,"* Nika said quickly. *"We'll leave immediately."*

*"No. Evil White killed our ancestors. You no leave alive."*

"What are they saying?" Gaitan whispered.

"You don't want to know," Nika said, his heart racing. "Be prepared to defend yourselves."

*"Get off,"* the man ordered.

Nika clutched Lilla-Belle protectively to his chest and swung his leg over his saddle. Just as he was about to drop to the ground, the skin on his arms prickled and a shiver ran down his neck. A flock of birds took flight at once, and the horses all grew jittery. The already red sky grew darker, and a single bolt of lightning cracked above them. The strange people shrieked and bolted for the trees, leaving Nika and his friends alone.

"What's going on now?" Yger demanded. Even she was spooked.

"I don't..."

The air above them sizzled and reeked of death. Nika leapt from Streek's back and drew his focus. He surrounded himself and Lilla protectively with his sprites, and sent Fin to protect the others.

"Get back!" he hissed, tightening his hold on Lilla-Belle. She wrapped her arms around his neck fearfully.

Another bolt of lightning shot from above, and hit one of the trees with an ear-shattering *boom*. The trees around it shied away in what Nika assumed was fright; the rest of the trees were shaking unnaturally. He summoned a splash of water and extinguished the flames.

Something fluttered above them that filled him with dread. A large, winged beast of pure darkness swooped into the clearing, its screech terrifying in itself. Lilla-Belle screamed and buried her face into his neck; he could feel her shaking as the beast hovered in front of him. It had the torso and arms of a decayed human that converged into a pointed tail, its skin the consistency of rotting leather. Its wings were equally as repulsive. The reaper's eyes were two black orbs devoid of any soul.

"Give me the child and I'll let the rest of you go," it said with a raspy hiss.

"Never! You'll have to kill me first!" Nika yelled.

He didn't wait for the reaper to make the first move; he sent an unsummoning spell at it, but to his dismay, it bounced off harmlessly. The reaper laughed and sent an attack of its own in retaliation. Nika blocked it just in time.

"Your unsummons won't work, Sarik. Du'Rakis didn't summon me, so you are powerless against me. Give me the spawn."

The reaper flew a little higher and readied itself to swoop. Nika drew energy from both the realm and the powers flowing around him, and imbued it into his sprites. As the reaper dived towards Lilla, he jerked his focus and formed an impenetrable ring of pure energy around them. The sprites spun in a circle, dazzling spikes of yellow and orange light that danced like flames. The reaper flew into the coloured spikes, and screamed in agony. The stench of burning flesh almost made him gag.

Nika continued drawing the power into him, and sent forth another attack, willing it to burn. The reaper shrieked as the orange ball hit dead-on in its chest and spread to cover every inch of its undead skin. Nika held it, trapped.

"Give Du'Rakis a message from me. If anyone or any*thing* tries to harm this child, there will be hell to pay!" Nika roared. "I'm coming for you, and when I find you, I WILL destroy you!"

He squeezed his hand, increasing the power of the burn. The reaper screamed in agony, and with a flap of its wings, it scrambled back up towards the sky. With another crack of lightning, the reaper disappeared.

Nika waited until he was sure it was gone, then

dispelled the last of the energy held in his sprites. He sheathed his focus, then dropped to his knees and pulled Lilla-Belle into a tight hug.

"Are you ok?" he demanded.

"Is monster gone?" she sniffed.

"It's gone, bubba. Don't you worry. I'll always protect you."

"Woah, what was that thing?" Gaitan asked, slapping Nika on the shoulder.

"It's called a reaper," Nika explained. "It's a form of ghoul that's manifested by pure evil. Let's hope we don't see many more of them around."

"What, you're not going to throw up this time?" Priye asked.

Nika was about to reply, but broke off as he heard the sound of hundreds of pairs of running feet and hooves coming towards them. He groaned and stood back up, and lifted Lilla once more into his arms. As he drew his focus, an army of the strange people burst into the clearing around them. Some were mounted on yaks, brandishing long spears and ready to fight, while the rest were on foot, shaking their weapons angrily. Nika was too tired to even think about fighting them all, and lowered his focus.

Instead of surrounding Nika and his friends, the fighters took defensive positions while jabbering nervously in their strange language. He slowly edged backwards until he was close to the others. One of the tall folk approached, his weapon lowered.

*"Evil White protected us. Saved tree. Chifa will come talk."*

Nika nodded, baffled. The clearing was swarming with fighters, several hundred at least. He watched as two older menfolk emerged from the trees, conversing animatedly. As Nika glanced around, he saw that more of the folk were joining them, only their skin was tinged with green, not brown. Some of the women were topless, but for once Gaitan averted his gaze.

A commotion broke out behind the two elders as someone barged their way through the army. Nika frowned as he felt yet another presence growing stronger, one he was more than familiar with. He frowned and wordlessly handed Lilla-Belle to Gaitan, his stomach twisting into knots.

"Hey! What am I supposed to do with her?" Gaitan objected.

"Give her here," Priye ordered, but Nika wasn't listening.

The person storming through the crowd reached the front, and stepped into the clearing, breathing heavily and his face a mix of anger and concern. Everyone stopped and stared at him in awe, and some reached out to touch him.

Their eyes locked for a split second; and then Nika was running as fast as he could, his arms open wide. Freyne caught him, and they came together in a tight hug, almost knocking each other over. They held each other for what felt like a lifetime, neither of them wanting to let go. Freyne's scent was joined with the slightest hint of lemon myrtle. Nika inhaled deeply, his heart thumping in his chest.

"Did you face him?" Freyne whispered so only Nika could hear.

Nika nodded.

"Twice. He wouldn't stay and fight, though."

"What do you mean?"

"He fled both times. He's either testing me, or waiting for something. I just wish I knew what he's planning."

"Shh. We'll worry about all that later."

Freyne released his grip just enough so he could kiss Nika on the forehead. Nika closed his eyes, wanting nothing more than to reach up for a proper kiss. One of the older menfolk approached, hissing and grunting angrily at Freyne. Freyne let go of Nika and responded just as harshly. The man bowed slightly and stalked away.

"Come on, everyone. We need to get back to U'Dav'lar

where it's safe," Freyne said urgently.

"What's going on?" Nika asked. He couldn't help feeling disappointed that their long-awaited reunion wasn't anything like he'd hoped or imagined.

"Du'Rakis' army of undead vastly outnumbers all of the people of Ayrillis. If humanity are to have any chance of survival, I need to convince the U'Dav'lar, A'Llun'bar and O'Gant'tok tribes to form an alliance with us. And given how they were treated by humans in the past, it isn't going to be easy."

"Oh. Ok."

Nika half turned to walk back to the others, his emotions almost getting the better of him. Freyne caught his arm and roughly pulled him back. Before Nika could argue, Freyne helped himself to Nika's lips. Nika's heart started racing once more, and he parted his lips, welcoming Freyne's kiss. For the first time since parting ways, Nika felt whole again, and as their kiss deepened he knew one thing for certain: he was ready. Ready to face Du'Rakis, and nothing, not even an undead army, would stop him so long as he drew air through his lungs.

"Let's go then," Nika said, pulling away with more determination than ever. "I have a Miscreant to vanquish, and we're not going to find him while standing around here all day."

*The story concludes in book 3, The Final Realm*

# About The Author

Amy-Alex Campbell is a queer Aussie author living in Western Sydney, Australia. In addition to writing, they love to draw fantasy maps for both commissions and fun. When they're not writing, Amex enjoys gaming, reading, and taking care of their two axolotls, Chernobyl & Pripyat.

# Books By This Author

**The Miscreant**
The Lowest Realm
The Darkest Realm
The Final Realm (forthcoming)
Tysion's Story (forthcoming)

**The Marsden Park Series**
Beneath the Grandstand

# Acknowledgements

I would like to sincerely thank Sarah for her love and support. My writing journey wouldn't have been possible without you.

Visit
amyalexcampbell.com
for lore, artwork, maps, pronunciation, and more!